BLOOD BORN

BLOOD BORN

A NOVEL

LINDA HOWARD

AND

LINDA JONES

BALLANTINE BOOKS • NEW YORK

A Ballantine Books Mass Market Original

Copyright © 2010 by Linda Howington and Linda Winstead Jones

Published in the United States by Ballantine Books, an imprint of The Random House Publishing Group, a division of Random House, Inc., New York.

BALLANTINE and colophon are registered trademarks of Random House, Inc.

ISBN 978-1-61664-346-1

Cover illustration: Don Sipley

Printed in the United States of America

To Robin Rue and Beth Miller,
for their unfailing support and enthusiasm

BLOOD BORN

The warriors have always been with us; they're the ones who were willing to die to protect the ones they loved, the ones who were honored to live another life afterward, and who had the courage to stand watch even from the other side, ready and willing to once more step into danger if they were needed. Once the warriors who live beyond this world were accepted, even revered. Then, for a long time, they weren't needed and they became myth, their stories passed from father to son, from mother to daughter. Now they are forgotten.

Immortal Warriors live in a very real world much like this one, a world far away and at the same time close enough to touch. Some think they are ghosts, or spirit guides, or even angels. But they are none of these things . . . yet all of these things. Some among us— blood descendants of these warriors—can see them, can hear them when they call. But how do you hear someone who has been forgotten? How do you understand why they are calling?

Each warrior once walked this earth. They lived, loved, and went to war. Now they fight forever, sacrificing their eternity in order to preserve the human race.

But only if they're called. Only if we learn to hear.

PROLOGUE

Los Angeles, California

She was losing her mind. There was no other explanation.

She hadn't slept more than thirty minutes at a stretch for the past three days. How could she, when the dreams were so vivid and came so quickly, one after the other, startling her awake every time her name was called? Some of the details were murky, but two things she always remembered very clearly: the man, and the way he called to her.

It wasn't fair. She was twenty-three years old, healthy, unattached—at the moment—and living in the bustling and exciting city of Los Angeles, far from the family she'd left behind in Missouri. She should be having the time of her life, the way she had been just a few days ago, and not dragging herself around in a stupor of fatigue. Normally she wouldn't complain about vivid dreams of a very large and muscular, mostly naked, dark-haired hunk who felt so real there were moments she actually forgot he was the product of a dream, but she needed her sleep.

Now it was getting worse; he was invading her waking hours, too, though, to be fair, for the past three nights it seemed as if most of her hours had been spent awake. She'd started hearing him at different times, and the way he called her name was getting more and more urgent. Hearing him! Really, truly *hearing* him. It might be a whisper of her name as she walked down the hall, or a very faint yearning call as she stepped into the shower. She wasn't imagining the voice. It was real.

Only it couldn't be real. She didn't do drugs, so that meant she was losing her mind. It was the only explanation. Fine. The mind could go, so long as she could get some sleep.

She'd been sitting slumped at the table, picking at an ordered-in meal, but she was too tired to eat and finally she gave up on the effort. Dragging herself to her feet, she cleaned off the table and tossed what was left of her supper into the garbage can. As soon as she lifted the lid, the strong, sour odor of several uneaten meals hit her right in the nose. Shit, she should've taken the garbage out before it got dark. Not that she was afraid of the dark, and the Dumpster for the apartment complex was in a well-lit area just a few yards from the end of the stairwell, but she'd already changed into her at-home grubbies, she was barefoot, and if she dared leave the apartment looking like this the odds were she'd bump into some really hot guy who'd take one look at her and decide she was about as attractive as her garbage. That was the way life worked. On the other hand, did meeting at the complex Dumpster qualify as "meeting cute"?

She could wait until tomorrow to take out the trash, but that would mean waking up to that smell. And that was assuming she actually got some sleep tonight. She was so tired, she didn't think anything could keep her awake, not even a naked dark-haired hunk.

She tugged the plastic trash bag out of the can and tied the top, tested the knot to be certain it would hold, then trudged out the door, down the flight of stairs just outside her apartment door, and around the corner.

"Johanna!"

Her hair stood on end as her name echoed both in her head and from somewhere around her. It was spooky, the way the sound seemed to come from everywhere at once. It made her want to run home like a scared little kid, to hide her face in her mother's lap.

And that was the last thing she wanted to do, considering how dead set her mother had been against her moving away. Things hadn't changed since then, either. Her mother was always warning her to be careful. L.A. was a big city. She hated the idea of her daughter being in such a heavily populated place. So many people! The lecture was delivered on a regular basis: *Lock your doors, don't go out alone at night, watch out for strangers.* Yeah, right. That last one was a hoot. She was a hair stylist, so she met new people every day. Moreover, she was fairly new to the area, which meant almost everyone she met was a stranger. Why bother to live in L.A. if she was going to close herself off in her apartment every night? She was here to make her reputation as the hair stylist to go to if you had a special event, someone who could make you look both elegant and edgy. One of these days she'd be stylist to the stars.

The strange sound came again. There was an urgency in this latest call of her name, as if it were a warning.

"Leave me alone," she whispered, focusing on the Dumpster straight ahead. The faint sound of her own voice made her sharply aware that there was no one in the parking lot of the small apartment complex at this time of night. People who had to be at work early were already asleep, probably having perfectly ordinary dreams. Those who worked at night weren't home yet. All she saw were a few cars, including her own, a lamppost, and the winding sidewalk that led to the pool. It was all comfortingly familiar. This was her home now; there was nothing to be afraid of, except the possibility that she was going nuts.

She tossed the bag of garbage into the Dumpster, turned, and stifled a shriek as she lurched backward, almost bumping into the trash container. A tall man with long blond hair stood right behind her, reflective sunglasses making his eyes look like giant insect eyes, with the lights reflecting in the lenses. "Shit!" she exclaimed, then put her hand over her heart as if she could physically calm its frantic pace. "I almost jumped out of my skin!"

He paused, his head tilting to the side. "Interesting," he said. "I didn't know humans could do that."

She would have laughed if she hadn't been so preoccupied with catching her breath. Where had he come from? She hadn't heard a sound, though he had to have been following almost in her footsteps. Surely she should have heard him leave his apartment, heard his door open and close.

She'd been right about something like this happening, she thought in disgust. Her hair was a mess, she didn't have a trace of makeup on, and she was dressed like a bag lady, so of course a trip to the Dumpster would bring her face-to-face . . . well, face-to-chest . . . with a hunk. He was dressed all in black; he had a serious Johnny Cash vibe going on. Still, she should have seen him, heard him, but she supposed she could only blame her foggy state of mind.

She tipped her head back to look at him. What was with those pretentious sunglasses? It was night. Not that there wasn't a more than fair share of pretentiousness in L.A., where everyone was a star or about to become one. This guy was no star. She would've remembered this face if she'd seen it before. *Wowza,* she thought dazedly. He could give her dream stalker a run for his money in the looks department.

Like she was in any kind of shape to admire hand-some strangers.

"Run!"

The voice was the one in her dreams, and for a moment she was stunned that he'd said anything other than her name. Then the urgency in the faraway voice seeped into her weary mind and uneasiness chilled her spine.

"Excuse me," she said, stepping to the side to allow him access to the Dumpster. He moved, too, his action mirroring hers, and like a slap in the face she realized he wasn't carrying any trash. The taste of copper filled her mouth. Every cell in her body seemed to tense as a rush of alertness seized her, but before her brain could quite send the message to scream he lifted his hand and used one finger to pull his sunglasses down so she could see his blue eyes . . . his *glowing* blue eyes.

The scream never came. She felt herself sinking into that gaze, and the odd thing was, she didn't *want* to tear herself free. The growing fear of a moment ago vanished as if it had never existed; instead, she was filled with a sense of warmth and pleasure. He was beautiful. She wanted to please him, to do whatever he wanted.

"Oh," she said in a voice of wonder, reaching out as if to touch his face.

He caught her hand instead, lifting it to his mouth in an elegant and old-fashioned salute. The touch of his lips was warm on her fingers. "Good-bye," he said, and slid eight inches of a knife blade between her ribs and into her heart.

That hurts, she thought, but without any urgency. "I don't want to leave," she said, faintly bewildered. "I want to stay with you." Why was it so hard to talk? Why did she feel as if she couldn't draw a breath? She blinked at him, trying to formulate an argument, but thoughts kept slipping away from her and time faded away. She became aware, on some distant level, that somehow she wasn't standing in front of him any longer but was lying on the ground in front of the Dumpster. That wasn't right. She would never . . . too many germs . . . she should get up.

And there he was again, the man in her dreams, as vivid as he had ever been. He said her name once more and this time he sounded so sad and angry. Then he faded away . . . and so did she.

Sorin stared down at the girl's body. He didn't rejoice in her death, but he did regret that he couldn't feed from her. The conduits had to be killed in a normal fashion— that is, a normal *human* fashion, to keep from raising the alarm. This one had been very pretty, so pretty that, under other circumstances, he'd have liked to spend some time with her, feeding and fucking. She would have awakened the next day feeling unusually weak but otherwise in good health, and all she'd have remembered was having a really great time. Instead, an accident of birth had signed her death warrant.

He could mark her name off his to-do list.

Northeast Alabama

Melody leaned against the passenger door of a black pickup truck, and relaxed in the warm evening air. A breeze kicked up, blowing warm Alabama air that smelled of honeysuckle across her skin. And there was a lot of exposed skin for that breeze to caress. Even back before she'd been turned, when she was just a silly human teenager, it hadn't taken her long to realize that men were suckers for big boobs, a flat tummy, and long legs. She had all three and didn't mind displaying them if it got her what she wanted.

She smiled as the door before her swung open and a couple walked out of the bar. Wouldn't be long now; it was getting late and there were only a few customers left. Before the door swung shut again Melody caught a glimpse of the men lined up at the rustic wooden bar, their beers or whiskeys sitting before them, their gazes cutting to her. They knew she was here. Well, *he* knew she was here, and that was all that mattered.

The conduit caught her eye just before the door closed. She managed to tip her chin in way of a greeting. He was cute—dark-haired and rugged, fit and tall. He had workingman's hands and nice eyes. It was his truck Melody was leaning against, and she was waiting for him.

Less than a minute later, he walked out of the bar. His stride was long; his jeans were faded and nicely snug. His pretty green eyes were tired.

"Why don't you come back in?" he asked as he walked toward her.

"I don't really care for alcohol," she said.

"Then why are you here?"

Three nights in a row she'd visited this bar, coming and going quickly, getting a sense of who this man was. She had to be sure.

"I dropped in that first night by chance," she said. "Since then I came here for you."

He looked a little surprised but not shocked. A good-looking man who had a decent job had to be in demand in this little town, which was seriously in the middle of nowhere. Melody smiled. She knew there was no one around here who could hold a candle to her when it came to blindsiding men. They were so predictable, so easy.

"Take me home," she said simply. "I can't stay around much longer. I have places to go, a job to do. But damn, I don't want to leave without getting a taste of you."

He was definitely interested, but still wary. "I'm not looking for anything serious. I got divorced just six months ago and the last thing I need—"

"I just want your body," she said, and that was the truth. "Why don't we go back to your place?"

He flinched a little, and said, "I don't want to go home."

There was a fear in his eyes that told her she had the right man.

She looked around, blew out a huff of air. "It's been a long time since I had a man in a truck, but you've got an extended cab and the windows are tinted, so I suppose we can give it a shot."

The keys were out of his pocket in a flash. Melody stepped out of the way. It was a shame, really, but she had no choice. The conduit was a soldier in a war he didn't even know he was fighting, but he was a soldier all the same.

A gentleman to the end, he took Melody's hand and helped her into the backseat. They'd be in cramped quarters, but that didn't matter. They wouldn't be here long. He joined her, closed and locked the door behind him, and she moved in.

Occasionally she'd been chastised by her elders for playing with her food, but her elders weren't here, and Melody didn't see any reason why she couldn't make the end pleasant. It wasn't his fault that he was a conduit, that he had the bad fortune to have the blood of an Immortal Warrior in his veins, that he'd been contacted. She'd give the good ol' boy a little fun, in his final minutes.

He could die now or later, but he was going to die.

There was a little bit of light coming through the tinted windows, just enough for him to see her face, though of course she could see his very well whether there was light or not. She smiled at him. She'd been turned in 1956, which made her all but a fledgling in the vampire world, but being so young—relatively speaking—meant that she still clearly remembered what it was like to be human, with all the flirting and drama that humans attached to sex. She still enjoyed some of those silly rituals. With vampires, it was fuck if you felt like it, and that was about as complicated as it got. Not that vampires didn't make great lovers—there was a lot to be said for both practice and stamina—but humans could be so *sweet,* both figuratively and literally. Why give that up when she could have both? She'd actually heard that some of the really, really old vampires eventually gave up sex completely, but she couldn't imagine that. She sure as hell wouldn't ever make that sacrifice.

Hell, she'd had to give up ice cream and sunbathing, and that was enough sacrifice for her.

The conduit was exhausted, robbed of sleep night after night by his warrior trying to contact him, but he wasn't so tired that he couldn't appreciate the view as Melody shimmied out of her clothes. When she was entirely naked she took his hand and guided it to her breast, where he held it as she slowly peeled his clothes off and trailed her mouth over each section of his body as she bared it. The anxiousness she'd seen in him for the past three days faded, replaced by desire.

She straddled him, took him in, closed her eyes and enjoyed the feel of coming together. Their position was awkward, thanks to the small space. His bed would've been better, but he didn't want to go home. Home was no longer a sanctuary for him, poor thing.

Home was where contact with one's warrior began, and sometimes ended. At home, alone, safe from uninvited visitors and the turmoil of public places, the conduits began to see or hear or simply sense the presence of their warriors. No wonder the poor boy had been sleeping on friends' couches and in this very truck, where he could have a few hours of peace.

The sex was fast and sweaty and satisfying for both. There was a touch of awkwardness that was almost endearing. He was manly but also shy. He wasn't a smooth operator with the ladies and never had been. If she hadn't made the first move, he never would've spoken to her.

When they finished, for a long moment they lay awkwardly tangled, sweating and sated. Melody lifted her head, shook back her thick blond hair, and looked him in the eye. Even in the dark, he saw her . . . and she saw him. She caught his gaze, pushed, and his mind was hers. She was charmed by how easy and pliable he was. She'd be tempted to keep him for a while, if she didn't have a job to do.

She extended her fangs, but because she'd already established a contact with his mind, he wasn't alarmed. She already had control, and he knew what she wanted. Obediently he tipped his head to the side, exposing a long, strong, salty throat.

Melody lowered her head and bit down, breaking the skin, opening a vein. She couldn't drain him; she'd been ordered to be cautious when killing the conduits, so there wouldn't be a trail of bloodless bodies that might lead the humans to the center of power and blow the whole revolution thing. He tasted so *good,* as if the basic sweetness of his nature flavored his blood. Melody hummed a little in delight, and because she was a generous person she reached down and stroked his penis while she fed. He gave a little moan and pumped his hips against her hand.

"That's good, sugar," she whispered. "Isn't it good?" Without waiting for an answer she drew deeply of his blood, lost in the moment, in the lovely feel of his body and the taste of his life force, in the energy that coursed through her as she fed.

Finally she made herself stop drinking; she didn't

dare take any more. With lingering movements of her tongue she licked his throat, waited for the healing to kick in and close the bite. That done, she placed a strong hand over his mouth and nose, cutting off his air. She hated that she had to use this method to kill when her own appetite was so much more efficient. It just made no sense to waste that much food. But she was a good soldier, so she did what she'd been told.

He didn't struggle, except for a brief twitch. She kept his nose and mouth covered until his heart had ceased to beat. Her job done, Melody patted him on the head, then touched his cheek. At least his last few minutes alive had been happy ones. She found some comfort in that thought. She wasn't a monster, she was just . . . *different.* More than that, she was *better.* Better than she'd ever been before, better than humans, who knew so little and existed for the benefit of those like her.

She took her time putting on her clothes, watching through the tinted glass windows as the last of the bar patrons came out, got in their various vehicles, and left. They didn't pay a bit of attention to the truck. He'd left it parked here a few nights lately, getting rides with friends when he was too drunk to drive, or sleeping in the backseat.

When the last patron left and the neon beer sign went out, Melody climbed out of the truck, closing the door behind her.

It bothered her that the conduit hadn't fought. Even though he'd been glamoured, his body should have struggled for air. Maybe she'd taken too much. She didn't have the kind of control an older vampire possessed, but that wasn't her fault, was it? She'd get older . . . eventually. But if she'd taken too much blood and some backcountry coroner got suspicious, she'd be in trouble. It really would be best if there wasn't enough left of the body for any medical examiner to study.

The good thing was, she had a natural talent that had come to life when she'd been turned, one that came in very handy when she wanted to hide some evidence. She lifted her hand, applied some concentration as she stared at her palm, and a small lick of flame flared to life there. She didn't feel any pain or heat from the flames, because it was *her* fire.

She stood back and with a flick of her hand sent that flame toward the pickup. It caught, licked across the seat, and with her mind she sent it racing through the cab, where it engulfed the body. Stepping farther away, she drove the fire onward, sending it in search of the gas tank. That took some doing, because she really wasn't sure where gas tanks were located, but by the time she struck pay dirt—so to speak—she was far enough away that the explosion didn't do much more than ruffle her hair.

A man came running out of the bar, alarmed by the noise of the explosion. Taken aback, Melody stared at him. She'd completely forgotten about the bartender. The older man raced toward her. "Dear God, what happened?" he yelled as he fumbled for the cell phone in his pocket.

Dammit! Under most circumstances Melody wouldn't have cared that her presence had been noticed, but her orders were clear: don't draw attention to what was happening, or else. She didn't want to find out what "or else" meant, though she had a very good idea. The last thing she wanted was to make Sorin unhappy. She had to handle this, and do it fast.

In the blink of an eye she moved in front of the bartender, startling him. "Wha—" he began, already stepping back, but she caught his gaze and he was hers. She saw the reflection of the fire in his eyes, then she was in his mind.

"I wasn't here," she said calmly. "That poor boy's

been sleeping in the back of his truck lately, and you knew that but didn't mind."

"I didn't mind," the bartender echoed.

"Poor fella," Melody continued. "He hasn't been himself lately. He's been moping around about the divorce, and he just seemed so sad." Slowly she walked away, and when she was out of the bartender's line of sight she released his mind.

She watched as he fumbled with his cell phone, listened to the frantic call. "Send the fire truck, the ambulance, whatever you got!"

Walking down the side of the narrow road in the darkness, Melody smiled to herself. That had been fun.

Another conduit would soon be hers. As soon as she reported in that she'd succeeded here, she'd be given another assignment. How would she kill the next one? Knife, pillow, gun, a shove off the side of a cliff . . . it all depended on who and where. She had to be more careful about taking too much blood next time, though, but when the rebels succeeded and vampires ruled, she wouldn't ever have to be careful again. *Cool,* she thought. Very cool.

CHAPTER
ONE

The Scottish Highlands

There was something special about Scotland in the summer that made it one of his favorite places in the world. It was more than the rain and clouds and heavy mist that called Luca Ambrus here; it was the taste of what had come before, a palpable history that flowed so vividly in his memory that sometimes he could close his eyes and hear the voices of people long gone, feel the impact and vibration of a sword in his hands during countless battles, smell the peat fires. He'd actually been born in Greece—his olive skin gave away his Mediterranean heritage—but he'd spent many more years in Scotland than he had in Greece and was far more at home here. Greece was too hot and sunny; he much preferred cool, misty, foggy places.

There were times when he craved the noise and movement and excitement of a city, but more often he preferred his own company and his own thoughts. If he hadn't been comfortable within himself, he'd have gone mad many centuries ago. But he *was* comfortable and grounded, to use the current phrasing, so he was very content to pass days, weeks, at a time without seeing another soul. The trick was to live in the moment, to enjoy each successive year for itself, for the changes that came both slow and fast, and for the things that never changed. He enjoyed life, and didn't necessarily require companionship.

His home here in the Highlands was an elegant cottage with all the modern conveniences, far away from the larger cities. He saw no need to sacrifice his comfort for solitude when he could have both. Once he'd have had to choose between them, but no longer. Times changed. What good was living through the centuries if he couldn't enjoy all that was offered?

The things he'd seen come into being during the past hundred and fifty years! Even he, who was seldom surprised by anything, had watched with bemusement as change piled on change. Electric lights, telephones, automobiles, airplanes—it was almost too much to take in, though he enjoyed them very much. He loved movies and television, the travel, the thrill of driving a fast car or getting on a plane and a few hours later being thousands of miles away. The humans had even managed to go into space; the audacity of such fragile creatures was either valiant or incredibly stupid, and despite two millennia studying them he hadn't yet decided which it was. Both, perhaps.

He had money, and he had time. If he was in the mood for city life he stayed in his place near Seattle, Washington. When he wanted peace and quiet, he came here. In a while he would tire of the quiet and move on, but for now . . . for now the solitude was as necessary to his survival as blood. Immortality didn't come without a price.

Still, he never stayed in one place very long—"long" being a relative term. A month might seem long to some, but to him it was the blink of the eye, a heartbeat. It wasn't in his nature to nest. He was a hunter at heart, and he enjoyed the thrill of the chase even more than the inevitable end when the prey was his. One day soon he would feel the call—or receive an actual call—and in a flash he would leave behind his beloved solitude to lose himself once more in the blood hunt.

When twilight came, Luca left his cottage and walked out into the cool fresh air. This was the time of day he liked best, when the fading light and gathering darkness accentuated the aloneness he sometimes craved as if it were as tangible as the earth he walked upon. He took a course that led him through a fragrant meadow, with the craggy mountains looming over him and deepening the shadows. His boots cut slowly through the tall grass. There was no hurry in his movements, no need beyond the moment. He was old enough that he no longer had to feed very often, unless he was burning a lot of energy, which allowed him to escape from the world for days, even weeks, at a time. The hunger, the *need,* would eventually come, and when it did he would feed.

But he wasn't hungry tonight. Tonight he was satisfied to walk these stark, dramatic hills and remember the battles that had been fought here. There was a lot to remember, because there had been so many battles, so many wars. Easily destroyed or not, his human fellow warriors had thrown themselves into war with such complete lack of caution that he could only marvel. It wasn't as if they didn't know they were mortal; they did. And still they fought, often long past the point where sanity or common sense should have kicked in. Even after centuries of watching them, preying on them, sometimes fighting beside them, humans could still bemuse him.

He didn't know exactly how old he was; he knew he was over two thousand, but he couldn't pin down a year or even a birth date, if he'd ever known it at all. Vampires in general weren't big on calendars, even assuming his mother had known the date he'd been born. He'd kept track for a while, the first four or five hundred years, but after that he'd lost interest because the number wasn't important; after all, no one would be throwing a birthday party for him. All that was important was his personal power, which had grown with each passing century and would continue to increase, until now the number who equaled him in some ways could be counted on one hand. In power lay safety, and one of the first lessons he'd learned was to always watch his back, even with his own kind, which was why he didn't live among them.

He had everything he needed here. In a lot of ways he was more comfortable with humans than he was with the kindred, because he could relax with humans. He didn't fear them, didn't have to be wary of them. They were puny in so many ways, a lot of fun in others, and best of all, they never remembered him.

A small village lay just over the farthest hill. When he had to feed, he went there. And when he left after feeding, the people he'd met, even those he'd fed upon, immediately forgot he'd been there at all. Every time he entered the village, the residents greeted him as a new visitor. That was his power, his curse, his salvation: no one remembered him. When he passed by, he passed out of their lives as if he'd never been there at all. Only the strongest of his own kind could resist the power, which meant he could come and go as he wished. To be forgotten as soon as he was out of sight was as good as being invisible, and gave him a freedom that other vampires could only dream of having.

He was engrossed in one particularly delicious memory when the portable satellite phone in his pocket rang. He cursed under his breath. The one thing he didn't enjoy about modern life was the ease of communication. In the old days, the Council would have had to send him a written summons, which, depending on where he was, could take months to reach him. Not that the length of time mattered, because no matter how long a rogue vampire had to go to ground, Luca always found his prey.

Dammit. His position with the Council required that he always be available, but he'd just completed an assignment and he needed to get away from the irritation he felt around crowds of people. Normally months, sometimes years would pass before the Council summoned him again, but the call had to be from them because few others knew how to reach him. He didn't blithely give out his number, not even to the older, stronger vampires who could remember him. What was the point? Vampires didn't call to chat. Besides, he made other vampires nervous. Even most of the Council members, who were powerful in their own rights, were wary of him. And as far as he was concerned, that was a good thing.

Politics didn't interest him at all, so his involvement with the Council wasn't entirely logical. The ruling branch of vampire society was as beset by back-stabbing, deal-brokering, lobbying, and special interests as any government yet devised by humans. But he had skills others did not, and for more years than he could count he'd been an integral part of the workings of the Council. His assignments gave him a sense of purpose, and besides, even this place bored him after a while.

Individually and collectively the Council had offered him a more permanent position, a seat at the table of power, but he'd turned them down so many times he thought they should long since have stopped asking. The Council members were as heavily protected as any American president, and he'd go stir-crazy if he had to live all but imprisoned in the Council headquarters. Their quarters were luxurious, but a prison was still a prison, no matter how high the thread count on the sheets.

They would keep calling until he answered the phone. Annoyed, he pulled it from his pocket and glanced at the number. His eyebrows rose as concern replaced his annoyance, and he thumbed the talk button. "Ambrus," he said. Hector wasn't the member of the ruling Council charged with assigning Luca's missions, but he was an old friend and he wouldn't call unless it was important. In the more than six hundred years they'd known each other, they'd also learned to trust each other, something important in the vampire world. Together they'd seen a lot of changes in the vampire community. They'd kept the peace, and they had protected the secret of their very existence, using whatever methods were necessary.

Hector hadn't been a young man when he'd been turned, and though he was strong he wasn't at a physical peak, the way Luca was. Hector's strength was in his mind, his shrewdness and his control.

"There's a serious problem," Hector said without preamble. It wasn't like him to be so abrupt. He was almost twelve hundred years old, so he'd learned there was almost never a need for haste or impatience.

Luca turned to walk back toward his cottage. A problem for the Council meant that, like it or not, he'd soon be on his way to D.C. "What sort of problem?"

Hector hesitated. "I think there's a traitor on the Council."

Luca stopped in his tracks. "A traitor . . . How?" It was a serious accusation, but not one he could easily dismiss, simply because this was Hector. Treason in the vampire world meant one thing: a vampire doing something stupid that could result in exposure to the humans. Still, exactly what did "traitor" mean? Attacks against the Council didn't count as treason, because Council

members, like all the other vampires, had to survive by
their own strength and wits. If they couldn't manage
that, then they were dead, and the stronger stepped
into their places.

"A rebel faction has formed. Their position is that
they're tired of living in the dark, that vampires are
superior to humans—which is true—so they want to
overcome the humans and take over the government.
One of the Council has joined them. I'm certain of it,
but I haven't been able to find out *who*."

Luca grunted, but otherwise restrained his reaction.
If Hector was right—and he almost always was—then
this was definitely a serious situation. Periodically
someone or a group of someones would decide it was
outrageous that vampires had to hide their existence, and
they would have to be dealt with before they could
expose the entire race. Never before had a Council member joined in that idea, though, which immediately made
the situation more dire.

With some common sense and caution, vampires
could live in relative peace because humans didn't
believe they were real. The Council made the rules that
ensured that peace, and whenever any vampire didn't
obey, well, that was where Luca came in. A vampire
who fed and killed indiscriminately risked them all, so
Luca was called in to handle the problem.

Because he could come and go pretty much as he
wanted, and no human remembered him, there were no
repercussions. Not only that, he was old enough and
strong enough that he could go out in daylight, which
meant most vampires were helpless against him. He
executed them during the day only under the most
extreme circumstances, such as if the vampire had gone
totally mad and any delay was too dangerous.
Otherwise, he faced his prey and at least gave them the
opportunity to fight. They never won—obviously, or he

wouldn't still be here—but the exercise gave him fighting practice. Executing a sleeping vampire wasn't any fun at all.

He could almost—*almost*—have some sympathy with the rebels. There were many vampires who considered all humans as far beneath them as a cow or a chicken might be to those humans. They were necessary for nourishment, but to be forced to hide from them out of fear, to be made to cower in the dark . . . some vampire egos couldn't handle it. Luca didn't quite see things that way. For one, he didn't cower. For another, he had fought beside humans, made love to human women, enjoyed their progresses and inventions, and sometimes laughed at their actions until he was exhausted and his ribs ached. Humans were endlessly entertaining, if nothing else.

"I'll be there tomorrow," Luca said as he resumed his distance-eating stride.

"Hurry," Hector urged, and his voice changed as his power surged, his tone and cadence sliding into the rhythm that said he was seeing the future. *"Battle is in the air. I smell it. I can almost touch it. Death is coming. Death is coming for us."* With a click, the call disconnected.

The powerful vampire sounded frightened, which alarmed Luca even more. Death. Vampires lived with death, but some clung to their new version of life with an almost panicked intensity. Others, after living for so many years, actually yearned for an end and would choose to die, but most didn't. Hector enjoyed life, even after all his years, but he wasn't afraid of death. What he feared was something bigger: the collapse of the wall of ignorance that protected the vampires from the humans.

Luca reached his cottage and began packing, making phone calls and arrangements of his own as he gathered what he needed. If Hector felt death was coming for them, as he'd said, then their world was in great danger and uncertainty.

Luca had many strengths and powers; as a rare blood born, conceived and born to a vampire mother and father, he was much stronger than those who'd been turned to the life. Prophesy, however, wasn't one of those powers. Despite the surety in his tone, Hector's gift of prophecy was relatively mild, and while Luca certainly believed Hector's prediction, he also knew there was just as much that Hector didn't see.

He'd have liked more time in Scotland, but as he prepared for the trip he felt his heartbeat increasing in anticipation for what was to come. If there was a huge battle, well, he hadn't been in a proper battle in a very long time.

Washington, D.C.

Chloe Fallon had just drifted off to sleep when the image popped into her subconscious: a long, thick, blond braid hanging right in front of her face. That was all, just a braid, but so real she felt as if she could reach out and touch it. The shade of blond was darker and more golden than her own, and it seemed to be streaked with several shades. Had to be a natural color, her dreaming mind thought; it would take forever for a hairdresser to work all those different colors in.

She started awake, absurdly surprised to find herself alone in her own bed. That was the weird thing— one of the weird things, anyway. She didn't feel as if she was truly alone. She almost felt as if all she had to do was roll over and she'd find the person attached to the braid lying there beside her. Unable to stop herself, she lifted her head to take a quick glance at the other pillow. Nope, no one there. Good. She had the bed to herself, as usual.

She flopped over on her back and stared at the dark ceiling. Of all things to dream about . . . a *braid*. She kept having the same dream, over and over, about a damn braid. Maybe she had some deep-seated desire to be a hairdresser, though she didn't think so. She didn't even like spending much time on her own hair, which was why she got the most maintenance-free cut she could, short of shaving her head. So what did it mean that she kept dreaming about a braid? There had to be a person attached to the hank of hair, but she'd never seen a face. She didn't even know for sure if the braid belonged to a man or a woman. Her first thought had been "woman," since long hair wasn't exactly in fashion for men, but she got a sense of power when she was in the presence of the braid. It was definitely a strange thing to be obsessing over.

The braid dream had been coming for several weeks now. At first she'd decided stress was the cause. Her job and college classes were both demanding. She enjoyed them, but they didn't leave much time for a social life. Relaxation, laughter, fun . . . she'd had to put them all aside, but now she was out of college for the summer and thought a break would cure all her ills. *Not.*

It didn't make sense. All she had to worry about right now was her job—assistant manager of an upscale restaurant in Georgetown—and her parents' planned visit at the end of August. She had to get the guest room in order before they arrived; thankfully she had a couple of months to get ready. That spare room was presently a cluttered storage space, but it would only take a few hours to turn it into a decent guest room. Okay, it would take longer than that, but it was do-able.

Yes, she was obsessing a little over the pending visit. What sane, single woman of a certain age didn't obsess when her parents, who couldn't understand why their only daughter wanted to live so far away, came to visit? Her mother couldn't quite pull herself out of her protective mode, even though Chloe was scaring thirty and was determined to live a normal life despite having an aortic aneurysm. The way she saw it, the aneurysm was small and stable, and might never change or grow to a dangerous size. The way her mother saw it, however, was that Chloe had a ticking time bomb in her chest and could die at any moment. Finding a balance between those two viewpoints wasn't easy, though Chloe suspected that, if their positions were reversed, she'd feel exactly the same as her mother did.

She growled at the ceiling, disgruntled at being awake and stressing over something that wouldn't happen for a couple of months. She loved her parents. They loved her. She could handle being coddled for a few days.

But, dammit, the latest encounter with the ownerless braid had left her wide awake. Sighing, Chloe rolled out of bed and headed for the kitchen. A glass of milk would help; she'd rather have hot chocolate, but chocolate had caffeine, so she'd settle for the milk. She could sleep late in the morning. She could sleep as late as she wanted, because she worked the evening shift at the restaurant.

After pouring herself some milk, she leaned against the kitchen cabinet while she drank, and stared at her blurry reflection in the window of the microwave. Huh. Maybe there was a little bed-head going on there, which wasn't fair considering she'd been in bed maybe fifteen minutes, tops. She wondered how she'd look with really long hair, like that braid. She kept her hair just long enough that she could pull it back, sleek and neat, to keep it out of her way while she worked. Right now she just looked kind of mussed and messy, in soft, gray cotton shorts and a matching sleeveless tee, but what kept pulling her attention was her own baby soft, blond hair. Dammit, forget about the hair!

Impatient with the dream and with hair in general, she moved so she couldn't see her reflection in the microwave and distracted herself by looking around for things she needed to do before her parents came to visit. All in all, she was very happy with what she saw. Her rental house was small, but she loved it. A friend of a friend had moved to California, but hadn't been willing to let go of the little gem, though property values in the district were so high surely there would have been a hefty profit in selling.

Still, she couldn't blame them. The house was well-maintained and the landscaping was great. It was the perfect size for her: two bedrooms, two baths, a decent-sized living room, and a kitchen. It was practically within spitting distance of a Metro station. What else did a single woman need?

The kitchen was square and well-equipped, and had been recently updated. Chloe liked to cook when she had the time, so a decent kitchen was a necessity. She kept hoping her landlords would decide the move to California was permanent and they'd offer to sell her the house—she'd told them she was interested, basically calling dibs—but so far they showed no signs of giving it up. Just as well. She needed to save more money for a down payment. The house was small, but this was a very desirable neighborhood and at the upper limit of what she could afford.

Her parents would freak if she bought a house in the D.C. area. They kept thinking that when was she was finished with school she'd come to her senses and move home to Atlanta. After all, there were plenty of restaurants there that needed managers, as they'd told her time and time again. The truth was, Chloe loved living here. She loved the people, her job, the energy of the city. She had friends—even if her social time was limited when school was in session—and she loved this house.

Maybe one day she'd have the man to go with it, even kids if they decided to go that route and her doctor agreed that the risk was acceptable, but for now she liked being independent. A few of her friends felt as if they had to have a guy in their lives or else they were at loose ends, incomplete somehow, missing out on life. Not Chloe. She valued her alone time and her independence. If and when the right man came into her life, that would be great. Until then, she wasn't looking, and she wasn't desperate. She'd watched too many of her friends end up with losers when they thought they couldn't snag anyone better. A time or two, she'd fallen into the loser trap herself. Okay, three times, before she'd come to her senses. She wasn't going to settle for Mr. Right Now because she was afraid Mr. Right wasn't ever going to materialize.

Chloe had often thought that if she had one major characteristic, it was that she was level-headed. Wow, wasn't that impressive? But she made a great assistant manager, and one day she'd make a great manager, with an MBA, her level head, and her organizational skills—which did not, she admitted, extend to her guest room. She'd get there, though.

She had the whole summer ahead of her to get the spare room in order, get her responses thought out and lined up for the inevitable arguments her parents would fire at her, and get rid of the weird braid that had invaded her dreams. In the bright light of the kitchen, that last detail sounded downright ridiculous. Who let a dream about hair keep her awake at night? Maybe she subconsciously wanted to dye her hair. The color of the braid really was nice. Maybe she'd seen someone on the street with a long braid like that one and she'd mentally filed it away without realizing it.

But what about the sensation that she wasn't alone? Maybe she did need to seriously consider looking for that elusive permanent man, even though she wasn't quite ready to settle down. She could start cruising bars until she found a willing and acceptable man—nope, wasn't going to happen. Her level-headedness said that kind of behavior was both sad and dangerous.

She'd have to take up jogging again, dammit. She should have been doing it all along, but she simply hadn't had the time. Now that she was out of school for the summer, she didn't have that excuse. Everyone in Washington jogged, so she'd get out and join the herd.

"Chloe . . ."

The voice didn't just surprise her, it shocked her like a slap to the face. Her half-full glass of milk slipped from her hand and shattered on the floor, sending glass and milk shooting across her bare legs and the tile floor. Wildly she looked around, certain that someone was there. The voice, that hoarse whisper of her name, had been right *there*. The sound had been directly in her ear.

No one. Nothing. She was completely alone.

She began shaking. She wasn't asleep, she couldn't write the whisper off to dozing in the middle of the kitchen while she stood there drinking milk and making plans to drag her running shoes out of the closet. The voice had been real, as real as the mess she had to clean up, as real as the thin trickle of blood where a sliver of glass had cut her leg.

After a minute she controlled her ragged breathing, and her panicked senses began settling down. Stepping carefully to avoid the broken glass that surrounded her, she concentrated on cleaning up the mess, focusing on the task so she didn't have to think of anything else. By the time every speck of milk and glass had been cleaned up and disposed of, she could take a deep breath and let it go. She hadn't really heard anything; her imagination had gotten the best of her, that was all.

It was either that or admit that she was losing her mind, and pragmatic Chloe couldn't allow herself to go there.

Across the city, Hector paced in his private quarters. His ability to read energies, to see bits and pieces of the future, had grown in his years as a vampire, but he couldn't see everything. What use was such an incomplete ability in a time of turmoil? How did he benefit from knowing someone close by was a traitor who had aligned him- or herself with rebels, when the precise knowledge of their identity eluded him?

It was the sensation of battle, of coming turmoil, that most disturbed him. The last thousand years had been relatively peaceful, and his six hundred years on the Council had been productive ones. Order was required for the continued existence of his kind. He had done his part to keep the peace, and everything within him told him that the peace would soon come to an end.

Hector had no great love for humans; he barely remembered being one himself. But humans were necessary for the existence of his kind, and as long as vampires were thought to be nothing more than myth or fantastical beings from horror tales, their survival was ensured. There were always a handful of vampires who thought differently, who wanted to openly take their place at the top of the food chain, but they had never had the strength of numbers and were easily taken care of.

Until now.

There was a knock on his door, and with that knock an increased sensation of the end. He didn't answer, but he knew the locked door offered only a brief delay of the inevitable. He wasn't a warrior, had never been a warrior. If Luca were here . . . but he wasn't, and wouldn't be for a few more hours.

All he could do now was use his ability, and Luca's, to pass on what he could. Concentrating, Hector did his best to fill the air with his thoughts, his energy, and his knowledge. He was looking at the door when it flew open, and in truth was not surprised to see who was on the other side.

He thought the name, whispered it, imprinted the face in his mind, and set it loose.

He fought, of course he did, but he'd been old before he was turned and his physical strength had never been great. The outcome was a foregone conclusion, one he had sensed approaching. And he was aware, at the very end, that there was another traitor in the hallway, listening, waiting, hiding from the power she knew he possessed.

She.

Out of respect, the attacker didn't drink Hector's blood before he drove a long-bladed knife into his heart. Three times, it took, before the heart was so damaged that Hector's long life ended in a burst of bitter, gray dust.

TWO

It was late morning when Luca arrived in D.C. The sun was shining brightly as he stepped out of the terminal building at Reagan International Airport, and he pulled on a baseball cap before sliding dark sunglasses into place to protect his pale gray eyes as he crossed to Parking Garage A to pick up his rental.

Unlike vampires who were either younger or weaker—the two weren't always synonymous—he could tolerate sunshine, but he didn't like it. He protected himself with the cap and sunglasses, as well as long sleeves, but sunlight was still an irritant, making his skin feel as if he was being scrubbed with a stiff-bristled brush. His eyes were the most sensitive; when he'd been a fledgling, all of his senses had been so acutely sensitive that he hadn't been able to tolerate anything other than complete darkness, and as he'd grown older he'd pushed his limits too far a couple of times and temporarily lost his sight. He didn't want to repeat that mistake. As far as he was concerned, sunglasses were one of the humans' best inventions, and it pissed him off that a vampire hadn't thought of dark lenses centuries ago. Hell, why hadn't *he* thought of it, instead of just enduring and waiting?

That was one of the weaknesses of being a vampire:

generally, his kind lived so long and were vulnerable to so little, that there was no need for them to be inventive. Humans, on the other hand, were vulnerable to almost everything and lived very short lives, so they didn't have the luxury of waiting. They were like bees in a hive, constantly working and adjusting and coming up with a million little ways to make the hive more comfortable. Vampires certainly enjoyed those creature comforts, the entertainments, but they usually were nothing more than recipients. More vampires now were working in various fields of science and engineering, but identification was problematic, as well as the fact that they didn't age, so anything long term was difficult to maintain.

His rental was reserved and waiting for him. He'd flown in under his real name, reserved the car under his real name. He had a very good forger who had provided him with the necessary documents for modern travel. If there was a traitor on the Council, and he trusted Hector enough to believe there was, then he wasn't going to risk exposing his other, carefully established, identifications, which he used to travel when he wanted to remain totally off the Council's radar. It would be child's play for the rogue Council member to glamour a human who worked for the airline industry into checking any passenger list, so Luca put himself out there front and center. Very shortly they'd know he was in town anyway, so there wasn't anything to hide.

He always preferred renting a car to taking taxis; not only did he still get a thrill at the speed—a hundred or so years wasn't *nearly* long enough to dilute that particular joy for a man who had spent over nineteen centuries getting around on horseback or in oxcarts—but taking a taxi was a pain in the ass. He'd have to talk nonstop, because if he let himself lapse from the driver's consciousness, even for a few seconds, the driver would forget he had a passenger and either stop to pick up someone else, which would at least cause some confusion and usually hostility, or Luca would find himself in a part of the city where he didn't want to be. If he wanted to amuse himself he might climb into a cab, but for the most part he didn't have the time to waste.

After locating his reserved SUV, he threw his duffel in the back and slid behind the wheel. He liked the room in an SUV because he was a big man—at a little over six-two he'd been a giant, back in the day—and he didn't like folding his long legs into a tiny tin can. He didn't bother checking into a hotel first, but drove straight toward Georgetown. At his age Hector didn't require much sleep; he usually napped during the day simply because there wasn't much else to do, but given the urgency of his phone call, even if he wasn't awake, he wouldn't mind being disturbed.

D.C. had been the seat of the Council for the past ninety-odd years, so Luca had spent a lot of time in the city and didn't have to consult a map as he drove. Before, the Council seat had been in Paris, but there had been an incident during World War I that had come perilously close to exposing the kindred, and the Council had thought it prudent to relocate to another continent. D.C. was a beautiful city, but Luca was always amused that the humans who lived here thought two hundred years was a long period of time, that buildings barely a hundred years old could be called historical.

Regardless of the subject, though, humans were endlessly entertaining. Take their obsession with jogging. They seemed to think that trotting around the city would make them stronger, lead to a longer life, when in fact even at their strongest their physical limits made them somewhat pathetic, and a human's longest-lived life was nothing more than the blink of an eye to him.

It made no sense at all to get attached to something so fleeting and fragile. He'd had his moments of weakness, though, and greatly enjoyed them, even though for him any relationship was pretty much one-sided. A few times he'd developed a fondness for a friend, or a woman, and watched over them as best he could, given that they always forgot him as soon as their backs were turned. Seducing a woman over and over again could be a real challenge, too, but was not without its rewards. The trouble was, if they didn't die from some disease or injury, they grew old and died; he watched them fade away while he stayed the same. Then they left, while he was still here. He hadn't let himself become attached to a human for a very long time now; he'd grieved enough.

In a way, Luca could understand the vampires who were tired of living what they saw as a subservient life. Humans were truly less powerful, but because vampires had to remain hidden, the weaker race was the one in charge, and all their rules and regulations made things much more difficult for vampires without the humans even being aware of what they'd done.

The world had changed, and for vampires not for the better. Once vampires had been able to set up their own cities in unexplored areas of the world. With select humans as servants and food supply, they had all they needed to survive. But now there was no suitable part of the world left unexplored. Humans had busily pushed their noses into every nook and cranny, climbing into tiny, cramped ships and sailing unknown waters for months, then settling on every acre of land they could find.

They were like a rash that never stopped spreading. Now they outnumbered vampires to the point where any pitched battle, if it ever came to that, would go against the kindred, even with their superior speed and strength. And then there was that damn spell, cast nearly four hundred years ago, which kept vampires from entering a human's home uninvited.

Once vampires, or at least their existence, had pretty much been common knowledge, though most of the existing vampire lore was pure fiction, invented by humans long ago who had comforted themselves by pretending they had weapons that were useful against vampires. That suited Luca just fine, because that meant he could live among the humans without raising suspicion, provided he followed a few precautions. In most ways, he was like them. He was a living being, not some walking dead person like they thought. His heart beat, he was warm—warmer than they were, actually—and he was solid mass, so he had a reflection in a mirror just as they did. Crosses didn't bother him at all, and holy water was just water. He could bathe in it if he wanted to. He didn't much like sunlight, but he certainly didn't explode or burn if he was exposed to it. Same with garlic; a human who'd eaten garlic simply didn't taste good, but if he were starving he wouldn't let that stop him.

A wooden stake through the heart would kill him, but so would a metal stake, or a shotgun blast. Destroy the heart or the head, and even the strongest vampire would turn to dust; immortal didn't mean invincible, just that he wouldn't age and die in the human manner.

But the bit about not being able to enter a home uninvited—that was true, and it was a real pisser. Several centuries ago a very powerful witch had cast the spell that effectively left vampires out in the cold; then some stupid vampire had let his temper get the best of him and he'd killed her before she could be forced to break the spell.

Luca had been dispatched to take care of the moron for putting the kindred at such a disadvantage, but the damage had already been done. As long as that spell stood, as long as humans could protect themselves by being inside even the flimsiest shelter, vampires were forced to fade back into the shadows and let the humans assume they were nothing more than myth. They couldn't take their place at the top of the food chain. Any battle between humans and vampires would be long fought and ugly, and in the end, the vampires would lose—because of that damn spell. There were very few vampires in comparison to the billions of humans, and with the spell limiting their access, humans always had the sanctuary of home from which they could fight.

Vampires couldn't even glamour a human into issuing the necessary invitation into a home, or convincing the human to step outside. Glamour stopped at the threshold. The protection of the spell went deep, and in over four hundred years no one had been able to break it. The vampires had tried; they'd paid witches, glamoured witches, turned witches into vampires in the hope that their witchy powers would withstand the turning. Sometimes they did, sometimes they didn't, but that didn't matter: The result was the same. The spell still stood. No witch, whether coerced, paid, or turned, had been able to break it.

Luca didn't have the mundane worries many lesser vampires did. Because people forgot him as soon as he passed by, he didn't have to worry about changing his residence before neighbors became suspicious when he didn't age. He didn't have to wrestle with a new world where everyone and everything was on the Internet. He'd gotten all the modern means of identification: Social Security number, driver's license, credit cards, simply because having them made things easier for himself, but he didn't *have* to have them. He liked the convenience so much, though, that he'd procured sev-

eral extra sets in different names, for those times when
he didn't want anyone to know where he was. If necessary, he could glamour airline employees into letting
him on a plane, but by trial and error he'd learned
doing that could cause problems if he took a seat that
had been assigned to some late-arriving passenger.
Actually buying a seat was a simple solution.

Damn computers. He liked using them, but without
a doubt they had complicated the lives of vampires,
some more than others. For him they were a minor irritant; no one remembered him, so no one checked up on
him. For almost all other vampires, they were a major
pain in the ass.

He found a parking spot in Georgetown, a couple of
blocks from the Council building, and walked the rest
of the way. There might have been a parking space
directly in front of the Council building, but he preferred parking where they couldn't see him coming; he
even took the precaution of circling the block so he
approached from a different direction. He was the
Council's executioner, but there were some on the
Council he preferred to catch off guard. It was a game
he played; he liked making them guess, making them
wary of him. Most of them were wary of him anyway,
and he played on that, making them think he was more
powerful than he was. When it came to vampire politics, his reputation was his greatest asset. He didn't
mind being the boogeyman, the one they were all afraid
of, because that bought him his freedom from a lot of
hassle and interference.

Walking also gave him the opportunity to see if anything unusual was going on around him. He wasn't
comfortable, with the sun high overheard, but the
looming trees provided enough shade that he could
ignore the irritation. The thick, heavy air was laden
with the lunchtime smell from a small tavern across the

street; the sidewalk tables were mostly occupied, and his acute hearing picked up the laughter and buzz of conversation.

Nothing caught his attention, so he tuned them out, but drew in deep, appreciative breaths as he continued down the street. He'd long since become old enough to not only tolerate the smell of human food, but to enjoy it—some of it, anyway. He couldn't live on it, but he could eat a few bites of, say, ice cream or some non-spicy food. He'd grown to love the taste of a good wine, despite the fact that alcohol had no effect on him. Same with coffee: good taste, no effect. Sometimes he was really pissed about that, but for the most part he was simply glad he could enjoy the taste even if he didn't get any of the side benefits.

Leaving the wonderful smells behind him, he turned the corner and the Council building came into view on the right, third from the end of the block. It was a three-story red brick, prosperous-looking without being ostentatious, ordinary in that it blended in with all the other buildings in the neighborhood. The interior, however, was opulent; not only did vampires in general love their creature comforts, but the nine Council members had every luxury. In Luca's view that didn't come close to making up for the crushing responsibility and lack of freedom, but to some the prestige and authority were acceptable trade-offs.

The area was stately and fairly quiet, though there was the occasional tourist and, of course, a steady stream of joggers. As Luca neared the Council building, a jogger ran at a steady pace down the sidewalk toward him. *Military,* Luca thought after a quick assessment, though Secret Service or even private security was also a possibility. Short hair, erect posture, excellent overall physical shape; he was sweating, of course, but his breathing was easy. The jogger looked Luca up and down, taking in the long dark hair, the long sleeves that were unusual for such a hot summer day, the sunglasses that hid the direction of his gaze. Instantly there was a new tension in the jogger's body, an awareness that Luca was a potential threat.

Luca kept his pace steady, his body language as neutral as possible. He was what he was, a man of war honed by centuries of experience into something truly scary, and it was obvious to people who'd been trained to assess danger. They might not realize exactly how lethal he was, never dreaming he was a vampire, but the signs were there in the power and fluidity of his movements. It helped that he wasn't carrying anything, and obviously wasn't armed. He kept his hands open, his posture relaxed, and the jogger passed by. Luca gave a quick look over his shoulder, watched the jogger's body relax by the time he'd gone three paces. He'd forgotten, already.

He turned up the sidewalk, leaped the shallow steps two at a time, used his fist to give two sharp raps to the door. There was an ornate doorbell installed beside the door, but actually using it guaranteed that the door wouldn't be opened unless a delivery was expected. The building was always locked, always guarded. He knew that a discreet surveillance camera had been recording him almost from the time he'd turned the corner.

Dammit, the sun was burning him. Not literally, but a midday summer sun was a lot for him to tolerate. Annoyed at having to wait even a short while, he gave another two knocks, this pair decidedly harder than the first two had been.

Abruptly the door was jerked open a bare six inches, and a narrow, suspicious face filled the gap. "We aren't expecting any visitors," the vampire said, without any hostility but also without any welcome.

The guard's name was Jasper. Vampires were as varied in their personalities and strengths as humans were.
Jasper was a little over two hundred years old, which
was kind of middle of the road for a vampire: not
dreadfully young, but not all that old, either. His powers were very mediocre; despite having first met Luca
over seventy years before, he never remembered him.
He couldn't fly, and he wasn't great at glamouring. He
could, however, stay awake during the day, which
made him perfectly suited to be a Council guard. He
could also tolerate a little sunshine, so long as it was
indirect.

"I'm Luca Ambrus," Luca said, reintroducing himself as he did every time he came to the Council building.

Jasper recoiled a little; what vampire wouldn't when
faced with the Council's infamous executioner? "Yes . . .
yes sir," Jasper said, automatically withdrawing and opening the door wide enough for Luca to enter. "Ah . . . who
should I . . . That is, is someone expecting you?" He
ground to a halt, his eyes widening as it occurred to
him that perhaps Luca was here to execute one of the
Council members themselves, or perhaps even *all* of
them. If anyone on the Council had been expecting
him, Jasper would have been notified to expect a visitor.

"Tell Enoch that I'm here," Luca said, closing and
locking the door behind him. Cool, blessed dimness
engulfed him and he gave a mental sigh of relief. He
would have given a physical one, but he never revealed
even the slightest hint of discomfort in front of another
vampire. Let them think he was invincible; it made his
job a little easier if his prey went into the fight expecting to die. He removed his sunglasses and slipped them
into his pocket. Jasper flinched from the clarity of
Luca's pale gray eyes. His eye color would have been

noticeable in anyone, but given his dark hair and olive skin, the contrast made them particularly piercing. There was no power attached to his eye color, but other vampires were never certain whether there was or not. After all, with a blood born, anything was possible.

Jasper turned to reach for a phone but hesitated as his keen hearing picked up the sound of someone hurrying toward the entrance. Luca had already turned to face the newcomer, recognizing Enoch's tread. Enoch had either been monitoring the security camera himself or someone else had been, and had awakened him.

A door opened at the end of the hallway and Enoch appeared. "Mr. Ambrus! I'm sorry, I wasn't notified you'd be arriving." He flicked a quick glance at Jasper. "That'll be all."

Jasper looked relieved at being excused from Luca's presence, and withdrew into the small room off the foyer where he monitored the security cameras.

Enoch was large, bald, and efficient. He was old enough and strong enough to remember Luca, and he was a powerful fighter, but by far his most valuable trait was his efficiency. He oversaw the running of the Council building, which essentially meant he made certain everything was as the Council members desired it. Despite being caught unaware, at a time when most vampires were sleeping, he was dressed in an impeccable Italian suit that had been tailored to fit his bulk. His dark eyes revealed a hint of wariness, as if he knew Luca's unannounced visit was going to cause an uproar. The Council members didn't like surprises, especially in the form of their own paid executioner.

"No problem," Luca said. "I'm here to see Hector."

Enoch blinked in astonishment. "Hector?" he echoed blankly, then recovered himself. "I apologize, it isn't any of my business. I'll call his quarters."

Enoch's surprise was understandable; Hector wasn't

the Council member whom Luca dealt with on official business; that was Theodore, another Greek, but not one Luca liked—or trusted, come to that.

He could have called Hector's number himself, but instead waited while Enoch stepped to an old-fashioned corded phone and dialed Hector's extension. There was a reason for the land-line phone; vampires were as electronically savvy as the general human population, which meant the Council was also very security-conscious. They all had cell phones, for convenience, but cell phone calls were easy to intercept unless they were encrypted, so for communications within the building they used a private land-line system. The calls weren't registered by any phone company, the phones worked during power outages, and the security measures needed were all passive, to guard against any eavesdropping from outside the building.

The idea of someone spying on them wasn't ridiculous; everyone in D.C. seemed to be obsessed with secrets, security, and espionage—and with good reason. What kept them mostly invisible was that vampire concerns ordinarily weren't the same as human concerns, though with three vampires in Congress, that line was beginning to blur.

Luca didn't agree with vampires getting involved in human politics; with the intense media scrutiny these days, no secret was safe, and deliberately making oneself a target of that scrutiny was opening the door to disaster. In the matter of congressional vampires, the Council was divided. Some of the members thought it was a good idea to have friends in high places, while others thought as Luca did, that it was inviting trouble. He just hoped he wasn't one day called on to permanently remove a sitting member of Congress, because that could get nasty. He could make the member disappear—literally—so that wasn't the problem; the resulting hue and cry was the problem, and that was exactly what he was supposed to help the kindred avoid.

Enoch hung up the phone. "Hector didn't answer. He must have left his quarters." He glanced at the ornate grandfather clock that dominated the foyer, a slight frown creasing his forehead as if he wondered what Hector was doing wandering around the building during daylight hours. Luca gathered that Enoch didn't like Council members to deviate from their routine, which was understandable. If he were the one responsible for meeting the wants and needs of nine very powerful, sometimes capricious vampires, he'd want them to be where they were supposed to be, too.

"I'll find him," he said to Enoch, striding to the elevator.

Enoch looked appalled at the idea of Luca doing his own wandering through the building, and hurried to enter the elevator with him. As Luca hit the down button, he hid his amusement; maybe Enoch also suspected he might be here to eliminate one of the Council members, though in that case what he thought he could do was a puzzle. Open a door for Luca, perhaps? Hold down the target in case he or she struggled? Bring him a glass of blood afterward, in case Luca needed refreshment? The one thing he wouldn't do was try to interfere with the executioner, which would sign his own death warrant.

Then another thought struck. Hector was old, but age didn't matter to vampires when it came to one particular area: sex. Could Hector be having an assignation, and Enoch knew about it? On the other hand, why would anyone care? And as worried as Hector had been yesterday when he called, would he then blithely settle down for a long round of sex when he knew Luca was due to arrive? Not likely.

The private apartments of the Council members took up two of the three underground floors of the building, which had originally been built in the eighteen nineties, then extensively remodeled in the nineteen twenties, when the Council had relocated from Paris. Even though the Council members were each able to withstand sunshine, without doubt they all rested more comfortably belowground, where they were more relaxed.

The bottom subterranean floor consisted of storage and three very sturdy cells, not that any vampire who might require a cell was likely to survive long enough to make use of one. Still, they were there, for the rare occasion when the Council wanted a vampire held for questioning. Aboveground were the public rooms where business was conducted and meetings were held, as well as the rooms a human would expect to see should one be allowed inside: a dining room (unused), a kitchen (also unused), a parlor, some private offices, regular bedrooms. To the outside world, the vampire headquarters was an old, elegant, privately owned building with nothing to distinguish it from the rest of the neighborhood.

The private apartments were opulent; each furnished according to the Council member's individual taste. They had all the modern conveniences, including whirlpool tubs, Internet, big-screen televisions, music systems, saunas—anything and everything they desired. Hector's apartment was on the first basement level; the elevator opened onto a richly appointed foyer, decorated with antique furniture probably bought directly from the maker, or plundered from a palace. Luca had never been much on furniture, so he didn't know a Louis of any number from a Hepplewhite or a Brandenburg or whatever the hell those guys' names were; he was much more of a weapons collector. From a hatchet to a fine Toledo blade to a Browning shotgun to a Sig Sauer nine millimeter, he knew his killing instruments.

He paused, but even with his sensitive hearing he heard nothing. If any of the Council members were awake, they weren't moving around or talking. There was something else, though . . . he stopped, the hair on the back of his neck rising in response to the presence of something with which he was well acquainted: his old friend, Death. The lingering violence wafted through these silent, luxurious halls like something he could almost smell, almost touch. Through all the hundreds upon hundreds of years that he'd lived, he'd become so intimate with violence that he could often read details in the echoes of energy that remained behind.

"I'm going into Hector's apartment," he said brusquely, striding down the hallway with Enoch a half-step behind. He kept all his senses at a high pitch, so acute that he could even hear the rapid thumping of Enoch's heart.

"But—"

Luca didn't pause, and Enoch bit back whatever objection he'd been about to make. Hector's apartment was on the left, at the end of the hallway. Luca gave one sharp knock and the door swung open beneath the force of the blow. Looking down, he saw where the heavy wood had been splintered, the metal of the lock twisted. Even though both the door and the lock had been industrial strength, they couldn't withstand the sheer force of a strong vampire.

He stepped inside, Enoch right behind him. "Hector!" Enoch called, his tone edgy with tension. "Hector, are you here?"

In a way, Luca thought, but kept the idea to himself. Hector had been right . . . but then he almost always was. Death *had* been coming for him.

Rapidly he gathered what impressions he could from the swirling miasma of leftover violence and the thoughts Hector had hurled out, not as weapons with which he could protect himself, but a means perhaps by which his murderer could be found. He would need more time to sort through all the impressions and thoughts, the essence of Hector's life that he'd left behind, but that time wasn't now. There would be no other opportunity for him to read the initial reactions of the other Council members to Hector's death, which meant he had to move now, before they could be fore-warned.

"Wake the Council members," he ordered, retreating from Hector's quarters and drawing Enoch with him. He kept his expression cold and blank, to keep from giving away anything. For now, he needed to keep what he'd sensed to himself. "Don't tell them why. Just say it's an emergency, and they're needed in the Council chamber."

Enoch looked as if he wanted to spew objections and questions, but Luca turned his pale, glittering gaze on him and despite himself Enoch looked away. Luca was the only one who knew the extent of his powers—and, conversely, his own limitations. Other vampires whis-pered and wondered, but the ones who had dared try him had all gone to dust at his hands.

"Yes, sir," Enoch finally said, and went to the near-est house phone to begin rousing the sleeping Council members. Luca stood beside him, making certain none of the members were given a heads-up about the situa-tion. Enoch followed his instructions to the letter, despite the complaints Luca could hear coming loud and clear from eight powerful and very unhappy vam-pires. After making those eight calls Enoch looked very unhappy himself. There had to be someone, or several someones, on the Council whom he would have liked to warn, but with Luca standing right there he couldn't disobey his instructions.

In a remarkably short time, considering how fractious and uncooperative the Council members could be when they weren't happy, Luca stood in the primary Council chamber and stared grim-faced at the eight seated members. Women had always outnumbered men on the Council, whether because they were more cunning or paid more attention to surviving rather than dominating; currently there were five women—Alma, Marie, Nadia, Eleanor, and Darnell—and three men—Theodore, Pablo, and Benedict. Of the eight of them, Luca couldn't think of a single one he'd trust with his life. But which one of them would undermine the Council's chosen path, and murder Hector to prevent him from interfering?

"If you're as smart as you think you are, you'll have a very good explanation for this," Theodore growled, his thick black brows drawing together. He sat down with a thump, drawing his extravagant ceremonial robe around him. He was the only one who had taken the time to put on the Council robe; the others were dressed in whatever had been at hand. Granted, with vampire speed they could have found anything they wanted and been dressed in it in almost the same length of time, but Theodore was the only one who had bothered. Being on the Council was a huge ego stroke to him, and he always dressed the part.

From the scowl on his face, it was obvious Theodore didn't like that Luca had arrived without his knowledge; as the one tasked with giving Luca his assignments he looked on himself as Luca's supervisor. Much as the humans had comforted themselves with completely useless bits of folklore about what worked to repel vampires, some on the Council, and especially Theodore, had convinced themselves, or were trying very hard to, that Luca was *their* tool, *their* employee, and subject to *their* orders.

Luca, on the other hand, regarded Theodore as nothing more than a pain in the ass and had made his opinion plain on several occasions. What was the Council going to do? Fire him? They could certainly stop giving him assignments, as well as the very nice payment that went with those assignments, but in the larger picture Luca would scarcely miss the income—and they would have to find someone else capable of doing what he did.

His reasons for taking the jobs weren't complicated; he saw a need for what he did, and he liked to fight. He was at heart a creature of war, and if living over two thousand years had taught him anything, it was to keep things simple and uncomplicated inside himself, no matter how tangled and problematic life on the outside might become. So long as pursuing rogue vampires gave him an outlet for his battle skills, he'd keep doing it.

On yet another side of the equation, the Council members looked to him for protection, if need be, and none of them would like it if he were no longer available, so while Theodore might posture and growl, he certainly didn't want to push Luca into quitting. He'd do just enough to satisfy his own ego that he hadn't been a wuss. The mere knowledge that Luca stood ready to meet any threat had undoubtedly, over the years, dissuaded many hotheaded, ambitious vampires from hostile acts.

The Council members were powerful in their own right, but having Luca as a deterrent was definitely a bonus even though that meant *they* then had to deal with him. Luca had played nice over the years, taking their assignments and not giving them cause to worry about him, but each and every one of them was aware that playing nice had always been his choice, not theirs, and he could change his mind at any moment.

Mutual distrust made for an interesting working relationship. To Luca's way of thinking, it kept him on his toes, kept him aware, on edge—and alive.

"Hector's been murdered," he finally said, ignoring Theodore's bluster and watching the faces before him. Vampires weren't known for their lively expressions, merely because of all those years of practicing self-control, but there were still small flinches and gasps, and not even a vampire could control whether or not his or her pupils dilated.

Darnell blinked her eyes once, slowly. "How do you know? Did you find his dust?" No one except she knew what name she'd been born with, in what was now Ethiopia, or why she'd chosen an Irish name. She was deliberate in manner and intensely private. She had always voted to maintain the status quo, but at the same time she was so contemptuous of humans that Hector had never been certain of her vote.

"I could tell," he replied, his tone flat. If they had no idea *how* he could tell, that was their problem, not his.

"From thousands of miles away? You *were* in Scotland, weren't you?"

"Enoch opened Hector's door for me." He'd always made certain that no one, not even Hector, knew exactly where his homes were located, but abruptly he decided that the fact they even knew the country was more than he wanted them to know. He had other bolt-holes, of course, but they were for emergencies only. Though he was safer from the Council than the average vampire—since no human ever remembered seeing him, no human could give directions to his homes—the Council members did have their own skilled hunters.

"And you saw his dust?"

"I didn't have to."

Marie, the oldest and the only blood born on the Council, sat back with a quick, tiny sip of air. "If Luca says that Hector has been murdered, I believe him. That means . . . one of us killed him. No one else in the building is powerful enough to have done it." She stared at him, then looked around at her fellow Council members, the faint shock in her eyes morphing to one of calculation as she considered all the ramifications and how she could use this to her advantage. Hector had been the head of the Council; perhaps she would be elected to succeed him. Her pragmatic Gallic nature meant she wouldn't waste time regretting that someone she'd known, served with, and respected had finally met an end to his long life; she was a political creature to the core.

"We're supposed to believe that you 'sensed' this?" Theodore demanded truculently, which was his normal tone. "How do we know *you* didn't kill him? That's what you do, isn't it?"

Not for the first time, Luca had the thought that the Council members were strong enough to kill him, if even two of them combined to attack. Also not for the first time, he assessed Theodore as not having the balls to be one of those two, because he would always expect the remaining Council members to turn on them. Did it follow, then, that neither would Theodore be likely to have orchestrated the attack on Hector? He thought so, yes. He didn't miss the irony that the member he least liked was probably the one he could most trust, at least in this matter.

"Enoch can vouch for me," he said, the slight hint of boredom in his tone letting Theodore know that his attacks weren't coming anywhere close to hitting a target.

Theodore turned to Enoch. "Is that true?"

"I've been with him since he arrived, less than half an hour ago," Enoch admitted, the normally unflappable house manager uneasy at being put on the spot. He made a tiny shift of his weight, which in a vampire was the equivalent of wringing his hands.

"And Hector has really been murdered?"

Enoch darted a quick glance at Luca. "He isn't in his quarters."

Nadia threw up her hands. "So we are having all this drama and no one knows for certain if Hector is dead or merely *elsewhere*?"

"He called me," Luca said, still watching their faces. "He said there's a rebel movement to bring open war against the humans."

"Why is that a bad thing?" Alma growled in her deep-throated voice. "I've said the same thing for years." She sat near the foot of the table, her pale green eyes slumbrous as she watched him. Alma was a piece of work—ancient, bloodthirsty, beautiful, red-haired, and power hungry. One of the newer Council members, having been seated barely fifty years ago, she was constantly advocating for change in their community and generally making a nuisance of herself with her complaining. Luca was surprised they hadn't booted her out years ago, though getting rid of a Council member wasn't as easy as adding one. She *could* be the traitor, but he reserved judgment on that.

A scan of the other faces at the table told him she wasn't alone in her opinion. It grated on most vampires that they had to hide their existence, that their *food* had more power than they did.

Sorting this out was going to be like swimming through a school of piranha. Council members were chosen for their age, their strength, and their commitment to maintaining the status quo, though that last sometimes depended on the mood of the moment. The youngest Council member had been around during the Wars of the Roses; one didn't manage to live that long, especially in the treacherous mire of vampire politics, without an innate cunning backed by mental toughness and unusual power.

Then Marie sat forward, her dark gaze pinned on him. "So. What you are saying is that one of us is a traitor."

Luca smiled, an expression that held all the humor and friendliness of a shark going in for the kill. "Exactly."

CHAPTER
THREE

They were all quick to make the connection, but then cunning and trickery were necessary parts of their lives. Hector could only have been killed by a powerful vampire who was already inside the building, and knew where his quarters were. Tie that with news of a brewing rebel faction, and his killer was obviously part of that faction. Yes, there were aides and servants inside the building, but the key word was "powerful." A vampire in a support position wouldn't fit that description.

This was the tricky part. The traitor had had help in killing Hector, which meant Luca was currently outnumbered and handicapped by not knowing who all the players were. He could feel his heartbeat speeding up in anticipation of a fight to the death—vampires almost didn't know any other way to fight—but he quickly focused and brought his heart rate back to normal. With their acute hearing, every person in this room could hear one another's heartbeats and he didn't want his to be racing. He'd been listening, but the only fast heartbeat he could hear was Enoch's, though the manager was settling down now. Whoever the traitor was, he or she was either very controlled or not at all worried—or both, which brought up some interesting possibilities.

First he had to make it out of here alive, and that meant making the traitor think he was safe, at least for the time being. The only thing Luca had going for him was that no one other than himself—and Hector— knew how he could read the remnants of energy, of both life and death. That was his ace in the hole, the thread he could pick up that would, with luck, eventually lead him back to the traitor.

He hadn't been able to pick up a betraying flicker of expression from any of them that would tell him who was behind Hector's murder. He'd hoped he could, but that had been an outside chance. Not one of them was unduly upset by Hector's death, and in the rarified air of the ruling Council, a vampire killing another vampire wasn't something they worried about. What concerned the Council—most of the Council members, anyway—was preserving the wall of secrecy that protected them all. A simple murder . . . bah! Unless it was done in a public manner, who cared?

He cared. Hector had been his friend.

Deliberately he dragged back the chair Hector had always occupied, the seat of the Head of the Council, and sat down. He didn't pull the chair up to the table; instead he kept it back and slightly at an angle, his long legs sprawled out and crossed at the ankles. He was just far enough from the long conference table that he didn't give the impression of taking Hector's place, but at the same time the fact that he'd taken the chair at all offended their egos. He liked to keep them a little off balance. He figured it was good for them—and in this instance might startle one particular member into making a tiny mistake.

Every one of them was highly conscious of their privileged status, and they didn't like the casual way he'd just put himself on their level. Even Marie looked taken aback, though for what felt like centuries—hell, maybe because it had been—every time there had been an opening on the Council she had lobbied him to accept the position.

He lifted his arms and laced his fingers behind his neck, the very picture of indolence. "No question one or more of you is working with the rebels," he said lazily. "The bigger question is what the Council wants me to do about it."

The eight of them looked at one another, weighing, considering. He could almost hear their thoughts: Which of them was the most likely to go behind the backs of the others? Who thought it was time to come out of the shadows? Who most resented the humans? Unfortunately, the answers to those three questions weren't necessarily the same.

Alma was the one who had always harped that they should resume their natural positions of superiority, but Theodore was the one most likely to go behind their backs. As to who most resented the humans . . . who knew? Possibly they all did, which meant that the answer became one of degree. None of this told him who *they* thought the traitor could be, just that any of them were possible.

"You're assuming Hector was correct about the rebel faction," Benedict finally said. He was Roman, a patrician, and had never liked associating with those he considered lower than himself, which was almost everyone, vampire and human alike. It amused Luca that, as blood borns, both he and Marie presented a dilemma to Benedict; they were members of the Rolls-Royce class of vampires, but their respective parents, in their human lives, had obviously not been as highly born as Benedict, so in his eyes they were tainted by low birth . . . but they themselves had never been human, which threw Benedict's value system out of balance.

"There was no point in killing him, otherwise," Luca pointed out.

"True," Eleanor agreed. She was tiny, as people often had been hundreds of years ago. Being made vampire didn't make the person suddenly grow taller; rather, they were preserved as they had been when they were turned, which was why the myth that vampires were all beautiful and physically perfect was only that: a myth. If people had been ugly as humans, they were just as ugly as vampires—much stronger, much faster, immune to aging and all diseases, but still ugly.

Eleanor was neither pretty nor ugly. What she was, was alert, wily, and a ruthless enemy. Hector had seemed fond of her, and often relied on her common sense to sway other Council members to his way of thinking. She drummed her nails on the conference table in a quick tattoo. "If these rebels are so organized that they've recruited one of us, I'm amazed that no intelligence regarding this has come our way. We all have kindred children, alliances, our own sources of information—" By that she meant "spies," but that didn't have to be spelled out. "We should have received warning. I don't like this at all."

"Hector wasn't infallible," Pablo pointed out. He crossed his arms over his burly chest. "Perhaps he was mistaken."

"Then why is he dead?" Marie snapped.

Nadia snorted. "We don't know that he is. All we know is that he isn't in his quarters, and Luca has assumed that he's dead because Hector called him in a panic about some rebels that none of us have heard about until now."

The very idea of Hector in a panic was enough to make several of them roll their eyes and snicker. Nadia set back in her chair, sulking.

Luca hid his annoyance at their behavior, though he'd seen it before. No matter how old or how power- ful the vampires, put them in government and their behavior began devolving toward juvenile. He didn't bother telling them again what he knew to be true. Instead he looked around the table and said, "Well? What do you want me to do? Anything? Nothing?"

Someone sitting at that table would be very relieved that he was evidently willing to let the Council direct him in this, though that someone would be greatly mistaken, because no way in hell would he let this go. Still, let them think they had control of the situation.

No one said anything. After a moment, Marie pushed her chair back and stood. "Obviously no one is going to make any decisions right now, but the one thing we can do is look around Hector's quarters." She glanced at Luca, silently asking if that was where he thought Hector had been killed, and he gave a slight nod. "If we find his dust, then we'll know Luca's assumptions are on target—as usual," she added, not above a jab at her fellow Council members.

"Are you in charge now?" Theodore growled, though everyone had risen to their feet, himself included.

"No, she isn't," Alma snapped.

"Oh, for God's sake," Marie muttered. "I said 'let's go look,' not 'I'm taking over.' "

"That's what you *said*," Pablo observed. "I'm not too certain that's what you meant."

There had always been a degree of tension between Marie and the other Council members, perhaps because she was a blood born and they feared her enhanced powers—much as they feared Luca—though of course none of them would ever admit to that. Jealousy came into play, too; blood borns matured until they reached the apex, the optimum physical and mental peak; for Luca, perhaps because of his size and the extra growing time he'd needed, his prime had occurred in his early thirties. For Marie, it had been at roughly age sixteen. Her skin was flawless, her teeth perfect, her hair thick and lustrous, her breasts nice and high. Even Alma, as beautiful as she was, looked like someone's aunt compared to Marie's youthfulness. Because of that, they were all alert to any sign of ambition in Marie.

God save him from politics, Luca thought wearily. It reduced ancient, powerful vampires to the emotional maturity of grade-schoolers.

Enoch nervously led the way to Hector's quarters. When he reached out to open the door, however, Luca said, "Wait," and he put enough power in his voice that all of them, even Marie, stopped in their tracks. Enoch visibly shivered, his eyes widening as he stared at Luca. Vocal compulsion wasn't a rare power, but the level of strength needed for it to work on vampires as powerful as the Council members was something that made all of them take notice.

He moved ahead of all of them, and Enoch stepped back as he approached. Deliberately he opened Hector's door and stepped inside. The first room, for the sake of camouflage should any intruder be able to enter the building, was a rather nondescript office. There was a desk and a long leather sofa, both well-used, with a thick rug covering the floor between them. One painting hung behind the desk; Botticelli, Luca noted, and likely not a copy. There were no plants, real or artificial, no knickknacks, just a jumble of papers and some files.

If any outsider were to stumble upon this particular room, it would give them no pause at all—unless they had an eye for art.

Hector's suite of private rooms sprawled beyond this square, austere office, but as he had before, Luca immediately sensed the swirl of recent and deadly energy here, in this room.

"Is this necessary?" Nadia asked. "If he's merely elsewhere, we're invading his privacy—"

Ignoring her, Luca moved farther into the room. Hector had died here; he felt as if he were drowning in Hector's life force, in his very essence. He allowed his mind to clear, to open, and then he thought of Hector. He captured and controlled the energy that danced here. There were many memories of the old vampire to call upon, and within those memories there was a particular energy that *was* Hector, his essence, his power.

There were energy pictures in this very room, as if Hector had taken a photo of his death and spat it upon the air. The murderer hadn't been working alone; death lurked in the room—and in the hallway. The danger that Hector had sensed had carefully remained hidden. Luca knew who had taken Hector's life, but still wasn't able to discern the power in command.

Hector hadn't gone easily; he'd fought for his life. The violence Luca sensed would have overturned furniture, broken lamps . . . but there was nothing out of place. He looked around, taking the time to notice every detail. The office had been straightened, the broken items removed and replaced. Lines in the thick pile of the rug revealed a recent vacuuming.

Vacuumed? Of course—remove Hector's dust, and there was no real proof that he was dead.

Luca crouched and touched one finger to the rug. The faint remnants of Hector seemed to shout at him, the impression was so strong. He looked over his shoulder, met the eyes of the one Council member he knew had a sense that was related to his, though not as strong. He was well aware that she could be the traitor, but so could any of the other seven. "Darnell," he said quietly. "Tell me what you feel."

She came to him, sank bonelessly to a crouch beside him. As he had done, she reached out one finger, dragged it through the pile of the rug. Lifting her finger, she stared at the gray dust coating it. Her large dark eyes were somber.

For a long moment she was silent, then she said, "Hector."

Behind them Theodore asked heavily, "You have no doubt?"

"No," she said. "None. Hector is dead. Here, on this rug."

"It's been vacuumed," Luca said, pointing to the track marks on the pile.

"So the rest of him is in a vacuum-cleaner bag somewhere?" Alma asked, not quite eliminating the snicker from her voice.

Luca slowly turned his head and pinned her with his pale gaze. The humor vanished from her face and she moved as if to step back before she remembered that she was a Council member and stopped herself. Anger and resentment flashed hot in her eyes.

Silence fell in the room. There was nothing else he could do here at the moment, and plans he needed to put into motion. Rising to his full height, Luca caught Theodore's eye. "You know how to reach me," he said. "Let me know what the Council decides."

Theodore gave a small, brusque nod of his head.

Luca strode from the room, down the hall to the elevator. The doors opened as soon as he punched the button.

"Luca . . . wait!"

It was Marie, striding toward him with a confidence that her small stature could neither diminish nor disguise. Her expression was a mixture of determination and exasperation. "I'll see you out," she said, for the benefit of any listening ears, and stepped into the elevator with him. No sooner had the doors closed than she muttered, "Morons."

"Anyone in particular?" he asked.

She looked up at him, her gaze narrowed and sharp. "Don't pretend you don't think the same thing."

Though they were both blood born, had known each other for hundreds of years, Marie had never been a confidante and Luca couldn't see making her one now. He shrugged and didn't answer.

"What are you going to do?"

He lied without hesitation. "Depends on the Council." He'd do what he wanted to do regardless of how the Council voted, if they ever got around to voting. He could almost see it now: First they'd have to elect a new member to replace Hector, then they'd have to elect a new Head of Council, then they'd have to discuss and debate the issue.

"The Council would be more decisive if you were on it."

He shook his head. "You don't give up, do you? Not just 'no,' but 'no way in hell.' " Not that she didn't have a point, considering what he'd just been thinking, but he didn't want to be a part of their decision-making.

The elevator stopped and the doors opened to a soft *ping*. They left the car, and Marie put a hand on his arm as he started toward the front door. "Luca . . . think about it. Don't automatically say no. I had to be persuaded to accept a Council position, too. Once you're on it, it's different from what you expected. And together, you and I could shape the Council the way we wanted. What you did with your Voice . . ."

"That was the upper limit of my power in Voice," he said wryly, again lying without compunction. "And all the other Council members, including yourself, will immediately begin working to strengthen their resistance to Voice, so don't bother stroking my ego."

Her dark eyes flashed, and in that millisecond the Council member was replaced by the woman; her look said she wouldn't mind stroking something else. For the most part, sex to a vampire was a casual, voracious appetite, frequently fed but seldom significant. Young vampires were prone to forming relationships, but older vampires generally knew better.

Having sex with Marie wasn't on his list of things he wanted to do, though. She was a Council member, and thus a suspect. He had fought wars and battles his entire life, and he looked at everything, even sex, from a strategic point of view. She was very old and very powerful, and the act of sex might provide a moment—such as during orgasm—that would leave him vulnerable. He didn't believe in vulnerability, especially when it involved someone as arrogant and powerful as she was.

Then the moment was gone as fast as it had appeared and she was her usual focused, determined self. "Do you have to leave immediately? I want to show you something," she said abruptly.

He needed to get some rest. He needed to feed. He'd been traveling all night, the sunlight was draining, and he hadn't fed in several days now, something he needed to do more often when he was exerting this much effort. Hunger was gnawing at him, fraying his self-control. The last thing he wanted to do was to put off feeding so long that he went into a frenzy. But his curiosity was sparked, maybe because he caught an air of banked . . . excitement? self-satisfaction? about her, and he wondered what could have brought that on. He said, "No, I can stay for a while."

"This way," she said, and led him through a door toward the back of the building, then up a flight of stairs. He wondered why they didn't take the elevator, but he preferred the stairs anyway—there wasn't enough room in an elevator to really fight, if he needed to—so he didn't ask. As they climbed she said with a sigh, "You are so stubborn. Together, you and I could easily rule the Council. Two blood born vampires, with our combined power and age—no one would dare to challenge us."

"I have enough power to suit me," Luca said easily. "I like my life as it is."

"You're a hired gun!" Marie argued. "We send you after rogue vampires and you dispose of them like any capable garbage man. You're better than that. You deserve more."

Luca smiled. He wasn't going to allow Marie to get a rise out of him, as she obviously intended. "Maybe I like being a hired gun. No worries and plenty of money."

"You have no idea of the amount of money you *could* have. Look at Valerik."

Valerik was one of the vampire senators. He'd changed his name, established all the proper records, and he was capable of withstanding daylight. Maybe he'd glamoured people into voting for him, but that wasn't Luca's problem.

"Valerik is a twit, and he always has been."

"That's beside the point. Now that he's in office, he's become a very *rich* twit."

They'd reached the second floor, and from there took a long hallway that led to a plain door that opened onto another stairway. The building was like a maze, purposefully confusing, with doors that led nowhere and other doors that led in circles. No one had ever invaded the Council headquarters, but if they ever did, finding what they were searching for wouldn't be easy.

"Where are we going?" Luca asked, looking around to note the details of this part of the building, where he'd never been before. He reached out to touch her energy, to read her, but she was too strong and too guarded for him to see beyond the surface.

"Here," she said, stopping before a door and fishing a key from the pocket of her black capri pants. "I have just what you need. She's pretty, young, and tasty." She looked over her shoulder and smiled at him. "And she likes it."

The door opened on a small studio apartment. There was a tiny kitchenette, a living area with a long couch and a flat-screen TV, and a full-sized bed butted up against one wall and set apart by a lacquered Chinese screen. A pretty, dark-haired young woman looked up when the door opened, and smiled as she got to her feet. Naturally, there were no windows—no threat of sunlight, no way for the pretty girl to signal for help, if she ever decided she didn't "like it."

"Kristi, darling, this is Luca. He's hungry."

Instead of being afraid, as most humans would've been, Kristi turned that beaming smile on Luca and began to unbutton her blouse. For a moment, Luca wondered why she was so accommodating, and then he saw her eyes.

"You've drugged her," he said, his tone flat. He didn't like that Marie had somehow known how hungry he was, and he didn't like the risk of kidnapping a human and using her against her will.

"I have not," Marie responded sharply. "Kristi has simply been glamoured."

"For how long?" Luca asked.

"Just a few weeks. When she goes home all she'll remember is this lovely villa and the view of the ocean, and the man with whom she had a short, but passionate summer affair. She might wonder why he doesn't call, she might try to find him, but other than that she'll be fine."

"She'll be a vegetable." Being glamoured wasn't without its side effects. A one-time, short-term glamour wouldn't cause any noticeable brain damage, but something this continuous would leave the girl a drooling idiot. It wasn't new, to keep food on-site, particularly where the Council was concerned. In the old days, it hadn't been hard to find and keep willing donors for many years. These days, with communication so widespread, that simply wasn't possible. When people went missing, the authorities mounted massive searches, unless the missing human was one of the homeless, which pretty much meant no self-respecting vampire wanted to feed from them anyway.

That left drugging and glamouring, but drugs left the blood bitter-tasting. Usually a human was kept only a short while, and glamoured into forgetting.

"No, she won't. I've been working on this, refining my touch. I use barely a breath of power. When we release her, she'll have suffered very little damage. Trust me," she added in a low voice, "she's better off here than she was where we found her."

Kristi shrugged off her blouse and unfastened her jeans. Luca held up a hand to stop her. He wasn't about to fuck and feed on an empty-headed girl who had given up her free will—or had it taken from her—and had probably spread her legs for every Council member, and probably the on-site staff as well, who was interested in having her. Certainly her blood had been taken; if anyone had given her blood as well, during sex, then she was on her way to being bonded and he didn't want to be the one who went over that threshold with her. The last thing he needed was to find himself bonded to a mentally handicapped blood donor. Marie might say Kristi would be all right, but that didn't automatically translate to reality.

Damn her, anyway. He needed to feed, and somehow she'd known that, dangling this helpless fruit in front of him. In the end, though, Kristi's lack of will helped him hold back.

"I like the hunt," he said, motioning for the girl to be seated. She sank back, her expression disappointed and even hurt.

"Don't we all," Marie snapped, then she shook her head and made a motion as if to wipe away her ill temper. "I miss it," she said wistfully, "the days when we could move around without having to worry about computers and identification and all of the other things we have to deal with now." She heaved a sigh, then gestured toward Kristi. "Command her to fight, if that's what you want. She'll do whatever you tell her."

"Knowing that kind of takes the fun out of it. Thanks, but no thanks. How many others have you kept glamoured this long?"

She shrugged. "It's been an ongoing project of mine, to minimize the risk we run when we bring food here. The less often it has to be done, the less likely we are to have difficulties. Intense, long-lasting glamour has always been one of my gifts, but for the past twenty years or so—not very long, really—I've been fine-tuning my touch. It's very delicate, like touching a butterfly with a feather. Their minds are so weak, the ordinary glamour is a sledgehammer to their brains."

"Is Kristi the only one here?"

"No, there are a dozen more on site. Male and female, all young, all pretty, and entirely ours. This is the way it was before, with humans serving us the way they should."

On the couch, Kristi whispered dreamily, "I can hear the ocean. It's so relaxing." She stared at one of the walls as if she were looking out a window at the pounding surf.

"What did Hector think of this new arrangement?" Luca asked. In the past, donors had been housed here for a few hours, perhaps a day, then their memories were wiped and they were returned to their rightful places in the world.

Maybe she heard the disapproval in his tone, because she stiffened and her dark eyes narrowed, but she contented herself with saying, "He saw the logic of the arrangement."

Maybe. If Marie could glamour that many people for that long without irrevocably damaging their minds, that would certainly make feeding the Council less of a logistical problem. He shrugged. "I can see the benefit, I guess, but I'm still not interested."

Marie shrugged, too, then closed and locked the door. If Kristi was so willing and the glamour so perfected, Luca wondered, why bother with the lock? Marie turned, headed for the stairway with a sway in her hips. "Find whoever killed Hector," she said without looking back. "I know you'll be looking regardless of what the Council says or how long it takes the fools to reach a consensus. The murder of a councilman can't be tolerated, or we're all at risk."

Was her concern genuine, or was she simply throwing up a smoke screen? After all, her insistence that humans should be subservient was in line with the rebels' way of thinking, but not unusual at all in the vampire world. Probably all of the Council members felt the same way, even though they bowed to necessity when it came to keeping their own existence secret.

Luca followed her back to the entryway, then let himself out. The hot summer sunlight seemed to eat at his skin, but he didn't show any reaction as he strode away. When he was out of sight of the building, he checked to see if he'd been followed—he hadn't—then he began backtracking. He knew who had killed Hector, but not the Council member behind the murder. How deeply did the betrayal go? How organized were these rebels, and how close were they to bringing disaster down on them all? Yes, he was hungry, and the hunt called to him, but he had control over even his most basic needs, and feeding would wait . . . for now.

FOUR

Potomac neighborhood

Her captors left her alone more frequently these days than they had in the beginning. Nevada Sheldon had been twenty years old when she'd been taken, a college student oblivious to the dark world beyond—and yet so close to—her own. She'd certainly had no idea that she was a witch. At first she hadn't believed them. True, she'd had good instincts all her life, and on occasion small wishes would come true, but she'd never considered those little oddities to be a sign of power. Everyone had things like that happen, right?

The power she possessed now would have been frightening and unmanageable for the girl she'd been then, but now she had the strength to move forward and make the best of what she'd discovered, what she'd become.

Nevada didn't know if the vampires who had taken her and her family almost three years ago thought she was totally cowed, or if they were so arrogant they didn't think she could possibly harm them or interfere with their plans. She voted for arrogance, because no one topped the vampires in that. Three years ago she hadn't known they even existed, but since then her survival had depended on learning as much about them as she could, and fast.

And yet, *they* needed *her;* they needed her to break the spell cast by an ancestor she hadn't known about until they'd told her about her witch blood, which was some-thing else she hadn't known about, much less that she was evidently descended from a long line of über-witches. Because they needed her, they'd assured her that she wouldn't be harmed, but at the same time, they had no qualms about threatening her parents and her younger brother and sister to make her do what they wanted.

She'd been terrified at first. She hadn't known what they were talking about, only that she and her entire family had been kidnapped by these monsters, then separated. She was kept in luxury in a large bedroom in a mansion, while her family was kept, the vampires said, in a dungeon somewhere. After being held in total seclusion, except for the monsters, after being scared half out of her mind, finally it had occurred to her that she had a weapon against them: herself. They used her family to force her to do what they wanted, but, by God, they had better keep them alive and at least rea-sonably well-treated or she wouldn't do a damn thing the monsters wanted.

Standoff. After trying unsuccessfully to bully her, they had finally relented and shown her cell phone pic-tures of her family, and every now and then they would place a call and she'd be allowed to talk, very briefly, to one of her family just to reassure her that they were still alive.

So long as her family was alive, she would *try* to do what the vampires wanted. They set up a work area in the middle of the huge bedroom, bringing in tables and a comfortable chair, and then they had brought her tons of really old books, books so old she was afraid to turn the pages because she kept expecting them to fall apart under her fingers, but they never did. There were so many books that they were stacked everywhere, piles of them, some of them so huge and heavy she couldn't lift them and had to either call one of the vampires for help or shove and tug at the books herself to get them out of the way. She did a lot of shoving and tugging, because as a general rule she'd rather eat ground glass than ask a vampire for help.

For the first several weeks, she'd been at a complete loss. A witch? Her? If she'd been a witch, wouldn't she have stopped them from kidnapping her family? But they'd told her she "must learn"—yeah, that was real specific—and the threats against her family had spurred her to at least *pretend* she was doing something, so she'd begun leafing through those old books. She didn't like touching them, had to force herself to look at the pages. They gave her a creepy feeling. The paper smelled . . . weird, as if wasn't really paper at all, but something else she couldn't identify. And some of the pages were stained with what she thought was blood, which *really* gave her the creeps. If these books were about witchcraft, it was the bad kind of witchcraft, not the kind that was all about being one with nature and treating people with respect, stuff like that.

Some of them were in some kind of weird language she couldn't read. How the hell was she supposed to "learn" if she couldn't read the language? On the other hand, if the vamps had been able to read the books, they wouldn't have needed her; likewise if they suspected she really had no clue how to learn what they insisted she learn, so she kept her mouth shut and dug into the books.

The books that were in that weird language she shoved off to the side—why waste time with them?— and began concentrating on those that were sort of, at least, written in English. Even though she understood all the words, they were strung together in ways that didn't make sense. *Light of the dark, dark of the day*— yeah, right. It was gibberish. But the monsters took their gibberish seriously, so Nevada tried her best to do what they wanted.

Then, slowly, the words in the books began to resonate with something deep inside her, began to take on meanings that went beyond the words themselves. She couldn't quite put her finger on exactly what it was, maybe something like a current she could ride, a door she could step through, or both. But there was *something*— and it called to her. So what at first she had been doing out of desperation she began doing willingly, and then even eagerly, though she hid that from her captors.

Six months into her captivity, she successfully cast her first simple spell. It wasn't anything much, she'd tried to reheat some food that had gotten cold because she was distracted by her reading—the food was pretty terrible because vampires weren't interested in eating at *all,* so being cold had pretty much made the stuff inedible—but the spell *worked.* She'd been so excited she had jumped up and down and done a happy dance, because all this reading and studying was evidently accomplishing something after all.

Then she had wondered what she was so happy about, because she was smart enough to figure out that, if she managed to reverse this spell the vamps were so concerned about, then she'd have no more value to them and they'd kill her *and* her family as casually as if they were swatting flies. It stood to reason that if she could reverse the spell, she would also be able to reinstate it whenever she chose, or lay some other nasty spell on them, so of course they intended to kill her.

Her only chance, and the only chance her family had, was to hide how fast her skills were developing until she was strong enough, skilled enough, to do . . . something. Another kind of protection spell, maybe. A liberation spell. Hell, she didn't know. Just *something*.

She'd played along as best she could, reassuring them that she was learning, demonstrating small spells for them when they pressed her for proof of her progress. The weeks and months had turned to years, and she would have gone crazy a long time ago if the work itself hadn't been so engrossing—and if it hadn't been for Sorin.

She didn't know what his last name was. Maybe vampires didn't have last names. No, they'd once been humans, so surely they *did*, but none of those she had met used a surname. She guessed that when you lived for hundreds of years last names stopped mattering, because it wasn't as if they were going to have kids and pass the name along. Nevada didn't understand why she liked him. No, it wasn't even something as simple as "liking." It was something more. Nothing sexual, nothing romantic, but some sort of tie she couldn't understand. She felt safe with him. Okay, not exactly *safe*, but safer.

Sorin was . . . well, she didn't know what he was. Not the leader, because that was the bitch who thought she was some kind of queen, but nevertheless all the others kind of deferred to him. It wasn't just that he was big and muscled and gorgeous, with blond hair and glowing blue eyes, or that he was like some kind of general in this battle or war they were fighting. (They weren't exactly forthcoming with her—she only got bits and pieces when they forgot she could overhear them. She tried to put it all together into a story, but huge gaps were missing.) The other vamps *respected* him. He was in some position of power, because they listened to him. Well, the bloodsucking bitch queen who ran this sick show didn't, but from what Nevada could tell she didn't listen to or respect anyone except herself.

And Sorin had protected her, hadn't allowed any of the others to feed from her. His reason had been completely logical: the work and study load they required of her was exhausting, even with her at her full strength; if they weakened her by feeding from her, she wouldn't be able to keep up the pace. They were on some kind of schedule, Nevada thought, one that she was now pushing to the limit. They wanted results, they wanted that spell broken, and they wanted it soon.

If Nevada could have arranged it, she wouldn't have had contact with any of them other than Sorin, not that he was an angel himself. Far from it, in fact. He came to her room every day—or rather, every night—to assess her progress, and he wasn't above using threats against her family to push her even harder. Sometimes, though, he tried to charm her with a smile—and, gawd, what a smile!—or a kind word, a reminder that he wasn't like the others, that he liked her and wanted what was best.

But Sorin *was* different from the others, even though she couldn't explain why. He was frightening, but he didn't frighten *her,* even when he was threatening her. He was a vampire like the others, but he didn't give her the heebie-jeebies. She actually looked forward to seeing him. Yeah, it was sick, but she still felt that way. At least he didn't treat her as if she meant nothing, the way the other vamps did.

She wasn't delusional, though; she never let herself think that Sorin would ever help her, ever put her above the vampires' interests. He was what he was, and if she sometimes saw flashes of the man he'd been long ago, the *human* he'd been, that was something she couldn't let tempt her into doing something stupid.

The fact was, she was getting close to being able to break the spell. Her power and knowledge had been steadily growing, but a huge shift had occurred about a year ago. Some of those large books written in that weird unknown language had been in her way and she'd been dragging them to the side when one of them had fallen open. She'd glanced at the page—and abruptly her entire body felt electrified, her hair standing on end from the shock. *She could read the book.* The language hadn't suddenly been transformed into English, it was still the same odd blend of swirls and angles that didn't look like any alphabet she'd ever seen before, but she could read it.

Hastily she dragged some of the other books to her, flipped them open. Some of them she could read, some of them were about halfway legible, and one of the really old books was still gibberish to her.

And suddenly she'd understood. The books in English were like primers, teaching her basic stuff, getting her ready for the next step. The books she could read now were . . . high school. The ones she halfway understood were the college courses, and the lone indecipherable one was for her master's degree—or doctorate, depending on how tough it was. When she could read it, then she'd know she was ready for the big leagues.

A year down the road, she still couldn't read that one last book, but a word here and there was making sense. Close . . . she was so close. The book was beginning to open to her. The vamps had no idea how far she had come, the powers she had practiced and pushed and expanded. They might keep her body imprisoned in this room, but thanks to the weapons they themselves had brought her—the books—she had just recently learned how to set herself free.

She could "see" beyond this room she was never allowed to leave. She had to be careful when she did it, though; she wasn't certain what went on with her body while she was mentally traveling, whether she looked as if she were asleep, if she was merely sitting with her eyes open, or if she was jerking and drooling. She hoped it wasn't the jerk and drool, but who knew?

The hideous monster who always delivered her food had just left. She had some time before Sorin could be expected for his nightly visit to check on her and push her for a progress report. He pretty much had to believe what she told him, because really they had no way of testing her, unless maybe they brought in another witch or vampire who was some sort of lie detector, but so far she'd successfully skated around the truth while at the same time showing enough growth in her powers to give them hope, to give them a reason for keeping her and her family alive.

She wanted to find her family. She wanted to see for herself that they were okay, that the vamps hadn't done something backhanded like recording her family's voices, then setting up those calls for her to hear them, when all the while they were long dead. Part of her whispered that Sorin wouldn't do something like that, but that was the part that thought she recognized the remnants of humanity in him. The logical part of her brain said *He's a vampire,* and she had learned how ruthless they were.

But thanks to Sorin the others left her alone, unless they were bringing meals to her, so she was grateful to him not only for sparing her from being a McDracula snack but also because she could pretty much count on solitude right now.

She hadn't realized just how lucky she was to have his protection until, during one of her first experiments with remote viewing, she'd mentally stumbled upon a vampire soldier feeding from a human who was kept a prisoner for that very purpose. It hadn't been pretty. They had fed from her so often that the woman was near death, and the savagery with which the vampire had torn into her . . . Nevada had jerked herself away from the scene, a sick feeling in the pit of her stomach. She didn't think the woman had survived.

Nevada went to stand at her workstation, a large, oblong table with books, crystals, stones, and cards scattered across the top. Her long red hair fell across her face and into her eyes; annoyed, she pulled the hair clip from the back of her head, gathered her hair, and resecured it. She really, really needed a haircut, but the vamps wouldn't let her have scissors.

With that irritant out of the way, she rolled her shoulders, settled, and focused. Tugging one particular book toward her, she opened it to the page she wanted, spread her fingers, and lightly touched all ten fingertips across the words of the spell. She closed her eyes, and began gathering her newly discovered energy, pulling it inside as she whispered the words of the spell, feeling a shimmer begin to spread through her body, through every cell, permeating the fabric of her being. She took several deep breaths, then sent her mind outward. At the very last second she thought, *"Sorin."*

She never knew exactly where she would end up, so she was trying to learn control. If she thought of a destination, maybe that's where the spell would take her. She didn't know where Sorin was, but maybe she didn't need to; maybe the spell could take her to a person rather than just a place.

In her mind, she opened her eyes.

She stood in the corner of another room, a very functional, utilitarian room without any windows, furnished with a computer, maps, files . . . yes, she had the impression it was in this very building. Sorin was there. She gave a triumphant pump of her fist—or at least, her spirit did. Yes! The experiment had worked! She'd gone straight to him.

There were other vampires in the room with him, and in this realm she could see that they were like him, and yet . . . not. She could see more clearly in him the man he had once been, but in the others . . . no. She could see only the monsters they were, with no shred of humanity left. She had to be careful of Sorin, and not let herself forget that he was a monster, too, perhaps the worst monster of them all, because he could hide behind his handsome face, suppress the monster when it suited him.

She could see them, hear them, but they couldn't see her. She wondered if she could walk among them, brush against their spirits, but as soon as the idea occurred she thrust it away. That would be stupid. Vampires were at essence creatures of magic, and they might very well sense the touch of another kind of magic.

One of the vampires in the room stuck a pin in a detailed map of D.C. "Chloe Fallon," he said. "Her warrior is trying to contact her, but she's still several weeks away from hearing the call. I don't think there's any hurry on her."

"Don't tell me about the conduits I don't need to worry about," Sorin growled. "Tell me about the ones I need to kill now."

"She's practically in our backyard," another vampire said, sounding annoyed. "Why wait until the last minute?"

Sorin gave the third vampire a narrow-eyed look. "Jonas will let us know when it's time. More and more warriors are trying to come in, and some conduits respond faster than others. There are only so many of us who can travel in the daytime, so we take care of the most urgent first."

Conduit. What was a conduit? And what was this about warriors? Didn't matter, Nevada thought as she listened to them talk. *The vampires were systematically killing these humans they called conduits, and Sorin was leading them. The vampires were planning to seize power, but first they had to kill these conduits who somehow could contact these special warriors. It didn't make sense to her, but she didn't have to understand to know that innocent people had been killed and even more were slated to die. She herself was part of this grand plan; she had to break a spell that kept the vampires from breaching human sanctuary. Until now, however, she hadn't realized there was another part to the scheme.*

The vampire who had stuck the pin in the map picked up a photo from his desk and handed it to Sorin. "This is Chloe Fallon." He rubbed a hand over his face; he looked exhausted, which was weird, because Nevada hadn't realized vampires could get tired. But this vampire wasn't tall and muscular like Sorin; in fact, he looked like a geek, with a scraggly build and a mild face.

Sorin looked down at the photograph. Nevada sent her spirit edging closer, so she could get a look, too, but she was careful not to get too close to Sorin. The woman in the photograph was a pretty blonde with a cheerful, infectious smile, but there was something fragile about her that Nevada couldn't put her finger on, as if she was in danger of fading away. She wasn't thin, wasn't sickly looking, but—

She was going to die.

Nevada felt a chill run through her spirit body. This pretty young woman who was innocent of any wrongdoing was going to die because she was a conduit, because she was the means of bringing one of these badass warriors into being. *The vampires must be scared*

*shitless of the warriors, must realize they couldn't win
the war they were planning if enough of the warriors
could make it to the fight.*

*These people, these conduits, were helpless, Nevada
thought. They didn't know vampires existed, much less
that the vamps were stalking them like animals and
butchering them.*

*But she could make a difference. She knew she could.
Physically she was bound, but her mind was free. She
could help defy the vampires, and they'd never know—*

With a deep intake of air and a heavy thump of her
heart, Nevada found herself solidly and completely
back in her room. Her knees wobbled and she sat down
hard, completely missing her chair and sprawling on
her ass. She sat there trying to gather her spinning
senses, marshal her thoughts.

She could do something. She had a real sense of who
and where this Chloe Fallon was located. She was here
in D.C., close enough that Nevada thought maybe she
could reach her. If Chloe had been in Alaska, say, that
was probably beyond Nevada's skill right now. But
every time she did this she got better, so if she managed
to warn Chloe then probably the next time she could
reach farther out, to other conduits.

Could she communicate beyond these walls? Once
she would have said no, but that was before she tapped
into the power that had lain dormant within her. If she
could listen in and observe what was happening a couple of floors below, why should there be a limit? She
didn't *know* that she could reach this Chloe Fallon and
warn her, but she had to try.

Quickly she scrambled to her feet and once more
stood at the table, absently rubbing her aching butt as
she leafed through the book before her. The spells
weren't in any order, weren't broken down by section
so she could just flip to, say, Warning from a Distance

and find what she needed. Looking through the book took more time than she liked, because the wording was so obscure that sometimes she had to read a spell three or four times before she understood the purpose of it. Eventually, though, she found a spell that she thought might work. What did she have to lose? What did Chloe have to lose?

Her life, that's what, if this didn't work.

Nevada whispered the words on the page, words that would give her access to Chloe's mind . . . if she was doing it correctly. She closed her eyes and pictured Chloe's face as best she could, casting out an invisible net that she prayed would reach far enough. The net soared high and wide, sparkling and glittering like huge crystal butterfly wings. She had a connection with Chloe that made the spell possible, and that connection was Sorin. He was the one who had seized Nevada from her home years ago, and now he had set his sights on Chloe. They shared a common enemy.

"*Beware,*" Nevada whispered. She was acutely aware of the passing time. The hour was late; Chloe might already be asleep, might think this contact was part of a dream, a dream to be dismissed or forgotten. She mustn't forget. "Listen," Nevada urged in a low chant. "Hear, and remember. Dear God, please remember. You must. *Remember.*"

She was so intent on getting through to Chloe that she didn't hear Sorin coming until the door opened. Nevada was severed from the spell so sharply and completely that she jumped and stumbled backward. "Dammit!" she yelped, her hand pressing over her heart in an instinctive motion, as if she could physically still the furious leap of fright. "You scared the crap out of me!" Dammit, for real. She hadn't been able to send Chloe all the information she'd intended to.

Sorin stopped just inside the door, his head tilted a

little to one side as he gave her a bemused look. "You humans say the funniest things when you're startled. What were you doing?"

You humans. His phrasing told her just how far Sorin was from those long ago days when he, too, had been human. She wanted to ask him if he remembered what it was like to be human, but instead she took a deep breath and thanked her lucky stars that, outwardly at least, she'd been doing nothing more than standing over the old book of spells. "I was concentrating on my work, just like you want. I was trying out a spell."

He studied her sharply, as he always did, and she felt that gaze to the pit of her stomach. "Did it work?"

"No," she said sourly. "You interrupted."

"What kind of spell was it?"

"As far as I can tell, it's for locating a lost object."

His gaze got sharper. "That isn't the spell we want you to do. Stop playing; we're running out of time."

"It isn't playing, it's using the spells I can do to expand my power base—" She stopped, made an abrupt dismissive gesture. "I'm doing the best I can." *And he'd just let slip that she didn't have much time left. If she couldn't break the spell by whenever this deadline was, they'd have no further use for her.*

He gave her an inscrutable look, tilted his head toward her in a formal, old-fashioned dismissal, and left as abruptly as he had arrived.

Usually he stayed longer, chatted with her, sometimes even teased her a little in a way that reminded her that he was hundreds of years old and she must seem like not much more than a toddler to him. After he was gone, Nevada felt oddly bereft. She pushed the feeling away and, bracing herself, went back to the book of spells and tried to resume where she'd left off.

It was no good. Whatever spark she'd discovered, whatever link she'd established, was gone.

CHAPTER
FIVE

Chloe's feet hurt. She'd been on them from the moment she arrived at work that afternoon; if *her* feet hurt, she could only imagine how the waitstaff felt. Business at the restaurant had been heavier than usual; traffic always picked up in the summer because of the tourist business, and they also kept their regulars, thanks to consistently good food, impeccable service, and, when required, discretion. Tonight had been non-stop, every table full and people waiting, which was good for bar business, plus a popular senator had brought his lovely wife in for dinner. The staff had smiled and greeted the senator as if he hadn't been there just last week with his girlfriend. What a schmuck.

At last, though, the place was quiet, the chattering crowd gone, the kitchen cleaned and silent, the lights turned down. Chloe reconciled the receipts with the night's take, put the cash and credit card receipts in a bank bag for a morning delivery and locked it in the safe, and, while it was on her mind, placed an online order for monogrammed napkins. She checked the kitchen to make sure it was properly cleaned and ready for the morning crew, and texted a message to Jerry, the day-shift manager. Then she wrote a note leaving him the same message, in case his kids got their hands on his cell phone and deleted the text message. It had happened before.

She got paid a little more for working the night shift, because of the hours and the extra work—the restaurant did more business at night—but it was Jerry's choice. He had a wife and kids and he liked being home in the evenings. That suited Chloe; she was a bit of a night owl anyway, and lately even more of one.

She could have put the restaurant to bed and been out of there, but she puttered about for a while longer, delaying going home. When she was at work, she didn't see braids or hear disembodied voices. She couldn't in all conscience delay for very long, though, because the bartender, Carlos, was waiting to walk her to the Metro station, as he did on the nights she didn't drive to work. She'd have preferred taking the Metro all the time, rather than fighting the D.C. traffic, but it was open late only on Friday and Saturday evenings. The other three shifts she worked, she had to drive.

All day she'd tried to come up with an explanation for what she'd heard in her kitchen last night after work. It would be so easy to write the episode off to imagination, but she didn't think she had *that* much of an imagination. She hadn't been drinking, and she had no history of mental problems—not yet, at least. Maybe. She hoped. The way things were going . . .

She might put what she'd heard down to some bizarre sound wave carrying from a neighbor's house, or a radio or television somewhere. Could sound waves do that? Weird things happened with electronics all the time. But the fact that the voice had called her name blew that theory out of the water.

She even tried to convince herself that she'd been sleepwalking, but dammit, she hadn't been; she'd been wide awake, which was why she'd been in the kitchen at that hour, drinking milk. If even one of these theories would at least stay in the damn boat, much less in the water, she'd be satisfied, but no, that one was blown out, too.

Even worse, during the busiest part of the night she had suddenly felt . . . weird. That was the only word she could come up with to describe it. Not exactly dizzy, not exactly sick, just suddenly disconnected, as if she were a half-second out of sync with time, and there was a kind of golden shimmer behind her eyes that faded in just a few seconds, and after that she felt perfectly normal. *Weird.*

The aortic aneurysm she'd lived with for so long wouldn't affect her brain. If she'd thought there was even a chance that that was the case she would've spent last night at the ER. She tried hard not to let the aneurysm affect every aspect of her life, not to tie everything that went wrong in her life to it; if she did that, then whether she lived a long life or died tomorrow, the stupid little thing won. Sometimes, though, blaming stuff on it was better than not, because then she'd at least have a reason; too bad it wouldn't work in this case.

None of the possibilities she was left with were good: she was down to brain tumor or mental illness.

The doors were locked, the restaurant quiet and in order. Carlos was waiting. Chloe sighed and got her purse, and together they went out the employee entrance. She set the security system, then locked the door behind them.

"You okay?" Carlos asked as they walked down the brick pathway behind the row of shops and restaurants. The lighting was adequate, and no one had ever had any trouble in this neighborhood, but she had to admit she'd always been grateful for his protective company. "You've been a little quiet to-night. Busy, but quiet."

"I'm tired. I haven't been sleeping much for the past several nights." Understatement of the year.

"Something wrong?"

"Nothing I can put my finger on. Just odd dreams that wake me up, then I can't go back to sleep." She wasn't inclined to share the details, to tell him about that stupid braid or the voice or the possibility that she might be cracking up. Some things weren't for sharing.

"Maybe you'll catch up on sleep tonight."

"I hope. I'm going to try drinking milk *before* I go to bed instead of waiting until after one of those stupid dreams wakes me up." That wasn't much of a game plan, but it was the best she had. She didn't want to start taking sleeping pills, though she didn't rule them out as a last resort. She just hadn't reached that point. But she couldn't swear that tomorrow wouldn't have her there.

The Metro station was convenient to work, and on the other end she had a brisk, ten-minute walk ahead of her. Carlos took the Metro home, too, though he got off at a different station and then got on a different line for the next leg of his trip home. Because it was a weekend, there were enough people on the train that she felt safe and comfortable; several of them even got off at the same station she did, and they all took the long escalators up to the street.

It was a nice, quiet night. The nearby businesses were closed and most of the people in the residential neighborhood she soon turned in to were long asleep. A sliver of moon was setting, just peeking through the heavy summer foliage. Even though the neighborhood was calm and respectable, Chloe followed her mother's orders and gripped her pepper spray in one hand and her keys in the other. She'd never had to use the spray and so far the keys hadn't been needed for anything other than unlocking the door, but she was enough of her mother's daughter to have them out anyway; if by some awful chance she needed the pepper spray and didn't have it in hand, she'd feel like the biggest moron on the planet, assuming she was still alive to feel anything. She wasn't afraid, but she was prepared.

Chloe liked her nighttime hours, liked that her timetable was slightly off from the majority of the people around her. She enjoyed sleeping late, when she could sleep, and she liked the silence of the night. She liked the sensation that she was completely alone as she walked the deserted streets, and she even liked the sound of her steps on the sidewalk, shadowed by the ancient trees in full leaf. The air on a warm summer night had that special, summery smell, of flowers and mown grass, and warmth that had been soaked up by the concrete beneath her feet. There was something peaceful about it all.

As she passed by one house, which was small and neat, much like her own, she saw the flickering of a television beyond thin curtains. So, someone else was awake in this neighborhood. Another home was completely dark, while yet another was well lit outside but dark inside. The differences made her wonder about her neighbors' lives, what kept them up late or sent them to bed early. Did they ever wonder about her, or did they go about their lives pretty much oblivious to everything except their immediate surroundings?

Her steps slowed. Her own house, half a block ahead, was dimly lit by the front porch light she'd left burning. Normally, by the time she reached this point, she was glad to get home, ready to wind down with the routine of washing her face and brushing her teeth, getting into pajamas, maybe indulging in a quiet hour of reading before she turned off the lamp and relaxed into sleep. Tonight, though, tension was already settling between her shoulder blades, tightening her scalp. What would happen tonight? More strange dreams? More voices from nowhere? Or would she finally get a decent night's sleep?

One of her friends had seen a psychologist for a while, after her husband had left her. Maybe she'd call her, get the shrink's name and number. That wasn't what she wanted to do with her savings when she was hoping to save for a down payment on the house and have extra cash in case her car needed a new something or other, and another semester of school was right around the corner, but none of those things would do her a bit of good if she didn't get her head on straight.

She had reached the short sidewalk that led to her front door when a sound at the end of the street made her pause. She cocked her head to the side, listening. Music? Then the music stopped abruptly and she heard the murmur of a deep voice, and she realized what she'd heard had been the ring tone of a cell phone. She couldn't see anyone, though, no matter how she strained her eyes. Just the knowledge that someone was out there made the hair on the back of her neck lift, because she never saw anyone else out and about at this hour, not in this quiet neighborhood.

"Chloe! Beware!"

The words had barely whispered through her mind when he moved, darkness blurring into the deeper darkness of the trees, before he stepped out onto the sidewalk.

A man stood at the end of the street, just barely caught in the light from a streetlamp at the end of the block. He held a cell phone to his ear, and he was still talking. Chloe narrowed her eyes, trying to see better. He was tall, and he wore a long dark coat that was too heavy for summer—*any* coat was too heavy for the humid heat of D.C. A whiff of a breeze caught his long hair, which was blonder, and longer, than her own. He wore sunglasses, and when he stepped forward, more directly into the light of the streetlamp, he smiled at her.

The bulb in the streetlight exploded, sending sparks raining down on the man, and that end of the street plunged into darkness.

Chloe bolted for front door, key in hand, her heartbeat suddenly hammering against the walls of her chest. Her hand shaking, she tried to jam the key into the lock while she looked over her shoulder, expecting to see the man looming out of the darkness as he tried to get to her before she could get inside—

No one was there. Or rather, no one she could see. Swearing under her breath, she forced herself to look down at the lock, but it still took three more tries before the key slid into the lock. To hell with swearing under her breath. She said, "Dammit!" in a fierce voice, turned the lock, and slammed the door open. As soon as she was inside she slammed the door again, this time closing it, and engaged the deadbolt before she gave the door a kick for good measure.

That was it. Okay, so this was the first time she'd gotten scared walking home at night, but once was enough. No matter how much her car sputtered and lurched, no matter how nice the weather was, no matter how short the walk was or how *green* she felt by saving the gas, she was driving to and from work from now on.

Something was going on. The dreams, the voice, the weird disconnect at work, and now what felt like her first official panic attack. Tomorrow—actually, when she woke up later today—she was calling her friend and getting that psychologist's phone number. Maybe she could move up the date of her annual checkup with her general practitioner, too, just in case. All was not right in Chloe's world, and she'd do whatever she had to do in order to fix it.

She wanted her peace of mind back.

But maybe, just maybe— Blowing out a breath, she stood there a moment longer, trying to decide if her imagination had just run away with her, big time, or if her instincts had been on target and she'd been smart to listen to that little voice telling her to run like hell.

Sorin was watching Chloe Fallon walk toward him relaxed and unconcerned when his cell phone rang. "Shit," he muttered, annoyed with himself because he hadn't turned off the phone, and with the caller for choosing that exact moment to make the call. No point in hoping she hadn't heard the phone; she'd stopped immediately, her head turned as she looked for the source of the noise.

Even from here he could hear the sudden thump of her heartbeat; she was already thoroughly spooked. For a split second the thrill of the hunt surged through him and he started to take her now, his fangs elongating as the hard, rapid beats of her heart pulled him like a lodestone.

Only the knowledge that the call had to be urgent stayed him, though it had been an effort to hold himself back. He reached into his pocket for the phone instead of bringing down the pretty blonde. "Yeah," he said by way of greeting, his gaze still locked on Chloe Fallon. A sudden perverse urge to tease her seized him. Should he stay hidden in the shadow of the big trees, or—

"We have a warrior coming through soon," Jonas said, his tone tired and excited all at once. "Melody's the closest, but I can't get in touch with her."

"Who's the conduit?" Sorin asked, at the same time

he was thinking, *Hell, why not?* Maybe if Chloe Fallon was on edge, she'd give him a better chase. Tease her a little, let her know he was out there . . . things had been a little too easy lately, and he was getting bored.

He stepped out of the shadow of the tree and smiled at her, letting some of his power lash out. Overhead, the streetlight exploded and sparks rained down on him like fireworks, and the little rabbit ran for her house as fast as she could.

"He's a soldier in North Carolina."

Soldiers were reliable and efficient conduits, which stood to reason; they were often able to make contact with their Warriors and bring them over in half the time other conduits could figure out what was going on.

North Carolina wasn't far, but the sun rose early in the summer and he wasn't as resistant to it as that bastard Luca. The queen wanted him to locate Luca, hunt down conduits, *and* keep tabs on his little red-haired witch, Nevada. How in hell he was supposed to do all that simultaneously he had no idea. His wayward child, Melody, was supposed to be taking up the slack, but Melody now and always did whatever she felt like doing. She was a top-tier hunter, but she had no discipline. Someday, he was afraid, that lack of discipline would be the end of her.

On the other hand, it was better that he, rather than Melody, face the soldier. If the Warrior was close to coming through, the soldier would be on high alert, and trained humans could and did take down even skilled vampires.

"Okay," he finally said. "Where exactly is he?"

"I'll send his picture and address to your phone." Jonas cleared his throat. "The queen called earlier. She wants to know if you have any leads on Luca."

There was both a wariness and a weariness in Jonas's voice that told Sorin the man was close to the breaking point. Even vampires had their limits, and Jonas was pushing his. The queen had had him working nonstop for months now, since she'd discovered his special talent of locating conduits and that he could even tell how close the conduit was to bringing over one of the warriors.

"So, you're now a messenger as well as a locator?" he asked.

"Apparently so."

"If she calls back tell her I have nothing new on Luca because I'm spending all my time trying to kill conduits, the way she wants, and keeping the little witch hard at work, also the way she wants. You might also tell her if she wants to replace me, feel free."

"I can't tell her any of that," Jonas said softly. "She really just wants you to find Luca."

"I'm not the one who lost him," Sorin pointed out.

"She said he's potentially dangerous."

Regina was right about one thing: Luca Ambrus was a dangerous bastard, a pure fighting machine who with just a look could make ordinary vampires piss on themselves. No one knew exactly how old he was, or exactly how powerful, but there were plenty of tales about some unbelievable things he'd done. One of these days, Sorin figured he'd test himself against Luca, because he himself was too much of a fighter to live in peace with himself unless he knew whether or not he could defeat the blood born. He might die in the attempt but what the hell, battle was a good way to go.

"Hector was his friend," Sorin said. "She should've thought of that before she killed him."

The queen—she had begun insisting that they call her Regina, as she would leave her old identity behind and adopt a new one when their uprising succeeded in upending the structure of power in their favor—was as cold and ruthless as any vampire he'd ever known. She would destroy anyone and anything in her way, in her determined rise to power, so it was far safer to be on her side than against her.

"Forget Luca, forget Regina," Jonas said tightly. "There's a conduit close to calling in his Warrior, and you have to take care of him ASAP. Do it yourself or send someone else, I don't care."

There were a few vampire rebels, Sorin's own soldiers, who could withstand daylight to some degree. He could send them out hunting Luca, because that's when he'd be moving around. "Check all the area hotels and motels again; Luca has to be sleeping somewhere." The first check hadn't turned up anything, but that didn't mean Luca hadn't since found himself a nice, dark little room somewhere. He was cunning enough to have delayed doing so until he'd figured they had had enough time to run the initial check, thinking they wouldn't bother to check again.

"So, I guess you're *not* going to forget Luca," Jonas said, his voice tired. "Fine, fine, I'll check again."

The unwelcome truth was, a lot of vampires were not exactly computer savvy. Computers were too new, and vampires had an innate dislike of them because the digital era had made life so much more difficult for all of them. Jonas was an exception to the rule; he'd taken to computers as if he'd been born in 1980 instead of 1780. Sorin had forced himself to learn something about computers, and of course they all used cell phones, but he'd learned just enough to help him evade showing up in all the data files.

Jonas was a bit hamstrung when it came to computer usage, since—as he was not exactly a willing rebel—he wasn't allowed computer access unless he was under guard. His cell phone was programmed to send and receive only from select numbers, as if he were a human child, not a powerful vampire. How that must grate . . .

"I'll head to North Carolina myself," Sorin said. "If I can locate the conduit right away and catch him outside his home, I'll be back within twenty-four hours."

"Call me as soon as you get back."

The phone went silent; Jonas had ended the call. Sorin supposed if he had anything else to say to him, he'd call back. If not, he'd simply send the required information.

He needed to be on the move, but he stood there for a moment staring at Chloe Fallon's closed front door and wishing he could simply walk through it to do what had to be done.

Soon.

God, he wanted this to be over with. The preparations were necessary, but they wore on his patience. He was ready for the real war to start, the war where the humans found out just how pitiful and lowly they were.

This uprising might be the most exciting thing he'd done since his turning, more than seven hundred years ago—seven hundred and twelve to be exact. When the war was over, he wouldn't have to hide ever again. He wouldn't have to change his name, move, or seek dark alleyways in order to feed, taking just enough to survive and then glamouring the unwilling blood donor into forgetting what had happened. A lot of times he'd gone hungry because he hadn't been able to feed as much as he had wanted.

His position in the uprising was high enough that when the war was won he'd be nicely placed in the hierarchy that would be set up. He wouldn't ever again have to pretend to be someone else, and he'd feed when and where and how much he chose. Humans would serve him, and he'd never again be forced to hide from those who were so far beneath him in every way. That was the way it had been when he'd been turned, and he longed for the old order, when vampires had been superior.

Everything was falling into place. First, they had Jonas, a vampire who could locate the specific energy a conduit emitted, so they could stop the Immortal Warriors from coming into this world. Without the Warriors on the side of the humans, the pitiful little worms wouldn't stand a chance. Then Regina had located a descendant of the witch who had cast the spell that kept vampires outside a home unless they were invited in, so for the first time they had a real chance of having the spell broken. Regina had quietly been building her army of vampire rebels for the past fifty years, looking for the ones who were outraged by the imbalance of power, swaying those who were on the fence, luring the strong. If they could avoid Warrior interference, humans wouldn't realize what had happened until it was too late. They'd be enslaved, serving their superiors as they should have been doing for all their short, miserable, meaningless lives.

This country would fall first, because the vampire community was already so large and organized here. The rest of the world would follow in time. At the very least, they would have to deal with the reality of vampires being in charge of the most powerful nation in the world.

As he walked away from the conduit's house, he started thinking about his little witch. Nevada was necessary, but her part in the rebellion was taking longer than it should. There were times when he thought she was holding out on them, hiding her power and her ability to break the spell even though her family's lives depended on her doing as she was told. He had no proof, he'd never caught her in a lie, but there was something about her . . .

It was her scent. It annoyed the hell out of him, and

if he could, he'd separate himself from her and have someone else monitor her progress. Regina thought it was funny that the witch relied exclusively on Sorin, that she had asked for him and didn't willingly deal with any of the other vampires at all.

Twice during the past week he'd caught a hint of that familiar smell even though Nevada wasn't anywhere near. It was disturbing as all hell. Tonight the scent had been so strong in the basement that he'd gone up to her room almost expecting to find that she'd escaped. Why else would he catch a whiff of her scent so far away from her second-floor room?

But she'd been there, engrossed in those damn spell books, obedient and pretty and very, very young—and, unfortunately, very necessary.

He tried to create her scent now, wondering if he could call it up whenever he wanted, which would at least be an explanation even if it was an unwelcome one, but . . . nothing.

It was all in the blood, he mused. The Warriors' connections with their conduits, who were always their descendants, and the power of the witch who could undo the curse that hampered all vampires . . . it all came down to the power of the blood.

CHAPTER

SIX

Despite the crappy day and getting scared out of her wits, which, after she woke, seemed more than a little silly, Chloe actually got some decent sleep that night. She had the braid dream again, but only after she'd slept over five undisturbed hours. Those five hours felt like heaven. When the dream finally came and woke her up, at least she wasn't exhausted. And she felt perfectly normal: no dizziness, no shimmering behind her eyes, no anything, just her normal, level-headed self. If something was wrong with her physically, wouldn't she feel weird all the time? If it was a brain tumor, would she even notice if she felt weird? Probably not, which meant she likely didn't have a brain tumor. Along the same vein, if she was going nuts, would she *know* she was going nuts, or would she think everyone else was? Food for thought, there.

Because she felt normal and had finally got some sleep, she put off calling her friend for the shrink's number; after all, it was the weekend, so she wouldn't be able to get in touch with the doctor until Monday anyway. She spent some time on the computer looking up her own symptoms and came up with some interesting stuff, none of which was very likely unless she wanted to get into witchcraft and spells . . . *not*. That was kind of reassuring; maybe there wasn't anything wrong with her at all; maybe the weird dreams were just that, and didn't mean anything. Maybe the voice she'd heard was . . . okay, so she didn't have an explanation for the voice. She still felt better about the situation than she had the night before.

When it was time to leave for work she got her bag and was actually on the sidewalk in front of her house, walking to the Metro, when she stopped and looked uneasily over her shoulder. No tall blond guy in sunglasses and a long black coat was standing at the end of the block, of course. Why had she been so frightened? All he'd done was talk on his cell phone, and smile at her. Wearing sunglasses at night was dumb, but she'd seen other people do it. The long black coat was also dumb . . . wasn't that something drug addicts did? Her overall impression of the blond guy wasn't of someone on drugs, though; he'd looked too brawny, too healthy, not that she'd been able to see a lot of detail.

But . . . why had he been there? She knew he didn't live on the street. She had made a point, at her mother's urging, of making a note of all her neighbors and what kind of cars they drove, so she'd know if someone strange was casing the neighborhood. Yes, her mother was paranoid about her daughter's safety, but that had still been a good idea. The blond guy hadn't been visiting anyone, either, not at that hour. Taking a stroll, maybe?

A chill ran up her spine, even though the bright sunlight had dispelled all the shadows and the street was empty of threatening characters. Abruptly Chloe turned on her heel and went back to the house to fetch her car keys. Her gut instinct for caution might be wrong, but she'd rather be wrong than mugged or dead.

She didn't like driving in D.C. traffic; the Metro was far more convenient. The only thing that made it tolerable was that she wasn't driving during rush hour; she went to work before the evening rush hour began, and came home in the wee hours long before the morning madness. But each time she made the drive, Chloe spent most of her time praying that her car wouldn't break down.

She'd had the burgundy Ford since high school, which meant it was on its last legs . . . wheels. She'd been putting off buying a new one because the old Ford was paid for. With school, rent, and all her other expenses, it had been nice to not have a car payment, too; she'd been able to save much more than she would have otherwise. But she couldn't put off getting a new car much longer; that night, after putting in another extremely busy shift at work, she had trouble getting the old car to start. Carlos, bless him, stayed until he was certain she was on her way.

As her car lurched and sputtered into the driveway as if taking its last breath, Chloe faced the inevitable. On Monday, she'd have to begin looking for a new car. She didn't need anything fancy, just something reliable so she could drive down to see her parents for the holidays and make it to and from work on the days when the Metro closed early, when it was cold, rainy, or when she'd been spooked by strange men on her street.

She was being extra cautious, but when she reached her street she drove to the end of the block, going slowly and letting her headlight beams light up the tree trunks. She didn't see anyone lurking in the shadows. After making a U turn in the intersection, she drove back to her house and parked. Maybe she seriously needed a vacation, but she still felt uneasy.

Chloe turned off the ignition and got out, automatically depressing the lock lever before she closed the door. The porch was maybe ten steps away, the front door just a few more. If she bought the house and stayed here, maybe she'd build a small garage out back, connect it to the house with a covered breezeway. That would be nice, especially during bad weather. She could even add a second story over the garage and make a visitor's suite. She could use the extra storage, too. Of course, the yard was very small, as all yards in this neighborhood were. Was there room to build on? She didn't know anything about the building codes, but she could find out when the time came.

As she stepped onto the first of the three steps that led to the porch, Chloe thought that she should probably buy the house before she started thinking about renovations.

She didn't have even a whisper of warning, before he was on her.

About damn time. Luca had been waiting over two days for this moment.

A dark-clothed figure slipped out of the building, using a back exit where the light conveniently hadn't been turned on. Recognizing his prey by both shape and movement, Luca rose silently to his feet from behind the heating and air unit he'd been using as both shelter and concealment, and floated from the roof to the ground.

Trailing a vampire, especially a strong one, was an exercise in discipline. He had to maintain absolute control over his body, because a vampire's senses were acute. He couldn't make a sound, not even an unguarded breath. Over the centuries Luca had learned how to reach out with his own senses and isolate his prey's heartbeat, synchronize his own heartbeat to that of his prey so the other vampire wouldn't hear that telltale second heartbeat and know someone was behind him, and he had to do it fast, within two beats at the most. If there was any wind he had to position himself so his scent didn't carry, and sometimes that was damn difficult. He also had to make certain that he moved only when he couldn't be seen.

Scent was the most difficult sense to bypass, because he couldn't control the wind. He'd tried; no dice. He also had to account for the possibility that his prey might have a heightened sense of danger awareness, something that developed with time; a vampire either learned and grew, or died young. Maybe it was his own force field of energy that set off the alarm in his prey, in which case Luca could do everything right and something would still alert the prey to his presence. It was a real pisser when that happened.

He was relieved to at last be doing something, anything. When he'd first left the Council building, almost three days ago now, he'd urgently needed to feed; being awake so long, being out in the daylight, had seriously sapped his strength. He'd done the most expedient thing, glamoured the next jogger he encountered, and took the woman to his parked rental. To anyone passing by, they would have looked as if they were making out, especially as the woman had her arms around him. Then he'd taken her back to where he'd found her, the small wound on her neck already almost healed. The only effect she'd feel was that she'd have to cut her jogging routine short because she was unaccountably tired.

Finding a place to rest, to get out of the sun, had been a calculated risk, but one he'd had to take. Using his secondary ID and credit card, he'd checked into a nearby small hotel, pulled the covers from the bed and dumped them in the tub, stripped off his clothes, then closed the door to the bathroom and settled in the tub for a few hours of refreshing total darkness. His entire body seemed to heave a sigh of relief. Despite the discomfort of fitting his six-plus frame in a five-foot bathtub, despite the hardness, he'd slept like a baby.

When he woke, it was almost nine o'clock at night, and full darkness was looming.

After tossing the covers back onto the bed he quickly showered and got dressed again, then headed back to the Council headquarters. He didn't approach the building itself; instead, he settled himself on the roof of the building next door. Then he waited.

For almost three long damn days, he waited. He did take breaks, to get away from the noon sun, to sleep a little, to feed, but he spent most of the time on that roof, waiting for his prey to leave the building, watching to see who came and went.

None of the Council members had left, unless there was a tunnel that came out in the basement of some neighboring building, but given the residential nature of the area he didn't think so. There was very little activity, which made it easy for him to keep watch but at the same time was boring as hell. If he guessed right, he almost didn't need to keep watch during the day, but he did it anyway, just in case.

He had almost decided that nothing was going to happen tonight, either, because the hours were ticking toward sunrise. The vampire he was following could withstand sunrise, to some extent, but most of the rogue vampires enlisted in the uprising wouldn't have the same ability. Either the errand or meeting was expected to be a short one, or his prey was up to something else entirely.

He stayed well back, often losing sight of his target but using his senses of smell and hearing to stay on track. It was a delicate game he played, one of balance; he had to stay close enough that he could follow, but not close enough that he could be detected.

Being followed evidently wasn't something Enoch had considered, because he never once stopped to check his surroundings, or so much as looked over his shoulder.

Luca had known from the first time he'd stepped into Hector's quarters that Enoch was the killer; even if he hadn't been able to read the residual energy, he'd have known from listening to Enoch's rapid heartbeat, from the smell of fear oozing from every cell. He'd been tempted to execute him on the spot, or at least take him into custody for questioning. He hadn't for one simple reason: he wanted to know who had given the orders. Enoch hadn't acted on his own authority. Hector had suspected that someone on the Council was a traitor and he'd almost certainly been right, but there was also the chance that the Council member wasn't the one giving the orders, that someone from outside was the actual leader. Personally, Luca thought the traitor had to be a Council member, simply because of the enormous egos involved. He couldn't think of a single sitting member who would willingly take orders from another member, much less from someone on the outside.

If he'd acted then, he wouldn't have found out who was behind it all. He had carefully watched Enoch's every move in the Council chamber, but Enoch was both smart and careful; not once had he looked at any member who wasn't speaking, not once had he volunteered any extra information in an effort to tip off his cohort. He'd been sweating it, though, spooked by how much Luca had already been able to tell but not knowing exactly what else could be read at the scene.

If the rebels were meeting anywhere, it wasn't at the Council headquarters, which only made sense. Therefore Luca's best bet was to follow Enoch and see where he went, who he met, maybe overhear a name. Then he'd kill the son of a bitch.

Enoch was bearing north and east. He was moving fast, using vampire speed, but there wasn't much risk that anyone would see him because of the hour. He did use some caution, staying in the deepest shadows much of the time. Luca stayed with him as Enoch moved deeper into an older, less affluent neighborhood. This didn't strike him as a good meeting place, Luca thought. People lived in neighborhoods like this for years and years, and they paid attention to who came and went, and what went on. What was Enoch doing here?

A bare, burly arm circled her neck and jerked her backward off the step, back onto the sidewalk. Chloe gasped, instinctively bringing her hands up to grip her attacker's arm as the pressure on her throat increased. Clamping his free hand over her mouth, he lifted her off her feet and held her there, choking. Panicked, she jerked her head back, slung her elbows, kicked at his shins, but it was like fighting with a rock.

Colored spots swam in front of her eyes, and in despair she realized she was close to passing out. The thought came, bitter and angry, that she wasn't paranoid, after all. If anything, she hadn't been paranoid enough. Her thoughts darted. Her keys, her pepper spray—*shit!* She'd dropped them in her instinctive fight for air, trying to loosen the killing hold around her neck.

She was going to die. The realization hit her like a fist to the gut. She was going to die because some punk *dick*head was too much of an asshole to *work* for a living, choosing instead to rob and kill women like her, and knowing that made her so furious that the world shrank to a tiny point, a point filled with nothing but wild determination to tear him limb from limb, to dance in his blood, to *stay alive.* Her muscles surged, heat flared until she felt as if her skin would melt. She couldn't scream, couldn't get a curse out, but a rhythmic snarl started in her chest and rolled up her throat, feral, savage. Wildly she threw her head back again, trying to catch him in the nose. She dug her nails into his skin, scratching as hard and deep as she could, marking the bastard so maybe at least the cops could find him and he'd—

He paid no more attention to her struggles than if she'd been a child, even laughing very softly, his mouth close to her ear. There was a strange, coppery smell coming off him as he whispered, "Do you know what you are? Have you heard him? How close is he?"

The words didn't make sense. She heard them, recognized them, but they didn't make sense. Still snarling, she reached back, digging for his eyeballs as she arched her back, heaving and twisting. He jerked his head away from her scrabbling fingers and tightened his grip around her neck, laughing again.

"Fight all you want," he crooned. "You can't hurt me. I'm not weak and mortal, like you. You're just an annoying little fly, and I am the swatter."

Black was closing in on her, she could feel her brain shutting down from lack of oxygen. Fly . . . swatter? Not fair. Her killer was a nut. . . . Might not stand trial, claiming nuthood. . . . Just wasn't fair.

Using the hand that continued to silence her, he pulled her head to the side, exposing the curve of her neck. Chloe hung on to consciousness, still trying for his eyes even though she was aware her hands were flailing uselessly now. His mouth moved over her neck, nuzzling, opening—

And then he was gone. Just like that. The arm around her neck, the big body pressed against her back—gone. Chloe fell limply to the ground, landed half on the sidewalk and half on the grass, choking and coughing and unable to think, to do anything other than lie there dragging deep, rough breaths of air into her lungs. Somehow she managed to roll onto her side and curled up in a fetal position, shaking and crying, unable to think.

Sounds . . . she could hear something. She didn't know what it was, some kind of thudding sound, but with a *wet* sound, too. Her chest heaving, she tried to focus her eyes. There were dark shadows cut by streams of light from her front porch and the streetlight that was several yards away, in front of her neighbor's house, shadows that seemed to swirl and blend until she wasn't certain what she was seeing. Two men . . . fighting, she thought, though they were moving so fast she thought she might be hallucinating. One of the men was her attacker; she saw his bare arms flashing. He was completely bald, and big—damn, was he big—but he fought with a speed and silence that was disorienting.

The other man . . . who was he? Someone passing by? Coughing, she struggled to her hands and knees, thinking only that she had to help him because the other man was so much bigger. But she couldn't get to her feet, couldn't help—

Her cell phone . . . 911. She had to call 911.

She silently repeated the numbers to herself as she looked around, as if she was afraid she might forget why she was looking for her purse. Where was it? It had been on her shoulder, but it wasn't there now, and the yard was too shadowed for her to see. Blindly she patted the grass and concrete around her, sweeping her hands out . . . there. Her hands shaking, she grabbed the strap and pulled the purse toward her. The effort upset her balance so much that she fell weakly to her side again, but she didn't lose her death grip on the purse strap.

The two men were moving so impossibly fast they were nothing but a blur. Her eyes and mind weren't working in sync yet, the effect dizzying, so she simply shut her eyes and felt around inside her purse for the sleek hard plastic of the little phone, right there in the side pocket where she always put it.

It slipped from her nerveless fingers, fell to the concrete. The back popped off, but the battery stayed inside. Panting, she grabbed it up again—and became aware that the sounds of the fight had stopped, and the silence was as terrifying as the attack. Which of them had won, her attacker or her rescuer?

A shadow of a man came around the car, and Chloe surged forward, a tiny mewling sound coming from her throat as she crawled up the front steps, fumbling with her phone, trying to punch in the numbers at the same time she kept darting panicked glances over her shoulder. His eyes . . . dear God, were his eyes *glowing*?

"It's all right, miss," he said in a deep, steady voice, the tone as calm as Sunday. "He won't bother you anymore."

She froze, staring up into those eyes as he moved fully into the light, and relief washed through her in a warm flow that eased all the tension from her muscles, all the terror from her mind. He wasn't her attacker. She didn't know who he was, but he definitely wasn't the huge bald guy. This man was tall and muscular, but with a lithe grace that made it seem as if he were flowing, instead of moving in the slightly clunky way most people walked.

He wore boots and jeans, and a dark, long-sleeved shirt, which as far as she was concerned was the best outfit ever for a man. His hair was long and dark, too, falling around his broad shoulders. Did she like long hair on a man? She wasn't sure. And when had she decided that boots and jeans were *it* for dress code?

Didn't matter, though; she liked it now. She was so relieved she liked everything about him. Vaguely she wondered if she should be relieved, and why she was. This guy was a stranger—a helpful one, but still a stranger. "I'm calling the police," she said, showing him the phone in her hand.

He smiled, and for a moment she forgot about the phone. "You don't need the police."

No, of course she didn't. How silly. The danger was over, the bad guy gone. She hadn't seen his face, anyway, so she couldn't give a description beyond "big, bald, bare arms." Yeah, that would really get his ass caught. She tried to remember why she'd been so desperate to call 911.

He sank to a crouch in front of where she half-sat, half-lay on the porch steps, reached out and touched her arm. "Are you hurt?"

"Just shaken." *Shaken, not stirred.* She almost laughed at the stray thought but her throat hurt, her knee hurt, her hand hurt, and she realized she had just lied. She turned her hand, looked at the scrape on her palm, blood darkly smeared there. "Maybe a little banged up, but not much."

"May I?" He took her hand, not waiting for her to actually give permission, but she was oddly charmed and comforted that he'd asked. His own hand was very warm, masculine, his long fingers hard and comforting as he turned her palm up. Chloe found herself staring at her hand, at the way it looked so feminine and delicate cradled in his, at the gentle way he touched her as if he, too, was acutely aware of how much bigger and stronger he was. She didn't usually feel like a delicate flower, and the sensation was a little bemusing. She was Level-Headed Chloe, who had— Hadn't she been about to call 911? Why had she stopped?

That was puzzling, but not enough for her to worry

about it. All in all, she was feeling very peaceful right now.

Then he lifted her hand to his mouth. The touch of his lips was soft on her scraped palm, the tiny licks of his tongue so light she could barely feel them. Wait. He was *licking* her?

"You can't lick me," she said sternly. "I don't know your name."

He looked up and a quick grin slashed across his face. "Luca," he said.

In his own way, he looked as . . . *brutal* wasn't the right word; *dangerous,* maybe? . . . as the other guy. Yes, dangerous was a good way to describe him. There was something very hard about him, not just that he was obviously in great shape, but a look, an expression, that said he was as tough mentally as he was physically. His features weren't exactly handsome, but they were so sculpted that she didn't think she'd ever forget exactly how he looked.

With that last thought, she had the impression that the very air around them began to shimmer. Yesterday the shimmering had alarmed her; tonight it simply felt all apiece with the night, the moment.

He was striking-looking, in so masculine a way that no one would ever associate the word "pretty" with him. His skin was tanned, and in contrast his eyes were strangely light. Whenever he caught her gaze she found it almost impossible to look away. Okay, flat impossible. She felt as if she were being cocooned in velvet, all her cares and hurts floating away as if they'd never existed.

"Luca," she repeated. "Is that an American name?"

"No." He lifted her hand to his mouth again, and his tongue once more began a slow, gentle movement over the scrape. She was okay with it now, because she knew his name. They'd been introduced . . . sort of. She knew his name but he didn't know hers, and that seemed wrong.

"I'm Chloe," she said. "Chloe Fallon."

He looked up again, his pale gaze meeting hers. "I'm very pleased to meet you, Chloe Fallon."

Her hand had stopped hurting.

"Sit very still," he said softly. "I'm going to heal your knee, too. You won't be alarmed, and you won't even remember that it was hurt."

"Of course I'll remember," she said automatically.

He smiled, eased her pencil skirt up over her knee, and bent his head to her leg where a thin line of blood trickled down from her bruised and scraped knee.

Chloe took a deep breath. Warmth flowed through her again, and it had nothing to do with relief. She looked down at his dark head bent to her leg, at the two strong hands cradling her calf and ankle, and she took yet another breath as images swirled through her mind, images that had to do with her skirt being pushed higher, with his mouth moving higher. Her breasts tingled as her nipples began to tighten. Oh, my.

He'd told her she wouldn't be alarmed, and she wasn't, but he hadn't said anything about "disturbed."

He lifted her leg a little higher, moving his mouth and tongue over her shin; cool air rushed under her skirt, all the way up her thighs. Chloe leaned back a little more to maintain her balance. She was all but lying on the steps now, her legs spread a little, the injured one lifted as if to his shoulder . . . *Stop,* her subconscious whispered. *Brakes on.*

"That's enough," she managed to say, though her voice wasn't very loud or very forceful.

For a moment she thought he was going to ignore her and she wasn't certain how she felt about that—good? bad?—as his mouth continued lightly moving on her skin. Then he rubbed his chin against her calf in a gentle caress and finally lifted his head. "There," he said, his tone slightly thick. "All better."

And it was. She stared down at her knee. The trickle of blood was gone, all the pain was gone . . . she couldn't even see the scrape. "That puts a whole new twist on kiss it and make it better," she said in wonderment. She lifted her hand, examined it in the yellow glow of the porch light. No scrape there, either. "Wow."

He smiled as he reached down and gripped her hand and pulled her to her feet. Her knees wobbled and he put his hand under her arm, held her steady for a moment until her balance settled.

"I don't know how to thank you," she said, feeling embarrassment heat her cheeks because she hadn't already thanked him; after all, he had saved her life. "He was . . . he was going to kill me." A slight frown knit her brow as she looked around. "Where is he?" Was he lying unconscious behind her car? Was he dead? Just . . . gone? And shouldn't she file a report, or something? Oh, right, Luca had said she didn't need the police, so no report.

"He's gone," Luca said. "He won't bother you again."

Well, that was a relief. She barely wondered why she would so blithely take his word for it, then the moment of doubt was gone and everything was okay.

She couldn't stand there all night, she thought. Nor was she inviting him inside for a cup of coffee—for one thing, she didn't want coffee, she wanted to go to sleep, but the main reason was that a thread of unease suddenly ruined her contentment. She didn't know him; she couldn't invite him in. She should find her keys, thank him again, and put an end to a very long and upsetting night.

Where *were* her keys? They'd been in her hand, so of course she'd dropped them. She sighed as she looked around, but they weren't in sight; for all she knew, they were somewhere in the shrubbery. "My keys are down there somewhere," she said ruefully.

"Here they are," he replied almost immediately, stooping to pick up something in the black shadow of a bush. He straightened with her keys in his hand.

She blinked at the dangling keys. "How did you find them so easily?"

"The streetlight was shining on them just right."

She took the keys, smiled shyly at him, and went up the steps to the front door. Her back to him, she inserted the key and turned it, then pushed the door open. She turned to look back at the man who stood at the foot of the steps. "Thank you again, Luca."

He went very still, an expression of surprise, almost shock, on his face. "It was my pleasure," he finally said.

Saying "thank you" didn't seem like enough. She needed to do something more, something tangible. "I'm the night-shift manager at Katica, a restaurant down on—"

"I know where it is," he said, a trifle abruptly.

"Come by tomorrow night and I'll see that you get a free meal." He still looked a bit taken aback by something, and less than thrilled by her suggestion, so she added, "The chef is really great. I can promise you a meal you won't forget, and a special bottle of wine."

"Thank you," he said, sounding rather formal. He even dipped his head in a truncated bow. "I'll stop by if I can."

"I'll look for you, then." Chloe stepped into her house, then closed and locked the door, set the alarm. She felt remarkably calm, considering all that had happened. She knew she should be shaky, but the horrible details seemed very distant, and all she could think about was maybe getting some sleep—

"*Chloe!*"

"Dammit," Chloe said as the voice suddenly whis-

pered urgently in her ear. There went the hope of sleep.
Something had to be done; this had to stop.

Standing outside, Luca stared at the door as it closed
behind Chloe Fallon. He felt as if he'd been body
slammed. *She had remembered him.* She had not only
remembered he was there, *she had remembered his
name.*

Not only was she not supposed to remember him at
all, he'd glamoured her into forgetting Enoch's attack
had ever occurred. He'd healed her wounds—and hadn't
that been an exercise in self-control, he thought wryly.
She'd tasted . . . God, she'd tasted the way he imagined
ambrosia would taste, and the scent of her had
wrapped around him, gardenia-sweet on a warm summer night. He didn't understand it. She was pretty
enough, not beautiful but definitely pretty: a normal
little human working a normal little job, her strength
puny, her senses dull in comparison to his—and still
he'd had to fight the sudden screaming urge to flatten
her there on the ground and take her, body and blood.

He shook himself, looked around. Enoch was nothing more than a pile of dust lying on the driveway on
the other side of Chloe Fallon's old car. The slight summer breeze was already dispersing him.

That had been close; if he'd been any farther away,
he wouldn't have been able to reach them before Enoch
killed her. He'd heard what Enoch asked her, if she
knew what she was, if she'd heard him yet.

She evidently had no clue, at least not yet, but Luca
knew. She was a conduit, and her Warrior was trying to
contact her—and the rebel vampires were evidently trying to hunt down and kill all the conduits before the
Warriors could come through, to set the stage for a
vampire takeover.

SEVEN

What the hell was going on?

There wasn't a simple answer, concerning either Chloe or the uprising, so Luca put the question aside for the moment to concentrate on the necessity of cleaning up after himself. He rounded Chloe's car to examine what was left of Enoch, which consisted of the clothes he'd worn, a pair of scuffed boots, the heavy gold ring that Council employees always wore, and a handful of dust. Luca scooped up everything but the dust, which would soon enough disperse in the gentle breeze. He'd dump the clothes in a trash bin somewhere; the ring went into his pocket.

He'd almost been too late for Chloe Fallon. He'd even hesitated a second when he saw Enoch seize her, thinking Enoch was simply going to feed. Then he'd heard what Enoch said, the questions he'd asked her, and realized there was something much bigger going on.

He was sorry he hadn't been able to question Enoch, but from the second he'd intervened he'd known how it would turn out. Enoch's eyes had flared with panic when he recognized Luca, knowing at once what it meant: that Luca knew he had killed Hector and had followed him. For Enoch, it had been a fight to the death, because he would rather die than let Luca take him alive. Unfortunately, he'd taken his knowledge with him.

This was one time Luca's reputation had worked against him. If Enoch hadn't been so frightened he wouldn't have fought so hard, and if he hadn't fought so hard Luca could possibly have subdued him. Instead, he'd been pushed to his own limits by the frenzy with which Enoch had attacked, and in the end had had to literally tear his opponent's head off. Luca was drenched in blood, something Chloe hadn't noticed thanks to the reassuring glamour he'd used.

Now he was back to square one. No, worse, dammit: Enoch had been his only lead, so now he had no lead at all.

The hell of it was, he wasn't completely unsympathetic to the rebels or their cause. When had the vampire community turned corporate? When had they become more concerned with maintaining secrecy and order than with living their long lives to the fullest? Luca could see how easy it would be for a strong leader to convince frustrated vampires that, with planning, a takeover would be easy enough. Damn, it probably wouldn't take much of an argument to convince Luca himself.

The problem was, he could see where such a rebellion would lead. The vampires might take the upper hand, for a while, but it wouldn't last. Humans had the numbers, and the ability to close themselves in their homes and simply not allow access. Any war between humans and vampires would come down to individual skirmishes across the country—and then the world. The vampires' natural weaknesses would be discovered, they'd be hunted down and slaughtered when they were at their most vulnerable, and then the few strongest who were left would have to virtually seclude themselves from the world to keep from being found out, emerging only when they absolutely had to feed.

He'd seen it all before. The outcome had never been a good one, for the vampires.

This uprising had a new slant, taking out the conduits to prevent the Warriors from coming through. *Damn* those bastards. The humans had a formidable ally in the Warriors, and they didn't even know it, most of them living their lives without ever coming in contact with one. The Warriors watched from whatever plane of existence they inhabited, and they decided when the human race was in trouble and needed help, reaching out then to contact their descendants so they could be called. Luca had even fought beside one or two of them in a few of his many battles—an uneasy alliance if ever there had been one—and he had a healthy awe of the sons of bitches.

If the conduits were being taken out, then the Warriors already knew, and they would already be trying to make contact and come through. Luca closed his eyes for a moment at a growing sense of impending doom, maybe not for him, personally, but definitely for the kindred as a whole. With the overwhelming numbers the humans enjoyed, they would need only a few warriors to lead them and the tide would be turned. Whoever was behind this uprising was either an idiot or thought he had a good chance of eliminating all the conduits in time.

Imperfect as it was, the status quo was preferable to all-out war with the humans, especially if—no, *when*— the Warriors became involved. No, their lives weren't as pleasurable and free as they had once been. Yes, they had sacrificed a lot of their power to the complexities of the modern world. But they didn't live their lives in constant conflict, they were no less powerful simply because that power was so seldom revealed.

Besides, Luca enjoyed being invisible. . . invisible to every human except Chloe Fallon.

Dammit, all he really cared about was finding out who was behind Hector's murder. Enoch had been the weapon, but Luca wanted the hand that had wielded it. Enoch's death put him in a bind. He had no contact on the Council, no one he could trust. The Council and those who served them was a closed circle—a family of sorts, even if a dysfunctional one. With Enoch dead, there was no one on the staff whom he suspected more than any other, so he had no idea whom to follow and whom to ignore. He had no idea where the uprising was being headquartered. He *did* know that conduits were being hunted down in an effort to prevent those bastard Warriors from showing their faces—

And he had a conduit right here, virtually under his nose.

Luca turned and thoughtfully looked at Chloe's door. A light in the back of the house was still on, so she was still awake. Then, as he watched, the light winked out.

She was safe enough right now, in the sanctuary of her own home. Enoch's boss didn't yet know that he hadn't survived the night, but they'd soon send someone else to do the job. Come daylight she likely wouldn't be in any significant danger; the next attack on her would probably take place after dark, when a vampire was at his peak and the night hid a lot of secrets. So the next night was logically the earliest they would try again.

Luca considered his options, which weren't as clearcut as he liked. First, though, he had to do something about the problem of Chloe Fallon. She could *not* be allowed to remember him.

He'd never had something like that happen to him before. It was unheard of, damned annoying . . . and intriguing. Why didn't his natural ability work on her?

Who—what—the hell was Chloe Fallon? Why was she apparently immune to the innate magic that made people forget him, a magic so strong that until now it had always been effective on humans, and even on most vampires; only the older, stronger ones could remember him. She wasn't resistant to a direct glamour; he'd calmed her down with the merest flick of his power as he took away her fear and anxiety. He hadn't glamoured her into forgetting him because he'd simply assumed she would, the way other people did.

He couldn't afford to be sloppy or overconfident at this stage of the game. He wasn't invincible, any more than Enoch had been. Maybe it was good that this had happened, now he'd be more on his guard.

And yet . . . she'd *remembered* him.

He was so accustomed to being forgotten, to being nothing more than a ghost drifting in and out of humans' lives, that he had long since accepted solitude as his natural state. Being so old, having so many people and vampires pass into and out of his life, had blurred many of the details of his memory; thankfully so, otherwise he'd have long ago been crushed under the burden of loss. He did have very clear memories, though, of trying time and again to establish some way of remaining in the memory of someone he'd loved, only to fail every time. There was a particular heartbreak in loving a woman, whether human or vampire, and having moments of connection as sweet as nectar—until that moment when she turned away to do some simple chore, and he vanished from her mind.

Eventually he had stopped trying, stopped loving, withdrawn more completely into himself. There were vampires who remembered him, of course, but he had so thoroughly severed his emotional ties that being with them felt odd. All vampires knew *of* him, but essentially he was set apart, unconnected. It had been a very long time since he'd even felt the hunger to be seen, to be recognized, to be remembered.

Until now. Until it had actually happened.

Maybe he shouldn't be surprised that there was the occasional glitch in his abilities. Maybe he needed the reminder that he was no more invincible than Enoch had been; he couldn't afford to be sloppy or overly confident at this stage of the game.

But *how* had it happened? Maybe there had simply been a delay; maybe she'd completely forgotten him by now. There was a strong probability that that was what had happened. No one was the same; whether vampire or human, they all had their quirks, their strengths and weaknesses. Maybe the synapses in Chole's memory fired longer, or whatever, so the brief period of time when she hadn't been looking at him hadn't been long enough for the memory of him to fade. By now she should have no idea anything unusual had occurred tonight, no idea she had almost been murdered, no idea he existed. He ignored the cold sense of desolation that filled him at the thought; he'd lived through it many times before.

He'd find out if she had truly remembered; he'd go to her restaurant tomorrow night. But whether or not she remembered him, he would be her shadow, because another vampire would be coming for her, and Luca had to be there, waiting.

Chloe climbed into bed and pulled the covers over her head; the covers she cocooned herself in weren't necessary for a summer night, but the warmth and the softness soothed her. She'd turned on the small TV that sat in the corner of her room, looking for, hoping for, a touch of normalcy. The muted sounds of an old movie on the television served to remind her, on a subconscious level, that even though it had been a rocky few days, all was right with the world. She'd been feeling so nice and peaceful, until that damn voice had started up again.

She expected to lie awake worrying about it, but instead she went to sleep almost as soon as she closed her eyes.

The dream came, but it was different; she wasn't catching glimpses of a long blond braid that made her feel so uneasy she immediately woke. Instead, she was in another world—very literally. She didn't know where, exactly, but the place felt real and not real, here and not here. There were rolling green hills and fertile valleys, gentle and lush, framed by majestic mountains. On the field below the hill where she stood, soldiers prepared for battle. No, not soldiers, exactly; some of them—most of them—didn't wear any kind of uniform. In fact, some were barely dressed at all, which was definitely interesting. Being as appreciative of the male form as the next woman, she took a moment to consider exactly how interesting.

But some of the others wore uniforms that marked them as coming from different times, different cultures. Revolutionary war uniforms, some that looked like WWII uniforms, some . . . *Roman?* There was every type of weapon imaginable, from slings and stones to automatic firearms. Some of the soldiers sparred, some of them were cleaning their weapons, some were exercising. It all looked so real. She could even see some of them sweating. Now that she looked closer, she could see some women mixed in with the men, women who looked as fearsome as the men did.

"Weird dream," she whispered.

"This isn't a dream."

Chloe wasn't surprised when the old woman moved to stand beside her, wasn't surprised to recognize her. This wasn't the first time Grandma Annie had visited her in something that felt like much more than a dream.

"If it isn't a dream, what is it?" As disturbing as the last few days had been, Chloe simply couldn't be upset when Grandma Annie was with her. It was as if the spirit of the woman spread a circle of peace around her wherever she went. In life, in death, in whatever this was . . .

"This is a very real place, as real as your world. It's the home of warriors who wait to be called, who live and die again and again in order to serve the greater good."

"Warriors," Chloe repeated. It was an odd word to use in a modern age. There were soldiers in the world, there were leaders, there were even heroes, but *warriors*? The word evoked primal, even brutal images.

"They can't come on their own. They need help to come into your world in a physical sense," the spirit said. "They need *your* help."

"Help?"

"Ask," Grandma Annie whispered. "Call them to you."

And then, in the way of dreams, Chloe was somewhere else. Grandma Annie was gone without so much as a wave good-bye; the warriors Chloe had been watching were gone, and she stood alone upon a sheet of ice. It was so real she could feel the cold rising off the ice. Her nose was freezing, and so were her feet. She was so cold and so alone, and she longed for warmth and her grandmother and the circle of peace.

Then she turned, and found that she wasn't alone after all. A figure covered in thick fur knelt before her, head down, sword in hand and ready . . . long blond braid falling forward. For a moment Chloe was literally frozen in place, staring at the braid. That was it! *The* braid, exactly as she'd dreamed it: the color, the length, the thickness.

"Are you one of them?" Chloe asked. "Are you a . . . Warrior?"

A shrill beeping intruded; before she could get an answer, Chloe was yanked from her dream and into reality. The alarm clock was beeping loudly and continuously, and she wasn't at all surprised to find that her bedroom was freezing, which was probably what had prompted the dream about being on the ice floe. There was apparently something wrong with her thermostat, dammit all to hell.

She slapped at the snooze button and pulled the covers up around her neck, curling into a ball and burying her nose in her pillow, searching for warmth. Chloe didn't often wish for a man, but right now it would be nice to have someone to warm her feet on, someone to add the warmth of another body to her cold bed. She needed something solid in her life, when it seemed that nothing and no one was real.

A face swam into her memory, a face that was chiseled and strong, with long dark hair falling around it and pale gleaming eyes that seemed to pierce the darkness. He'd been here last night. He'd fought off her attacker, and everything had been all right. A sense of peace began to fill her, and she smiled a little. For a moment his name eluded her, and then it popped into her head crisp and clear: *Luca.*

CHAPTER EIGHT

Sorin arrived back in D.C. just before dawn, and he began threading his way through town to his secret lair. He could have slept at the mansion in Potomac, but that would have required a level of trust in his fellow rebels that he simply didn't have. From the time he'd been turned he'd always preferred having a secret place to spend the day. Sure, sometimes he'd dozed with a woman he'd just had sex with, but when he was tired and really needed to rest, like now, he wanted to be alone.

He was later getting back than he'd wanted. First, locating the soldier conduit had taken longer than he'd expected, and during the drive back it had been raining like piss pouring out of a boot (had to love those human expressions) in North Carolina, which had slowed traffic on the interstate to a crawl. *He* had been able to see perfectly, but the poor humans had been feeling their way along in the dark and the rain.

The mission hadn't been an easy one, either. The soldier had been a fighter, a real fighter, not someone who just filled a uniform and performed office duties. He had also been frighteningly close to realizing and accepting what was happening to him. There hadn't been any confusion, no doubts about the stability, or

lack of it, of his sanity. The human had begun to realize he was the route through which an Immortal
Warrior would come into the world. He hadn't known
why, or how, but when Sorin attacked the man had
very quickly realized exactly what he was fighting . . .
and why. He hadn't given up, he'd fought hard until his
last breath.

How many other conduits were teetering on the
edge? This was taking too long. They were cutting it
too close. Eventually some of the Warriors would make
it through, and things would immediately become
exponentially more difficult. At what point would their
numbers become too many for the vampires to handle?
There was nothing he could do to hurry the process,
though; Jonas was already pushing himself to exhaustion, trying to locate all the conduits as they became
active, and evaluate how ready they were.

Sorin had chosen the best hunters from the vampires
who had joined the rebels, but they weren't plentiful;
counting himself, there were only ten. He'd sent Enoch
after the Fallon woman only because she was local; all
of the other hunters were scattered around the country.
Enoch was a strong vampire, and though he'd spent
the last hundred years or so being what amounted to
a majordomo for the Council members, that hadn't
diluted his strength any; his patience, maybe, but not
his strength.

Frankly, the ten of them were stretched so thin he
didn't know how they'd be able to keep up. The Warriors
undoubtedly knew what was going on and would step up
the pace of contacting their conduits. Sorin mentally ran
through the names of the vampires at his disposal; he
already had the best of them hunting, but he needed reinforcements. The next group chosen obviously wouldn't
be as good, but they could take the less-urgent targets, the
easy ones, such as the Fallon woman.

He was tired, he hadn't fed in two days, and dawn was coming. When his cell phone rang he seriously considered turning it off without answering it. He glanced at the Caller ID—*Unknown*—but he recognized the number: Regina. He bit off a curse as he flipped the phone open. "Yeah."

"Enoch hasn't returned."

Sorin pinched the bridge of his nose. The girl should have been an easy kill, much easier than the soldier in North Carolina, which was why he'd sent Enoch. "He doesn't answer his cell?"

"He didn't take it with him. It was found in his room."

That was both bad and good. If Enoch needed help, it was bad that he didn't have his cell. If something had happened to him, it was good that he didn't have his cell, because then no one would be able to find out who had called him, and who he had called. Carrying a cell was always a risk, but one that so far had been a small one.

The risk factor might be going up, though. Enoch could have met with any number of accidents, a few of which could be fatal even to a vampire—say if he was hit by a train and decapitated—but Luca Ambrus was out there somewhere, angry and unaccounted for. Sorin had to assume that Enoch might now be a captive, though for the rebels' sake he hoped the man was dead. Dead was better. Dead didn't talk; dead didn't give up names and locations.

The good thing was, Enoch had no idea about the mansion or where it was located. His knowledge revolved completely around Council headquarters. If he told Regina's identity, that was tough shit for her.

Even if Enoch gave her up to Luca, the executioner might have trouble getting into Council headquarters. The security was superb, designed with an eye toward keeping out Luca himself, on the theory that if Luca couldn't get in, no one could. How was that for irony?

"What about the Fallon woman?" he finally asked.

"She's still alive," Regina replied, her annoyance touched with a hint of fury.

So Enoch hadn't even completed his mission; whatever had happened to him, had happened before he got to her. Something else to worry about, then, another little detail that affected his strategy. "Has her status changed?"

"According to Jonas she's further along, but her status isn't urgent. There's still time."

Sorin drummed his fingers on the steering wheel. That was good news. Still, if some other conduit didn't go hot and he was pulled away again, he'd go after her himself. After all, a conduit was a conduit; they all had to be eliminated, and this one was right under his nose.

Sorin sometimes enjoyed his visits to the witch, but when he went to her room that day just after sunset, he was still feeling grim about losing Enoch. No sign of the vampire had turned up. Regina was both frightened and angry, which meant she was a bitch to deal with. Actually, she was always a bitch to deal with, but today she was worse.

If Sorin wasn't happy with the witch, the feeling was mutual. Sometimes she seemed glad to see him; this wasn't one of those times. She was sitting on the floor, her hands flat on the open pages of one of the larger spell books. She could have called any of the vampires guarding her to lift the huge book to the table, but no, she was too stubborn; she'd rather sit on the floor than ask any of them for anything. When he opened the door without knocking—he deliberately never gave her even that much advance warning—she jerked her head around and glared at him.

"Do you ever *think* that I might be in the middle of something delicate," she snapped, "and when you barge in like that it destroys everything I've done? I was trying to get a spell started, but forget about that now. You want me to break your precious spell, but you won't *leave me alone* long enough for me to concentrate on anything!"

She was in a mood, all right. He liked that she was getting temperamental; she was a far cry now from the terrified girl she'd been when he'd first brought her here. She was gaining power and confidence along with, or because of, her expanding skills.

"A knock on the door would be just as much of an interruption," he said coolly, stepping inside and closing the door behind him. "The only reason you'd want me to knock would be so you'd have time to hide something you were doing."

She rolled her eyes. "Yeah, like I can pick up this book and stuff it under the couch or something. There's nothing here you don't know about, and nothing comes in that you don't provide. I practice doing spells. That's what you freakin' brought me here to do, right? But *sometimes*—just a thought, here—I might be changing clothes and I'd like to do that *in private*!" She was yelling at him by the time she finished, so angry she was arguing about something that hadn't happened.

Sorin glanced at the book in front of her. It was one of the books in one of the incomprehensible languages. She had indeed progressed far, if she could now understand the writing. The smell of magic was in the air, not the heavy magic he'd scented before when dealing with death spells, but something lighter, more delicate, something tinged with Nevada herself. "You can read the book?"

"I'm *beginning* to understand *some* of the words,"

she said in a testy tone, pushing her long hair back out of her face. "I'm feeling my way along, trying out different words to see how they work, using the process of elimination to—never mind, you can figure it out." She scowled at him. "What do you want?"

Nevada Sheldon was a pretty young woman, petite and fresh-faced, with long, rich, red hair and pale skin from three years in captivity, never seeing the sun. She even had a few very endearing freckles sprinkled across her pert nose, but they had faded some. She was twenty-three years old now, the prime of her young womanhood spent locked in this room.

She looked so innocent, so normal, but she was a direct descendant of the Welsh crone Briallan, the powerful witch who had cursed vampires to be physically unable to enter a human's home without invitation. It was Regina who had traced Briallan's lineage, discovered Nevada, and sensed the huge potential in her. Their capture of Nevada and her family had made this rebellion possible. With her blood, her heritage, the inborn talents she'd tried to refuse—and the proper motivation—Nevada could learn how to lift the curse.

He wouldn't be who he was if he didn't on occasion wonder how Nevada would taste. She looked like forbidden sunshine, and she smelled . . . she smelled like . . . someone he'd once known. An unbidden, unwelcome memory swam to the surface. For a moment he froze in shock as he was spun back in time, a very long way back, and he had an impression of a small woman with a sweet smile, sitting in front of a fire with a shawl draped around her bare shoulders as she nursed a baby, his baby . . . his daughter. That was it, he realized with an inner shock. She smelled like Diera, his daughter. He hadn't been able to watch Diera grow up; she had been his youngest child out of six, the only girl, and he'd been turned when she was just four. He couldn't remember her face, and after all these centuries he almost never thought of the human family that had been left behind so long ago, but her scent . . . yes, he remembered her scent.

Now that he knew why Nevada's scent got to him, he thought grimly, he could be on guard against it. Still, it was just as well that feeding from the witch—or glamouring her—was forbidden. Nevada needed all her strength to do what had to be done, and her mind couldn't be dulled by blood loss or glamouring, not even a little bit. If he'd ever fed from her, then realized she smelled like his daughter . . . everything in him rebelled at the idea. Even though she wasn't his daughter, the very idea brought back too clearly the time after he'd first been turned, when he had retained just enough sanity to know that he had to go far, far away from his family to keep them safe from him. His blood hunger had been so strong that if he had stayed, even without meaning to, he would probably have killed them all.

"We're running out of time," Sorin said, prowling around the room and taking a good look at everything. She had spell books scattered everywhere—not just on the worktable and the floor, but on the bed, the couch, the chair; he even spied one on the counter in the bathroom. She was working hard to give them what they wanted, but why wouldn't she? It wasn't just her life at stake, but the lives of her whole family.

She glared at him. "I'm doing the best I can. It isn't easy."

"If it was easy someone else would have done it years ago." He stopped by the worktable and ran his fingers through a pile of crystals.

Nevada reached out and slapped the top of his hand, quick as a snake. "*Stop* it!" she snapped. He jerked his hand back, outraged that she'd been able to even touch him; with his vampire speed, he should have been able to evade her without even thinking. But he hadn't been thinking about the crystals, he'd still been distracted by the unwelcome memories of his human family.

Nevada threw up her hands. "I had them arranged the way the book said, now I have to start all over again. Just *go away*! Damn! Don't touch anything else, you hear? Nothing!"

Sorin snarled at her, his fangs elongating a little as his own temper spiked, but then he reined himself in. She was doing exactly what they'd told her she must do. "My apologies," he said stiffly. "I didn't realize they were arranged in a certain manner."

A moment of silence, then she drew in a deep breath. "I'm sorry, too. I shouldn't have hit you." She paused, then in a small voice said, "I didn't mean to hurt you."

Her little slap had hurt his dignity, not his hand. The idea that she could hurt him physically was laughable, but he didn't feel at all like laughing. He wanted her to figure out how to break the damn spell, because the other part of the equation—killing the conduits before the Warriors could come through—was becoming more of a problem with every passing day. Surely to hell *one* part of the plan could go well.

This would be much easier if she had known all her life that she was a witch capable of amazing power. Instead, she had grown up as a normal human girl, completely unaware of what she was and of her potential. She had to learn everything from the ground up in a very short length of time, an almost impossible learning curve for anyone. And yet, every day she displayed more power, more confidence in who and what she was, what she could do. Soon, very soon, she should be able to lift the spell.

It had better be soon, or everything was lost.

"How are Emily and Justin?" she asked, as she did

every day. She had been very close to her younger sister and brother.

"They are well."

"My folks?"

"Also well." His answers to both questions were true, but he didn't say how frightened her parents were. They had figured out who, or more important *what*, had taken them. In another day and age, that knowledge might've been a death sentence, but once the rebellion began in earnest the existence of vampires would no longer be a well-guarded secret. The entire family had been spirited away when Nevada's existence and dormant powers had been discovered. She thought they were being held somewhere else, but in fact her family was housed in the basement of this very house.

"When can I see them? I need to see them."

"Not until you do what you were brought here to do. They're alive, and that's all you need to know. Just be thankful I let you speak to them."

Kidnapping her family had been the only leverage they had to force her into doing what they wanted. If he'd thought he could glamour her into serving him he would've done so months earlier, but glamoured humans never had full possession of their faculties, and Nevada needed every brain cell to be at maximum working order.

He might've turned Nevada—and might still, in time—but a new vampire was often weak and he needed her to be strong. She was likely to be so overcome by her new hunger that she wouldn't be able to give her task its proper focus. And there was no guarantee that her natural powers would survive the change; becoming a vampire might very well completely wipe away her gifts. There were so many variables, there was simply no way to tell how she might react to being turned.

No, this was the only way. But after the spell was broken . . . then he might turn her. That might well be the only way to save her life. Regina would already have faced the fact that a witch powerful enough to break the spell of sanctuary would also be powerful enough to recast it. Nevada wouldn't be allowed to live, at least not as a human. But if she were vampire . . .

Even that wasn't a guarantee that she would be allowed to live. If her witch powers survived the turning intact, Regina might insist that someone so potentially powerful be killed before that power threatened to surpass her own.

"I'm doing everything you asked. Letting me see them, just for a few minutes, wouldn't hurt anything and it would stop me from worrying—" She broke off, but he knew what she was about to say. She worried that they were dead, and he was tricking her somehow. She shoved her hair back again. "I've learned so much, I can do things I'd always thought were impossible, but . . ."

"But what?" Sorin asked when she hesitated.

"But there's a block of some kind, a shield I can't get past. The spell you want me to break is very strong."

"If you want it badly enough, you can get past that shield. You're strong enough, you just have to learn *how*."

She looked down at the table that was scattered with crystals, cracked leather-bound books, tarot cards, and vials of dull-colored powders. All the tools were there, if she learned how to use them. "Maybe I'm the block," she whispered. "Maybe I'm more afraid of what the world will be like if you win than I am of losing those I love."

"It'll be a good world," he replied.

Nevada tilted her head back to look him in the eye. "For you."

"Things will go on pretty much the way they do now, but vampires will be in control. Government won't operate on emotion and politicians prostituting ideals just to get re-elected." He paused. "We already have three of us in Congress."

Her mouth fell open, then after a minute she began to laugh. "Bloodsuckers in Congress! What a surprise—*not!*"

He was almost insulted—almost. Instead, he grinned back at her, because he'd had the same thought a time or two. For a moment they shared a look of complete agreement.

Then she sobered, and heaved a sigh of fatigue. "I want to go home," she said, her voice so low she might have been talking to herself. "I want to not be afraid all the time. I want my family safe, and more than anything else I want not to know what I know."

"About yourself or about us?"

She didn't answer. Didn't have to.

"I can give you many things, Nevada, but I can't return your ignorance." Not without completely wiping her mind, anyway. Her witch blood had ingrained the knowledge too deep, until it was so much a part of her that a simple glamour wouldn't return her to what she'd been before.

Moodily, he surveyed her. Everything he wanted hinged, in large part, on this small human who smelled so hauntingly familiar. Victory was close; Sorin could almost touch it, it was so close. The life he desired stretched before him, a life without secrecy, without being forced to hide from those who were beneath him. The fighting might continue for years, in pockets of resistance across the country—and then across the world, as the war moved beyond the United States. But in the end, he and those like him would win. Once they had access to every home, once there was no place for the fragile humans to hide, the war would effectively be done.

Against his will, he'd become fond of the little witch. Without doubt Regina would want to kill her, so he had to decide what *he* wanted to do. Turn the witch, or not?

How vicious would Nevada be, when—if—he turned her? How strong? Turning a human was always unpredictable. Some spent years unable to do more than feed; their new hunger eclipsed everything else. Those usually didn't last long, because their hunger was more important to them than the codes they were required to live by—including the all-important secrecy, which was strictly enforced by the Council.

Then again, other new vampires were more balanced, more powerful from the day of their new birth. Part of it depended on the strength of the vampire who did the turning; vampires were not created equal. He suspected Nevada might be one of the stronger . . . if she were allowed to survive.

NINE

Luca's cell phone vibrated gently in his pocket. He had been sleeping—again in the bathtub with all light banished, in another motel—rebuilding his energy after the long vigil before following Enoch. He'd also fed beforehand, choosing a big guy who had just left a gym; not only did the adrenaline make his blood pump faster, but a large human could give more than a small one, and not feel the effect as much. Luca preferred feeding from women, simply because they tasted sweeter, but he wasn't after a sweet taste now; he needed volume. He had planned to feed a second time if the first one wasn't enough, but the big weight lifter had come through with flying colors. Luca hoped the guy didn't have a competition coming up within the next week; he wouldn't fare very well if he did.

The message was from Theodore, and was unusual in its brevity: *Don't come in.*

Luca's eyebrows rose. That was interesting. Doubly so, if he had to consider the possibility that someone had stolen Theodore's cell phone and texted him pretending to be Theodore.

He and Theodore had never been best pals. In fact, he'd have said that Theodore would have voted to give him the boot at any time if he'd thought he could convince the rest of the Council to back him. So this text telling him to stay away was . . . what? A warning? Or was Theodore the traitor, and using this method to make sure Luca didn't interfere?

There were so many variables to this latest development that Luca needed to think about them for a while. He was a hunter and a fighter, not a damn politician; figuring out what anyone on the Council was thinking at any given time was enough to make him wish he could get drunk. His own gut, however, told him to stay away from headquarters, and his gut he would definitely listen to. But he was interested, to say the least.

He shifted in the tub, stretched out his legs by propping his feet on the wall. Now that he was awake, he realized how uncomfortable he was. He needed to find a place with blackout curtains, so he could sleep in a bed. Yawning, he rubbed his hand over his face and heard the rasp of beard. He hadn't shaved in—what?— four days now? If he hadn't glamoured Chloe, she probably would have run shrieking from the sight of him.

He checked his internal sense of the sun's position: almost sunset. By the time he showered and shaved, twilight would have deepened to the verge of complete darkness. Chloe Fallon should be safely at work, surrounded by people. He'd check out of the motel and arrive at Katica in plenty of time to see if any vampires arrived to lie in wait for her outside the restaurant.

He'd also find out for certain that his power had worked, that for whatever reason it had simply taken a few seconds longer for her to forget him. She might have some little quirk that kept her from forgetting as fast as everyone else did, but the end result would be the same: He would be as anonymous as ever.

* * *

Chloe glanced at her wristwatch: little more than an hour until closing time. There were a handful of customers still sitting at their tables, but they had finished their meals and were just chatting and sipping wine or coffee. It had been another good night, with a steady stream of customers. She was proud of the restaurant. Proud of the decor—which was warm and intimate, with a lot of brick and leather, a real wood fire burning in a huge central fireplace in the winter. Proud of the cuisine—which tended toward Pacific Rim but sometimes the chef went off on French tangents, sometimes on a southern tangent, which tended to keep the clientele guessing about what they might get. Everyone seemed to like it, because they kept coming back.

She had wanted to show off her restaurant. Well, not hers literally, but hers in that, for her shift five days a week, she had total responsibility for it. Chloe hated to admit it, but she was more than a little disappointed that Luca hadn't shown up to claim the free meal she'd offered him.

At the same time, she was terrified that he *would* show, because something strange was going on. Every time she thought about him she caught a glimpse of that strange shimmer behind her eyes, which should make her very nervous, only she wasn't. Thinking about him made her feel very peaceful. Shimmery, but peaceful. Okay, if something was wrong with her—and seeing a golden, transparent shimmer definitely fell into the "something wrong" category—then she should be seeing the shimmer all the time, and not just when she thought of Luca. Something didn't add up, and Chloe wanted to know what it was.

On the other hand, maybe she should count her blessings. She didn't know him, didn't know anything about him, not even his last name. He could be an ax murderer, or a lobbyist, for crying out loud.

Well, a very nice-looking ax murderer. She refused to
think he might be a lobbyist; that would just be so
wrong. Regardless of what he was or did for a living,
with his pale eyes and that sculpted face, he would
stand out anywhere. Add in the long dark hair, falling
around those broad shoulders like some . . . the word
"model" came to mind, but she instantly rejected it.
What he sort of reminded her of was the movie
Braveheart, the way the actors had looked in their roles
with their long hair and kilts. Yum. Now, if he'd just
had on a kilt—hmm. She tried to bring to mind what
he had been wearing, but the memory just wouldn't
form. Something dark, she thought. Maybe. But his
face . . . yes, she remembered every detail of that face.

Valerie Spencer walked by and lightly bumped Chloe
with her shoulder. "Are you okay?"

Chloe gathered her thoughts. "Sure, why?"

"You've seemed kind of distracted tonight."

That was the understatement of the year, Chloe
thought, but before she could answer a late group
spilled through the door, laughing and talking.

"Oh, shit," Valerie murmured. "The kitchen is going
to be so pissed." The kitchen staff was winding things
down, or trying to; a large group like that, if they
ordered full meals, made for late hours for everyone.

"I'll warn them," Chloe said, watching as Valerie
went to greet the late arrivals, her tall, slender form
swaying in a way that pulled men's gazes. She had an
exotic flare, from her boyishly cut dark hair to her
slanted dark eyes, but regardless of how many men
watched her, Valerie was cautious about who she
dated. She'd been burned a time or two, so she wasn't
in any hurry to jump out of the frying pan again.

Valerie was, well, she was just kind of on the same
wavelength as Chloe. She worked at Katica five nights
a week, usually as hostess, though she had been known

to fill in on the floor when the waitstaff was short-handed. She was five years older than Chloe, divorced, a D.C. native, and over the past few years had become one of Chloe's closest friends. They commiserated about men, went to the movies, had dinner together at least once a week, and basically kept each other sane. Chloe's other friends were either younger and more interested in a party lifestyle than she was, or married and always on the go with husbands and kids. Valerie had done the party scene and wasn't interested in it now, so they jibed in a lot of ways.

Chloe felt relaxed with Valerie; she could bitch when she was in a bitchy mood, let loose on the sarcasm instead of having to be nice all the time the way she did at work, and Valerie understood whenever the pressure built up and Chloe had to unload all her frustration and fear. For her parents, Chloe put on a brave face and pretended that the aneurysm didn't worry her; with Val, she could blow off steam about not being able to plan for the future when she didn't know if she even *had* a future.

The fact was, no one knew what might happen. Her aneurysm was fairly small and stable, and no surgeon she'd found wanted to touch it. The surgery to repair an aortic aneurysm was so dicey that evidently they did it only when it was a necessity, and Chloe hadn't reached that point. They couldn't, however, assure her that the aneurysm wouldn't suddenly blow, no matter how small and stable it was at the moment. Still, she was lucky in that hers had been found early, so they could keep an eye on it, blah blah blah. It was enough to drive her nuts.

Wait—maybe she was *already* nuts.

If Chloe had been inclined to tell anyone about the dreams and voices, it would have been Valerie, but she wasn't ready yet to tell anyone. It sounded too strange, even to her. Braid, voices, the dream about Grandma Annie and all those warriors . . . oh, and don't forget about being attacked last night and almost killed, before being saved by a hunk with long dark hair. But she *did* keep forgetting about it, at least the attacked-and-almost-killed part, which was really weird. She should be a nervous wreck, having flashbacks or something, but she wasn't. Instead, she felt very mellow about the whole experience, and if *that* wasn't weird, she didn't know what was.

When she got to the kitchen she warned the staff about the late arrivals, earning some groans and weary sighs. "Maybe they'll just order appetizers," she said. "But regardless of what they order, even if it's the most complicated item on the menu, we don't cut any corners." She knew they wouldn't; the chef was proud of her work, proud that Katica had a reputation for good food.

She left the kitchen and the first thing she saw was Luca, standing just inside the entrance. She stopped so abruptly it was as if her feet were suddenly glued to the floor. Her heartbeat speeded up, excitement raced through her veins at the sight of him. There was something about him . . . he simply wasn't like anyone else she knew. All he was doing was *standing* there, and she had the sudden impression that he was the most dangerous thing she'd ever seen, as if a hungry panther had suddenly strolled into the restaurant. Whether it was the way he moved, so fluid and graceful, or the almost arrogant tilt of his head, the expression in his eyes that said nothing surprised him and he could handle just about anything that came his way—she didn't know what it was about him that made him so noticeable, couldn't pin it down. Maybe it was the sum total of all those things.

Valerie was still getting the group seated, the menus

distributed; Chloe signaled to her that she would handle this one, and threaded her way through the tables to the hostess station. She was tempted to do deep-breathing exercises to settle her pulse down, but she was afraid he'd notice. Good lord, if anything, he looked even better than she remembered, she thought as she approached. His long dark hair fell freely around those muscular shoulders, his pale gray eyes glittered in contrast to his olive-toned skin. Tonight he was wearing black pants and a charcoal-colored shirt, and he looked like walking sex. She could feel her heartbeat speeding up, her skin heating in automatic response. His mouth . . . warm, mobile . . . the flick of his tongue on her skin—

Good lord, where had that come from? Both horrified and amused at herself, she shoved the thoughts away. Thank goodness he couldn't read her mind!

"Luca, I thought you weren't going to make it," she said, holding out her hand to him, and because she had embarrassed herself with her own thoughts she tried to dampen the warmth in her voice, but she was afraid it came through anyway.

She got the impression that he'd been about to say something but at her words his face went blank and still. She stopped, her smile fading to uncertainty, her hand dropping to her side. "Is something wrong?"

He didn't reply; instead his gaze moved slowly over her features. The intensity in his eyes made her blush pink, all the more because she felt as if she must have an ink smudge or something on her face. She cleared her throat, summoned up every ounce of professionalism she had, and said, "I believe I promised you a meal you wouldn't forget. Let me get you settled at a table—" She looked around, saw that a very good table was now empty and clean, and plucked a leather-bound menu from behind the hostess station. "Is there anything you want from the bar? I'll put in the order so you won't have to wait."

He finally spoke, his voice as smooth and deep as a summer night. "I can't stay for a meal."

Chloe stopped in her tracks, unaccountably disappointed. "I know it's late— Never mind. If you can't stay, you can't stay. The offer is good for any night I'm on duty. A glass of wine, then, if you have time?"

He hesitated, that unnerving gaze never leaving her, then he said, "Wine sounds good, but I really don't have time. I just wanted to stop by and see if you were all right."

A little frown knit her brows. "Why wouldn't I be? Oh! You mean last night. I'm fine." Why wouldn't she be fine? She'd been scared, but it all seemed very vague now, like something that had happened years ago.

"No bad dreams?"

Startled that he'd mentioned dreams, she jerked back a little. For a moment she was unnerved. What did he know about her dreams?

Then she realized he didn't know anything, that the question was rhetorical. She gave a short laugh. "Dreams, yes. Bad ones, no." Dreaming about a braid was a far cry from having a nightmare. She'd been annoyed, not scared.

"Good." His pale gaze went over her again. "I have to leave now, but I'll see you again, Chloe Fallon." Then he turned and walked out the door, quickly fading into the darkness beyond the mellow lights at the entrance.

Huh. Well, that was a letdown. Irritated, Chloe returned the menu to the stack at the hostess station. Why had he bothered to come in if he wasn't going to stay? And why be so brusque about it? Yeah, he'd thrown in that "I'll see you again" bit, but she distinctly felt as if she'd just been brushed off.

* * *

Luca barely paid attention to where he was going as he jaywalked across the street. He reached the other side, instinctively blending into the shadow of a tree, then common sense kicked in and he stopped, carefully looking about, reaching out with all his senses to see what was around him. Unless a vampire had arrived during the few minutes he'd been inside the restaurant, he was clear, but sometimes timing was a bitch.

He felt as if he were reeling out of control, a sensation so completely foreign to him that he could barely form a coherent thought. There was no doubt about it, no plausible explanation that there had simply been a slightly longer delay before the inevitable happened; the inevitable *hadn't* happened.

She remembered him. His face, his name—she remembered. Her expression had lit with recognition the moment she saw him. He'd had his senses dampened, because hearing so many human heartbeats confined in one small space tended to make him hungry, but still he'd heard the hard, solid thump her heart gave, then a radiant smile had lit her pretty face and she'd come straight toward him, her hand held out in welcome as she called him by name.

His throat tightened, and abruptly he found it hard to swallow. In all his long life, that had very rarely happened with the kindred, and certainly not with a human. Most vampires were wary of him, for good reason; whether or not they were able to recognize and remember him made no difference in that. They knew about him, knew he was out there, and knew that if he came for them their long lives were at an end. As for humans, none of them had *ever* remembered him before, so the possibility of being recognized and welcomed had never been on the table.

What was different about Chloe Fallon that the
magic didn't work on her? It wasn't something he con-
sciously did; it was something that had developed as he
matured, as much a part of him as his pale eyes. By the
time he'd matured enough that he could endure even
the slightest bit of light, and learned how to dampen his
painfully acute senses so he could hunt by himself, the
magic or power or whatever the hell it was had kicked
in. Except for a very brief time, as a percentage of his
lifetime, when his parents had formed a somewhat
reluctant partnership in order to care for him and see
him to adulthood, he hadn't normally experienced the
common state of being that was enjoyed by everyone
else in the world, vampire and human alike: that of
being known.

He felt . . . awkward, which was an astonishing sensation for someone over two thousand years old.
Before, no one had ever remembered what he said or
did, so he hadn't worried about his behavior. After all,
what did it matter? Now, suddenly, he felt as guilty as
a misbehaving schoolboy, and he didn't know why.

*She didn't remember just him, she remembered last
night, too.* He had glamoured her. She shouldn't
remember any of it. But evidently she did. Why did she
remember last night?

This was wrong. Something was wrong. Either that,
or Chloe Fallon was somehow different, on a genetic
level, from every other human he'd met over the past
two thousand years.

She was a puzzle he'd have to explore, but right now
he had the more immediate duty of watching to see
who next tried to kill her. He put away all thoughts of
the mystery that Chloe represented, instead concentrating on the here and now. He waited, listening, scenting,
but nothing unusual registered. Attacking her here
would be the least logical place, anyway: too many

people around. Enoch had done it the smart way, waiting for her at home, attacking before she could get
inside. Luca would make certain he was there before
she arrived, waiting and watching.

Finally the last customer was gone, the door locked,
the restaurant cleaned and ready for the next day.
Chloe rolled her shoulders, trying to ease the tension in
her tired muscles. Once again, she'd been on her feet
almost the entire shift, and had managed to snag
roughly five bites of food in the past eight hours.

"Want to try to catch a midnight show?" Valerie
asked.

For a moment Chloe was tempted, then reality made
her shake her head. "I'm beat. I didn't sleep much last
night, either. All I want to do is get out of these shoes,
put my feet up, and relax."

Valerie's eyebrows danced. "Can I assume it was a
man who kept you from your beauty sleep?"

"Yeah, but not in a good way." After a pause, Chloe
told her friend about the attack, and Luca's appearance.

Valerie's full mouth quickly settled into a disapprov-
ing frown "You called the police, I hope."

"No. I wasn't hurt and I couldn't really give a
description of the guy, so it didn't make much sense to
file a report." Even as she heard the words coming out
of her mouth, Chloe wondered at herself. For crying
out loud, she *should* have called the cops, at least made
the report.

"For all you know, it was a setup. Those two
might've been in cahoots. One scares you, the other
saves you, and you end up trusting a complete
stranger." Valerie paled a little. "Tell me you didn't ask
him into the house."

"No, *Mom,* I didn't ask him into the house." If she

was going to tell, she might as well tell it all. "I did kind of . . . ask him to come by so I could buy him a meal."

Valerie sighed in obvious disapproval. "You told him where you *work*?"

"He already knows where I *live*."

"Yeah, but . . ." Valerie pursed her lips. "Sorry. I do kinda sound like your mother, don't I?"

"Yep."

"It's just . . . we single women have to be careful, we have to look out for each other." Valerie smiled at the customer who stood, waved, and headed for the door. "So, what did he look like?"

"I told you, I didn't get . . ."

"Not the attacker, this Luca person."

"You saw him. He's the man who came in while you were seating that last group. He couldn't stay, though. He just stopped by to see if I was okay."

Valerie frowned. "I don't remember anyone coming in. How did I miss that?"

"I signaled to you that I'd handle seating him, remember?"

"I remember you walking that way, but, sorry. Guess I wasn't paying attention. Anyway, what does he look like?"

Chloe pictured his face, and that odd shimmer danced behind her eyes. "He's very striking—not pretty-boy handsome, there's something all *man* about him. Olive complexion, but light-colored eyes. Like I said— striking. At least six feet tall, maybe taller. Long dark hair, down to his shoulders. Strong, but not muscle-bound. Like I said, he isn't pretty, but he's definitely hot. Nice ass. Good hands. Really sharp jawline."

Valerie made a low, humming sound "Now I'm sorry I didn't see him." She smiled. "And going strictly by your description, I have to confess that maybe I wouldn't have been nearly as cautious as you. I think I would've had to take a chance and ask him in for a drink, or whatever."

"I was too tired for a drink, and I don't *whatever* with men I just met."

Valerie smiled wickedly, her earlier concern gone. "We both desperately need a little *whatever* in our lives." The smile faded a little. "Unfortunately, unless you buy one at a specialty store, penises come attached to men, who almost always turn out to be more trouble than they're worth. You're not taking the Metro home tonight, are you?"

"Nope. For the duration, I'm driving." Sputtering from place to place was a more accurate description, but since she was off work for the next two days she was going to get her disobedient car to the shop and have that taken care of. "And you'll be happy to know that I had my pepper spray in my hand." For all the good it had done her, since she'd dropped it when she was grabbed. But Valerie had given her the pepper spray for her birthday, so she wanted her to know the gift was being put to use . . . almost, anyway. The intent had been there. Maybe she should also think about buying a taser, but wouldn't that be overreacting? After all, she hadn't been hurt, had she? No, she didn't think so. She couldn't even find any scrapes or bruises this morning.

On the other hand, was it possible to overreact to being attacked in her own front yard? On the upset scale, that ranked in the upper third, at least. She should definitely be upset; should be, but wasn't. Weird.

Chloe pushed back that memory. Now would be the time to tell Valerie about the voices, if she was going to take that step. It was hard to admit even to a good friend that she hadn't slept in days, weeks, that she was hearing voices and having weird, vivid dreams that made her question what was real and what was not.

Even though she had almost decided the cause of her

auditory hallucinations was physical, not psychological, there was one detail that gave her pause. She only heard the voices when she was home alone. Never at work, or on the drive or walk home. Chloe had to wonder: if she had invited Luca in last night, if she had asked him to stay, would she still be questioning her sanity and her health today? Would a visitor, any visitor, bring blessed silence to her home?

"Why don't you come by the house after work?" Chloe asked.

"I thought you wanted to sleep."

"We can crash in the living room and catch a movie on TV. I know I need to sleep, but I'm not sure I can."

"Still shaken from last night?"

Chloe nodded. She didn't have to explain to Valerie exactly why she didn't want to be alone. They were good enough friends that they were there for each other, no questions asked . . . not many, anyway.

Valerie followed Chloe home and parked behind her. Walking from her car to the door without sprinting was difficult for Chloe. Last night the big bald man had come out of nowhere, and there were a lot of shadows in and around her small front yard. All day long the memory had been vague, as if it had been in a movie she'd seen, but tonight, taking that same walk, it all came back. She didn't breathe deeply until she was inside the house, with Valerie, with the door locked behind them.

They talked about work for a while, watched a movie on TV, ate microwave popcorn, and drank too much diet soda. Chloe didn't want to talk about Luca, and fortunately Valerie didn't mention his visit to the restaurant. Odd for Valerie, but maybe she sensed that Chloe didn't want to go there.

Since the movie wasn't very good they talked more than they watched. They made fun of the movie and laughed a lot. It was a laid-back evening, relaxed and very nice. There were no disembodied voices, not with Valerie in the house.

Unfortunately that couldn't last forever, and Chloe was aware that sooner or later her respite would end. Valerie wasn't going to move in; she wasn't going to give up sleeping in her own bed to crash on Chloe's couch, not even for one night. The movie ended, Valerie started to yawn, and finally the moment came. She had to go home.

Chloe stood in the open doorway and watched Valerie make her way to her car. She held the can of pepper spray in her hand, just in case the bald freak jumped out of nowhere. Valerie was right; she should've called the police, but it was too late now. They'd think she was nuts if she called to report something that had happened more than twenty-four hours ago. What could they do at this point? Nothing.

Tonight all was quiet. Of course, last night had been quiet, too, until the psycho had jumped her. Chloe didn't rest easy until Valerie was in her car, the engine revved, and she was driving away on the otherwise deserted street.

She was still standing in the doorway when the voice whispered in her ear. *Don't deny me.*

Chloe jumped, startled into a shriek. Her heart thudded in her chest, so hard and strong she could feel it. She didn't know if she wanted to run into the yard to escape the voice, or slam the door, sink to the floor, and scream at the top of her lungs. The yard won. Bald mugger/rapist and all, the yard won. She'd rather face something that was real instead of the gremlins in her own head. Gripping the can of pepper spray in her hand, Chloe ran across the porch, down the steps, into the grassy yard. There she dropped to her knees and wallowed in blessed silence.

How long would it last? In the beginning she'd only heard the voice in her dreams, and then in that half-asleep state between dreams and reality. Now it came when she was wide awake in her own home, but when she was away from the house she was safe from it. How long did she have before the voice began to follow her outside? To work? How long before the voice was so much a part of her she could no longer tell where reality ended and insanity began?

Out of the corner of her eye she caught some movement, darkness against darkness. Another wave of panic washed over her, along with a sense of outrage. What, she wasn't safe either inside or outside? That wasn't fair. *Pick one*, she wanted to shout at the Fates, or whatever was behind all of this.

She was too vulnerable in her kneeling position; she lunged to her feet, her finger resting firmly against the trigger of the pepper spray canister as she shakily backed toward the porch, ready to defend herself. "Stop right there," she ordered the shadow. "Or I'll fry your eyeballs."

The shadow moved again, stepped out of the darkness beside her house into the light, and everything in her relaxed as if her moment of panic had never been. "Luca, it's you." She remembered Valerie's theory that he and the big guy might have been in cahoots to rob her, and her gaze scanned the yard behind him. She couldn't see anyone else, though. She looked back at him. "What are you doing here?"

He had his hands in his pockets, his shoulders relaxed. "I'm restless at night. I don't sleep much, so I thought I'd just walk by and make sure everything was all right here."

"You live nearby?"

He jerked a thumb to the east and nodded. "I haven't been here very long. I'm still learning the neighborhood."

If he'd recently moved to the neighborhood, it was logical that she hadn't seen him before, given her odd hours. That also explained how he had happened by last night.

Disjointed thoughts raced through her mind. She didn't want to be alone. Valerie wasn't coming back, not tonight. Which was worse, to take the chance that a man she'd just met wasn't a psycho? Or take a chance—*no, know without doubt*—that if she went back inside alone the voice would torment her?

She was tired of being tormented. She was tired of the voice, of doubting her own sanity. The simple truth was that if Luca had wanted to hurt her, last night or tonight, he could have. Her pepper spray might slow him down, but it wouldn't stop him.

And still, she didn't run for the door. She simply couldn't make herself go back inside, alone. "It's usually a quiet neighborhood."

"Still worried about the man who attacked you last night?" he asked, watching her closely.

"Duh."

He smiled at her response. That smile was very nice, almost mesmerizing. "The guy was drunk. From what little he said, I believe he thought you were an ex-girlfriend. But he won't be bothering you again. I, uh, made sure he got the point."

"That's good to hear. Thank you again. I can't tell you how glad I am that you were there. At any rate, I'll definitely be looking over my shoulder for a while."

"He made you jumpy."

Chloe nodded.

"I'm sorry to hear that." Luca came closer, but he moved slowly and there was still a decent distance between them. His voice was soothing, "If I could make the memory go away, would you want me to?"

Chloe actually smiled, a little. "I guess that would be

nice, if it was possible, but then if he did come back I wouldn't be prepared."

"Are you prepared now?"

"Maybe. Definitely more aware of what's going on around me."

Luca seemed a little distracted. He wasn't obvious about it, but she got the distinct impression that he was giving her only half his attention, that his mind was elsewhere. He seemed to be listening, though she had no idea for what. Then he looked back at her, the focus of his gaze sharpening. "You should go inside, where you'll be safe."

She felt an odd compulsion to do what he said, but knowing she would hear that voice again made her resist. "Is it really safe? I mean, no matter how many locks I have on the door, if someone wants in they're going to find a way."

"Your home is safe," he said, still in that soothing, convincing voice.

But to Chloe, being alone in the house was far removed from safety. Alone . . . when she was alone anything was possible.

"Would you like to come in for a cup of decaf?"

Luca was obviously surprised by the invitation. So was she, to be honest. Though her instincts told her he wasn't a danger, could she trust her instincts when her world was being turned upside down?

"Just for coffee," she added. "I'm not . . ." *That kind of girl. Desperate. After your body—well, not much.*

"I'd love a cup of coffee," Luca answered before she could fill in the blank.

CHAPTER
TEN

She was nervous, twitchy. Maybe she didn't invite men into her home very often; maybe whatever it was that was different about her let her sense his otherness. Luca watched Chloe carefully as she prepared a pot of decaffeinated coffee, trying to get a read on her. He kept getting distracted, though, by the little glances she'd throw his way, glances that weren't full of surprise as if he'd suddenly appeared out of thin air. He had learned to handle the surprise; it was the lack of it that was jolting.

So this was what it was like for everyone else. He had always circled on the periphery of life, watching, participating, but always unconnected in the most basic of ways because for most people he simply didn't exist beyond the moment. For Chloe, he existed. With Chloe, there was a connection, whether he wanted it or not. He hadn't made up his mind yet if he was dizzy with joy or if what he felt was panic and he should be running for the hills.

No, no way was he leaving until he discovered who was responsible for Hector's murder. That was his first priority, and for that he needed Chloe. Afterward . . . maybe then he would devote some time to studying her.

Good thing he'd learned to appreciate the taste of

coffee, he thought as he watched her open a cabinet door and select two mugs from a huge selection. Why did one woman, living alone, need so many coffee mugs? Evidently she drank a lot of the stuff.

A long time ago he'd learned to eat and drink without letting his aversion to human food show; it was part of blending into the woodwork, part of existing in a world that was not welcoming to his kind, like walking slowly instead of moving at vampire speed, and smiling at inane jokes. Eventually, though, some of the tastes had grown on him, and coffee was one he sincerely enjoyed. And hell, it might as well be decaf, because caffeine had no effect on him.

No vampire had been waiting when she came home—no vampire other than himself. He wondered if it meant anything, that no attempt had been made on her life tonight. Would the rebels assume Enoch had carried out his assignment and simply not check to verify whether or not Chloe was dead?

If they did, that was piss-poor strategy. He himself would have verified as a normal course of action, so he had to assume that whoever in the rebel faction was in charge of eliminating the conduits would at least send someone to verify that Enoch had accomplished his mission. Tomorrow, surely.

He couldn't hang around forever, Luca thought, but he might have to give it a month at the very least, even though that wouldn't be easy, especially since she remembered him. Each time he had that thought, the shock of it was like a punch to the gut; damn, that complicated things.

He couldn't spend all night, every night, in the street outside her house. Other humans wouldn't remember him but she definitely would. He couldn't saunter by her house every night and hope she'd ask him in for coffee, or conceal himself nearby and wait, listen for her screams, assuming she'd have time to make a sound. He hadn't romanced a human in centuries, but it was possible he'd have to either befriend or romance Chloe.

Cautiously, because she was so jumpy and uncertain.

Luca hadn't interacted much with humans—other than as food sources with a relatively short shelf life—in hundreds of years. He no longer tried to blend in. He didn't surround himself with human servants, lovers, or playthings, mainly because it was so much damn *work* when they didn't remember they were supposed to be lovers and playthings. He fed on them, and then he was forgotten. Simple.

He wasn't sure he even remembered how to seduce a human. They were much less direct in their physical dealings than those of his kind were. Women in particular clung to outdated romantic notions of love and forever, when in fact love was a pretty word for physical attraction, and humans had no real concept of forever.

He switched his attention to Chloe as she brought the two mugs of coffee to the small kitchen table. "Sugar? Cream?" she asked as she set them down.

"No, thanks."

She added both to hers, then sat down directly across from him, and took a sip. Studying her objectively, he could see that Chloe Fallon was an attractive human. Her hair was one of her best features. It was soft, feathery, and golden, falling almost to her shoulders with oddly cut sections that framed her face and swayed when she moved. That face was very pretty, with even features, a nice mouth, and somewhat innocent brown eyes, eyes that carried an expression he couldn't quite read. Wariness? Fear? Of *him* or of something else? She was definitely spooked.

Was she still shaken by Enoch's attempt on her life? Luca had soothed her fears last night, so they shouldn't have resurfaced. The only other explanation was that his own presence disturbed her even though she had invited him into her home. Then he caught her looking at his throat—not in the same way he would admire hers, given the chance—before she too quickly glanced away and took a sip of her coffee.

That was easy enough to read, and he almost smiled. Though it had been a long time since he'd bothered with a human, he suspected she'd be easy enough to seduce. If that's what it took to stay close, it would hardly be a chore. In fact, it would be a downright pleasure. There was always the option of glamouring her into compliance, but where was the fun in that? Besides, anything beyond a moment's simple glamour might damage her mind. Humans were so fragile there was always that possibility. There was no need to leave Chloe in worse shape than he'd found her.

On the other hand, his glamour hadn't exactly worked on her the way it should have, because she still remembered the attack. It should have been completely gone from her mind; she should have remembered having a normal, uneventful night, and nothing else. He was either losing his touch, which brought up the horrifying possibility that his skills and powers were deteriorating—something unknown in the vampire world, because vampires were the opposite of humans, becoming more and more powerful as they aged instead of weaker and weaker—or she was somehow immune to glamouring. He had to find out, because the answer, no matter which answer it was, affected everything. If he was deteriorating, he needed to know. He didn't think he was, because his powers still worked on everyone else, and he felt completely normal, but this wasn't something he'd take on faith.

"So," she said, looking at him again. "What's your last name?"

"Ambrus. Luca Ambrus."

"I don't think I've ever heard that name before," she said thoughtfully. "Ambrus, that is."

"It's Greek." He hadn't been born with any surname at all, but over the centuries the name, which meant "immortal," had become attached to him and he'd taken it as his own.

"But you aren't from Greece, are you?" She tilted her head, studying him. "I mean, you have the olive skin, but you don't have an accent."

He almost laughed aloud. His accent morphed with the times, and it was automatic for him to adapt the speech of his surroundings. When he was in Scotland, for instance, he had a perfect Scots burr. "I was actually born in Greece, yes, but I'm an American citizen." That much was true, and he had the paperwork to prove it. True, the papers were forged, but as far as the government was concerned they were legitimate, and that was all that mattered.

"How long have you been in the D.C. area? Are you renting a house or an apartment?"

"A house," he responded, amused by her version of twenty questions. "And I've been in and out of D.C. for years."

"What do you do for a living?"

"I fix things."

Chloe bit her lower lip for a moment, then released it to ask, "Cars? Air conditioners?"

He smiled. "Nothing so uncomplicated."

"So, you're a spook. Imagine that—a spy, in my own neighborhood."

"No, not a spook. I'm a corporate troubleshooter." That was the truth, as far as it went. He leaned forward a little, his movement drawing her attention as he'd known it would. He caught her gaze and held it, watched as her eyes dilated slightly. He allowed himself a split second of pleasure in her automatic response to him, then with a gentle mental push he was there, in her head, in control of her thoughts. He would try something simple, so light a touch that it wouldn't damage her—something that couldn't fail, if everything was working as it should. "Chloe, stand."

She had been about to take another sip of her coffee, but at his words she placed the mug on the table before her and rose slowly to her feet. Immediately, she looked confused, as if she couldn't remember standing, or why. "What am I doing?" she said in a bewildered tone. "Was I about to get something?"

Good. She didn't even remember his words. So, it was possible to glamour her, and yet his most important ability was useless where she was concerned—and she remembered Enoch, which she shouldn't have done. Fascinating. She was a complete mystery, a normal little human who in one tiny way was completely abnormal.

Abruptly her head snapped to the side, and she stood frozen as if she'd heard something. That was impossible, because his hearing was infinitely better than hers and he had heard nothing beyond her breath and the beat of her heart. But he watched her pupils contract in shock, watched the color fade from her cheeks.

"Go away," she whispered. "You're wrong. That's impossible."

"Chloe?" Luca stood, concerned, and was about to round the table to reach her when the truth came to him in an unpleasant flash. He couldn't hear what Chloe was obviously hearing, but he could *feel* the flow of energy in the small kitchen, an energy that wasn't his but was somehow connected to her, an energy that wasn't of this world. She was a conduit, as he'd suspected, and her Warrior was trying to contact her.

Was that why she was somehow able to remember

him? Was the Warrior interfering, trying to make Chloe recognize him for what he was? That made sense, but at the same time he didn't remember this ever happening before, and over the centuries he'd had contact with the Warriors before, sometimes even fighting side by side with them. At least the possibility was an avenue he could explore.

She pulled herself away from contact with that other world, looked up at him with a quiet sort of terror in her wide, dark eyes. "I think I'm losing my mind," she whispered.

"You're not," he said with certainty, but she shook her head in silent refusal of his assurance.

"I am. I'm hearing voices, and if that isn't nutsville, I don't know what is." Tears gathered in her dark eyes but she blinked them back, squared her shoulders, and said, "I'm sorry, Luca, but I think you should leave."

He didn't want to leave. His instinct was to stay, to question her, to find out exactly how far along she was in the recognition process, but it was so early in the game that if he pushed too hard she might panic and withdraw, order him out—and if she ordered him to leave, in effect she would be rescinding her invitation into her house and he wouldn't be able to enter again unless she specifically invited him again. He needed to play this just right.

"All right, if that's what you want," he said gently, to reassure her. Rounding the table, he took her hand in his, feeling the race of her pulse under his fingers. Immediately he knew he'd made a mistake; touching her, when he'd already tasted her blood, brought temptation and hunger roaring upward. For a moment he hovered on the edge of striking. The warm, sweet scent of woman rose to envelop him. *He could have her.* He'd have to glamour her, but the thought was there, the need was there. Both his fangs and his cock began to lengthen in response.

But where was the challenge, the fun, in that? He controlled his blood lust, retracting his fangs, and firmly clamped down on the urge to take her in his arms and sink his fangs into her neck, to drink from her as he fucked her long and hard. That time would come, but not quite yet.

He leaned down and kissed her temple, feeling the flow of blood against his lips.

"You're not crazy," he reassured her again. "Sit down, and tell me what's going on."

Chloe looked up into that strong face and felt inexplicably reassured; he didn't look concerned or wary, simply interested in hearing what she had to say. Her legs were shaking, so she sat. Why had she stood in the first place? It was as if she'd blacked out for a few moments, because one moment she'd been sitting there sipping her coffee and the next she'd been on her feet, with no memory of getting up or a reason for doing so. Then that damn voice had started in again, and this time it hadn't been content with simply calling her name. No, the disjointed words that had echoed around her had said things like "not human," and "monster," and "danger." For a nauseating moment nothing made sense; Luca's face had swam in her vision, but off to the side, when he was sitting right there in front of her.

There were no monsters but the ones in her head.

So much for having a visitor in the house to keep the voices at bay. This was worse than before! The minute she'd left her chair and risen to her feet, the whisper that had been tormenting her for days had returned with a vengeance.

Inviting a man she barely knew into her house at this

late hour—at any hour—wasn't the smartest thing she'd ever done, but he'd actually *protected* her from danger, which made her inclined to trust him. How far gone was she when taking a stranger into her home was preferable to being alone? Right now, though, she was pathetically grateful that he was there, that he hadn't immediately decided she was nuts and left at a dead run.

He got the coffeepot and poured some hot coffee into her cup, topping it up. "Tell me what's been happening," he said. "Maybe I can help."

She gave a faint smile as she studied the coffee swirling in the cup. "Unless you're a neurosurgeon as well as a troubleshooter, I don't think so. If you can't fix my brain . . ."

"You've been having abnormal dreams, haven't you?" he asked calmly.

Chloe's head jerked up, and she stared wide-eyed at him. His voice had been calm, but there was something fierce and intent in his gray eyes.

"Yes," she whispered. "How did you know?"

"Seeing any odd kinds of light?"

Her heart skipped a beat. How did he know about the dreams and that strange shimmer? She gave a jerky nod.

He seemed to consider her answers for several moments longer than was necessary, then he dropped to his haunches in front of her, so they were practically face-to-face. He took both her hands in his. His eyes were like pale storm clouds. "I'm going to tell you something you won't like hearing."

"I know what you're going to say. I'm either crazy as a loon, or I'm dying from an inoperable brain tumor." She managed a crooked smile. "I go back and forth between the two possibilities."

"No, that isn't it at all. Listen to me, Chloe, with an

open mind—and believe. When I'm finished, you may wish the answer *was* something as simple as insanity. I wasn't going to tell you any of this, but now I think I have to."

He leaned in closer. Despite her worries, she found herself suddenly distracted by his nearness. He had absolutely perfect skin, she noticed. Not a scar, not a nick, not a blemish. And his hair . . . most women would kill for hair like that, thick and heavy and falling perfectly, and also looking as though he'd simply washed it and let it dry that way. Maybe he was one of those men who spent hours in the bathroom making himself look naturally beautiful. Maybe his muscles were the result of hours spent in the gym, and the perfect face the result of a lot of money spent on skin care products, and behind that facade he was vapid and dull. Except she already knew he wasn't, and—

And here she was, terrified and shaking, trying to figure out how the man before her managed to look so damn good. Was this another sign she was losing her mind, or was it simply an attempt to escape reality, just for a moment?

After that harsh prelude, which left her dreading what he might possibly say, Luca stopped to consider his next words for several moments that seemed way too long, long enough that she began to panic. What could be that bad?

The doorbell rang. Startled, Chloe came out of her chair like a shot, almost knocking Luca down. She did bump into him, but he recovered his balance with a swift, powerful grace that was so inherently masculine her mouth went dry. How could he move that fast? He caught her arm to steady her, standing so close her shoulder brushed his chest. He towered over her, his heat and nearness burning straight through to the core of her.

She shook herself back to earth. "Who could that be at this hour?"

"You aren't expecting anyone?"

"Like I said—at this hour? Maybe Valerie forgot something."

"Valerie . . . is she the woman with the boy hair?"

He must have been lurking outside for far longer than she'd realized, if he'd seen Valerie leave. He hadn't just happened by when she'd bolted out into the yard, he'd already been there. Abruptly uneasy, she was suddenly glad the doorbell had rung, glad she wasn't alone with him right now. Something was going on, something that gave her the sudden feeling that she needed to be running for her life.

She went to the front door, acutely aware of Luca following her. Though she could feel him behind her, she did not hear him at all. A man as big as he was shouldn't be able to move so silently. She reached for the doorknob, and the voice in her head whispered, *No, no, no, no* . . . She paused, trying to ignore the words, but at the last moment she decided on basic caution and looked through the peephole.

It *was* Valerie standing there on the front porch, looking tired and totally out of it, as if she were seconds from falling asleep. She wasn't alone. A tall man with long blond hair stood behind Valerie, with one arm around her in a strange sort of hug.

Chloe opened the door. Valerie's face remained blank, but the man holding her gave a reassuring smile. "Your friend had an accident. May we come in?"

Chloe stepped back, opening the door wider. "Oh my God! Of course—"

"No," Luca said sharply, looming behind her. "Don't invite them in."

"But she's hurt—"

"He's here to kill you."

What? Chloe jerked back, her gaze darting between the two men. Luca's statement made no sense at all. First the big bald guy tried to kill her, and now this blond Adonis supposedly wanted to kill her, too? She didn't own anything of importance and she didn't know any state secrets. What the hell?

"Ambrus," the blond man said in a flat tone as his gaze switched to Luca. He didn't look angry, and he didn't deny that he was here to kill Chloe.

"Sorin," Luca responded in the same tone.

Wait. They know each other?

"What the hell's going on?" she demanded, outrage flaring. Dammit, if they were playing some kind of sick, twisted game with her, trying to make her think she was going crazy—

Sorin's arm tightened around Valerie, who seemed to be completely unaware of, well, everything. "You've chosen the wrong side."

"Have I?" Luca moved in front of Chloe, subtly and slowly easing her away from the door frame.

She didn't want to be eased away. She shoved back, resisting his efforts. Regardless of what these two men were doing, there was something wrong with Valerie. Had she really been in an accident? There was no blood, no bruises, but she was obviously dazed.

"What happened to her?" she demanded, glaring at this Sorin guy, and with a shock she realized that he was the man who'd spooked her a couple of nights ago. He wasn't wearing sunglasses at the moment, but yeah, he was the same man.

"She needs help," Sorin replied. "Let me bring her in."

"No," Luca said.

"You're making a mistake," Sorin said, annoyed, his attention snapping back to Luca. "Everything is changing, and fast. We'll be who we are for the entire world to see. Humans will be serving *us*, the way it should be. No more hiding, no more pretending."

"Do you think they'll roll over and let you win?" Luca asked.

"They might as well."

One word stuck in Chloe's head, as the men continued to talk. *Humans?* What the hell were these two if they weren't human?

Sorin nodded his head in Chloe's direction. "You know what she is, you've obviously figured out that much. She's a fly in the ointment is all. What's coming will happen more smoothly without her interference, but it'll happen anyway, so there's no point in protecting her now. Besides, if she knows too much, the Council will insist that you get rid of her, or at the very least have her memory wiped clean. I could easily strip her brain of every useful function. You're just prolonging the inevitable."

"Indulge me," Luca said with a smile that wasn't a smile at all.

Sorin smiled, too, and Chloe fell back with a gasp. Sharp fangs appeared, transforming that smile into one of horror. He moved so fast she didn't really register the movement, lowering his mouth to Valerie's throat and biting down, sinking his fangs deep into her neck.

Valerie gasped, her body arching in his grip, but she didn't fight against the attack. Two small rivulets of blood ran down her throat. With a raw cry Chloe launched herself forward, but Luca's arm shot out and barred the way. "No," he said, his expression calm.

Chloe was anything but calm. "He'll kill her!" she shrieked, shoving at him, trying to move him aside. It was like trying to move a rock. Behind her, that . . . that *monster* was, oh God, actually sucking at Valerie's neck as if he was drinking her blood. Desperately Chloe tried to duck under Luca's arm, only to have him grip her around the waist and haul her tightly against him, preventing her from moving.

"Probably," he said, sounding completely unconcerned. "But if you leave this house, he'll *definitely* kill you. You're safe as long as you stay inside."

"She's my *friend*!" She screamed the words at him, kicking and fighting for all she was worth, jerking on his hair, kicking his shins. None of her efforts seemed to bother him at all. Enraged, terrified, she fumbled for the pepper spray in her pocket, aimed it at his face. "You let me go! I can't just stand here and watch this happen! If I die, I die, but I won't let him kill her without even *trying* to stop him!"

He made another of those movements so fast the action blurred, jerking the pepper spray from her hand. He tossed it away without even glancing at it, and gave a sigh. "Fuck," he said, in an almost conversational tone, then tossed her aside and was through the door faster than her eyes could register the motion. A half-second later, Valerie came flying inside, landing hard on the floor and rolling a short distance before her limp body came to a stop. With a cry, Chloe flung herself beside Valerie, frantically looking around for something to stop the bleeding from the dreadful wound in her neck, which looked as if an animal had bitten her. There was nothing she could use so she jumped up and raced to the bathroom, grabbed several towels, and ran back. Through the open door she could see . . . *blurs*. There was thudding, snarls, the sound of blows, but she couldn't focus on anything long enough to make out details. She could make out the impressions of flesh and hair, and red smears of what had to be blood, but the two men—men?—themselves were moving so fast she could barely tell they were there.

Let them kill each other, she thought violently, pressing a towel to the puncture wounds on Valerie's throat.

God, what was going on? Nothing made any sense, unless . . .

What she'd seen tonight—the fangs, the biting, the unearthly speed with which they moved. What she'd heard—*humans, worse than insanity, monster.* Bits and pieces that fell into place—she'd invited Luca in, but Sorin hadn't been able to simply bring Valerie inside, he'd asked permission—*and waited for her to give it.* The long hair, the *otherness* she'd sensed—it all made sense now.

Except it didn't. Her senses spun as she tried to get a handle on the impossible thing she was thinking. This couldn't be real, but Valerie was lying there on her living room floor, bleeding from a bite to the throat. That was real. The unearthly struggle going on in her front yard was real.

Dear God. Luca was right: she *would* almost rather be insane, or have a brain tumor. Vampires were fucking *real,* and for some reason they wanted her dead.

CHAPTER
ELEVEN

In battle, Sorin was almost his equal. He was strong, a man born to battle as a human and one who had continued to hone his skills after being turned. There was also a part of Luca that made him reluctant to kill a man he'd fought beside in the past, one he actually admired.

He was hampered by his need to take Sorin alive, for questioning. Sorin had no such limitation; he fought hard and fast, his intent plain. With Luca out of the way, Chloe would be dead the moment she set foot outside her house. Within thirty seconds, Luca knew he was in the fight of his life; taking Sorin would be difficult enough even if he wasn't holding back a little.

"You've been practicing," he grunted as he dodged a blow that might have caved in his skull.

Sorin grinned, his face alight with the joy of battle. "You haven't," he taunted.

Their battle was fast and savage, moving from the porch to spill across Chloe's small yard. They didn't need weapons beyond their hands and feet and teeth, though so far they both held back from using their fangs because neither of them wanted to move in that close to the other. They moved faster than the human eye could follow, each blow unnaturally strong. Luca didn't go for the death blows to the heart or head, but he deliberately maneuvered so they were moving farther and farther away from Chloe's house.

Sorin feinted with his right and Luca moved his left arm to block it, for a fraction of a second leaving his heart unguarded. Sorin's left fist came in, faster than sight; Luca simply let his momentum keep him turning and he moved in closer, taking the blow on his right shoulder before Sorin's punch could reach maximum force. The force of the blow rattled the teeth in his head, but he ignored the shock of impact and drove his elbow into Sorin's solar plexus.

Sorin wheezed and immediately retreated just out of reach. Luca leapt, taking advantage of Sorin's momentary disadvantage, and slammed the big blond Romanian full force into a tree trunk. A lesser vampire would have been stunned into unconsciousness, but Sorin instinctively fought back, fought through his temporary daze. Seeing a brief opening, he took it, sliding away from the tree so he was no longer pinned between the trunk and Luca's attack, gaining himself a second of relief.

"Not bad, old man," he said, needling Luca, trying to get under his skin. Human or vampire, battle tactics were the same.

Luca gave a brief snort. The day "old" was an insult to a vampire was the day he'd know the world was at an end.

Was Sorin holding back, too? His eyes were blazing with fierce pleasure, the same pleasure Luca had to admit to feeling. All too rarely did he have an opponent who could test his mettle, who gave him a real battle. In that respect, he and Sorin were much alike. They were, at heart, more at home on a battlefield, sword and ax in hand, pitting themselves against worthy opponents.

Luca, at least, still had the occasional battle—such as with Enoch—but Sorin must be starved for the kind of competition that fed his soul. Was he deliberately prolonging the battle rather than trying to end it quickly?

A kick to Luca's side sent him reeling, but he recovered, rounded, came right back with a fist to Sorin's face. The skin split and he felt the splash of blood on his hand. The scent of their blood filled the air, clear to Luca's sensitive sense of smell. Sorin came in low and fast, catching Luca in the gut with his shoulder, and they fell to the ground together, rolling and punching. Sorin got his hand around Luca's throat as they rolled across the grass, but Luca took advantage of the opening and drove his fist into Sorin's chest, pulling the punch just enough to keep from stopping Sorin's heart.

Instinctively Sorin retreated from what could have been a death blow, throwing himself backward, then they were on their feet again and he was aiming for Luca's chin with a savage uppercut. Luca did a backwards flip, the power of Sorin's punch coming so close that he felt the wind of it on his face; the flip brought Luca around and up, coming in below Sorin's guard and forcing him to fall back even more.

This wasn't accomplishing anything, he thought, his initial pleasure giving way to annoyance. He and Sorin could continue this way all night and into the morning—that is, if Sorin was able to tolerate sunlight, though at his age, with his strength, he probably was. They'd both be weaker beneath the sun, and the wounds that were inconsequential by moonlight would take on more meaning, more danger—plus a lot of humans would be out and about, and be witness to the battle of the supernaturals taking place on Chloe's lawn. Sunrise was hours away, though, and while he'd rather question Sorin than kill him, if this continued much longer he might not have that choice.

A wailing noise in the distance grabbed his attention, and he swore. Sirens. Dammit, Chloe had called 911.

Sorin heard the noise, too. He backed away, breathing hard. The two of them surveyed each other. Both had been hurt to some degree, but their various wounds were already healing.

"Why are you doing this?" Sorin asked angrily. "She's just a human. We're your own kind, you should be on our side."

"Why do you want her dead?" Luca countered, though he already knew; he simply wanted to see what Sorin would tell him.

The sirens grew closer. Sorin backed farther away. "There's something bigger going on than this little human. Stop wasting time with her."

"The uprising?" Luca made a scoffing sound in his throat.

"Don't laugh. We're so much more than these miserable little humans, and you know it. We shouldn't have to hide what we are, we shouldn't have to sneak our food like a child sneaking cookies. Tell me one way, just one, that we're inferior to humans. We aren't. You should join us, Luca. The Council has outlived its purpose, keeping the kindred safe by keeping us hidden. We can seize control now; we're the future."

"I'm not here to debate politics," Luca said.

Annoyance flashed over Sorin's expression, but the sirens were getting closer and closer. He kept backing away, and pointed at the house. "You can't always be here. I'll come for her again, or someone else will. You can't guard against us all."

Then he was gone, moving with such speed he effectively disappeared. The sirens came even closer, and Luca had to make a decision, fast. He could leave Chloe to her own devices, or he could stay and watch over her. Sorin had said he, or someone else, would be back. If a vampire came to her door posing as a woman in distress, a repairman—hell, anyone—she'd invite death into her house. Her life would be over before she even realized what she'd done.

He shouldn't care. There were other conduits in the world, others who could bring in the Warriors. And it wasn't as if Luca had any love for the Warriors themselves, the self-righteous bastards. The Warriors could, and would, kill vampires with ease. They knew how, and they wouldn't hesitate. Luca wasn't a fan of the rebels' cause, but neither did he want to see his own kind slaughtered because a few of them wanted more power in the grand scheme of things.

But though there were other conduits, there was only one Chloe—Chloe, who remembered him.

In an instant he was at her door. She'd invited him in, so he had no trouble crossing the threshold and closing the door behind him. She was kneeling beside her friend, trying to staunch the bleeding, and for the moment she didn't realize he was there. She had no weapons, no self-protection skills. Without him, she was basically a sitting duck. If nothing else he had to explain to her what was going on, warn her of the danger. And then . . .

If he left her to her own devices, she wouldn't live another forty-eight hours, probably not even that long. From what he'd seen, she was in the process of connecting with her Warrior, but was not so far along that the vortex might open within that short time frame. There was still a distance between the two energies he sensed—Chloe's, and that from the other side. Before the Warrior came through their energies would have to merge entirely and Chloe would have to understand what was required of her. That hadn't even begun to happen; she was still in the "I'm going crazy" stage of denial.

He was more than a little torn. The rebels' argument definitely had some merit. Keeping the existence of vampires a secret wasn't an easy task. Sometimes it was galling to be forced to structure one's life around inferior beings. What vampire wouldn't want to be openly at the top of the food chain? It was humiliating to be forced to hide from lesser beings. On the surface, victory should be easy enough for those with superior strength and intellect.

And yet . . . Luca saw a different possible result. The rebels had forgotten what they themselves had been like before they were turned, and they were discounting how stubborn, willful, and downright insanely resistant humans could be. Humans would never completely bow down to vampires; the war would never end. In the end, a lot of vampires would die, maybe more than they could afford to lose. Humans definitely had the advantage of numbers, so they could afford to suffer far more losses than vampires could.

The world would change, and not for the better. While it was easy to dismiss humankind as being far beneath the kindred, there was an innocence and a beauty about these foolish, troublesome humans that shouldn't be lost. Chloe Fallon, who would rush toward certain death to defend her friend, shouldn't be lost.

Besides, he still didn't know why she was immune to his magic. Until he knew why she could remember him, she was a puzzle, a curiosity . . . a gift.

At this point, Luca was alone. He didn't know who he could trust, and who he couldn't. Every member of the Council, every employee of the ancient ruling body, was suspect. There was no way of knowing who among his acquaintances had joined the rebels, and it wasn't as if he could go to the human authorities.

Which left Chloe—Chloe and her Warrior. At the moment, they were his only allies.

* * *

Chloe suddenly became aware of Luca's presence behind her and she whirled around on her knees, bloody towel in her hand. He was standing no more than six feet from her. There was a spot of blood on his jaw, another on his forearm, though she couldn't see any actual wounds.

Vampire! her subconscious shouted in warning. No shit. Thanks for the warning, but at the moment she was short on crosses and garlic. The only thing that prevented her from descending into shrieking panic was the knowledge that twice now Luca had saved her from other vampires.

"Is he gone?" she asked.

"For now. We need to get our story together, now, before the police get here."

Chloe glance down at Valerie to check on her; she had passed out, but was breathing slowly and regularly. "You called the police?" she asked in surprise.

Luca's eyebrows lifted slightly. "No. I thought you did."

She had certainly considered doing so, but what the hell was she supposed to say? *Help! Two vampires are brawling in my front yard!?* She didn't think Valerie was in any immediate danger, unless the vampire's bite carried some sort of disease that no hospital could help her with.

Her dazed mind kept going back and forth between being relieved that she wasn't crazy, and being stunned to discover that beings she'd always thought of as fictional actually existed. It wasn't as if she could deny what she'd seen with her own eyes. Maybe tomorrow she'd think this was all a dream; maybe Luca would use some vampire woowoo on her to make her forget.

She hoped so. She didn't much like having her world

turned upside down. Forgetting would be very, very good. On the other hand—there was always that other hand, dammit—how could she protect herself against something if she didn't know the danger existed?

Outside, the sirens grew louder, closer, then passed on the connecting street, on their way to some other destination. Lucky cops, she thought; whatever had happened at that destination, it couldn't possibly be as interesting as what had happened here. Ignorance was bliss.

First things first. "Will Valerie be all right?"

Luca walked closer, looked down. He studied Valerie as if she were an inanimate object—with curiosity but no concern. He made a sort of put-upon noise, then moved so quickly Chloe didn't have a chance to tell him to stop, or ask him what he was doing. He scooped Valerie up into his arms and carried her to the sofa, where earlier in the evening Chloe and Valerie had talked and watched television as if the world wasn't about to change.

He went down on one knee beside the couch and bent to put his mouth to Valerie's throat. Chloe cried out, darting forward. "No!" she yelled, grabbing his shoulder and pulling at him.

He covered her hand with his, lacing his fingers through hers a little as he looked up at her. "It's all right. I'm going to lick the wound. My saliva will make her heal much faster than she would on her own."

Despite herself, Chloe was a little disarmed by his touch, the intertwining of their fingers. Fiercely she tried to remind herself that if he was a vampire, he could play all sorts of mind games with her and that made her more determined to hold on to her instinctive hostility. She'd been bowled over by him from the moment she first saw him, and now . . . now she didn't know what to think. "You aren't going to bite her?" she demanded suspiciously. "You don't want a taste?"

Was that a sparkle in his eyes? Maybe, because he almost smiled. "You know what I am."

"Not being blind or stupid, yeah, I do."

"Good," he said softly. "Then you know that if I want to feed from her, there's nothing you can do to stop me. But I'm not hungry, and she doesn't appeal to me on any other basis. I'll heal her, and I'll make her forget everything that happened tonight. On the other hand, I'd very much like another taste of *you,* if you offer."

Chloe's heart lurched, then began racing from a tangled combination of fear, anger, and excitement. Taste her *again?* When had he tasted her the first time? She felt that odd shimmer in her brain, behind her eyes, and abruptly she had a vague memory of him hunkered in front of her with her skirt pushed up and his tongue gently licking over her leg. Her knee . . . yes, her leg had been scraped, and he'd taken care of her. You'd think she'd been leaking chocolate, the way he'd seemed to savor her blood. Oh, God. Her legs turned to spaghetti as the memory brought a rush of physical longing that rattled her with its intensity. Level-headed Chloe simply didn't get lost in lust, but with Luca, she was afraid that might actually be possible.

She took a deep breath, forcing her thoughts away from that direction. Valerie was what was most important here, that and the sudden sea change her world had just undergone. "Can you make *me* forget?" she asked with a tinge of bitterness, because what she wanted most was for all this weird shit to just go away.

Luca shook his head. "In your case, forgetting could be deadly. You have to be on guard, and you can't be if you don't remember."

"What if I don't want to know what I know?"

"You don't have that option. Chloe . . . " He paused, squeezed her fingers before releasing them. "You're different."

Great. The one time in her life she wouldn't mind being perfectly ordinary, and he tells her she's different. She narrowed her eyes at him. "Are you going to explain that a little further? Because, frankly, that doesn't tell me squat."

"Later. Let me take care of your friend first."

He'd even distracted her from Valerie. Chloe felt as if she should smack herself in the head. Yes, what had happened had her rattled, but it hadn't made her stupid, she hoped. "Yes, of course. Valerie first, then . . . explanations. Lots of them."

He gave her a quick, wry look before leaning forward again; he slowly began licking the two puncture wounds in Valerie's slender throat. The tip of his tongue danced repeatedly over the twin wounds. His long hair fell across his face, obscuring her view, and that gave her the strength to look away, to suck in a long, calming breath.

And it struck her that for the first time in a while, the whispering, tormenting voice had gone silent.

CHAPTER TWELVE

Valerie briefly regained consciousness, but was agitated and confused until Luca said in a quietly compelling tone, "Valerie, everything is all right. You drank too many margaritas and decided not to drive home. You won't remember anything about being attacked. You're very sleepy now, and you'll sleep until the middle of the afternoon."

"I'm so sleepy," Valerie had murmured, the words slurred, then she'd dropped right off to sleep.

"Holy crap," Chloe blurted, her gaze ping-ponging from Luca to Valerie, then back to Luca. "What did you do, hypnotize her?"

"In a way. It isn't exactly hypnotism."

"What is it then, exactly?"

"It's called glamouring." He slanted a cool gray look up at her. "Don't ask me how it's different from hypnotism, because I can't give you a textbook answer. For all I know, it's the same thing, except faster—instantaneous to be exact."

"Can you do that to me?" she asked suspiciously, because she didn't like the idea of not being in complete control of herself.

"I *have* done it to you," he'd replied, which left her terrified, outraged, and momentarily speechless as he effortlessly lifted Valerie and indicated to Chloe to lead the way to her guest room.

She hastily cleared off the bed, then Luca deposited Valerie on it and stepped back while Chloe eased off Val's shoes, removed the bloodstained blouse so she could wash it, then pulled the sheet over her friend. Valerie never roused. When a vampire voodooed someone to sleep, they stayed asleep. Even if Valerie had been lying on a concrete slab, she was evidently going to sleep until midafternoon.

Luca stood back, watching. Chloe could feel his presence behind her like a human (maybe) thunderstorm looming in the room. She was all but choking on her sense of ill-usage. He'd done . . . whatever it was he did . . . to her! The worst part of it was, she didn't know what he'd done or when he'd done it, so for all she knew he could be lying to her and making her feel like a fool for no good reason. This could either be some sort of con, or the government was involved. She couldn't think why the government would be involved, but in this town anything was possible. All she knew for certain was that she was pissed, and she couldn't even trust her own eyes, much less anything that Luca had said or was about to say.

She *thought* the wounds on Valerie's throat were almost completely healed, marked only by red spots, and even the spots seemed to be fading. But if Luca had hypnotized her, or whatever, was she really seeing what she was seeing or did she only think she saw it?

The possibilities made her head hurt. "Aaargh!" she said furiously, and punched him in the stomach before stomping out of the room. Granted, it wasn't much of a punch because she'd never learned how to really put some power behind it, but it was the thought that counted—and in this case, the thought was that she was completely pissed off at him. He stood frozen for a second, an expression of utter surprise on that chiseled face, then he strode in her wake.

"What was that for?" he demanded, what sounded like indignation in his deep voice. What right did he have to be indignant? She was the one who was being jerked around like a pull-toy.

She stopped in her tracks and whirled on him, planting her hands on her hips as she glared at him. "What do you mean 'What was that for?' It was for everything! For telling me you've hypnotized me so now I don't know if anything I've seen is real and I've just made a fool of myself for even thinking I've seen it, and if it *is* real, then for being here at all! What the *hell* is going on?" She wanted to shake her hand, because his stomach was as hard as a rock, but she was damned if she'd let him know that she'd hurt herself when he hadn't even had the courtesy to give a small "oof." Instead she turned around and resumed her stomping. The kitchen seemed like the best destination, because at least there were knives there, in case she needed to defend herself.

After an impossibly fast detour into the hall bath— she heard the water running and thanked the heavens he was washing the blood from his face and arms— Luca steamed in her wake; she couldn't hear him—his movements were absolutely silent, which was spooky as all hell—but she could *feel* him, all but breathing down her neck.

"In case you've forgotten," he growled, "I've saved your life—twice, in fact. That should be worth a little respect, rather than a punch in the stomach." He sounded rather put out by that measly little punch, when she knew she hadn't hurt him at all.

"That's what you say, but I don't know whether you've saved my life or not. After all, you've hypnotized me, so I don't know what's real."

"Glamoured. Not hypnotized. *Glamoured.*" Oh, he was definitely steamed. He sounded as if he were grinding his teeth together.

"Glamoured, schmamoured," she scoffed. She stopped in the middle of her nice, normal kitchen, feeling as if she'd fallen down the rabbit hole. So much had happened since the knock on her door that she felt as if hours had passed, but when she picked up her abandoned cup of coffee she found it was still warm. Incredulous, she looked at the clock. Had fewer than twenty minutes passed? Honestly?

"I've glamoured you twice," Luca said from behind her, ill-temper plain in his tone, as if he wasn't used to explaining himself. "The first time was last night, because you were so upset and scared after being attacked. I calmed you down, told you to let me heal your leg, then I told you to forget the attack."

She snorted. "I hate to tell you, but it didn't work. I remember." Except . . . the details were fuzzy, and wouldn't something that traumatic be a razor-sharp memory? And she hadn't remembered about him licking her leg until tonight. How could she forget something like that? Even now, after everything that had happened and how out of sorts she was, she felt a curl of warmth through her body at the memory, so shouldn't she have been remembering it all along?

"I know," he said curtly, sounding more than a little annoyed that his glamouring hadn't worked. "You being a conduit may have something to do with that."

Conduit?

She sighed, suddenly so exhausted she could barely stand. He kept throwing new things at her, not giving her time to get her mind around one incredulous detail before hitting her with another. "Okay, I'll bite. What's a conduit?"

Abruptly he was standing in front of her; she hadn't been aware of him moving, but there he was, his expression grim. Startled, she fell back a step, and the cup of coffee began slipping from her hand. Had she blanked out for a second, just now?

He reached out and took the cup from her, the movement smooth but fast, too fast for her to really follow. "I don't know if you're making all these double entendres deliberately, or if you're oblivious," he muttered.

"I must be oblivious. I think." She didn't really know what she was, other than confused and angry.

"Before I explain what a conduit is, let's get something nailed down. You said you know what I am."

"I know what I thought before." But that was before he'd said he hypnotized her—all right, *glamoured*—so now she didn't know anything for certain. Maybe the safest course was to assume he was lying every time his lips moved.

"Then I'll say it: I'm a vampire. So was the guy who attacked you last night, and so is Sorin." He stood with his arms crossed, his pale eyes intent on her face as if it was somehow imperative that he convince her of something preposterous. Yet now that she'd had time to think about it, her earlier conclusion had to be the result of panic, not logic.

She made a skeptical sound in her throat. "Uh-uh. Right. I know there are vampire clubs around where people pretend to be vampires—"

His eyes narrowed. "I'm not pretending anything."

"Prove it," she shot back.

"Fine. Maybe this will convince you." He put his arms around her and pulled her close, tucking her against his hard, warm body, and convincing her that he had a partial erection, though how that was supposed to relate to him maybe being a vampire, she didn't know. On the other hand . . . wow. Her heart gave a thump, and that curl of warmth started low in her mid-section again, so low that she might as well give up the pretense and admit it was between her legs.

She shouldn't be having this response to him. She should be running for the hills; she did manage to brace her hands against his chest, preparatory to pushing him away, but instead temptation gnawed at her. The beat of his heart thumped under her palms; the heat of his skin burned through his shirt, warming her, luring her closer. She wanted more, more of everything: more touching, more heat, more *him*.

Marshaling her defenses was an uphill battle, but she managed to say, "Making a pass is supposed to convince me? I don't think so."

"Close your eyes," he whispered, and bent his head.

"Don't kiss me," she ordered, gathering her wits just in time, because his mouth was almost on hers.

"I won't," he said, and kissed her.

Okay, so he lied. Her eyelids fluttered shut and she lost herself in the experience. He wasn't the first man to kiss her and she doubted he'd be the last, but good God, she couldn't imagine anyone being any better at it. His mouth was warm and firm, angling across hers to find the perfect fit. He tasted like coffee, like man, like sex. His tongue moved leisurely, played with hers a moment before moving deeper, taking more. Her hands slid up his chest to curve over his shoulders, clinging when the ground seemed to fall away beneath her feet. His arms tightened around her, lifting her and holding her so close she felt as if he were trying to pull her into him.

Just for a moment, she thought. She'd let this go on just a few seconds more. Then she'd put a stop to it and—

He lifted his mouth. "Open your eyes," he murmured.

Chloe swallowed, opened her eyes, and stared at him. This close she could see the tiny specks of black and white that made his pale gray eyes so penetrating. She could get lost in those eyes, in the power and intensity burning there— Something wasn't right. Something flat and white was almost touching their heads, and behind him was . . . a light fixture?

Bewildered, she looked around, and shrieked. "Holy shit!" Desperately she threw her arms around his neck and hung on for dear life.

They were hovering several feet in the air, their heads almost touching the ten-foot ceiling.

"What the hell are you *doing*?" She craned her neck from left to right as if looking for a solution to this utterly impossible situation, but the fact was she was still floating in the air, held up only by his arms.

"Convincing you," he said calmly, and they sort of floated to the floor. As soon as her toes touched the floor tile she shoved away from him, putting as much distance between them as she could in the small room. Too late she saw the block of knives sitting on the counter next to the oven; she should have grabbed one while the grabbing was good.

"You don't just . . . just float someone in the air like that!" she shouted, so beside herself she was almost frenzied.

"Why? Is there some human law against it?"

"No, but—" But what? It was rude? It was pushy? She bit her tongue to hold back everything she wanted to yell at him, because most of it was ridiculous.

He began to rise into the air again. Furiously Chloe rushed forward, grabbed his belt, and pulled him down. "Keep your feet on the ground!" she snapped. "I can't have a serious conversation with someone who's doing a balloon imitation."

He began softly laughing. "Are you convinced yet?"

"I'm convinced you can float, but for all I know you're just full of hot air."

He smiled, and razor-sharp fangs turned his smile from heart-stopping to nightmare-inducing. It wasn't that he looked deformed or horrific, simply that he was instantly the most lethal-looking man she'd ever seen.

Chloe fell back, silenced, and for a moment there was no sound in the kitchen except that of her own rapid breath. "Okay," she finally said, her voice shaky. "You're a vampire."

His fangs retracted and he looked up at the ceiling as if to say, *Finally.*

She remained on the other side of the kitchen, shaking from head to toe. A vampire was in the house with her. *She'd invited him in.* Jumbled bits of vampire lore raced through her mind: Would garlic powder repel him the same as a clove of garlic? Could she hold up her fingers in the sign of a cross, or did she have to have a real cross? Didn't it have to be silver, or something, or was she thinking of werewolves?

"Now that that's settled," he said, "let's have some coffee and talk about what's happening."

In short order she found herself sitting on the sofa with Luca beside her, the television dark, their cups of coffee sitting on the table in front of them. She didn't know why they'd bothered to get them, because she didn't know if she'd ever be able to swallow again.

Evidently there were Immortal Warriors on another plane of existence; they were the greatest warriors who had ever lived, and they all died in battle fighting for good against bad, or something like that. From this other plane, they watched over human kind, and whenever there was a great need they'd come back to Earth, or the present, or reality—whatever you wanted to call it—to go back into battle again.

Then there were the vampires. Rebel vampires were

organizing to destroy the status quo and resume what they thought of as their rightful place in life, which was a position of power. The man, vampire, who had attacked Valerie was part of the insurrection. Luca had protected her because . . . okay, she wasn't real clear on that part. Something about following whoever attacked her back to headquarters and finding out who was behind the murder of his friend, only he hadn't done that; instead he'd stayed with her, which defeated the purpose. She didn't know if he was a good vampire or a bad vampire, or if he simply had a different agenda right now and would turn on her when he'd accomplished what he wanted.

Not that he came out and actually said that, of course. Instead he told her about the Warriors and the vampire rebels, speaking as calmly as if he wasn't talking about something so far beyond her experience that he might as well be talking about flying to Jupiter. "They can't just come through, though; they have to be called, by one of their descendants here in the present. You are one of those descendants, a conduit for the Warrior. The dreams you've been having, the voice you've been hearing—that's your Warrior, trying to contact you. The connection will gradually become stronger and clearer, until you can call the Warrior home." He gave her an assessing glance. "Your Warrior probably has other descendants, of course, if your parents are still alive, or you have siblings or cousins, but you must be the most clairaudient."

Lucky her. She was clairaudient. Of all the things she'd ever wanted to be, that had never even blipped on her radar.

She sat in silence for a while, trying to absorb what he'd said. Light blazed all around her; the television might be dark, but every other light in the house was on. Before she'd let him lead her into the living room, she'd raced around the house flipping switches and turning on lamps, banishing every shadow. Even then, she felt safer with Luca sitting beside her on the sofa rather than in a chair, which was sort of like a bird feeling safer under the cat's paw. But every nerve in her body felt raw and exposed, and a part of her expected some new boogeyman to jump out of a closet or a dark corner; she couldn't do anything about the closets, but a boogeyman would have a hard time finding a dark corner in her house.

It would soon be dawn, but Chloe didn't think she could sleep. She might never sleep again. On the other hand, she was utterly exhausted, and wanted nothing more than to lie down. Failing that, she leaned her head back on the couch and closed her eyes. "Let me see if I have all of this straight. I'm a conduit, Sorin is a vampire rebel, the guy that jumped me last night is also a rebel . . ."

"Was," Luca interrupted.

"Was what?" she asked, opening her eyes to look at him.

"The man who attacked you last night. His name was Enoch, and I killed him."

She shouldn't be surprised to hear that, but a chill ran down her spine. Luca said the words so calmly, so matter of factly, as if killing someone was everyday business for him. She shook off the chill and continued. "Anyway, Valerie had the misfortune to be my friend, and to be in the wrong place at the wrong time. But what about you? You didn't follow Sorin when you had the chance. Why not just let him kill me, then you could do what you intended to do. Why save me?" Twice.

He gave her a hooded look. "There are several reasons I won't go into right now."

Chloe sighed. "You're kidding, right? What could

possibly be worse than what I already know? Vampires, warriors, rebels . . . what else could there be?" She almost hoped he didn't answer that question, as her mind took her to places she didn't want it to go. If this was all true, what else might be waiting around the next corner? What other monsters must exist?

"All you have to know about me right now is that I'm on your side, and I'll keep you safe."

That was honestly reassuring, though she knew it shouldn't be. Luca had a strength about him that gave her confidence, even now. There was an aura of power she was drawn to—if she believed in auras, which she didn't. Well, hadn't. Tonight she didn't know what to believe.

Maybe he was somehow forcing her to trust him. She had to at least consider the possibility. "How do I know you're not going to make me your own personal meal wagon and voodoo me into doing whatever you say, like I'm some sort of Renfield?"

No reaction. "What's a Renfield?"

She sat up, staring at him incredulously. "Oh, come on. A vampire who doesn't know who Renfield is. What, you don't watch Dracula movies?"

He snorted. "Why would I? They're always wrong."

"Renfield is a fly-eating guy who calls vampires like you *master*, does whatever the master orders, and has this really freaky laugh as he betrays his own kind."

"Got it. You don't see vassals very often in this day and age, and I've never met one who ate insects. Or laughed very much either, come to that. A deep glamour capable of turning a human into that much of a slave would cause a lot of brain damage."

Chloe's eyes widened, and she instinctively backed away.

He rolled his eyes, such a human gesture that she

blinked at him in surprise. "You don't have what it takes to be a Renfield," he assured her. "Only someone weak can be glamoured so deeply, and even then it takes a very strong vampire to exert such long-term control." He paused, his expression going still as if he'd thought of something he didn't like. "You aren't that weak-minded," he finally finished. "And I promise I won't feed from you, ever, without your permission."

Interesting. She couldn't help but notice that Luca didn't deny that he was powerful enough to do . . . whatever, but he did promise not to feed on her without permission—as if she'd ever go there. An even larger question was, could she believe him? Should she? Hell, what choice did she have? "One more question, and then I'm going to try to sleep."

He nodded.

"Why hasn't this Warrior been talking anymore since Sorin's attack?"

Luca shrugged. "Maybe he knows I'm here to guard you. Don't worry; you'll hear from him again."

"*Him.* So, this Warrior is a man."

"Most Warriors are men," he said with simple logic. "But you've heard him; can't you tell?"

If only it were so simple. "I've seen a long blond braid and heard a genderless, husky whisper. That's pretty much it."

"Hmm. The vast majority of Warriors are men, of course, but not all. The blond braid is interesting. Do you have Nordic ancestry, or Celtic?"

"I can't even tell you where my great-grandmother lived. My folks were never much into genealogy."

"Into it or not, the connection exists."

"Tell me about it," Chloe muttered. She yawned, feeling exhaustion sweep over her even though just a little while ago she'd been thinking that she couldn't possibly sleep. Pulling her feet up on the couch, she curled into herself. "I'm so tired," she muttered.

"Then sleep. You're safe here, in your house." Luca reached out and touched her hair; his touch was very gentle, so light she could barely feel it, and yet it seared through her body. Her emotions and senses were on edge, at the surface, so it wasn't surprising that she felt that touch everywhere: in her toes, in her fingers, in the pit of her stomach.

"Humans," he said as he stroked her hair. "I'll never understand you. Tonight you were willing to die in order to help your friend, even though I told you plainly that Sorin would kill you both."

"I couldn't just stand there—"

"You enjoy life so much, but you'd throw it all away in an instant. It's never made any sense."

"I swear, you sound as if you're talking about aliens, like you don't have any clue what I felt when I saw Valerie standing there with Sorin all but tearing her throat out. You should remember; you were human once, too, weren't you?"

"No," Luca said, his expression remote. "I was never human."

She dozed off with that disturbing little item in her brain, but started awake just a few minutes later, both oddly alert and disoriented at the same time. Luca was still sitting close beside her, stroking her hair, and when she'd dozed off she'd slumped against him. His arm was around her, and he had her settled comfortably against his chest.

Chloe said the first thing that popped into her head. "I don't sleep with dead guys." Then she blushed hotly, because that had to be pretty close to the most awkward remark she'd made since she was three years old and announced to her Sunday school class that Daddy and Mommy wrestled naked. The other children hadn't understood, of course, but her Sunday school teacher had burst out laughing and, of course, told her parents.

Luca gave her an amused look. "Good. I'm not dead. Never have been."

"But—" Vampires were dead, weren't they? Dead people who got infected with the vampire mojo and sort of came back to life?

"I'm immortal. Think about it. If I were dead, would I need food? I'm warm, I have a heartbeat, my hair grows. But I won't look any older than I do now. I don't get diseases, and the food I need is human blood."

He was definitely warm, so warm she almost felt scorched sitting next to him. He breathed—in and out, in and out—and there was certainly life in those pale eyes of his. And in that body. And in his mouth . . .

She forced her unruly thoughts back under control. It would be much too easy to seek comfort in sex, in the illusion of intimacy. She might fantasize about him naked, but the fantasy was far safer than reality.

Best to change the subject. "What happens when a Warrior comes through?" The look he gave her told her that he knew exactly what she'd been thinking, but he accepted the change of subject. "They fight whatever war they've been called to fight," he said simply. "Some of them live, and some of them die."

That couldn't be right. Even as tired as she was, she knew that didn't make sense. "He can be killed?"

"Yes, of course."

There wasn't any *of course* about it. "Then he's not exactly an *immortal* warrior, is he?"

Luca smiled, his gaze going distant as he looked at something she couldn't see, something far in the past. Just how old *was* he? There was a lot of knowledge in those eyes, the kind that was gained by experience. "Immortal Warriors can die again in battle, but at death their spirits return to the other side, where they wait to be called again."

Chloe knew beyond a doubt that she wouldn't care for fighting war after war after war, for all eternity. "Are they being punished?"

"No," Luca said softly. "They are being rewarded."

"Doesn't seem like much of a reward to me."

"But you've never had to give your heart and soul, your very life, for what's right."

Chloe closed her eyes, because she was tired and because she couldn't bear to look at Luca a moment longer. He stirred her up inside, in ways she neither liked nor trusted. "So, they don't like vampires?"

"I suspect not, but the fact that we're vampires isn't central to their coming; it's the threat posed. If they come, they come into the world to preserve the human race as we know it."

A shudder walked down Chloe's spine. Logically, the vampires couldn't be thinking about exterminating all humans, because if they did they'd lose their food source. But to enslave all humans . . . she could see them wanting that, and it couldn't be allowed to happen. Was that why the Warriors were evidently so concerned?

The voice whispered through the air, power and magic shimmering all around her. *"Yes,"* it said. *"Yes."*

THIRTEEN

She'd *punched* him.

Chloe Fallon, an insignificant human woman the top of whose head barely reached above his collarbone, had *punched* him. Even strong, feral vampires were nervous in his presence, he had powers that could devastate her both mentally and physically, but she hadn't hesitated, she'd simply wound up and let him have it. Not only that, she'd done it knowing what he was, that he was a vampire, and as such could have killed her with a flick of his hand. Luca didn't know whether to be insulted, enraged, or amused. In the end, he was none of those things, because simple lust crowded out everything else.

He wanted her. She was funny—inadvertently, most of the time—and the scent of her was like a magnet, constantly pulling at him, dragging him closer. The taste he'd had of her was as potent to him as a good scotch was to humans. Above all that, though, what he liked most about her was simply that she was valiant, in that headlong, insane way of humans who would ignore their own best interests to go to the aid of a friend. Didn't she know how fragile she was, comparatively speaking, to a vampire? Hell, even compared to a human male. But there she'd been, clawing to get past him even though she'd known Sorin would kill her the instant she stepped over her threshold. She'd suffered her fair share of fear tonight, but she hadn't panicked, hadn't lost control . . . except perhaps when she'd punched him. He admired that kind of rebelliousness, though he suspected it was going to cause him some grief in the days to come.

She was asleep now, slumped against his shoulder. Luca sighed. She'd drift off to sleep, then wake with a start as if her subconscious kept prodding her awake. Maybe her damned Warrior was trying to talk to her. Couldn't the fool tell she was exhausted, that he should let her sleep? The Warriors pushed their conduits to the point of both collapse and insanity, in their ruthless drive to make contact. What would it hurt to let her rest for a few hours, replenish her strength.

Dawn had arrived. He watched the light gather beyond the drawn curtains. He was relatively comfortable, but he could use some sleep himself; the battle with Sorin had been hard and fast, and he was tired. He wondered if Chloe would let him sleep in her tub, or if she'd freak at the idea. He could always go to his rented room, but Sorin put a new wrinkle in the situation. Sorin was one of the vampires strong enough to endure sunlight; if he was hunting her, then Chloe wasn't necessarily safe during the day.

Sorin was powerful in many areas; if he'd joined the rebels, then the situation was far worse than Luca had thought. Having Sorin on their side was the human equivalent of getting a nuclear weapon. He was a born fighter, but he wasn't just a sword; he was a thinker, too. The traitorous Council member would have had to advance a good argument to sway Sorin to the side of the insurgents.

Chloe made a little sound in her throat, shifted, settled more comfortably against him. Luca looked down at her, leaned closer to take in her scent, which he shouldn't have done because it was damn distracting. He had to decide what to do about the rebels; he frankly didn't give a damn about their cause, but at the same time he understood it. He didn't have to deal with the frustrations of the average vampire. No matter what happened in the coming war, he could carry on pretty much as normal.

It wasn't in his nature to sit on the sidelines during a war, though. He knew himself well enough to know that wasn't going to happen. So the question was, did he fight for the rebels, or did he come down on the side of the status quo? He could find who had ordered Hector's death even better from the rebels' side, if he went that route.

The deciding factor was Chloe. If he chose the rebels, then she was dead. It was that simple.

He'd never been human, but he was definitely a man, and any man would appreciate that sweet scent, the curve of her breasts and hips, the shape of her lips. Other men might not care so much about her pale, slender throat, but he couldn't deny the beauty of it, or the beat of her pulse beneath that smooth skin. He could see it, smell it, hear it.

He would have sex with her before this was done. He very much wanted to know not only how she tasted, but how her body felt clasping his, the internal heat and cling of her, how she responded, the sounds she made when she came. Luca had never been content to simply imagine his pleasures; he'd do everything he could to seduce her, but the word was "seduce," not "glamour." Glamouring a woman into having sex was no challenge at all.

In the past five hundred years or so, he hadn't had many human women. They were too naive, too vulnerable, as if they weren't *finished* in some way. A real relationship was impossible, as they never remembered him. And it wasn't as if there weren't enough willing female vampires for him to enjoy, with the added bonus that he didn't have to worry about hiding his strength, or his feeding needs.

Chloe was different. He couldn't put his finger on the exact difference, but she seemed more finished, spiritually older. She knew what he was; he wouldn't have to hide anything from her. And she *remembered*.

She shifted yet again. He knew she was waking even before her breathing changed and her eyes fluttered open. He watched her blink up at him, saw the unguarded moment when heat entered her eyes. Her heart rate increased, and she took a deep breath that made her breasts rise against him. Unconsciously she licked her lips.

Luca took his own deep breath. He'd have her, when she was ready to come to him of her own free will, and he didn't think he'd have to wait very long.

Then she realized where she was and pushed herself upright. Color surged into her cheeks. "Sorry," she muttered. "I can't seem to stay awake."

"Then go to bed," he said. "I'll keep watch."

She glanced at the curtained windows, then her head snapped back around to him. Her brows drew together. "It's daylight. Shouldn't you have burned to a crisp, or something? Don't you have to crawl into a coffin? Where do you keep it stashed, anyway?"

"I've never owned a coffin," he admitted, unable to hold back a smile.

Disillusionment crossed her face. "You mean that's wrong, too?" She sounded disgruntled at being misled, though he didn't see how humans could fall for that coffin bit. Coffins were big, and noticeable.

"Not only that, I can go out in sunlight. I don't like it, but it doesn't kill me. Vampires are as varied as humans; some can tolerate sunlight, some can't."

"Garlic?" she asked in a hopeful tone.

"Don't like the taste of it."

"Holy water? Crosses?"

"No problem."

"Well, crap." She folded her arms, scowling. "Everything we know about vampires is wrong?"

"Pretty much."

"Is there *anything* I can do to kill you?" A second later she realized how she'd phrased that and she burst into laughter. "Sorry. I don't want to kill you, honest. Is there anything I can do to kill *Sorin*?"

Her laughter made him smile. What wasn't to enjoy, watching those soft dark eyes sparkle, her face light up? "You can cut off his head or destroy his heart; that'll take care of just about anything living."

"Yeah, I'm sure he'd stand still for that." Wry sarcasm colored the words. "I mean that literally, because he'd *have* to stand still. There's no way I could catch him."

"Once vampires reach a certain age, they've pretty much grown strong enough that their only danger is from other strong vampires, unless a human is really lucky. Usually a human can manage to kill only a younger, weaker vampire."

"Huh." She cut her gaze to him, speculation in her eyes. "So, how old are you?"

"Old."

"*How* old?" She poked him with a finger. "Come on, spill. I'll tell you my age if you'll tell me yours."

He snorted. "That isn't nearly as tempting as *I'll show you mine if you'll show me yours*." He was oddly reluctant to reveal his age. He thought she probably wouldn't blink an eye if he said four or five hundred years, but two thousand was in a different category altogether. He'd seen the fall of the Roman Empire. He hadn't been in the region, but he'd been alive during the time of Jesus. He'd seen London burn in the sixteen hundreds, he'd lived through earthquakes and volcanoes, he'd actually spoken to Shakespeare, the scrawny goat. She might find that intimidating, because in comparison her life experience was miniscule. He didn't want her intimidated by him, he wanted her . . . hell, he wanted her to punch him, if she felt the urge.

"Forget it," she fired back. "I'm not showing you anything of mine."

He reached up, twirled one finger in her hair so the soft blond strands curled around his finger. "Are you sure about that?" he drawled.

She batted his hand away. "I'm sure," she replied firmly, and got to her feet. "I'm sleepy, and I'm going to bed. If you aren't going to burst into flames during daylight or anything, you can bunk down here on the couch, if you need to rest. I probably won't sleep long." A shadow crossed her face as she remembered the insistent Warrior who kept disturbing her sleep. "Anyway, good night. Or good morning. Whatever."

She took herself off. Luca stretched out his long legs and spent some time thinking about the situation. When he heard her breathing even out in the deepness of sleep, he stood up and prowled through the small house, familiarizing himself with it. Her friend Valerie was still sprawled on the bed in the crowded guest room, as he'd known she would be. She didn't interest him, for feeding or anything else.

He quietly opened the door to Chloe's bedroom, and was instantly struck by the darkness. With his vampire-sharp vision he had no problem making out the details of the room, but the lack of sunlight was a distinct relief. She had blackout curtains! It made sense; she worked at night, slept during the day, so she needed to block out as much sunlight as possible.

A slow smile crossed his face, and he stepped into the bedroom, closing the door behind him.

* * *

Chloe woke instantly when there was a brief knock on her bedroom door, then the door opened and Valerie walked in rumpled, red-eyed, but blessedly whole. Chloe glanced at the clock on her bedside table. Nearly three in the afternoon! The sun had been up before she'd crawled into the bed, but still . . .

"Thanks for letting me crash here," Valerie said. "I'm headed home. Just wanted to let you . . . well, *hello*."

The change in Valerie's voice and the widening of her eyes accompanied a shift of the mattress that had Chloe jerking around to stare at who—what—she knew had to be lying beside her in the bed. She glared at the reason why her friend looked so stunned . . . and impressed. Even as ticked off as she was, she had to admit there was plenty to be impressed with. The light from the hallway gleamed on the muscular slant of Luca's bare shoulders, highlighting the long, powerful muscles in his arms, the dark shadow of curly hair on his chest. He was propped up on one elbow, his long, dark hair mussed, his eyes sleepy and seductive and plain sexy as hell.

"I didn't mean to interrupt," said Valerie, plainly amused.

"You're not interrupting anything," Luca said, his voice like dark silk. "You must be Chloe's friend Valerie."

Valerie nodded, as if dumbstruck. Chloe knew the feeling. She hadn't yet managed a single word.

"I'm Luca. It's a pleasure to meet you."

"Likewise," Valerie said, as she self-consciously ran a hand through her short hair, which was too short to get mussed but some gestures were ingrained.

"I'll let myself out," said Valerie, backing away. "It's *really* nice to meet you, Luca." She smiled and closed the door behind her.

Chloe glared at him, which didn't seem to bother him at all. He looked so smug she wanted to slap him. Even worse, he looked completely comfortable, as if he belonged in her bed. "What are you doing here?" she asked sharply. "You couldn't have slept on the couch?"

"No," he responded simply. "You have blackout curtains."

"I— Oh." What was there to say? She'd been thinking he'd jumped at the chance to get naked with her, and instead he liked her curtains. She supposed blackout curtains *would* make a vampire happy.

Besides, she wasn't naked. She peeked under the sheet. Yup. She was wearing exactly what she'd put on before going to bed—a T-shirt and boring underwear—so he evidently hadn't even tried to get naked with her. She was thinking that she was either very lucky or completely unattractive when she glanced up and saw the way he was looking at her, his expression so intent and male she might as well have been wearing a teeny slip of silk, or worse (better?), nothing at all.

That expression cut deep to her bones, in an entirely sexual way. It made her breath come short, made her want to turn in to his arms and let whatever happened, happen. She fought the impulse away, because sleeping with a vampire struck her as an inherently stupid thing to do. She supposed, though, that given the existence of vampires, a lot of people had slept with them both knowingly and unknowingly, and if there had been an epidemic of people dying from being bled out the news agencies would have been all over it, so presumably vampires could have sex without sucking their victims dry. And wasn't that a cheerful thought?

"Exactly when did you get in bed with me?" she asked suspiciously, though she couldn't have said why it mattered. When she'd gone to bed, he'd been sitting on the couch. She'd assumed—foolishly, as it turned out—that he'd remain there.

"Not long after you went to sleep. I was tired from the fight, and I needed to rest. There was too much light in the living room, so I got into bed with you. You never knew, and I didn't touch you. I thought about it, though," he finished with a devilish gleam twinkling in his eyes.

"You can think about it all you want," she retorted. "Just don't do it." She needed to get up, she needed to go to the bathroom, but she was reluctant to get out of bed and let him see, well, probably nothing spectacular, if she was honest with herself. She was obviously bra-less under the T-shirt, but her boobs were on the small-ish side, her panties covered more than a bikini, and he could see more by going to a park and watching some of the joggers.

Well, hell. She might as well get up. On that thought, she threw back the covers and got out of bed, still grousing. "First you stop by the restaurant, and now this. Valerie will tell everyone at work that I have a boyfriend."

"No, she won't," he said calmly, sitting up so the sheet fell to his waist. His bare chest was sculpted and hard, essentially mouth-watering, if her own mouth was anything to go by. She swallowed. Was he wearing *anything*? She glanced around the room, looking for his clothes, but they were either on the floor on his side of the bed or he was an extremely neat vampire and had hung them up somewhere. Oh, shit. Could he tell that her heart was now beating like a drum in a marching band?

"You don't know. This kind of gossip is too juicy to keep to herself. She'll tell everyone. Maybe not everyone, and if I ask her she'll try to keep it to herself, but one way or another it'll slip out," she said glumly.

"I don't see why you care what others think," Luca said, supremely unconcerned. "So what if you sleep with me?"

"For one thing, I don't make a habit of sleeping around, so finding out that I have a sex life at all would get them interested. Maybe Valerie can just not mention your name. The last thing I need is all my cooks and waitstaff Googling your name to see who the boss is sleeping with. What the hell are they going to find?"

"Nothing important," he said simply. "It certainly won't say: *vampire*. I have all the necessary paperwork for traveling, but for the most part I fly under the radar."

"In more ways than one," she muttered, and left him lying there, looking very much at home in her bed—too relaxed, too comfortable, too tempting. She didn't need this complication, she fumed to herself as she shut herself in the bathroom. When a man—even one who was of another species, or magically enhanced, or cursed, or whatever the hell Luca was—ended up in a woman's bed, sooner or later he'd expect more than sleep. Probably sooner.

She didn't bother with a shower, just dragged a brush through her hair, hastily brushed her teeth, then pulled on the robe she seldom used, but kept hanging on the back of the bathroom door just in case.

She found Valerie in the kitchen, pouring herself a cup of freshly made coffee. "I hope you don't mind," Valerie said when Chloe came in. "I'm in desperate need of caffeine, the more the merrier. You have the night off, but I have to be at work in a couple of hours, and my head is killing me. Whatever possessed us to make margaritas? And so damn many of them?"

The glamour really worked. Chloe hid her reaction. She'd love to tell Valerie there had been no margaritas, but in this instance the lie was a gift. It was better that

Valerie remember a pitcher of margaritas and a hang-over, rather than vampires and fang marks. She studied Val's pale face. The lack of color could definitely be attributed to a hangover rather than a bloodletting. As for the fang marks . . . they were gone. Not even red spots or bruises marked where Sorin's fangs had torn into her flesh.

Chloe took a deep breath and slowly exhaled. "Listen, about Luca—" She should've practiced this speech on her way to the kitchen, but it had happened so fast she wasn't sure where to start.

Valerie took a sip of hot coffee, leaned her hip against the counter, looked Chloe in the eye, and asked, "Who's Luca?"

CHAPTER FOURTEEN

Sorin strode down the stairs into the basement of the Potomac mansion. His little witch upstairs was completely unaware that her family was in the basement, but the area was used for other things than their prison. The basement walls and ceiling had been fortified and secured against both invasion and eavesdropping. Even more, there was an underground entrance through which they could come and go without being seen. The size of the grounds was what made the tunnel possible, because otherwise they'd have run into the same problem they had at Council headquarters: properties too close together, water and sewage lines, underground cables—all things they hadn't had to worry about in the past, but now seemed to frame almost every waking minute.

He wasn't in a good mood. The fight with Luca had left him more drained than he liked; damn, that bastard could fight! It had been a long time since Sorin had been in a battle that came even close to testing his mettle; he'd enjoyed the exercise, but the suspicion that Luca had just been playing with him really pissed him off.

Now *she* had come here, which was far too risky. Luca's presence at the conduit's house told Sorin that somehow the assassin had put together far more pieces of the puzzle than was comfortable. If anyone could sow confusion and fear in the insurgents' ranks, it was Luca Ambrus. Just knowing he was against them would make some of them either drop out, or switch to the other side.

Luca had obviously followed Enoch from headquarters to the conduit's house, which explained Enoch's disappearance; he'd no doubt gone to dust at Luca's hands. What Sorin didn't know was whether or not Luca had been able to question Enoch first, but given the fact that Luca knew the Fallon woman was a conduit, Sorin suspected the worst.

He entered the private underground room where she waited. To his relief, she was alone, which meant he could speak frankly.

"You shouldn't be here. You're safer in the Council headquarters."

She waved his concern away. "I wanted to check on the witch's progress." She gave a thin smile. "Seeing me always seems to make her work harder."

That was true enough, because Nevada was both terrified and repulsed by the vampire they called Regina to disguise her true identity. She always went into a frenzy of studying and practicing after a visit from Regina, but on the other hand, Sorin thought she was less productive when she was so frantic. He didn't think pointing that out to Regina would make any difference; she had a cruel streak that might enjoy frightening Nevada even more.

"Won't the other boys and girls at the clubhouse miss you?" he asked sharply, though he knew that daytime was when the other Council members were less likely to miss her. Her visits were usually brief and made in the middle of the night, when she was at her strongest. While she was able to go into the sunlight for brief periods of time when necessary, exposure to the natural light weakened her, and to get here she had to very briefly brave the light. This wasn't her best time of day.

Regina gave Sorin a cold smile. "There's nothing on our agenda, and all of us may come and go as we please. I owe no one any explanations. Besides, they've been catered to and mindlessly obeyed for so long, they've forgotten how the real world works. The majority of them don't even believe there's a rebel faction. They'll never know I'm gone, but even if they find out, they won't think anything of it." Her smile faded away, her gaze sharpened. "The D.C. conduit is dead?"

"No."

Her expression showed pure displeasure, lips thinned, eyes darkening and then turning ruby red. "Why not? Surely two of you couldn't have failed to kill the same human! I know she isn't far along in contacting her Warrior, but she's right *here,* practically under my nose. If she has a strong psychic bond, the connection could be made faster than we expect, and I want her gone. *Now.*"

"She has a protector," Sorin said grimly. "Luca was there."

Regina didn't gasp, but her red eyes flashed back to their normal dark color as shock overrode her anger. "Are you certain?"

"I fought with him. He protected her, he literally placed himself between us."

"You fought— If you're here, then why isn't he dead?"

"We were interrupted by the police."

She stared at him, and he could almost see the wheels turning in her head. She wasn't a natural strategist, at least not in the field of warfare, but she'd survived for a very long time on her wits and instincts, so she was quick to grasp the nuances of the situation.

He didn't like her, but liking wasn't required. She was necessary. She was difficult, vain, proud—and powerful. Without her, there would be no rebellion. She'd been the one who had searched ceaselessly, for literally centuries, for a witch who could undo the sanctuary spell and finally located Nevada; she had been the one who had made the connection between Jonas's ability to locate rogue vampires—he'd often worked with Luca in the past—and his ability to identify and locate the conduits so they could be killed. Jonas hadn't exactly been willing, but Regina had been ruthless enough, cruel enough, to force him to her way of thinking.

Her increasingly strong gift of glamouring made it possible for the rebels to have human servants among them. As a Council member she had food provided for her, but the rebels' situation was more problematic. They needed servants for food, for handling the details of everyday life while the sun shone and the vampires were either fatigued or hiding in darkness; though only the humans with the weakest minds were suitable for such tasks, they were essential to success. Trying as she could be, Regina *was* the rebellion.

"If Luca was at the conduit's house he must have followed Enoch," she said, reaching the same conclusion Sorin had. Her skin was so white it couldn't be said that she paled, but her pupils constricted. "If Enoch talked before he died—"

Sorin had changed his opinion about that in the past few minutes, subconsciously processing strategy even as he talked. "He may have talked some, but I don't think he gave away your identity."

"How can you assume that?" she snapped. "If anything, I have to assume that he *did*."

"You're still alive," Sorin pointed out. "If Luca knew your identity, you'd already be dead. All of the security at Council headquarters couldn't keep him out, and you know it."

She took a deep breath, fear warring with his logic. Luca Ambrus was every intelligent vampire's worst nightmare, but Regina was also a supremely logical being, her decisions made coldly, uncolored by emotion. "You're right. He wouldn't even have to force his way in. No one knows what he does or doesn't know, so he might come to the front door as usual, and I couldn't argue against letting him in or all the other Council members would immediately know I'm the rebel queen."

Not exactly, Sorin thought. They'd know she was the traitor. The queen part . . . that was her ego talking.

"I'm strong, but if they all turned on me . . . even if only two or three turned on me . . . I wouldn't have a chance."

That was true enough. Council members weren't chosen because of their personalities. They were, one and all, among the most powerful of the kindred.

"Your being there is a strategic advantage for us," said Sorin, "because we'll know what they plan, but there'll come a time when you won't be safe there. You'll have to be the judge of that, because I'm not on site."

Those cold eyes thoughtfully examined him. "It occurs to me, Sorin, that you're now a liability, too. Luca knows about you. He could follow you back here. He might already have done so."

She'd kill him without hesitation. Sorin knew that, but then he'd always known that. Most vampires were concerned, first and foremost, with their own survival. For that matter, she knew that he'd sacrifice *her* without a qualm, too, if it came down to a choice between her life or his.

"He didn't. He stayed to protect the conduit. I watched

from a safe distance to make certain he did." Sorin gave her a cocky smile. "Not only that, if you kill me, the witch will stop cooperating." He couldn't say that Nevada was exactly comfortable with him, but she far preferred him over the other vampires she'd met, and refused to talk to them, so, ipso facto, he'd become the liaison between her and Regina.

"She will if I begin tearing out her family members' throats in front of her."

Savagery was her answer for everything. Usually she was right, but there were times when more finesse was needed. "Then you don't know her at all. If you harm any of them, as far as she'll be concerned the deal is off, and she'll use whatever power and knowledge she's gained to hurt you in any way possible. Don't discount the power of witchcraft; look what happened the last time one of us didn't take it seriously."

"I can kill her, too, before she can complete a spell. If she rebels, then she's of no use to me, anyway."

He said casually, "So take your chances with an incomplete spell, which may begin with your eyeballs melting out of your head, but then you kill her before the spell is completed and you're left with melted eyeballs." Sorin barely held back a grin as he put forth this fairly preposterous supposition. A spell had to be completed before any part of it could work, as far as he knew. But Regina's weakness was her vanity, and he'd use whatever argument he could to protect his little witch. That she reminded him of his daughter didn't do anything to negate his sense of protectiveness toward her. He *wanted* it to, he didn't want to feel responsible for any human, but the connection was there whether he wanted it to be or not. All he had to do was catch her scent, and it was almost as if he could pick up his child again and swing her around, hear her joyous giggles.

He pulled himself away from that long-ago memory, and watched Regina mull over the possible horrors of an incomplete witchcraft spell. He knew he'd won when she shrugged. "Then *you* must make her study harder. Jonas said more and more conduits are getting close to contact. We don't have a lot of time left, a few weeks at the most."

He didn't ask her how he was supposed to hunt down and kill conduits and at the same time force Nevada to study more, how he couldn't be in two places at the same time, but kept his mouth shut. Nevada was doing all she could, and pushing her harder wouldn't accomplish anything except add to the pressure on her, which would be counterproductive.

"I'd love to bring Luca to our side," she said, tapping a finger against her cheek. "He's so incredibly powerful, no one knows for certain exactly what he can do; did I tell you he used Voice on the Council members? We were all so shocked, we didn't know what to do. Think about it: a vampire wizard, a blood born. If he switched to our side, success would be inevitable, because very few would take a stand against him." A malicious gleam lit her eyes. "He'd make an acceptable king."

If she'd wanted to annoy him, she'd succeeded. Not that he'd thought about being king in the new regime— too many restrictions, plus he seriously didn't want to fuck her—but judging by the sparkle in Regina's eyes she knew her jab had landed. To too many of their kind, Luca was the be-all and end-all of the kindred. The hell of it was, even Sorin liked the bastard. Sort of. And he'd be a lot more confident of their success if Luca was on their side.

"Don't pout," she said without remorse. "You're a perfectly acceptable second in command."

"As long as Luca Ambrus doesn't see the error of his ways," Sorin said sarcastically. "I don't think that'll happen; if he had ever wanted to mate with you, it would have already happened."

Red flashed in her eyes again, and he grinned. Jab at him, and he jabbed back. She was the type who kept jabbing until she got a reaction, so Sorin always gave her one, and if his reaction wasn't exactly what she wanted, then she'd better learn to stop jabbing. He'd give her respect, he'd give her loyalty, but he wouldn't be her punching bag.

She fiddled with the amulet she wore. For her excursion away from Council headquarters she had dressed in modern clothing, leaving the identifying robe behind and opting for a hideously expensive and perfectly fitted black suit and very high heels. But the amulet . . . she never removed it. Every Council member had one as a mark of their position, and her ego wouldn't let her part with anything that signified her power, her position, her place in their world. She sighed. "You don't have anything to worry about. Luca doesn't change his mind. If he's protecting the humans, he won't be joining us. That's a shame; it's such a waste of strength and possibility."

"Do you want me to kill him?"

"Of course I want you to kill him." She lifted her hand in a dismissive wave. "But not just yet. Give him a few days to settle in with our little D.C. conduit. Maybe he'll get to know her and decide she's not worth the effort, because Luca's very pragmatic. He might decide to sit out the action this time, or at the least he'll relax somewhat. Even Luca isn't infallible. Assign two or three of our more expendable soldiers to keep an eye on them. If Luca sees reason and gives up on her, then all the better."

"Expendable?" That was the word which caught his attention. He was a soldier; none of his people were expendable, not in the sense of logistics and strategy.

"If Luca catches them, they *will* die," Regina said without even pretending concern. "You might as well not send your best."

Sorin's hands clenched and unclenched. "And what am I supposed to do while Luca Ambrus picks off my weakest soldiers one by one?" It went against every instinct he had as a soldier to simply sacrifice his men for no good reason.

She was obviously unconcerned with the loss of a soldier or two. "Another target has been located, one who is apparently further along than Luca's pet." She seemed somehow displeased with the news. "I swear, if Jonas doesn't pick up the pace, the Warriors will start coming in long before we've eliminated all the conduits."

Poor Jonas, Sorin thought. He'd been cajoled, bribed, and then tortured, in order to get what Regina wanted from him. Nothing made the answers come any faster, and it would never occur to her that she was actually slowing down the process.

"I can't tell you how annoying it is to have the one conduit that's right under my nose protected by the only creature in the world who might actually keep her safe."

In his opinion, there was very little chance they'd be able to eliminate all of the conduits in time, but a handful of Warriors, while formidable, wouldn't be enough to organize the humans and realistically have a chance of winning. Even then, if Nevada didn't succeed in breaking the sanctuary spell, the vampires were doomed to fail. The war would be costly to the humans, but as long as they could withdraw to a safe place the vampires couldn't penetrate, couldn't harm in any way, they *would* win.

She shrugged then, putting the subject aside for another. "Have you ever been to Atlanta?"

"Many times." Just not in the past sixty years, or so.

"That's where the next target is located. You leave tonight, so get some rest today."

Good enough. At least when he was out hunting he wasn't called to her audiences. That's what his meetings with her felt like lately. Instead of being her second in command, nearly an equal, he could tell she was beginning to look at him as merely a subject. She habitually treated everyone as inferior, but lately it had begun to grate.

After she left, he did as ordered and assigned two soldiers to watch Chloe Fallon's house when night fell. Regina might not approve, but he also warned them to steer clear of Luca, to keep a safe distance, and to inform him immediately if the two separated for any reason.

With that chore done, Sorin climbed the stairs to Nevada's room. She'd been keeping vampire hours for most of her time here, working at night, sleeping during the day, so he knew she would be hard at work.

Nevada couldn't remember when she'd last slept well; not since coming to this place, at any rate. She woke often during the night . . . well, during the *day*, which had become her night . . . thinking of her family, of the life she'd lost, of the monsters who held her here. Sometimes she wondered why no one had found her; she wondered if anyone was even looking. Probably not. The vampires had left little to chance. What did her friends think had happened to her? Did they believe she was dead? Touring Europe? Since her family was also being held, did the cover story involve them, too? Probably.

It was likely everyone from the real world thought them all dead. A house fire or a horrific car accident would explain their exit from the world better than any other story. She hoped not, because that meant some other people had died in their places, to provide bodies for the authorities to find. If that was the case, would any of them ever be released?

Since discovering that she had a talent for remote viewing, Nevada had tried to reach out for her family, to see them, to know they were alive and well. Alive, at least. She'd cast her net far and wide, thinking of her parents, her brother and sister, trying to find them in a big, chaotic world, but she couldn't find any trace of them. She knew they were alive, or had been recently, because Sorin occasionally let her speak to them, very briefly, on his cell phone. But if she could just *see* them, visit them even if only in spirit, she'd feel better, feel as if something good could actually come from what she was doing.

Though she couldn't see beyond these walls, and she didn't have a clock to mark the hours, she was pretty sure it wasn't full dark yet. At night the vampires became more active, they moved about, made more noise, filled the house with the energy Nevada had learned to feel. So, not yet dark; in these early-evening hours she was rarely disturbed by the vampires. It was easier to concentrate on her task when she didn't expect to be interrupted for an hour or so.

Instead of searching willy-nilly for her family, it had occurred to her that she might have more success if she started at the center, and slowly widened her net of awareness. Taking a deep breath, she settled herself with her fingertips spread on the proper page in the book of spells, and drew all her energy in. Slowly, slowly, she began pushing it out, taking her time, examining every surge whether it felt familiar or not—

And there they were. Her family. Shock almost broke her concentration, but desperately she gathered all her strength and energy and held on to the vision. They weren't beyond her, they were *below* her, in the basement of this very building. Their windowless room was much too small for four people, and the walls were bare and gray. There was little furniture—two cots, some blankets, and a dim light—and no amenities that she could see.

But they were together, and alive, and oh, so close.

She sent her spirit soaring, out of her body and away from the physical world. In a flash Nevada stood in the corner of the gray room, washed in the love and fear her family emitted. She could see and hear them, and in that moment that was all she needed, she didn't care that they couldn't see her, that they had no idea she was with them. Anxiously she examined their throats, looking for signs of biting. Sorin had promised her none of the vampires would feed from her family, but why should she believe anything she was told by the monsters? Even though part of her whispered that he was different, he was still a vampire. It was a relief to see for herself that none of her family members bore any marks, no scars or bloodstains.

The tears that ran down Nevada's cheeks were real. They dripped down the cheeks of the body while the spirit, in another place, felt the pain. She walked toward her parents, who sat side by side on one of the narrow cots. They were both thinner, older, and so very tired. She felt their fatigue, of both body and spirit. They were almost broken beyond repair. Her mother's hair was now more gray than red, her face deeply lined. Her father had lost what little dark hair he'd had left on his head. Nevada reached out to touch them but her hand fell through their bodies. She didn't truly exist here; she couldn't touch them.

Justin, sitting on the other cot, had grown so much taller and thinner since she'd last seen him. He was now seventeen years old, tall and lanky. His auburn hair had grown long and tangled, and the expression on his face was so angry. He had much to be angry about, to be trapped here, to have his life taken away. She couldn't offer him any comfort, couldn't reassure him.

Emily sat on the floor in the corner of the small room, her head down, her knees drawn in. Her hair was a fine light red like Nevada's, her skin was pale . . . more pale now, since she hadn't seen the sun in such a long time. Emily was fourteen . . . no, it was summer now, which meant Emily had just had her fifteenth birthday. They had always been so close, and even though she knew it was useless Nevada reached out to touch Emily's hair, a gesture she'd been making since her little sister was born. She couldn't comfort Emily, but perhaps she could comfort herself.

But as Nevada's hand passed through her little sister, Emily's head popped up. Her eyes widened and she looked wildly around. "Nevada?" she whispered.

Nevada was shocked out of the small gray room, away from her family and into her own body with a gasp and a lurch. She grabbed the table before her to keep from falling to the floor. Dear God, how was it possible? The others hadn't realized that she was there, but Emily had known. How?

She swallowed, trying to control her rapid heartbeat. The vampires would hear it, would know she was upset or excited, and they would come to investigate. She needed some time to gather her composure, to think about what could have happened.

And then she knew. Emily had inherited some of the same powers the vampires had discovered in Nevada. The vampires would use Emily if they knew. No matter what, she couldn't let them find out there was more than one witch in the family, and they certainly couldn't find out that Nevada had discovered a way to reach beyond these walls. Somehow she had to warn Emily to hide what she could do, what *they* could do.

The door swung open and Sorin walked in, as if he'd been drawn by her agitation. What she wouldn't give for a lock on that door! The vampires were constantly in and out; they never knocked, never announced their unwelcome presence. Yes, Sorin was more welcome than the others, but she would rather have privacy.

He was what he was. As much as she'd come to care for Sorin, she knew that if he found out she'd discovered the ability to spy on them he'd kill her, and her family, in an instant. He was too dedicated to his purpose to allow her to spoil his plans.

"I'm leaving for a little while," he said. "Until I get back, Loman will be in charge."

There were some days when Nevada thought she might love Sorin, in some weird way. Other days she hated him intensely. But she never doubted that he was the lesser of many evils. She knew full well that inside he was as much a monster as any of the others, but he seemed to be more in control, less openly vicious. She saw the man he'd once been buried deep inside, where in the others she saw only hate and monstrosity. Just because he was handsome and occasionally kind to her, just because she occasionally saw his face when she closed her eyes to go to sleep, that didn't mean she'd forgotten what he was.

Nevada shuddered. "I don't like Loman."

"Do you like any of us?" he asked drily.

"No," she snapped, lying just a little. "But some of you are worse than the others." Loman was in the category of "worse." He was short, squat, ugly, and vicious, as much an animal as a man. He resembled a missing link, as if he'd never been quite human. He was rather troll-like, and openly devoted to the bitch.

She was terrified of Loman, who'd been one of those

guarding her since she'd been taken. It wasn't just his appearance, it was the feral expression in his animal eyes that scared her. She lifted her chin with a forced strength. She rarely asked for any favors, afraid of what the price to her family might be if she overstepped her bounds. Knowing that they were so close, that they were truly alive and relatively well, gave her a new surge of strength.

"Can't you put someone else in charge, anyone else?" she asked, her voice low. "I'm terrified of him. I can't concentrate, knowing he might walk in at any time."

He gave her a shrewd look. "If you study harder and learn how to break the spell, then you won't have to worry about Loman. Time's short, Nevada. You have to show us some progress."

Maybe if she'd spent all her time trying to break the spell she might have already accomplished it, but a lot of her energy had been directed toward other things. She glanced down. "It's coming along," she said, trying not to feel guilty.

"It's been *coming along* for months. You've been *close* for nearly a year. If you aren't making progress—"

"I am!" she argued. "Watch this." She hadn't intended to show him this just yet, but she had to be flexible in her plans. She made a shooing motion with her hands. "Move back."

Sorin obediently took a few steps away from her. Nevada closed her eyes and spread her arms. She inhaled, exhaled—five deep breaths—and then she began to chant words in a language she knew he wouldn't understand, because it was the language of the books.

She didn't have to open her eyes to know that a green energy was beginning to form and shimmer around her. She could feel it, feel the deep, warm tingle on her skin. It enveloped her, a bubble, a shield, a shimmering force

she created with her will and her words and the talent
with which she'd been born. The bubble grew until it
had expanded several feet around her. Eyes still closed,
she whispered, "Sorin, come closer."

He tried. She could feel him try. His steps were difficult, almost halting, as if something primal inside him
was warning him to go back. When he reached the
green shield, he couldn't come any closer to her; it was
as if a physical barrier existed. She could sense him
pushing against the shield, trying to break it, but even
with his enormous vampire strength he couldn't reach
her.

Within the circle, Nevada opened her eyes and smiled.
"It occurred to me that I had to be able to cast the spell,
before I'd know how to break it. This is a small, a very
small, version of the original spell." She said a few of the
old-language words, waved her hand, and the barrier fell.
It literally dissolved, drifting down in a cloud of sparkling
green dust and then disappearing.

"Impressive," he said, and she could tell he meant it.

"I might have to recast the original spell, and then
remove it."

"Will that work? Can you remove both your own
spell *and* the original?"

"I don't know. It's difficult enough to cast a spell
even this small, because it's so powerful. To cast a spell
strong enough to affect the entire world . . . I don't
know that I can do that." Nevada glanced down at her
worktable. "Some days I think I would be better off
dying here, and leaving the spell intact," she said bitterly.

"Your family would die, too."

"I know. They're all that keeps me going." She
squared her shoulders. "Some of the others, like Loman,
they're not like you. They're dark and mean, and to let
them loose on the world . . . "

"I'm a vampire, Nevada. Never forget that."

"I don't," she said quickly. "But sometimes . . . sometimes I see a part of what you were as a human. You were a good man, I think. How can that completely go away? Something in you must still care, on some level."

"No," he said bluntly. "I don't care for anyone."

Illogically hurt, Nevada once more looked down. Sorin took her chin in his hand and lifted her face. "I'm a vampire," he said once again. "For me, time is nothing. For humans, time is an instant in which they grow old and die. It doesn't make sense for me to care about something that won't be here very long. I might as well love a squash."

After he was gone Nevada stood there, breathing deep and trying to control her emotions. She wanted to save Sorin, but how could she save him from being a vampire when his only other option was death? Something in her wanted to love him, maybe did love him in a weird way, but she had to let him go. She had to concentrate on the humans she could still help, like Chloe Fallon.

She had tried several times to reach out, to find the conduit; maybe she could tell whether or not the earlier spell had taken. Unfortunately, sometimes it seemed as if her growing powers and skills were like the tide, coming and going, strengthening and fading. She hadn't gotten far in her original attempt at contact. *Remember.* What good would that do the poor girl?

But what if there was another reason she couldn't reach Chloe? What if the conduit was already dead?

FIFTEEN

Chloe was vulnerable. No matter how he looked at the situation, Luca kept coming back to that inescapable conclusion. If he wasn't here, or if he was asleep—and he had to sleep sometime—all Sorin or any other vampire had to do was capture one of her friends, a neighbor, someone off the street . . . hell, even a puppy would do, and Chloe would try to go to the rescue. They probably wouldn't go that far, though; Sorin had used that ploy simply because an opportunity had presented itself. A more simple plan of action was to catch her leaving work, glamour her into following, and that was that. No more Chloe.

The situation was complicated, so complicated that he hadn't even tried to examine all of his conflicting thoughts and emotions. He had two objectives: protect Chloe, and find the Council member behind Hector's murder. On the surface they seemed to be diametrically opposed, because if he aggressively hunted down the traitor on the Council, he would be leaving Chloe unprotected. Looked at logically, though, he didn't have to accomplish them simultaneously.

He *would* avenge Hector's death. But Hector was already dead, and nothing he did now would change that. If he concentrated on protecting Chloe, he'd be

saving her from the same person who had ordered
Hector's murder; he would still discover, eventually,
who that person was, and then he'd have his revenge,
which really was a dish best served cold, anyway. He'd
know more by then, and could make his plans without
all these distractions . . . such as Chloe.

He sat on the couch in her living room, TV remote in
his hand, flicking through channels that he wasn't
interested in, mainly to give himself something to do
whenever Hurricane Chloe whirled through the living
room. She seemed completely unable to sit still. She'd
done laundry, she'd vacuumed, she'd gone into a
frenzy of folding and packing in that disaster of a guest
room. Every so often she would get on her computer,
and he figured she was Googling his name or trying different people searches in an effort to find out something about him. She could have saved herself the trouble by simply asking, but he wasn't in the mood for
conversation, so he kept quiet.

If he wanted to keep her safe—and he did—the only
way was to go into hiding with her. Otherwise, she was
dead, and the only unknown factor was "when."

Even taking her into hiding wasn't foolproof. The
rebels would have hunters of their own—Sorin, for
instance. Sorin was damn good, probably the next best
after Luca himself. And again, Luca couldn't mount a
twenty-four-hour guard over Chloe for an unknown
length of time that might well stretch into months. He
had to feed, and he had to sleep, and she'd be unguarded
during those times.

All of that might be managed, somehow, but she
simply wouldn't go along with the plan. For one thing,
she wouldn't want to be stashed away in another
country for an unknown length of time. For another,
she didn't trust him enough to go away with him.
Other handicaps were that she was physically weak,

compared to even a fledgling vampire, and she could be glamoured.

No matter what angle he came up with, Chloe was vulnerable in one way or another. The only solution he could think of was to bond her to him, and everything in him shied away from such a drastic action.

It wasn't the sex. God knows, he'd love to have sex with her. But sex was the smallest equation of being bonded. He'd bonded with a human once, and once was enough. Her name had been Ena. He could no longer remember her face, but like a sharp blade he remembered the pain. He'd fallen in love with her, and bonded with her hoping that the bond, the blood tie, would let her remember him, but it hadn't. She had always responded to him physically—bonding did that—but for her it had always been like sleeping with a stranger she simply couldn't resist. Because she couldn't remember him, and it wasn't fair to keep her from ever getting wed and having children, he'd taken himself out of her life and let her get on with living, while he kept watch over her from afar.

On his part, he'd always been aware of Ena, even when they weren't together. He'd felt her emotions, her pain as well as her joys. And when she'd died in childbirth, at the age of twenty, he'd thought the grief and pain would drive him mad. She'd been a part of him even though he hadn't been a part of her as he'd hoped. Her death had shredded a part of his heart.

His heart had long since recovered, but he had never bonded with anyone else again. He had never let himself be so tied to another human. Their lives were too short even in the normal course of things, and when he added in their foolhardiness . . . no. A thousand times no. Bonding was simply asking for pain, and Luca hadn't reached such an old age by ignoring the lessons of life. Enduring eternity meant simplifying, and bonding with a human was the perfect illustration of a complication.

He gave an inward snort at his own thoughts. As reluctant as he was to bond with anyone, Chloe's response would be twice as negative, especially when he explained the process.

Yet bonding would protect her in several different ways. The main one was that no vampire, not even him, would be able to glamour her. The second was that it would give her enhanced strength and speed; nothing approaching vampire levels, but enough that she would have an extra second or so in which to escape, and sometimes that was all the time that was needed. The third advantage was that they would be able to sense each other; he would always know where she was, always know how she was feeling. And if something alarmed him, he wouldn't have to take the time to explain things to her; she would simply know.

Reluctantly, he knew he'd have to offer her the option, but a huge part of him hoped she'd refuse. The emotional price, for him, was too high. Not that there was a snowball's chance in hell that she'd take him up on it—yet he didn't know how he could keep her alive if she didn't.

Chloe couldn't settle down. For one thing, she had a vampire in her house; never mind that he was sprawled on her couch calmly watching television, he was still a *vampire*. Anxiously she watched the sun sink lower and lower in the sky. What would happen at dark? Would he keep watching television, or would he get hungry? And if he got hungry, was she dinner?

She tried to keep herself busy, between laundry and dishes and finally getting a start on straightening out the guest room, but there was only so much she could do unless she wanted to sit next to Luca on the couch to watch television, which she didn't. Besides, he'd appropriated the remote. It was interesting that being a vampire hadn't negated the male attachment to the gadget.

So . . . if she had a vampire guest in the house, it seemed smart to find out as much as she could about vampires in general. She got on the computer in the kitchen and Googled "vampire." It gave her a lot of literary references, some demonic stuff, "living dead," yada yada, but nothing that was at all pertinent to the reality, or useful when it came to the care and feeding of one. While she was searching the Web, he came to check on her, and braced one hand on the back of her chair as he leaned over to read the article she'd pulled up. She didn't click off the page, because she didn't care if he knew what she was researching.

"That's all wrong," he said calmly, but with an amused smirk on his face.

"I know that." If she sounded irritable, well, she was. "I Googled your name, too. You don't exist."

"What did you expect to find: 'Luca Ambrus is a rare specimen of his breed, a blood born—'" He stopped and straightened, a peculiar expression crossing his face.

Something in that expression zinged her *gotcha!* gene. Chloe swiveled in her chair, her eyes narrowed as she stared up at him. "Whoops. You let that slip, didn't you?"

He didn't reply, simply stared back at her with that remote gray gaze of his, as if he wasn't connected to earth or anything on it. She swiveled back around, pulled up Google, and typed in *blood born*. The first thing it asked her was if she meant *blood borne*. There were a couple of movies—or the same movie but a couple of entries, but nothing that was pertinent.

"Don't bother looking," he said. "There isn't a National Registry of Vampires."

"But how do you get around? How do you get on an airplane, or get a bank account so you can pay your utility bills, assuming you actually *live* somewhere, instead of hanging upside down in a cave. You exist, so there should be a trail of information."

"There are always aliases," he said carelessly. "And, yes, we live in houses. But those houses may belong to dead people, or nonexistent people, or a corporation. There are always ways to get around regulations. And for the record, I have lived in a cave, but I don't believe I hung upside down in it."

"Do you pay taxes?" She was unwillingly fascinated— if there was a way to avoid paying taxes, she wanted to hear about it.

That amused look was back. "If I must. If I can avoid it, I do."

"Well, just a hint: you need to do enough to show up in a Google search. If anyone else does a search—and trust me, they will—the fact that there's no information on you at all will be suspicious."

"Why would anyone do a search on my name?"

"Because that's what people do."

"You're the first human who ever has."

She snorted. "Yeah, right. You keep right on believing that."

He simply looked down at her for a moment, long enough that his cool, pale gaze began to make her uncomfortable. She finally snapped "*What?*" then hoped the answer wasn't, *I'm hungry.*

He glanced around, hooked one of the kitchen chairs around, and sat down in it, then swiveled her chair around so she was facing him. Leaning forward, he took her hands in his. The heat of his long, hard fingers wrapped around her hands, and he rubbed his thumbs back and forth over the inside of her wrists. "We need to have a very frank discussion," he said. "You won't like what I'm going to tell you."

"Let me guess," she said, trying for a brisk tone even though her heart was suddenly double-timing. "You're hungry, and you're going to suck me dry."

A wry smile touched his lips. "No, I'm not hungry. As for sucking you . . . that's something else entirely."

Make that triple-time. Her heart was pounding as if she'd done a five-mile jog. He looked at her chest and she knew he could hear her heart slamming away inside, feel it in the beat of her pulse in her wrists. Heat washed over her, until she felt as if she were red from her feet to the top of her head, flushed and hungry with her own needs, her nipples pinching until just touching her bra made them feel raw and achy.

Abruptly he released her hands and sat back, as if he had to break contact with her. He scrubbed his hand over his face and she heard the rasp of beard, which distracted her a little, because who knew vampires grew beards? She could use a little distraction right now; unfortunately, that wasn't enough, because he immediately pulled her attention back to him.

"I've been thinking over your situation," he said, "and it isn't good."

Chloe drew a deep breath. She hadn't been thinking ahead. In fact, she'd been trying not to think very much at all, concentrating instead on the here and now. All of that about Warriors and a vampire uprising . . . that was big stuff, and there wasn't a lot she could do about any of it. Still, hearing that Luca thought she was in big trouble wasn't a good thing.

"I can protect you while I'm here," he said, "but I'll have to leave in order to feed, and I have to sleep. If, while I'm gone, a vampire drags your next-door neighbor to the door and threatens to kill her if you don't step out, what will you do?"

Chloe gave him a wry, faintly sad smile. "You can't live life if you hide all the time," she finally said.

"That's what I thought you'd say."

"I live every day knowing that I might die," she said calmly. "This isn't anything new for me."

His gaze sharpened. "What do you mean?"

"I don't tell a lot of people, because then they'd . . . they wouldn't feel comfortable around me. They wouldn't want me to pick up anything, or go jogging with me, or just be normal. I don't want to live that way. But I doubt you'd want to go jogging with me anyway—"

"Not really," he said drily.

"So telling you doesn't matter. I have an aortic aneurysm. Mine was found after a car accident when I was a teenager. I may have had it all my life or it may be a result of the accident. No one knows. It's too small for surgery to be an option, because the surgery itself is so dangerous."

He was silent a moment, then said, "I don't know a lot about human physical problems."

"It's a weak spot, like a bubble, on my ascending aorta, above my heart. Mine is stable, for now, but it can begin growing without warning. It can burst. If it does, then I'm dead. Unless I was already in a hospital, then maybe I'd have a chance if they could get me into surgery within a couple of minutes. Otherwise . . . no." Her voice was dispassionate as she explained the situation. As she'd said, she lived with it every day. Life was what it was; she could either live it, or she could curl up in a corner and not have any sort of life at all. "It can remain stable all my life, and nothing will happen. Or it can begin growing, to the point where I can have surgery and have it repaired. I don't know. No one knows."

His face was very still as he looked at her; she couldn't read a single emotion in his expression, didn't know if he were even feeling any emotion at the moment. Probably not; after all, what did she matter to him? And yet she could feel the weight of his gaze as if it were a tangible thing, a probe going straight to her soul. Was he wondering what it was like to know you might die at any minute? Did the passing years weigh on someone who was immortal? Did he ever wish that his life was finite? Did anyone? Everyone she knew wanted to live long and prosper.

Finally he blew out a breath that sounded a little ragged to her, but he continued as if she hadn't said anything at all. "Another option is for us to leave here, for me to hide you somewhere until this is over. Your Warrior can still contact you wherever you are."

"That's a plus?"

Her tone was so skeptical that it drew a smile from him. "There's nothing you can do to stop it, and maybe now that you know what's going on the process will be easier."

"How long would I have to hide?" she asked. "I have a job, I have a family—"

"There's no way to tell. Months, possibly."

"Then . . . no. I can't do that."

"I didn't think you'd be willing." He drew a deep breath. "That leaves one other option."

"I don't want to be a vampire," she said rapidly, in case that was what he had in mind.

He shook his head, his long dark hair falling about his chiseled face like some ancient god. He gave no reaction to the unintentional insult she'd just thrown at him. "It isn't that. I can bond you to me."

That didn't sound good. In fact, it sounded even worse than being made a vampire. "Like Renfield?" she asked incredulously.

That was evidently the wrong question, because he looked pained and pinched the bridge of his nose. "Forget Renfield," he finally said with what sounded like strained patience. "Renfield was glamoured— Hell, what am I talking about? Renfield is *fiction*. Got it? Fiction!"

"So this bonding thing doesn't have anything to do with glamouring?"

"No. In fact, it'll prevent any vampire, even me, from glamouring you. You'll be stronger, quicker, and for what's coming you'll need every advantage you can get."

Cautiously she said, "That sounds like the upside. What's the downside?"

He drew in a breath. "It's a lifetime bond. We'll always be linked. I'll know if you're happy, if you're sad; you'll know if I'm nearby. When a vampire and human fall in love, they'll usually bond."

His gaze was getting more and more remote and his tone was flat. Chloe studied him, picked up on the reluctance he couldn't quite hide. A little pang hit her, and this time she was the one trying to hide her reaction. Still, she couldn't stop herself from asking, "Have you bonded before?"

"Once," he said, his tone so final it was like hitting a verbal brick wall, and she knew she didn't dare pursue that subject any further.

But all in all, bonding didn't sound all that drastic, so she knew there was more or he wouldn't have offered this as the last option. She waited, staring at him.

He met her gaze, then held it. "The way bonding is accomplished," he said gently, "is through sex and blood."

"Sex and blood," she repeated, something in her going cold.

"I take your blood, and I give you mine."

"During sex," she said, just for clarification.

"Yes."

Chloe shoved her chair back, stood, and walked away. That was certainly an original pickup line, she thought as she went into her bedroom and firmly closed the door. She hoped he took the hint and didn't come in, because she didn't know what she'd do if she had to talk to him right now.

She sat down on the bed and laced her trembling fingers together. Yes, she'd had a strong physical reaction to him from the start. If things had been different, maybe they could have had something together. But he was a vampire, and in her mind that had put sex between them in the "can't happen" category. That hadn't done away with the longing, the heat; she couldn't deny both were still there, as strong as ever.

The hell of it was: how did she know he was telling the truth? People lied all the time to get what they wanted. Men pretended to fall for a woman just to get sex, women pretended to be crazy about sports or a guy's friends, some people lied just to be lying. She didn't know how vampires operated. Was deception part of how they got what they wanted, namely sex and blood?

At least he'd been up-front with her, telling her what was involved. And she couldn't assume that he was lying. After all, he'd twice saved her life, endangering himself at the same time. She'd been too dazed to really know what was going on when Enoch had attacked her, but she had no doubt he'd been about to kill her, until Luca stopped him. And Sorin . . . she'd been preoccupied with Valerie, but she'd seen enough of the fight to know how fast and brutal it had been. No pretense, there.

So far, she thought Luca had told her the truth, about everything.

But did she want to be bonded to a vampire? No.

Not even to Luca, who looked like walking sex. It wasn't even that he was a vampire; she wanted to stay completely herself, a separate and autonomous human being. She would love to be in love, to one day have a husband and children, a family, and that was a bond, too, but it was an emotional and mental one, not something that sounded like an implant by which she could be tracked.

Sex and blood.

What he'd been telling her was that, because she was one of the conduits for these damn Immortal Warriors, she was a target and he couldn't protect her. She would be hunted down and killed, and unless she was willing to completely abandon her life, run away and hide, there was nothing else he could do.

Should she run away and hide? Would that even work? Or would the vampires then go after her parents, thinking they'd know where she was?

Chloe got up, restlessly pacing around the small space of her bedroom. If she stayed, were her parents any safer? No matter what Luca said, yes, if one of the vampires dragged her mother in front of her and offered to exchange her life for her mom's, she'd do it. And if she stayed, would they perhaps concentrate more on catching her here, and not in locating any of her family members, who, thank God, lived hundreds of miles away? Could she be the rabbit on the racetrack, keeping them chasing after her instead of hunting her family?

Blood and sex. She could bear the idea of giving him her blood, and taking his, easier than she could think of having sex with him. Blood was just blood. Sex would mean too much. He'd gotten to her, not just because of the physical attraction but in ways she didn't want to admit, and having sex with him would tear all her emotional defenses down.

And if she did, then what? He was a vampire; he wasn't going to hang around after this uprising was over. What could interest him in her? He was God only knew how old, while she wasn't even thirty yet; their experiences were, literally, aeons apart. She hadn't been good at history in high school, while he'd *lived* it.

So he would move on, and she'd be left here, something inside her always longing for him, measuring the men she knew against him and they'd always come up short, because how could they not? They would be bonded, she and Luca. She would always yearn for him.

Did that mean he'd yearn for her, too, at least physically? She hadn't missed how deeply reluctant he'd been to even offer bonding as a means of helping her through this. He said he'd bonded with a human woman once before; even if he'd done it for reasons other than love, such as now, evidently the link was very strong and ended only when the human died. It must be emotionally wrenching, to have such a deep connection and then to have it severed so abruptly, so finally.

She had never before had such a deep sense of transience. In comparison to his life, hers was on a par with a fruit fly, short and inconsequential.

She took a deep breath. It was time for brutal honesty. Yes, she wanted to have sex with him. No, even that was wrong. She wanted to make love with him, something that was very different, but that offer wasn't even on the table. She was more fascinated by him, with him, than she'd ever been before in her life, but circumstances being what they were she could never have any kind of life with him. She felt cheated, she felt outraged and bitter and, dammit, fucking angry about the whole situation.

What were her options? Oh, yeah. Run and hide or

bond. None of them guaranteed that she wouldn't still be killed. Sorin and his band of merry followers would still be hunting her. Whatever life she seized now might be all she ever had.

So what else was new?

A strange sound caught her attention and she stopped her furious thoughts, her head cocked as she listened, identified the sound. It was running water . . . the shower. He was in the second bathroom, taking a shower.

He knew what her answer would be, she thought bitterly. He might not know all her reasons why, but he knew the end result. An angry tear streaked down her face as she got up and went into the master bedroom's connecting bath to take her own shower.

When she was ready, she unlocked the bedroom door and stepped out. He was in the living room again, because she could hear the television channels flipping as he gave the remote a workout. She hadn't gone to any effort to make herself look attractive, hadn't put on any makeup, had simply dragged a brush through her hair. She was dressed, though, in a long-sleeved white blouse and a simple black skirt—not the stylish pencil skirts she wore to work, but something fuller, which better met her requirements.

She sucked in a steadying breath, then another. She could do this. Bracing her shoulders, she went into the living room.

He was dressed as before, but his long hair was still damp, and brushed straight back. The only light was from the flickering television, washing over the clear, cold lines of his face, highlighting here, leaving deep shadows there. Chloe stopped at the end of the couch and stared at him, seeing a sort of lethal menace in him she hadn't noticed before. It wasn't directed at her, it was no more and no less than a part of him, like his eyes, or the shape of his hands. The realization brought a sharp awareness that while she knew *what* he was, she didn't know *who* he was, and she was still about to begin something with him that couldn't be undone. There couldn't be a breakup, or even a divorce. There was no new beginning. This was literally *till death do us part*, minus the marriage.

"I'm ready," she said bluntly.

"Are you?" He wasn't being sarcastic; he even sounded concerned. He turned off the television and got to his feet. The room was dark now, but enough light still spilled from her open bedroom door that she could see him as he abruptly loomed over her, so close she could feel his breath.

She didn't answer.

"Chloe . . . " He said her name softly, little more than a breath of sound, and gently he stroked his hand down her arm, from elbow to wrist. "Don't be afraid," he murmured, the sound rich and deep. "I won't hurt you. I'll take your blood first, then give you my blood. I won't drink much, and I won't let you take too much."

"What would happen if I did?"

"You would become a vampire."

"How much is too much?"

She could feel his sigh, one that felt laden with sadness. "It varies from human to human, vampire to vampire. The size of the human, the strength and power of the vampire . . . it all factors in. Bonding takes place with the exchange of a certain amount of blood during sex. A human is turned to vampire at whatever point the vampire blood overwhelms the human blood."

She considered all that, for just a moment. She was what she thought of as normal size, though on the slim side because she had to keep her blood pressure down, due to the aneurysm. Was he a strong and powerful vampire? She thought he must be, not just because of the two battles he'd fought in her behalf—and evidently won—but because of that indefinable *something* she could sense in him, that frisson of power that leaked off him like electricity humming along a power line. "Is sex necessary for that, too? Or just for bonding?"

"Just for bonding. Otherwise, sex is optional."

"Optional," she muttered, and didn't voice her wish that it was optional in this case, too. "All right, let's get it over with."

She turned and led the way back to her bedroom. She had already prepared by taking an old blanket from the top of the closet and spreading it over the bed, because she didn't want to ruin her sheets. Wasn't that a cheerful thought? She'd like to have a cheerful thought right about now, instead of being filled with this angry bleakness.

As he entered the room behind her he turned off the light and she said, "No. Turn the light back on."

He paused a moment, then flipped the switch so light flooded the room again. Her jaw set, Chloe reached up under her skirt and slipped her underwear down, stepped out of the circle of cotton. "Just do it and get it over with," she said. "No undressing. No kissing. No pretending. There's nothing loving or romantic about this, it's just sex. Sex and blood." She could do this if she kept it on a purely physical level, and somehow it seemed important that she not be naked with him, that their only point of connection was genital, except for the biting part. She didn't want his arms around her, she didn't want anything except for this to be *over*.

The overhead light threw deep hollows under his pale eyes as he studied her in silence. She didn't know what he saw, but finally he said, "Lie down."

She hoped he couldn't tell how she was trembling inside. She didn't want him to see all the anger dammed inside her, or how hard she was fighting to keep all of this at a distance so she could still function. She didn't meet his gaze as she sat on the edge of the bed, removed her shoes, then stretched out full length. Self-consciously she smoothed her skirt down, even though he would very shortly, of necessity, pull it back up.

Luca stood beside the bed, looking down at her. She very determinedly kept her gaze fixed on the overhead light, but she heard him unzip his pants, then he put one knee on the bed and the light was blocked out as he lowered himself on top of her.

Despite all her efforts at compartmentalizing this, even through the layers of their clothing, the heat of his body was shocking. It seeped through cloth, skin, warmed her despite her need for cold. The weight of him on her was male, solid, both crushing and enveloping. The scent of him, hot and clean with soap, underlain with something sharp and wild, filled her head with every breath. She couldn't not breathe, so it was there, inescapable, already inside her body even though he hadn't yet—

He pulled up her skirt, sliding his hands up both her legs and taking the skirt up as they went. Her hands, straight down by her sides, grabbed the old blanket and clenched. His knees went between her legs, moving her thighs apart, and he settled on her.

Chloe heard her own breathing, far too fast, almost panting as she tried to stay on top of the bitter tide of resentment, so she wouldn't drown in it. Luca's breathing was still calm. She could have hated him for that.

He reached down, lowered his pants, freed himself. He was touching her now, his warm hand brushing against her bared flesh as he positioned his penis at her opening and gently began pushing. Suddenly she couldn't bear it any longer and squeezed her eyes shut. She hadn't said *no touching,* because obviously there had to be touching, but she— Oh God. Oh God oh God oh God. She dug her heels into the blanket and clenched her teeth against the pain. This wasn't going to work. She was too dry, she should have thought of that, especially being fresh from the shower.

The pressure between her legs eased as he drew back. Without a word he slid down, cradled her hips in his hands, and lifted her to his mouth.

She couldn't stop the low sound that hummed in her throat, but she tried to control the warm rush of pleasure as his tongue stroked and probed, moistening and softening her resisting flesh. Her thighs quivered, relaxed, tightened, did it again. She could feel their subtle movements, like butterfly wings around his head, and there was nothing she could do to stop it, not when he was alternating slow licks of her clitoris with deep kisses that penetrated her body so very gently, as if he knew she hovered on the edge of a dark cliff and he was trying to coax her back.

Tears seeped beneath her lashes. Chloe refused to give in to them, refused to even acknowledge them. "Do it," she said harshly.

He flowed back up her body and this time her body was moist, open; with a heavy surge his penis slid in, thick and hard and deep. Her flesh reverberated with shock; one moment she was wholly herself, and the next she was penetrated, stretched to the fine edge of pain, seared from within by his heat. He pulled back, slid home, did it again and again until she was moist enough that each withdrawal didn't pull her body with him, until her flesh settled into the instinctive lift to meet each thrust.

It felt too good when she didn't want to feel anything at all. The only way she could remain whole was if she gave him nothing, gave herself nothing. The danger was that he would take too long, that despite herself the pleasure would build and build until she couldn't resist it any longer, that she would break, and give him . . . everything. In a way she sensed even if she didn't completely understand it, she needed to hold herself apart.

The long seconds wore on, became minutes, and still he kept up the same slow, steady push and drag. Under other circumstances, she would have reveled in his control, in the drawn-out play of delight. Not now. Now she could feel the pull of temptation, the need to just give in and let the flood of pleasure sweep through her. She didn't want to feel any pleasure, she just wanted this done. Could he resist the offer of blood? He was going to take it anyway, but he was putting it off, in his way resisting the end just as she was. Which was the crescendo for him, orgasm or blood? Or were they so combined he couldn't separate them? If she gave him blood, would that trigger his orgasm?

Deliberately she turned her head to the side, arched it back so her neck was exposed. He made a harsh growling sound, and inside her his penis seemed to grow and harden even more. But his rhythm didn't falter, and though she could hear the rasp of his breathing now he didn't go for her neck, didn't let the call of blood break his concentration.

She whimpered, and knotted her fists in the blanket. No. She wouldn't give him that, wouldn't let herself . . . she couldn't. She simply couldn't. He had to hurry. There was a throbbing deep inside now, building and growing stronger as her inner muscles began to clench at his penis with every inward thrust, as if every cell in her body wanted to hold him there. She couldn't put it off much longer—

"Take my blood." The words were a command, panted, tight with strain. "Taste me. Drink me." She

relaxed one of her hands, cramped from being fisted
for so long, and stroked the side of her neck. Could he
smell the blood coursing through her veins? She lifted
her hand, touched to his lips the fingers that had just
stroked her neck, tempting him.

His long hair hung around his face, shadowing it
from the bright light overhead, but she saw the hot
glow that turned his pale eyes darker, almost blue. He
caught her hand, held it, lightly traced his tongue over
her fingertips—then he laced his fingers through hers,
bore her hand down until it rested beside her head, and
shifted his weight forward. His rhythm changed, the
strokes coming harder, faster, shorter, until there was
no let-up between the waves of sensation, until she
could feel the break coming and she screamed wordlessly at him, her mind saying *no, no, no* but her body
ignoring that pitiful resistance. Then everything crested
at once, wave after wave of intense pleasure shuddering through her until her vision blurred and everything
around her faded away, until there was only this, his
body in and around hers, all that she was given over to
the moment.

The almost painful tension was beginning to ease, the
pleasure ebbing, when he made a deep, hoarse sound
and began shuddering in his own release. Long seconds
later he hung over her, braced on his powerful arms, his
head down as he sucked air in and out, and Chloe tried
desperately to gather her scattered senses.

He hadn't bitten her. He hadn't taken any blood.

She was the biggest fool living.

She slapped his face as hard as she could, so hard
that her palm stung. "You *bastard*!" she shrieked, so
furious that her throat constricted and the words were
half-stifled. "Was all of that a line of bullshit so you
could have *sex*?" She slapped him again, shoved violently at his shoulders. "Get off me. Get *out*!"

As infuriated as she was, she saw it, saw the way his pupils contracted. He snarled, the sound as feral as an animal's. There was a flash of fang, and he struck.

It was like being body-slammed, such a complete assault on her senses that she was dazed, mind and body. There was pain, sharp pain in her neck, but it was somehow distant. What wasn't distant was the heat that engulfed her, an instant fever burning along every cell. He drank, long and deep, then he lifted his head and thrust and she began coming again, arching beneath him. When she finally relaxed he held her down and drank some more, sounds of pleasure rumbling in his throat.

Blur. Everything was a blur. He leaned over her, tore his own wrist open with those sharp white fangs, held the open wound to her mouth. "Drink," he said, the single word a growl of sound. She did, and the world spun around her. Lightning ran through her flesh, her mind, her soul. Her entire body convulsed, another orgasm, and he was thrusting hard and fast, he was coming, too.

Again. Again. Blood and sex. Sex and blood. She wanted to take more, she wanted to give more. She faded to black, but when she resurfaced she was naked and so was he, and he was at her neck again. She clung to him, unable to bear even an inch of separation. The orgasms didn't seem to stop, the next one rolling in on top of the other, and he was feeding her more of his blood. She drank, deeply. Through it all he fucked her, endlessly, taking her body and giving her his—and lightning struck again.

CHAPTER
SIXTEEN

Chloe came slowly awake, pulling herself from the undertow of combined exhaustion and sexual satiation. Luca leaned on his elbow and watched her, more anxious than he was willing to admit, at least to her. He couldn't see any bruises or marks on her; the bite wounds had mostly healed, of course, and the blood she'd taken from him would quickly erase any other marks. To anyone else's eyes, she would look completely untouched.

But his eyes weren't anyone else's. She was his, in a way that went far deeper than any sense of sexual possession. There wasn't any way to separate sex from the bond, it was a part of the whole. She was his, he was hers. And if he didn't wipe the worry from his thoughts, she'd pick up on it.

He would never be able to stop worrying about her, though, until the instant of her death. A sharp pang went through his own heart at the thought of that inevitable day. He would lose her; this plucky, valiant little soul would vanish from his life, and a part of his own soul would be forever bereft at her absence. All humans died, eventually, and unless they died very young they all knew that day would come, but he imagined for most of them death was nothing more than an abstract theory until it was actually upon them. Chloe, though, with her aneurysm, had lived every day knowing it might be her last, and still she had carried on as if everything was normal. She had looked at death, shrugged, and done her laundry.

She was everything he admired the most, and understood the least, about humans.

He'd liked her, before. Wanted her, before. But then she'd told him about the aneurysm, and something had hit him low and hard in the gut, touched him in a way he'd never been touched before, that a being as inherently frail as all humans were, and this one even more so, could be so damn courageous. When he had suddenly been afraid—he, Luca Ambrus, afraid—that she would refuse to bond with him, he'd known what had happened. He didn't like it, but neither did he hide from it. They were bonded now. For the privilege of knowing her, having her, for the relatively few and precious days of her life, he would pay a steep price—and gladly.

Maybe his blood would help her, give her additional strength in case the aneurysm did burst, maybe even prevent that weak place in her aorta from ever getting any weaker. He hoped so, because he didn't dare give her any more. Things had gotten out of hand during their bonding, and he'd taken more blood, given more blood, than he'd intended. She could be hovering close to the point of being turned, and she didn't want that.

He didn't know the exact point; no one did, when it came to turning someone vampire. The tipping point in every human was different, depending on a lot of factors. But he was a blood born, and his powers were intensified. Added to that, Chloe was a conduit, and God only knew what effect that would have.

She stretched and yawned, finally coming awake. Luca couldn't resist the arch of her body, so sleek and female. He stroked his hand from her hipbone upwards, over the curve of her waist, the softness of her belly, to cup one of her small breasts in his big hand. His thumb swept lightly over her nipple, chafing it, and he watched it tighten as it turned a darker rose in color.

The light blush of arousal tinged her entire body. He looked into those soft brown eyes and something in him relaxed, because the anger that had been there before was gone. "Hello, sweetheart," he said, and couldn't even feel embarrassed that he'd sunk to using endearments.

"Luca," she murmured, turning in to him and sliding her hand over his shoulder, around his neck. He still felt a sense of shock every time she knew him, but this time there was also a piercing sweetness at hearing her say his name. The heaviness of his growing erection pulled at him and he rolled on top of her, his mouth hungry on hers, her response as urgent as if they hadn't had each other in days. Already there was nothing more natural than moving between her legs and sliding home into the clinging heat of her body.

One. Bonded. Beloved.

East Texas

Jim Elliott hadn't been sleeping well for the past two months. At first he'd thought the problem was with the new vitamins his wife, Sara, had been making him take, so he'd started slipping the capsules into his pocket in the morning, making her think he was taking them but secretly dropping them into the trash when she wasn't looking.

But he didn't sleep any better once he stopped taking the vitamins. In fact, things got progressively worse. The disturbances moved from his strange dreams to when he was awake, from nightmares about very realistic, bloody battles, to seeing things he knew couldn't be there. It had started with bits of light he saw out of the corner of his eye and had gradually turned into light-filled shapes that no one else could see. The shapes had become more distinct over time, and what he now saw was undeniably the figure of a man—a figure that came and went at all hours of the day and night.

He was seeing things that couldn't possibly be, and dreaming about battles that felt too real. But hell, he'd never been in a battle. He was too young for Vietnam, then the military had gone to all-volunteer, so he hadn't served during any of the Gulf wars, either. So why in hell was he having what felt like flashbacks to battles he'd never fought? They weren't even modern battles, for crying out loud. Soldiers didn't use horses and swords now, and while he knew which end of a horse was which, he didn't know diddly about swords.

He didn't tell anyone about his problem. Privately, he looked up the definition of schizophrenia, but that didn't seem to fit. He was hearing voices—a single voice, really, but it wasn't telling him to do weird shit, and he knew the visions he was having were visions, so that wasn't schizophrenia. He didn't know what the hell it was.

Beer had dulled the problem for a while, but he'd ended up being drunk more than half the time. That hadn't helped the situation at all, because three weeks ago he'd lost his job. Dozing off at the bank and waking up screaming hadn't gone over well, but when he'd started showing up drunk, well, that had been the kicker.

A week after he'd lost his job Sara had decided to go visit her parents in Alabama. Judging by the tears in her eyes and the expression on her face as she'd left the house, she wouldn't be coming home anytime soon. If he'd told her what was happening and asked for her help, she would've stayed, maybe. She was a good woman, most of the time. She thought the problems were a midlife crisis and out of control drinking. Sara wouldn't walk out on a sick man, but if he was just a crazy drunk, that was another matter. So she was gone.

Just as well. Jim hadn't slept in days. He hadn't been drinking, either, since alcohol had only made matters worse. And something odd had happened.

He couldn't say why it happened, but it was like a switch inside him had been flipped. The fighting he dreamed about, the indistinct shape that came out of nowhere . . . he had finally accepted the truth: it was real. He wasn't crazy, and his mind hadn't been dulled or damaged by too much beer. There was a world beyond this one, a real world, and the man he saw was trying to contact him. He didn't know why, or what would happen next, but he knew without a doubt that change was coming, and for some reason he didn't grasp, he would be at the center of that change.

He'd tried, but he couldn't think of a good way to tell Sara what was going on, though he missed her more than he'd thought he would. She'd think he had truly gone off the deep end. Maybe it was best to keep her in the dark, for now. He sensed that the farther away she was from him right now, the safer she was.

He certainly couldn't tell Jimmy, their only child, who was in his final year of college in Austin. The boy needed to concentrate on his schoolwork; he'd have enough reality to deal with once he graduated. Until then, Jim would have to handle this problem on his own. While he'd accepted whatever was happening to him as real, he wasn't sure he wanted to be a part of whatever this was. The violence in the dreams was so tangible, he sometimes woke smelling blood and aching from wounds that were not his own. And in those first few seconds of wakefulness there was a name on the tip of his tongue, a strange name he couldn't quite catch. Something with a strong "R" sound.

He'd read somewhere that if you saw a ghost you could send it on its way by telling it to move on, or something like that. He hadn't paid all that much attention, didn't know if he had to call in someone special, or if maybe he himself could get rid of the ghostly figure he saw. Would that somehow bring the nightmares to an end? Ignoring the ghostly man didn't seem to be doing a whole lot of good. Screaming at it—him—hadn't helped, either. Even if it was real—and it felt real—didn't he have a choice in the matter? Maybe he didn't want to be involved with whatever the hell this was.

In the meantime, he drank a lot of coffee so he wouldn't sleep, watched a lot of television to distract himself. When the doorbell rang just after midnight he was surprised but wide awake and still dressed, in an old pair of jeans and a faded T-shirt. No shoes, but hell, who cared? His heart quickened as he neared the door. Maybe it was Sara. Maybe she'd had a change of heart and come home, but he really hoped not; she shouldn't be here until he found a way to be rid of the dreams and visions.

Besides, Sara wouldn't need to ring, she'd have a key. That thought occurred to him just as he opened the door, then the blonde who stood there wiped Jim's mind clean of all thoughts about his wife—about everything, to tell the truth.

Immediately he knew he hadn't seen this woman around their small town, because he would've remembered her. She was young, tall, curvy, gorgeous, and dressed in next to nothing. The "next to nothing" part got his attention more than the rest of it. The denim shorts that hugged her hips were so tiny that if she turned around he'd surely see her ass hanging out. The pink T-shirt was form-fitting and cropped to show her stomach, and it was fine and firm. And she was so tall the high heels put her close to his own six feet. Who wore heels with shorts? Not that he was complaining, because it made her legs look a mile long.

A six-pack of beer hung in one manicured hand, and the car parked in the driveway behind his was a red Porsche.

She was a distraction at a time when he desperately needed one.

The woman smiled. "Shoot," she said, her southern accent familiar, like warm honey. "I've got the wrong house."

"Who you looking for?"

Something funny happened. Out of the corner of his eye, he caught a glimpse of that now-familiar burst of light. That was unexpected, because it had never happened before when anyone else was around. Jim briefly turned his head. The transparent man, so familiar now, held one hand up, palm out, in the universal sign for *stop*. For the first time Jim saw the man's features, and it looked as if the man from that other world was shouting *No*.

No, what? No, don't talk to this pretty woman who'd shown up in the middle of the night? She sure as hell wasn't packing any kind of weapon; with what she was wearing, he'd have been able to see it. Besides, if she could afford a car like that Porsche, she didn't need the little bit of cash he had on hand.

"I thought Harley Barrett lived here," she said, giving him a slow, lazy smile.

Jim knew all his neighbors. He shook his head. "I don't recognize the name. Sorry."

"Oh, shoot, I'm totally lost," she said, a pout on her full lips. "Is it okay if I come in and use your phone?

The battery in my cell died, and I don't think they even make pay phones anymore."

Again the transparent man shouted *no*; Jim could easily read his lips, but he ignored the warning. That damn apparition had caused him nothing but trouble. It had cost him his sleep, his sanity, his job, and his wife, in that order. Thanks to the interference, Jim hadn't enjoyed the company of another human being in weeks. He wouldn't do anything with this girl, he was still married after all, but that didn't mean he couldn't pass a bit of time in the company of a pretty girl who didn't know that he had gone around the bend.

"Come on in," he said, opening the door wider.

"Thanks, sugar," the woman said as she crossed the threshold.

"I'm Jim, by the way," he said as she passed by him, her eyes scanning the living room.

She spun around, another smile on her face. "I'm sorry, how rude of me! I'm Melody."

"Melody. That's a pretty name."

"You're cute," she said, putting the six-pack on the end table by the couch.

No one had called Jim "cute" in a very long time.

"Do you like to party?" she asked. "Maybe I don't need to call my friend after all. I mean, I'm here, and you're cute, so . . ."

"I'm too old for you," Jim protested mildly. "And I'm married."

The transparent figure gave him a sad look, and faded away. Good riddance. For that, Jim supposed he could thank Melody; it was probably her mere presence that had made the figment go away.

"Oh, I bet I'm older than you are," Melody said as she came closer. Jim didn't move away as she wrapped her arms around him. Wearing those heels, she was tall enough that they were nose-to-nose, though he had quite a few pounds on her.

Jim laughed, and for a moment he wondered if Melody wasn't a figment of his imagination, too; if the lack of sleep and the visions hadn't actually driven him so crazy that he was having delusions that felt real. Things like this just didn't happen to ordinary middle-aged men like him. It was like something out of a porn movie, or a *Penthouse* letter.

Melody laughed, too. She put her mouth on his throat, and his thoughts scattered. Screw it. Sara had left him, after all, and it wasn't as if they hadn't maybe been heading for a divorce anyway. For the first time in a very long time, he was content. He was aroused and surprised, holding a beautiful woman, a beautiful *stranger*, in his arms. Melody took Jim's hand, lifted it, guided it to her full, firm breast. She sure felt real enough.

An unwilling comparison surfaced, because Sara was sorta flat-chested. Jim had never before fondled a breast like this one. Okay, he wouldn't have sex with her—he owed Sara that much, and the girl really was too young for him—but that didn't mean he couldn't touch, just for a moment.

"There's no reason this can't be pleasant," Melody whispered against his throat.

A sharp pain stung him in his neck; he instinctively gasped and tried to pull away from the girl. He dropped his hand, no longer mesmerized by one large breast. Melody was surprisingly strong, and she held him tight, very tight. After that quick flash of pain, there was nothing but warm pleasure. Jim's eyes closed as all his strength seemed to flow out of him. He touched her breast again, fondled it, but after a moment he found he didn't have the strength for even that, and his hand fell to his side.

Soon Melody was holding him up; his legs wouldn't support him. He heard a sort of slurping sound, soft and steady, and everything around him started to go gray.

Then she lifted her head, and with his fading vision Jim saw Melody's smiling face before his. Sharp fangs were extended, and her luscious mouth was stained with blood. His blood.

"See there, sugar?" she said softly. "That wasn't so bad . . ."

In Austin, Jimmy Elliott came awake with a start. Someone had called his name, but who the hell—? He looked around the dark bedroom of his apartment, then down at the girl sleeping by his side. Kate was sound asleep, breathing deeply and evenly, her short dark hair standing on end, as it did in her sleeping *and* waking hours.

Looking at Kate made him forget about thinking someone had called him. It was just a dream, was all. Kate, on the other hand, wasn't a dream, at least not in that sense. One day soon he was going to have to introduce her to his folks. They'd been dating almost a year now, seriously and exclusively for the past seven months. He loved her; he had no doubt about it. She was the one. As soon as he graduated and had a job, he was going to ask her to marry him.

Jimmy was about to graduate with a degree in mechanical engineering. Kate kept changing her major, but she knew what she wanted to do with her life. She wanted to be a ghost-hunter. Okay, so they didn't exactly have a clear and easy path ahead of them. They'd make it work. He liked that she pulled him away from the solid, logical world of engineering. They balanced each other; he'd keep everything in order and running, and she'd make life fun.

He'd been holding off introducing Kate to his parents because she was what his dad would call a flake. She believed in things that couldn't be seen; she owned her own tarot cards and a freakin' crystal ball; she was positive the two of them had been lovers in a former life. At first he'd thought all that woowoo crap was a quirk he could live with, as long as it didn't get out of hand, but he'd seen some freaky stuff in the past few months that had kind of made a believer out of him. The tarot cards were too often right on the money, and one night a few weeks back Kate had gotten some very specific information about a lost earring, using a small crystal dangling from a string to contact her spirit guide.

Finding the earring, which had been lost in the couch cushions for weeks, was a cute trick, but there was more—some of it not so much fun. War was coming, according to Kate's cards and the spirit guide. Unfortunately, the information she was able to get about this war hadn't been nearly specific enough. As far as Jimmy could tell, there was always a war somewhere, so he was less impressed with that. Any damn fool could say "there's war coming." The thing was, though, Kate wasn't a fool.

She kept telling him that he had a sparkling aura, that he was a psychic of some sort. He didn't know how he felt about that. Wasn't a sparkling aura kind of, well, gay? She'd said a hundred times that she'd be glad to help him discover and hone his talent, but he was putting that off even though he suspected that maybe she was right. There were times when he just *knew* things. He'd take a different route for some reason, and later find out there'd been an accident on the road he usually drove. He'd instinctively grab his weatherproof jacket on a perfectly beautiful day, and it would come in handy when a sudden rain shower popped up that afternoon.

All his life, but particularly in the past year, he'd been told he often reacted a moment sooner than he should. He'd start to turn around a split-second *before* someone called his name, or brake just *before* the kid on the bicycle or a dog ran in front of his car. He'd ignored those oddities all his life, but Kate wouldn't allow him to continue to turn a blind eye.

The truth of the matter was, Jimmy didn't want to be different. He didn't want to hone any talent that made him a freak.

He lay beside her, staring into the darkness. Now that he was awake, he couldn't shut off his brain again. He'd known for weeks that it was time to go home for a visit—past time, really. Something was going on there. His mother always called him a couple of times every week, but lately her voice was strained, and for the past couple of weeks she'd been calling from her cell, not the home phone. She'd finally admitted that she was staying with her parents for a while. What was going on? He hadn't talked to his dad for more than a month, and that wasn't normal. His mother assured Jimmy that his dad was okay, even though he hadn't been answering his phone.

There was definitely a problem at home. Jimmy wasn't sure he wanted to know what it was, didn't want to get involved. His mom and dad were adults, and they'd been married twenty-five years. They'd work things out themselves. Every couple had their bad times, he supposed. He'd give them some space, for a while.

Maybe *they* were okay, but there was some other kind of trouble. He felt a deep uneasiness, and in the night silence he heard the echo of the voice that had called his name.

Gently he touched Kate's hair, wishing she was awake, but not wanting to be the one who woke her. He couldn't go back to sleep. Everything in him, every instinct, was screaming that something was very wrong, but for the life of him, he had no clue what that something might be.

Nevada stood beneath the hot shower spray, hoping that here she wouldn't have to worry about being interrupted—for a while, at least. She couldn't stay here all night or someone might come in to check on her. No, someone *would*. Since Sorin had left there had been two new female guards who'd delivered food and checked on her progress through the night. They were slightly less frightening than Loman, but only slightly.

She was doing this without the book of spells, but she remembered the words, and maybe she didn't need to actually be touching the book. Maybe that was just a habit she'd fallen into. If it was, she needed to know, so she wouldn't think she had to have the book right at hand. She closed her eyes, focused, and because now she knew exactly where her family was being held, her spirit went there immediately. She held her breath, looked around. The low-watt bulb overhead still burned, but they were all asleep. She hoped they stayed that way, all except for Emily.

Her dad and Justin slept on the floor, huddled on pallets, each covered by a single thin blanket. Their mother had one cot, Emily the other. Maybe they slept that way all the time, or maybe they took turns with the two cots. Knowing her family, Nevada bet they took turns. Nevada concentrated on her sister. She wasn't sure how long she'd be here, wasn't even certain she could make contact.

"Emily," she whispered as she touched her little sister's cheek. "Wake up, but for God's sake, be quiet about it."

Emily stirred, slapped at the place where Nevada's hand touched, and tried to turn away.

"Come on," Nevada whispered, "I need you to hear me."

Emily's eyes fluttered open, and she looked right at Nevada. "Am I dreaming?" she asked.

Nevada put a finger to her sister's lips. "Shhhh. They can't know I'm here."

"You're not here, not really," Emily whispered. She came more fully awake, gave Nevada a scandalized look. "And you're naked!"

"I'm in the shower. I don't know how long I can stay, so listen carefully. Don't let anyone know that we can talk this way."

"But Mom . . ."

"No one," Nevada insisted. "The vampires will sense any change in their attitudes, they'll see . . . hope. We can't let them know that you have a gift, or that I can travel this way."

"You'll come back, won't you?" Emily said.

"As soon as I can."

"I have so much to ask you . . . wait, you're already fading . . ."

Nevada found herself fully in the shower, wet, naked, crying. She slapped a hand against the wet tile wall to steady herself. To stay with her sister and communicate was harder than she'd thought it would be. Doing it consistently, being able to control it, was going to take more practice.

She didn't know how long she'd been in the shower, but the water wasn't exactly hot now, so she figured she didn't have much longer before they checked on her. She stepped out of the increasingly cooler water, but left it running. She didn't have much more time, but she wanted to reach out to Chloe, the conduit who was, or had been, the target of the vampires. Knowing what the woman looked like, that she was close by, that they had connected once before, should make it easy. Closing her eyes, she pulled in her energy, refocused it, concentrated.

But either Nevada had depleted her resources in visiting Emily, or Chloe was already lost, because there wasn't even a flicker of connection.

She turned off the water, dragged herself from the shower. Her efforts had left her completely exhausted. She wanted to sleep, to get lost in good dreams and memories, but she never had good dreams now.

Sorin had sometimes tried to reassure her, but no matter what he said about her future, she had all but lost hope for her own freedom. Still, if she could see her family free she'd consider that a victory. It was likely the only victory she'd have.

SEVENTEEN

"Pack a bag. We need to leave before sundown."

Chloe gave him a cool look. "This bonded thing doesn't mean I have to obey you, you know."

Luca sighed. "I know. Believe me, I know."

He sounded so long-suffering that Chloe had to smile. She thought she'd been very accommodating since that whole bonding blood and sex thing—if by "accommodating" she meant having sex until she didn't know if she could do it again any time within the next decade. Vampires had unbelievable stamina . . . at least Luca did. She, on the other hand, was human, and she'd had enough for a while.

The most disconcerting thing wasn't the sex, it was the care and concern she felt for him. If anyone could take care of himself, it was Luca, but logic didn't make any difference to how she felt. She pointed at the window. "The sun's shining, in case you haven't noticed. It'll continue to shine for several more hours. Won't you explode or melt or something if we go outside?"

"No," he said patiently.

"Another common misconception, I suppose, like not being able to see your reflection in a mirror or the whole dead and cold thing."

By now Chloe knew very well that he was neither dead nor cold. "Exactly," he said in a dry tone.

She was delaying, and he knew it. Even worse, she knew that he knew it. All the logical reasons in the world didn't change the fact that she was leaving the house she loved, a job she loved, and she didn't know when or if she'd ever be able to return. She had worried at the problem all day, both aloud with him, and privately with herself: she could call her boss and arrange for some time off, but she had only two weeks of vacation time and taking both weeks back to back would really put him in a bind, especially on such short notice. If she was gone beyond those two weeks she probably wouldn't have a job to come back to.

Unfortunately, that might not matter, to either her or her boss. If the vampires succeeded, none of the humans were safe.

She trailed her hand over the arm of the couch, pensively looked around. The house wasn't a showplace; her furnishings were ordinary, chosen more for comfort than style, but the place was hers. "They can eventually find me, no matter where I am."

"Eventually, yes. But we can buy time. Moving every so often is probably our best bet; you'll be safer when I have to feed or sleep if they're constantly playing catch-up."

He didn't sugarcoat things for her. No matter how bad things were, Chloe faced them. Now that they were bonded and she was his in a soul-deep way she hadn't been able to understand before, he could feel her waves of emotion as if they were his own. He hadn't experienced emotions like this since Ena; no, not even with Ena, because that poor girl not only hadn't remembered him, her life had been far simpler than Chloe's was. Chloe's inner turmoil reminded him forcefully why he'd bonded with a human only once: human emotions were messy and irrational, and led to problems that could be avoided if they operated on simple logic.

Chloe was a tangle of emotions at the moment. Despite the concern he felt coming from her, she both hated and loved him, those two strong emotions so entangled she couldn't separate them. She was scared and angry; one part of her wanted to hide, while another part wanted to wage war on those who'd brought this to her: on all the rebels, on Sorin, on Luca himself. She'd recognized the necessity of bonding, but at the same time she hated that she was dependent upon him for her safety, hated that they were so tied together even though she reveled in parts of that bond. Sex between a bonded vampire and human was . . . combustible.

He didn't know what the future held. If Chloe survived, the only thing that would lessen the hold of their bond was if there was a great distance between them, and even then he would always long for her, and she for him. He didn't know if they could build any sort of life together, given that they were two different species. All of those questions would have to wait until the rebel uprising had played out, one way or the other. It went against his grain, his instincts, to wait for them to make a move. His next course of action, then, was to take the fight to them.

Regina smiled at Benedict as he made an argument for increasing their efforts to bring Luca in for questioning. Idiot. The entire Council was in a tizzy because their assassin had gone missing. Her people had been able to find him, but she wasn't about to share that information. Even if the Council somehow succeeded, no one forced Luca to do anything. Who were they kidding?

The Council members would be disturbed by the report that their assassin had decided to take up with a human, but she didn't tell them that, either. Just the fact that he wasn't answering their calls had them in a snit. What would they say if they knew he'd sided with a human over his own kind? It was all she could do not to laugh out loud. The Council had become what they'd once despised: bureaucrats. They were so entrenched in their laws that they'd been all but defanged.

The early hour of this meeting was a testament to the depths of their concern. They should be sleeping, resting, feeding in luxury and solitude until well after dark. Even though the sun didn't shine here, they all felt the rise and setting of the sun within. They were, and always would be, true creatures of the night. After dark they were all stronger, sharper, better. But instead of lazing away the afternoon hours they were all here, gathered around the familiar table trying to make sense of the latest disturbances in their world.

"First Ambrus comes to us with a tale of rebellion and conveniently discovers Hector's murder, and then he disappears. What are we supposed to think?" Benedict leaned back in his chair. "Perhaps he's a part of this rebellion. It makes sense to suppose that Luca himself killed Hector and disposed of Enoch because Enoch knew too much."

"If that's the case, why would Luca tell us about the revolt?" Theodore asked.

"Perhaps to confuse us," Benedict said. "To throw us off his scent." He grimaced. "Hell, he might've come here to gloat."

They were all definitely confused, she thought with amusement.

"Maybe Enoch simply left of his own accord," Pablo suggested. "He and Hector were close. I'm sure he was upset; the fact that both Luca and Enoch disappeared at the same time could be coincidence, nothing more."

Regina ground her teeth. Enoch was dead, not missing, but she couldn't say anything without giving away that she knew more than she'd let on.

"Why don't we contact Jonas and have him pinpoint Luca's location?" Eleanor said, her voice deceptively sweet. Bitch. Jonas had worked with Luca in the past, helping him locate rogue vampires, so of course it followed that if Luca had gone rogue Jonas was the one who could locate him.

Good luck with that . . .

"He's not answering his cell," Benedict grumbled.

Nor would he, Regina thought.

"Perhaps we should ask ourselves what we would do if we did locate Luca Ambrus?" Eleanor continued, pursuing another line of thought. That was what she did, offering first one argument and then another, until no one knew where she stood on anything. "In my opinion we're fortunate that Luca simply left. Who among us can take down Luca Ambrus, if it becomes necessary? Increasing our efforts to find him is rather like a human coming after one of us. The odds are *not* in our favor."

Regina rose slowly. She didn't have an imposing height like Benedict or Theodore, but the Council members respected her. The eyes of the other females were all on her; they would allow her to speak for them. She'd laid the groundwork for a division between the males and the females of the Council long ago, and stoked the fires when she got the opportunity. In the end some of them would come with her, though they would not be her equal in the new order.

"Eleanor's right," she said calmly. "Whoever you send to collect Luca will die."

"He isn't so strong," Benedict began.

"He is." Regina stared at him. "Don't you remember that he used Voice on us—and there was nothing we could do? We're strong, all of us, but he has powers that we don't. Luca isn't entirely like us," she added softly, though those words were more powerful than the ones that had preceded them. "He won't answer the phone if it doesn't suit him, and he won't come running because we call. He served the Council for a very long time, but only because it suited him. He doesn't care what we want, he never has, and I hope none of you were foolish enough to believe otherwise. Leave him be, for now. If he isn't involved in the rebellion, he'll likely come back to us soon enough." Not if she had her way, but the others needed to believe that Luca's return, and allegiance, was possible.

Her strength and calm had gained the attention of the others. They all looked at her expectantly, as if she had all the answers to their problems. "What should we do about this revolution?" Benedict asked. He was trying to take control of the meeting, trying to assert his authority, but he didn't have any answers to all of the questions they faced.

"How do we know for certain there is a rebellion?" she asked reasonably. "Hector apparently told Luca there is a rebellious faction, and maybe it's true, maybe it isn't. We told Luca to bring a rebel to us and he hasn't, so maybe they don't exist. If that's what he found, it's possible he's simply disappeared for a while. He's done it before." They all thought she and Luca had a special connection, which they didn't and never had, but they thought it because over the centuries she had carefully cultivated that perception. She leaned forward. "However, we must also consider that it's possible Hector never called Luca, and his presence here is a part of some plot we do not yet understand. Is Luca tired of answering to us? Does he think himself better, more capable of leading? Perhaps the revolution, if there is one, begins and ends with Luca Ambrus."

She continued to remain outwardly calm, carefully controlling her breathing and the beat of her heart, as she remembered stepping into the doorway of Hector's room as Enoch drove Hector's own sword through his heart, watching with some satisfaction as the Head of Council exploded into a spray of fine gray dust. Hector's talents had told him there was a traitor near, but he hadn't seen that it was her, had never even suspected her. He'd sensed that death was coming, but he hadn't realized until Enoch walked into his room that death had come for him at the hands of an old friend.

She'd felt such satisfaction in watching Hector die. He'd been an old fool, and weak. There wasn't any place in her order for weakness.

There were others at this table who could ferret out the truth if they put in the effort, but they, and their gifts, had atrophied over the years. Accustomed to having their food brought to them, used to having others of their own kind do their bidding, they had become lazy. Their talents slept and faded. More than a thousand years of peace and loyalty within the vampire community had spoiled them all—except for her.

When the matter of Luca was dismissed they moved on to the next order of business: the election of a new Head of Council. Regina knew the position could be hers if she fought for it, and she would not have to fight very hard. The others respected her; they saw her strength. But she didn't have the time or the patience to take on that duty, even for a short while. She had too many other things to do. Besides, in such a position of authority she'd be watched much too closely. So she nominated Pablo, who had a Napoleon complex and a sick fascination with one of the blood donors kept on site. His ego and the glamoured girl would keep him occupied and out of her hair. Benedict was annoyed that the others, who were thinking only of Pablo's age and experience and who knew nothing of his latest obsession, didn't see fit to champion him as an alternative.

They decided to take their time before choosing a ninth Council member to replace Hector. Regina knew it didn't matter, because soon the Council would be irrelevant . . . and then it would be destroyed.

Sorin returned from his latest assignment anxious to see if Nevada had made progress while he'd been gone, but she wasn't his first chore of the day. Traveling in daylight was tiring, but these days, every minute was precious. It had been too long since he'd slept, and he couldn't see a time for sleep coming. Not that he couldn't function, but he had to be careful not to let himself get so tired, or hungry, that he made mistakes. A single error could bring it all crashing down around their heads. That mistake would *not* be his.

When he returned to the mansion, his first order of business was to see Jonas, who looked as if he was about to have a nervous breakdown. The rate at which conduits were being activated had increased to the point where he could hardly handle the influx of information—mentally or logistically. The vampire was rightly terrified of disappointing his queen, horrified to think that he might be too late in some instances.

Because Jonas would also be able to sense the energy when a warrior came into this world, the rebels knew they had not yet been too late in taking out any of the conduits. Not yet, anyway.

Not so long ago, Jonas had been a relatively strong vampire, though his powers were more mental than physical in spite of the young age at which he'd been turned. His smallish stature and long brown hair gave him a deceptively safe appearance, which he'd used to its full advantage. The life of a vampire had agreed with Jonas, until now. He'd worked for the Council, alongside Luca on occasion, and spent his leisure hours glamouring pretty girls and leaving them brokenhearted—and oddly weak and pale, though not so drained or brain-damaged that they wouldn't soon recover. That had been before this new twist to his gift had been uncovered, before Regina had discovered that his talent for pinpointing energies extended well beyond rogue vampires, to conduits and their warriors.

The queen's initial recruitment of Jonas hadn't gone as planned. Jonas didn't want to be a soldier; it wasn't his style. Instead of cajoling or making reasoned arguments, Regina had kidnapped and tortured him in order to get what she wanted.

Sorin wondered if Regina realized that with a little effort she could've coerced Jonas to her side. She probably didn't care. The rebel leader much preferred a show of strength to coercion. She didn't ask twice.

Regina wasn't present now. She had an important Council meeting today, one she'd said she could not miss; her absence left Sorin in charge, thank God. He enjoyed being in charge, always had.

Jonas flitted about the small basement room where he worked, slept on a hard cot, and fed on the donors Regina had sent to him—just often enough to keep him alive and functioning. Gone were the days when he'd fed at will, leisurely and with great pleasure. These days he didn't receive a human for feeding until he was near starving, which didn't bode well for the human.

This was Jonas's world for now. Maps covered two walls, and a large corkboard hung upon another. A long plain table in the center of the room held notepads, pens, and pencils. Regina allowed Jonas the use of a laptop computer, but only when he was being closely supervised. That computer, and his carefully programmed cell, were his only contacts with the outside world. There was not a stick of comfortable furnishing, no rug to soften the concrete floor. It was a prison, as stark as Regina could manage to make it.

The thin, harried vampire flitted from one map to another with a handful of pins. Yellow for the recently activated, red for one who was close to bringing in a warrior, black for those who'd been eliminated. Sorin was glad to see that there were a fair number of black pins in Jonas's maps. He was disturbed to see a new profusion of yellow, as well as a dozen red.

"How can we stop them all?" Jonas asked softly, as if he were talking to himself. "They're everywhere. Paris, this morning, and now London. Why? The rebellion is here, in this country. Warriors are supposed to come in close to the site of battle, right? They don't have the time to be traveling all over the world. It's not like they can hop on a plane, not without money and identification and . . . and why are they starting to come in so far away?"

Sorin suspected that the warriors, who resided in a very real world beyond this one where they lived, waited and watched, realized what was happening and were taking drastic measures to ensure that some of their number arrived in time.

And look at this!" Jonas flailed a hand toward one map. "Eight in New York. Eight! How are we supposed to stop so many?" He shook his head. "She's going to be so mad. She's going to be angry as hell." His entire body shuddered. An angry Regina had become his greatest fear, and with good reason. While no scars were left behind, thanks to Jonas's vampire blood, the pain she inflicted upon him when it suited her was very real.

Sorin was concerned by the new developments, but

he wasn't alarmed. Regina had spent the last several years bringing over subjects, her own devoted children, who would serve her faithfully when she ruled. She treated them better than poor Jonas, and thereby kept them loyal, but at the same time she made sure they always knew who was in charge. Their numbers had grown, and though many in her army were newer vampires who had not yet discovered extraordinary talents, humans didn't have a chance against even the weakest vampire—as long as they didn't know what was coming and how to fight it. There were a number of veterans among the rebels, too, ancient vampires like Sorin who were tired of hiding in the dark corners of the world. He'd send veterans to handle the red, fledglings to the yellow. Soon they would all be black.

There remained only one pin in the D.C. area of the map that was not black, and it was an unalarming yellow. Sorin hoped Regina was right and Luca would soon tire of the human. It would be much easier to eliminate Chloe Fallon and stop her ancestor from coming in so close to the seat of the rebellion if she were not in the protection of one of the most powerful vampires in existence.

Sorin left Jonas to his mumblings and pins, issued orders to those who were waiting for them, and then swiftly climbed the stairs to Nevada's quarters. In a few hours he'd leave for New York. Before then, he needed to do what he could to spur her on.

While he'd always championed a more subtle approach with Nevada—out of necessity, as a wounded and weak witch would be of no use to them at all—he sometimes wondered if Regina's methods would be more effective. He shuddered at the thought of one so young and vulnerable in the kind of pain Regina could inflict, and he found himself glad that it had never come to that. Nevada was soft, her emotions her weakness. The threats to her family kept her in line. If one of those family members was disposed of before her eyes, would she work harder to save the others? Or would they lose her entirely? If he threatened to allow Loman to feed from her, would she find a reserve of strength to complete the spell?

He couldn't allow her scent to distract him. Now that he'd identified why that smell was so familiar, he should be able to dismiss the memories and the unwanted weakness those memories brought forth. Nevada was a tool, nothing more.

One of the new guards was at the door, bored and disdainful of her new position. She'd rather be killing conduits, had all but begged to be taken on as a hunter. Sorin nodded to Danica and walked into Nevada's room.

Nevada's head snapped up in obvious alarm, her eyes widened. Was it his imagination or was she thinner than she'd been just a few months ago? He pushed the thought aside. He didn't care, as long as she ate enough for her body to function until she'd done what she'd been brought here to do.

He was surprised that she didn't glare at him for entering without knocking, as if her complaints had ever made a difference. "Wait right there," she said softly.

"I don't wait," Sorin responded, but he did stop several feet away from Nevada and her worktable.

Nevada closed her eyes, stretched out her arms. She looked ethereal, with her fine red hair hanging around her shoulders, with the loose robe she wore clinging to her body here and there, flowing freely in others. Yes, she was thinner than she'd been, even a year ago. She hadn't seen the sun for three years, and her naturally pale skin was delicately creamy, unblemished, and unmarked but for those light freckles. He might turn her, he thought idly. Then she'd be more pale, more beautiful, more powerful. If she kept her witch's powers after being turned, she would be incredibly important in the new order.

There were only two choices for Nevada. She would be turned or she would die. If she had the power to undo the old spell then she could also cast it all over again, and that could not be allowed. If she were one of the kindred, she'd have no reason to work against them—if any of her innate witchcraft remained within her.

She began to whisper. He knew several languages, and this was not one of them. As Sorin watched, the shimmer he'd noticed on other occasions came to life. It grew. Sparks of light danced within the circle of magic Nevada created. The shimmer became a bubble that surrounded her, encased her. It grew until it almost touched Sorin, and then it stopped. He'd seen her do this once before.

Nevada opened her eyes. "You're not welcome here," she whispered. "You cannot come in."

Unconcerned, Sorin took a single step toward her . . . and ran into the shield she had created. He could go no farther. He shouldered the transparent bubble, tried to push his way through the shimmer, but it was no use. She was entirely protected.

It occurred to him that if they didn't have her family as leverage, Nevada could protect herself so none could touch her; she could effectively take "home" with her, wherever she went.

And then she said, "Come in."

This time when Sorin stepped forward, he easily passed through the shield of protection. He was within it, with Nevada.

"This isn't new," he said, displeasure in his voice.

Nevada looked disappointed. "This recent spell is much stronger than the first one. Can't you feel it?"

"No."

"Man, I can feel it. It's like the whole world is buzzing, like the magic is crawling on my skin, but not in a bad way. It's so *cool*."

"How close are you to breaking the original spell?" Sorin asked. Nevada was obviously experiencing a rush caused by the power of her magic, but he felt nothing. He was glad she was enjoying herself, but Regina was losing her patience, and he didn't have an abundance of patience himself. How much longer would Regina give Nevada to finish the job that had been forced upon her? "How long before this is finished?"

"Days, I think," she whispered.

"Good." He moved closer to Nevada. She didn't flinch, didn't look away. It had been a long time since he'd scared her, though if he tried . . .

"I have a request," she said, looking at his chest rather than into his eyes.

It was unlikely that any of her requests would be honored, but it wouldn't be wise to tell her so, not if she was close to breaking the spell. "What do you want this time?" As if he didn't know.

"Release my family. Once I know they're safe, I'll break the spell for you."

"This is becoming tiresome . . ."

"It's what I need to do this. If I'm going to be responsible for letting vampires loose on the world, I should get *something* in return."

Sorin didn't have any qualms about making promises and not keeping them. Still, he hesitated, as if giving the matter some thought. Finally he said, "If you insist."

She raised her head and looked him in the eye, studying him too closely. "I'll require proof."

Nevada was no longer the trembling girl he'd brought to this place. She'd found a new strength.

Perhaps he should complain, but it was that strength that would allow her to break the spell.

"As I will require proof that the spell can be broken before I allow your family to go free."

She nodded, and in that moment he saw the truth. Nevada wasn't lying. After three years, she was finally and truly close to breaking the spell.

When no vampire could be denied access to a human's home, an era of chaos would begin. Sorin smiled. There had been too little chaos in his life of late.

EIGHTEEN

How was she supposed to pack when she didn't know where she was going or what she'd be doing, how long she'd be gone, what she'd need? *Basics,* Chloe thought. She had to think basics: underwear, socks, jeans, T-shirts. Black yoga pants, and a light-weight sweater. A black knit dress that wouldn't wrinkle, and a pair of black pumps, because who knew if a war with vampires might require some-thing a little dressy? Yeah, she was feeling more than a little pissy about the whole situation, remembering that . . . that *fuckfest* last night, wondering what she'd gotten herself into, scared and annoyed and excited all at once. Anyway, if the need arose for a dress, she'd have one. That left enough room for a bag of toiletries and a pair of pajamas, though if last night was any clue, she wouldn't be needing the pajamas.

As she packed, she could hear Luca moving about in the living room. No, *hear* wasn't the right word, because he didn't make any noise. The man was as silent as a cat. But she knew precisely where he was, and when he started walking toward her bedroom, toward *her,* she was instantly swamped in anticipation, hope, and a pounding need that threatened to wipe away everything else. It was annoying as hell, and so sexy she almost couldn't bear it.

She was aware of his presence the moment he reached the doorway. She felt more connected to him simply because they were now breathing the same air, and she didn't know if this bonding deal was a good thing or bad, if perhaps she'd made the biggest, worst mistake of her life. She had bonded herself to a vampire. On the surface, that couldn't be good. But . . . *Luca*. Her heart leaped simply because she thought his name. She felt his gaze like a touch, a sense of electricity that hummed between them. He was watching her, watching her more closely than anyone ever had before.

"You called the restaurant?" he asked, his deep voice slicing through her as if the words had taken on a life of their own and physically touched her.

"I did." She rearranged a pair of socks, staring into her bag so she wouldn't have to look at Luca. "I told them I was sick—vomiting and diarrhea, to be precise— and would probably be out for several days. No one wants a restaurant employee with the stomach flu to show up for work, no matter how shorthanded they might be."

"They believed you?"

The simple question touched a nerve, but then she already felt raw and exposed. She was now well *beyond* annoyed. "Why shouldn't they?" she snapped. "I'm an honest person. I'm dependable. Maybe that's not exciting, maybe you don't think it's much to brag about, but it's who I am. I don't stay out of work, I don't call in sick when I'm not sick, and . . . and . . . ."

Unwanted tears stung her eyes, and she blinked them back. "Dammit, I'm going to lose my job," she said, her voice quivering despite her effort to hold it steady. "If I lose my job, I'll lose my house, and none of it matters anyway if I'm dead, so forget I said all that." She bit her lip and turned away, not wanting him to see what a mess she was. "I thought if we bonded I wouldn't have to hide."

He blew out a breath. "Bonding links us. It makes you stronger. It gives you certain advantages. But you aren't, in any way, on a par with a vampire. You're still vulnerable, just less so. It frees me when I need to leave you to feed, because I'll still be connected to you. If you hadn't agreed to bond, my only other option was to kidnap you and take you away. As it is, you'll still have to hide and avoid your regular routine."

"Until *when?*" she asked in despair.

"Until your Warrior comes through. After that, there's no point in killing you, because the Warrior will already be here." He suddenly went still. She didn't have to see him to know. "I wonder how they knew you're a conduit," he murmured. "Fuck. I should have thought of that before."

Hearing the word "fuck" from his mouth, even in a context that had nothing to do with sex, was like touching a lit match to dry kindling, at least as far as her body was concerned. She closed her eyes and carefully sucked in her breath, trying not to alert him that every cell in her body was abruptly focused on sex.

It was a useless effort. He said "Chloe," and just that one word, her name, in a tone gone almost guttural with need, made her knees go so weak she began swaying where she stood.

He moved closer, his body hot against her back, and placed his hands—hands strong enough to tear another vampire into pieces, and wasn't that a cheerful thought?—on her shoulders. Despite knowing what he was, his touch was comforting, and a whole lot more than just comforting. Low in her mid-section, a rhythmic throb began to beat. It was as if she needed him the same way she needed air. So much, so soon—or was it *too* much, *too* soon? Either way, this was a lot to handle. It was as if she had to have him just because he was here, as if he were an addiction. She was such a sucker for— Okay, bad choice of words, all things considered.

He leaned forward, placed his mouth on the side of her neck and gently bit down. Chloe held her breath, waiting. Was he going to really bite? She should shrug him away, tell him to back off, but she'd enjoyed the sensation of his teeth on her skin—*in* her skin—enough to be more hopeful than afraid.

She was sick, standing there holding her breath, hoping he would bite her, praying he wouldn't, yearning for that sensation that joined them in a way she'd never expected to know. Understanding that it was wrong didn't make her *want* any less, and was it wrong, when she had willingly entered the bond with him? Was it wrong when he was as caught in this trap as she was? She didn't know why he'd come in search of her, maybe to make certain she was actually packing, but now she could feel the hard jut of his erection against her bottom, feel his heart pounding as surely as he could feel hers. He moved his hands to firmly cup her breasts, and increased the pressure on that sensitive curve where her neck flowed into her shoulders. The lash of sensation through her body wrenched a thin, helpless cry from her as her head tilted back against his shoulder.

He knew what she wanted. Of course he did. He wanted it, too, and she knew him as well as he knew her. He was inside her, in her head and her body, in whatever it was that made her who she was: soul, spirit, essence. He protected her; in a way she didn't want to explore too closely he *owned* her. Chloe wasn't the kind of woman who would ever agree to being owned by anyone, but she couldn't fight what she felt, what she knew. The sex allowed her to forget, for a while, and she really needed to forget.

Luca lifted her bag from the bed and dropped it on the floor. Pulling her close, he nipped at her throat, drew a drop of blood, licked there. Slowly. And everything inside her melted. She felt different when he touched her, different inside and out—more whole and sound and at the same time on the edge of completely losing control. For someone who never lost control that experience should be frightening, but instead she liked it. She wallowed in the new feeling. It was like flying—and she wanted to fly.

Chloe put aside worries about her job, her life, and turned to face him. "Sex can't be the answer to everything," she said as she draped her arms around his strong neck.

He bent his head to hers. "For now, it can," he said, and kissed her.

Her body knew his as if they'd never been strangers, as if he'd always been a part of her. His scent, the weight of his hands, the warmth of his mouth. And more, the way they were drawn together.

She'd been bewitched. No, she'd been *taken*. She'd been changed. And at the moment, she didn't mind at all.

She had thought Luca was determined to leave here before dark, but he didn't touch her like a man in a hurry. He unbuttoned her blouse and slipped it down her arms, dropped it onto the top of her bag. He removed her bra, and at least this time it survived the effort; last night, her clothes had ended up in shreds around her. As he pushed her jeans and underwear down, he looked at the juncture of her thighs so intensely she almost came then and there, embarrassingly easy. Going down on one knee, he gripped her naked bottom and brought her forward to his mouth, his tongue playing with her clitoris. That was enough. She trembled, moaned, and began coming.

The next thing she knew she was flat on her back on the bed, stark naked, with only a hazy memory of being moved at dizzying speed. Luca was shucking out of his own clothes so fast she hoped they survived. He came down on top of her, positioned her, entered her. Oh, God. She arched at the sensation of being stretched by his thickness, her body instinctively trying to find the best angle and fit, but he didn't give her the time. He simply gripped her hips and began thrusting and that was, after all, what she needed and wanted.

What did it say about her, she wondered a while later, that with her life in turmoil and the fate of the world in jeopardy, she could put all that aside and concentrate on nothing but being skin to skin with Luca? When he touched her, there was nothing in Chloe's world beyond the bed. In truth, there was nothing beyond Luca.

She didn't want to think about the fate of the world, didn't want to think about warriors and vampires and wars she had somehow gotten herself smack dab in the middle of. Sated, happy to leave her troubles behind for another moment or two, Chloe rolled on top of Luca and took his wrists in her hands to hold him down—not that she thought she could actually restrain him. He was incredibly strong, but he was content to play along, for now, a faint smile on his face as he looked up at her.

"The biting thing is very freaky, but I don't suppose I can act like I don't enjoy it."

"No, you can't," he said drily. He'd bitten her several times, very lightly, and the sensation was still like having lightning run through her veins straight to her crotch. Where he'd bitten her once had left her screaming from the force of her orgasm, and then when he'd licked her afterward to heal what was a very minor wound, well, the outcome had been much the same.

She leaned down, placed her face close to his. Knowing he could extend his fangs at any moment, knowing he was so much stronger than her, knowing that he had an inborn need to feed on her blood . . . she still wasn't afraid. It didn't make sense. For years she'd had a hard time getting close to men, trusting, allowing herself to be even a little bit uninhibited, all because she couldn't let herself rely on them to stay after finding out about her medical condition. Luca was practically a stranger, albeit an intimate one, and a vampire to boot—and yet she was more herself with him than she'd ever been with anyone. This wasn't love, she understood that, but it was . . . something.

His body stiffened, and she felt a rush of concern, of unpleasant anxiety. "We're bonded, Chloe. That's all."

It was very irritating that he could get into her head that way.

In a flash Chloe was sprawled on her back, naked and satisfied and wanting nothing more than a nap and maybe some chocolate, and Luca was standing by the side of the bed, half-dressed in no more than a heartbeat.

"Whoa!" she said, blinking at his speed. Okay, if even thinking the word "love" was enough to send him into warp speed, she wouldn't go there.

"Playtime's over," he said. "We have to go."

He was right, dammit.

Dazed, Jimmy Elliott reined in his focus and listened hard, nodding now and then to show that he was paying attention while the sheriff attempted to explain what had happened to the elder Jim Elliott. If Kate hadn't been sitting beside him, gripping his hand so hard her knuckles were white, he probably couldn't have held it together. His emotions were on a roller coaster of despair, anger, sadness, fury, grief. Most of all, he was confused. He had a hard time believing that any of this was real.

His mother sat at his other side, placing Jimmy in the middle of the trio. Sara Elliott had just returned home from a long trip to see her folks, and seemed more numb than angry. Like her son, she couldn't believe any of this could be happening.

On the night Jimmy had awakened to the echo of a voice and knowing *something* was wrong, his father had been murdered. He had blamed himself a hundred times since he'd heard the news. If only he'd called someone, if he'd realized precisely where the danger was, maybe he could've done something to save his dad. Though according to the sheriff's timeline, Jim Elliott had likely already been dead when Jimmy had been jerked awake by that call—not that Jimmy had told the sheriff, or anyone other than Kate—about his dream, or premonition, or whatever the hell it had been.

When they'd first heard that his dad had died that night, Kate had suggested that maybe it had been the spirit of his father Jimmy had heard calling his name, the spirit's newly dead presence that had alerted Jimmy's sixth sense that all was not right with the world. A year ago he would've dismissed her as a nutcase, but now . . . now he had to consider that maybe she was right. How else could the timing be explained? Besides, Kate wasn't a nutcase. She was open-minded; she was as steady as a rock; she had a good head on her shoulders.

There was so much to do he couldn't seem to keep it all in his head—funeral arrangements to be made, a will to sort out, and fire and water damage to be taken care of. How was he going to handle all that when he was still in shock? He couldn't expect his mother to take care of things; she was in worse shape than he was.

Why had things gone to hell in a handbasket so fast? He'd thought maybe his parents were going through a rough patch, but no more than that. Now he was learning that things had been much, much worse: his dad had lost his job, and his mother had basically left her husband because he'd also apparently lost his mind. She wouldn't tell him more precisely what had happened, and because she was so obviously in shock he didn't press the matter. But he couldn't help but wonder if the recent changes in Jim Elliott's life had anything to do with his death. What had the man gotten himself involved with that could tear his life apart this way?

It wasn't until after his mother excused herself to go to the ladies' room—though Jimmy suspected it was nerves, more than anything else, that made it necessary for her to leave the sheriff's office—that the sheriff truly looked at Jimmy for the first time.

The sheriff had gained some new wrinkles since Jimmy had last seen him. He'd also lost some weight and cut his once-full gray hair close to the scalp, which only made those wrinkles more pronounced. Jimmy stared at the deepest wrinkle, a crooked one set right between close-set mud-brown eyes. The sheriff had always had a disconcerting resemblance to a possum. Now he looked like a gray-haired, wrinkled possum.

"I didn't want to say this in front of your mother," he said in a lowered voice. "But there was something very odd about your dad's murder."

As though there were ordinary murders happening every day in this small town. "How's that?" Jimmy asked, as calmly as he could manage.

The sheriff glanced toward the doorway. "I don't

want to upset Sara, but the truth is, your dad didn't have hardly a speck of blood in his body when he was found. There wasn't any at the scene, either. Not a drop. I swear, I think he was killed somewhere else and drained, then dumped back at home, but that doesn't make any sense." He wrinkled his nose, squinted hard. "None of this makes any sense at all. If a neighbor hadn't spotted the smoke and called the volunteer fire department, the house might've been destroyed and we would've never known, but as it was the fire didn't do a lot of damage before it was extinguished, and your dad's remains were intact. I just don't know how to explain his condition."

Kate's grip on Jimmy's hand grew tighter, and she leaned forward expectantly. "Sheriff, were there wounds on the body?"

The older man looked at Kate as if he'd forgotten for a moment that she was present. Jimmy knew that in a larger town, in the city, the family would be told nothing, or next to nothing, about the details of an unsolved murder. But his dad and the sheriff had been fishing buddies for years; the sheriff had even coached Jimmy's Little League team for a couple of years. The residents of this small Texas town were a family, and they didn't keep secrets if they didn't see a real need for them.

Kate wasn't family, though, and she wasn't from there. On the other hand, from the way she and Jimmy had locked their hands together, it should be plain that she was as good as family, that it was just a matter of time.

"Nothing to speak of," the sheriff said when he finally decided to answer. "Just a couple of small puncture wounds on his throat. I assume that's where whatever godawful device the killer used to take Jim's blood was attached. Or maybe it was some kind of animal bite, though I can't think of an animal that would take all the blood and not—" He stopped, as if the mental image he was conjuring up was too much for his mind to handle. "The coroner hasn't had any luck identifying the wound. I don't know what the hell caused it." He raised his hand to caution them. "This information is just between us, now. I don't need a panic on my hands, and I sure as hell don't want to try to explain any of this to a bunch of goddamned reporters."

Jimmy nodded. The pressure on his hand grew tighter, as Kate gave it another squeeze. His mother came back into the room then and the sheriff leaned back in his chair; he'd said all he was going to say.

Functioning on automatic, Jimmy filled the next couple of hours driving his mother around, making funeral arrangements, picking out flowers for the casket blanket, then going to the next-door neighbor's house—the neighbors had generously opened their home to Sara—where they accepted the condolences, and offerings of food, of their friends and neighbors. Later on, a deputy escorted them to their damaged home, and they were allowed to go in very briefly, to collect some things. Investigators had been over the place thoroughly, but they hadn't found anything to explain what had happened that night, so the investigation was ongoing. It might be days before they'd be allowed in to clean up and pack up.

They'd stay with their neighbors, the Lessers, for a few days, at least until after the funeral. The Lessers had been friends with the Elliotts for years, and with their kids grown and gone they had the room for guests. Jimmy knew he and Kate couldn't stay long, because they were both taking summer classes. As soon as his father was buried and his mother was settled, they'd have to go back to Austin.

The feeling of being separate from everything that was happening around him never entirely faded as the day passed, but Jimmy did what had to be done; his mother was incapable, at the moment. He tried not to think about the way his father had died, tried not to dwell on the strange facts. Kate helped just by being there, by being herself. She introduced herself to those who stopped by, cleaned the Lessers' kitchen, put food away, hugged him whenever she got the chance.

Now and then she looked at him with a meaning in her eyes he couldn't decipher, and he knew she wanted to talk about what had happened. They hadn't had a moment alone all day.

He thought his dad would have liked Kate; he thought Kate would have liked his dad. Now they'd never meet, and it was his own fault. He'd been uncertain how his dad would react to a woman so different from everyone else, and that had kept him from taking her home for a weekend. If he hadn't been a coward, his father would've known Kate before he'd died.

It was early in the evening when he, with Kate's help, talked his dazed and exhausted mother into going to bed. When that was done, and the last of the callers had left, Kate took Jimmy's hand and with a hint of urgency led him out onto the front porch. It was just past sunset, the beauty in the western sky in sharp contrast to a perfectly shitty day.

Kate faced him. She had a death grip on his hand. He knew her well enough that he could tell she was working up her nerve to say something, knew when she made up her mind. She squeezed the hand she held and looked into his eyes and bit her lower lip for a moment, and then she whispered the single word that shook his world:

"Vampire."

CHAPTER NINETEEN

Three down, one to go.

Before leaving D.C. Sorin had memorized the information Jonas provided on the New York targets, and as usual he'd done a bit of research on his own. It was ironic that the Internet, which often made life so much more difficult for his kind, was such a tremendous help when it came to tracking down the humans. Last night he'd caught the conduits going and coming as usual, sticking to their regular routines, unaware that their lives were as good as over. All three had shown varying signs of distress, mental and physical, so Sorin could see that their warriors had been strong enough, close enough, to make their presence known, and the conduits had been fighting against them—and losing.

And this was supposed to be a gift? According to the Warrior lore, the conduits were chosen, honored, *special.* Sorin figured he was doing them all a favor by ending their misery, though they likely didn't see dying as a gift. Their problem, not his.

One conduit remained on his list, and when that job was done he'd return to D.C. It was past dawn, but he didn't want to stop now. He was on a roll. He'd dressed for protection: sunglasses, a hat, long sleeves, gloves. He wasn't at his strongest during the day, but he was still stronger than most, and definitely stronger than any human.

The final kill of the trip was a student who attended school during the day, though Jonas hadn't specified which school. Most schools were out for summer vacation, so Sorin assumed this conduit was a college student taking summer classes, or maybe an older man who'd decided to go back to school late in life. A high school student? Not a very good one, if he was in summer school. Not that it mattered; Phillip Stargel's dreary days of academia would soon be over.

Jonas hadn't been able to find much information about Stargel on the Internet, but he had come up with an address, which was really all Sorin needed, though he preferred having at least a picture. He wanted to know with some certainty that he'd eliminated the right target. If he'd had time, he'd have preferred doing reconnaissance first, but their warriors had been too close to coming through. He was lucky that the other New York targets had been easily identified and taken out. He'd had to spend several hours tracking two of them, but one had been a cakewalk. If you posted on a public Facebook page that you were going to a particular bar with a friend, you really shouldn't be surprised when someone you didn't want to see shows up there.

Phillip Stargel was apparently a more private person than the others; he didn't have a Facebook page, or any other kind of Internet page. There weren't any pictures of him, no personal data, nothing but an address—and the address was the most crucial piece of information, the one piece that would bring death to his door.

Stargel's house wasn't in the New York City metropolitan area, but was located farther upstate, beyond the commuter train lines, and it was a bitch to get there. Sorin preferred either rural or big-city settings; in rural areas there was no one to see what happened, and in urban settings no one gave a shit. Small towns were the worst, because the busybodies paid attention to everything.

Phillip Stargel lived in fucking Small Town America, in a neat, lower-middle-class neighborhood. The house was yellow clapboard, with lace curtains in the windows at the front of the house, plain vinyl blinds over the windows in back. Not a lot of money to go around, but the place was kept up, as were most of the houses around. It was ordinary, unassuming, and, for now, protected. He couldn't go in and get Stargel, he'd have to wait for him to come out.

Sorin placed himself in the shade of a neighbor's garage, and watched the front door of the Stargel house. The neighborhood was awakening. If he put forth a little effort he could hear it all; the heartbeats of the humans inside the nearby houses, the sputter of a coffeemaker, a gentle snore, a baby's cry. Life.

He pushed aside all the sounds and concentrated on the Stargel house. A newspaper waited at the end of the walk, and there would eventually be mail to collect. There would be classes to attend, maybe; college schedules were erratic. It didn't matter. An unsuspecting target likely wouldn't stay in that house all day and all night. Sorin just wished Stargel would come out so he could finish the job and get back to D.C.

Standing there, with no immediate course of action available to him, Sorin had time to think—too much time, maybe, because he began thinking about a complication he couldn't ignore for much longer: Regina. Queen, Council member, power-hungry leader of the revolution, whatever you called her, she'd revealed some cracks in her armor of late. Sorin was all for vampires coming out of the shadows and taking control, all for openly embracing who he'd been for the past seven hundred years and not having to hide his strength and superiority. In that respect, he and Regina were in complete agreement.

But in her mind, everyone was expendable: the other Council members, humans, those vampires who didn't follow her commands. Anyone who got in the way of her plans was at risk. The way she treated Jonas was a perfect example. Without Jonas, they'd be nowhere; dozens of warriors would've arrived by now if not for Jonas. But because he'd refused Regina's initial offer, he was kept prisoner and brutalized into doing what she wanted.

That ruthlessness was what made her indispensable, at this point. She was the fire, the drive, behind the uprising. The same quality made her a danger to everyone around her.

How soon before he became expendable? Sorin walked a fine line, and he knew it. He had to be indispensable to the cause without jeopardizing Regina's position and power; necessary yet nonthreatening. How long before that line blurred for her? Whenever she was crossed, she retaliated first and assessed later. He couldn't trust that being indispensable would always be enough.

The workday was beginning. Soon people were leaving their houses, getting into their cars. Whenever someone glanced his way, Sorin nudged their minds a little, just enough to make them forget they'd ever seen him. Luca's gift would be nice for times like this, he thought sourly. He had to keep doing the same thing over and over, and it got boring.

Finally the sound of a back door slamming caught Sorin's attention. He couldn't see anything, but his acute sense of hearing told him the sound came from the back of the Stargel house. He straightened, refocusing on the task at hand.

A woman called, "Phillip, stay where I can see you."

A boy's voice responded. "Okay, Mama."

A chill ran up Sorin's spine. Surely Jonas would've warned him if Phillip Stargel was a child—if he knew. Sorin wasn't sure how Jonas's ability worked, exactly how much he saw or sensed where the conduits were concerned. The information the hunters were given varied from conduit to conduit, as if some info came through clearly and some didn't. There hadn't been any children among the conduits so far, but that didn't mean it wasn't possible.

If Stargel was a child then the lack of specific information about him on the Internet made some sense. "Low-life Warriors," Sorin muttered as he made his way between the houses, toward a chain-link fence that surrounded a neat backyard. They knew what was going on, they knew they were putting the conduits' lives in danger, and still, they were trying to come in through a kid. How desperate were they to put a child at risk this way?

Pretty damn desperate, given how Sorin and his hunters were currently kicking their asses.

Then again, what did they care, Sorin thought as he watched a boy maybe ten years old or so playing with a soccer ball, looking down, kicking the ball, then chasing after it. The Warriors didn't give a damn about anything except their battles and their victories. They didn't give a shit about those who gave them the ability to come back to this world.

Sorin watched the kid for several minutes. He wasn't a natural athlete; his arms and legs were stubby and he ran with a clumsy gait, sometimes missed kicking the ball even when it was lying right in front of him. But he seemed to be having fun, so his lack of skill didn't bother him.

A thought occurred to Sorin: maybe this was Phillip Stargel *Junior,* and his father, who was still inside the house, sleeping or watching the morning news or try-ing to deal with the confusion caused by the Warrior's efforts at contact, was the one Sorin was looking for. That would be great. More trouble, because he'd have to wait even longer for the older Stargel to come out of the house, but . . . better.

Without making a sound Sorin leapt over the fence, landing gracefully and silently on the soft green grass. The other yards he could see from this vantage point were deserted at this time of the morning, so if he got the job done quickly he wouldn't have to deal with any nosy neighbors. There was still the woman, Phillip's mother, but she wouldn't be a problem.

Maybe he could talk Phillip Junior into inviting him into the house. Wouldn't that be a kick?

Sorin moved silently, quickly coming up behind the child who was focusing so intently on the soccer ball at his feet. "Phillip," he said softly, and the kid turned around and looked up.

The kid had a flat, round face, and widely spaced, slanted blue eyes that regarded Sorin with open curiosity. Sorin caught his breath, slowly let it out. Now it was called Down syndrome, though he couldn't remember when the terminology had changed. He had no experience with children like this, had no idea how much the kid would understand.

"Hello," the kid said. "Who're you?" His words were a little thick, oddly framed, but understandable. He should be alarmed to find a stranger in his back-yard, but he wasn't.

"My name is Sorin."

"That's a funny name."

"It's—" Sorin started to say it was Romanian, but stopped himself. "Yeah, it's funny. I get kidded about it all the time."

"My name is Phillip Anthony Stargel. This is my backyard. I have to go to school soon. I go to a special school. Where do you go to school?"

"I'm too old for school," Sorin said, his voice calm though inside he was anything but. This was so wrong . . . "Is your father's name Phillip, too?"

"Phillip Anthony *Stargel*," the kid corrected. "That's *my* name. My father's name is Stephen Harrison Stargel. He doesn't live here anymore. He lives in heaven with Jesus and Grandma Laverne."

Sorin felt as if a boulder had settled in his gut. This was the conduit, the only Phillip Stargel at this address, perhaps the only blood relative of some bastard warrior desperate to find his way into this world. Fucking Warriors; didn't they have any boundaries? Didn't this one have a conscience?

"Why are you dressed like it's winter?" Phillip asked. "It's summer. I like summer. I don't like the snow. You don't need a hat and gloves in the summer. Why are you wearing gloves when it's not cold? Won't you sweat?"

The back door flew open and Phillip's mother came hurrying out of the house, a cell phone in her hand and both fear and anger in her eyes. She hadn't called for help yet, but she was prepared to if she found it necessary.

Sorin turned toward the woman. Even from this distance she was easy to glamour. She was exhausted and lonely, and any natural shields she might've had had been destroyed long ago. He caught her eye, filled her with ease and comfort, and commanded her to be still and quiet. She stopped where she was, relaxed, even smiled wanly. The hand that held the cell dropped to her side.

Sorin turned back to Phillip Stargel, the conduit he'd come to kill.

"You're different, aren't you?" the kid asked, and kicked the soccer ball. It was a pretty good kick, the best he'd made yet, and he crowed with delight as he ran after it. He positioned himself carefully, and kicked the ball toward Sorin. "You're like my new friend, but not exactly like him. You have a funny light around your face like he does."

The soccer ball rolled against Sorin's boot. He looked down at it, gave it a very light kick back in Phillip's direction. "You have a new friend?"

"Yeah." Phillip tried to field the ball with his feet, missed, and sat down hard on the grass. He immediately scrambled up and with growing enthusiasm kicked the ball again. This time it went wide to the right, and Sorin shifted to intercept it. "He visits sometimes, but not for very long," Phillip continued. "I want him to stay for a while, but he isn't really here. He pretends to be here. Can you pretend to be somewhere you really aren't? I think that'd be fun."

"No, I can't do that," Sorin said, giving the ball another tap toward Phillip. This time the kid got in front of it, blocked its progress, and beamed with delight.

"He can't really be here until I figure out what his name is. I wish he'd just tell me what his name is like you did, but it's a game we play, just the two of us. I'm not even supposed to tell Mama, but sometimes I forget. She thinks he's an imaginary friend, but he's not really imaginary. He has a sword, like a pirate."

Sorin had carried a sword in the past, but right now his only weapon was in his pocket, a knife with a razor-sharp six-inch blade. His plan had been to cut Phillip

Stargel's throat and move on, his fourth target in twelve hours down, the trip an unqualified success. It had been a good plan, a simple one; the simple ones were always the best, less chance for something to get fucked up.

Phillip looked toward his mother, and his smile faded. "Is Mama all right? She looks funny."

"She's just resting," Sorin said. "She's fine."

That assurance was enough for the kid. "Good. I love my Mama. Isn't she beautiful?" He was beaming again as he booted the ball toward Sorin.

Actually, no, she wasn't; she was tired and worn and a little plain, but seen with love she was beautiful to Phillip. "Yeah," said Sorin. "Your mother will always be beautiful."

Sorin bent down and picked up the soccer ball, motioned for Phillip to come to him. The kid trooped over, a big grin on his face. Sorin went down on one knee, so he was more on a level with the kid, almost face-to-face. Phillip tilted his head as if he were listening to something, frowned, but didn't move away. "My friend doesn't like you very much," he announced.

"Yeah, I know. The feeling is mutual." Was it ever. If he ever got the chance, he'd gut that son of a bitch warrior.

"People should like each other. Maybe when he gets here we can all play soccer and you two can be friends. You can't have too many friends. Mama will make us cookies, if I ask her to. I like chocolate chip." Phillip reached out and laid a plump, soft hand on Sorin's cheek. His slanted eyes knit together with concern. "You don't have many friends, do you? I can help you make friends. I'm very good at making friends. Everybody loves me." He smiled widely, flashing a crooked, unrestrained grin filled with joy.

Sorin looked away from that open, joyful grin. How long had it been since he'd felt a child's loving touch on his face? The knife was heavy in his pocket, a rock weighing on his soul. *Fuck* this. Fuck everything. A black pit was yawning in front of him; he'd crossed a lot of black pits in his long lifetime, but not this time, not this one.

He gripped the kid by both arms, careful to keep his touch gentle. "Phillip, I want you to make me a promise."

"Okay," Phillip said agreeably, before he had any clue as to what the promise would be.

"I want you to stay in the house until your new friend can come to stay." Sorin knew without a doubt that Regina would try to kill him if she realized what had happened. It all depended on Jonas, who would know that one of the New York conduits was still alive and active. Whether or not Jonas would tell her . . . that remained to be seen. But even Sorin had limits. He hadn't known where those limits were until this moment. The decision was easy, so easy it came without him really having to think at all. "Don't go to school, don't play in the backyard. It's very important that you not go outside until your new friend comes."

"Not even to play soccer?" Phillip asked, concerned.

"Not even to play soccer."

"But I need to go to school . . ."

"I'll make sure your mother knows to keep you at home. Your friend will be able to come visit easier if you stay at home." The woman was easy to glamour; he could tell her to stay in for a few more days, tell her to keep Phillip inside. A few days was likely as long as it would take, given how close the warrior was to coming through. He could glamour Phillip, too, he supposed, but it wasn't necessary. Phillip's brain was different. Even a simple glamour might do irreparable damage.

If Regina knew that a conduit he'd been sent to take out was still alive, she'd send someone else to do the job, someone who might not have even a modicum of scruples. But once the warrior arrived, there would be no need for Phillip to be killed. He'd be safe then, or as safe as any human would be when the world changed. Until that happened, he simply had to stay inside his home . . . he and his mother, because a hunter would have no scruples about grabbing his mother and using her to lure Phillip outside.

The kid's eyes were filled with trust, complete innocence, and love—for his mother, his life, even for his new friends though one of them had come with the intent to kill him.

"It's very important, Phillip Stargel," Sorin said. "For you and for your mama." If he had to meet one more warrior in order to keep this child safe, then so be it. "Both of you are to stay inside your home until your new friend arrives."

"Do you know his name?" Phillip asked, his tone hopeful.

Sorin shook his head. "No, I don't, but it will come to you soon. And when he gets here, can you give him a message for me?"

Now the kid looked doubtful. "I'll try," he said.

"Tell him he's a—" *Fucking lily-livered cowardly asshole.* No, he couldn't say that to Phillip. "Tell him I'll be waiting for him."

He handed the soccer ball to Phillip, then glamoured the kid's mother into doing what he wanted. He even asked her if they had enough food to get by for a few days, without leaving the house. He saw the child and his mother back into the house, then walked away. Just before he leapt over the fence again, he looked toward the house and saw Phillip's smiling face pressed to the window as he enthusiastically waved good-bye.

Sorin's jaw was clenched as he strode back to his rental. If anyone ever found out what had happened here, his time as Regina's right hand would be over. The rebels would oust him; hell, they'd do their best to kill him, though he'd give them a good fight if they tried. He'd thought he was willing to do anything in order to get what he wanted, what was right for his kind. He'd been certain any sacrifice was possible.

He'd been wrong.

TWENTY

Jimmy and Kate couldn't get much time alone over the next day or so. Funerals were time-consuming, and no one would leave them alone much. Friends came to sit and talk, offering the comfort of their presence, bringing still more food even though the Lessers' refrigerator and freezer were bulging with food already. They ate until Jimmy thought he'd pop, trying to make a dent in the offerings, and still people brought food: cakes, pies, pot roasts, potato salad, anything and everything that could be thought of. He thought the strangest was orange Jell-O with broccoli chopped up in it; he made a mental note to stay far, far away from the woman who brought that particular dish.

The only time he and Kate had to talk was at night, after everyone had gone to bed, and even then they had to talk in whispers because the walls were thin. He was so tired, worn out by stress and long hours, that he couldn't stay awake long, but he managed to ask some questions and get some answers, even though he didn't like those answers. Kate was convinced that vampires had killed Jim Elliott, but Jimmy couldn't get his mind around that. Maybe he could accept spirit guides and ghosts and mental powers, but vampires? They were monsters, fictional characters. The other beings Kate sometimes talked about were from beyond this world; vampires, if they existed, were very real and living in this one. *That* he had a hard time accepting. Maybe he simply didn't want to accept it; hell, who would?

Thank goodness Kate didn't try to sell the idea to anyone else. The knowledge that his dad had been murdered was hard enough to live with, but vampires? He didn't want his girlfriend being dismissed as a nut-job on her first visit.

But if she was right . . .

When he had a moment alone, Jimmy spent some time in Mrs. Lesser's basement, which had been tricked out as a home office slash recreation room. Using their computer, he did searches on vampires, blood-drained bodies, strange murders that might tie into his father's. Most of what he found was total crap. That was the Internet for you, so he wasn't surprised. There were references to movies, books, creepy goth clubs. He found one rambling blog written by someone who'd used the unimaginative pseudonym "Van Helsing." Yeah, right. This Van Helsing went on and on about vampires living among us. The way the blog meandered from one unprovable and unlikely sentence to another made Jimmy less inclined to believe a single word.

He was staring at the computer screen, concentrating hard as he tried to make sense of what had happened and wishing that Kate had kept her suspicions to herself—though he'd never tell her that—when a voice whispered in his ear.

He'd heard the voice before, the night his dad died. He knew the tone, the timbre of it. What the voice said wasn't a word though, not a word he recognized. It sounded like *Roar,* with a hard "K" sound at the end.

It was pretty damn bad when disembodied voices didn't even make him jump anymore, when the light cast from a flash that shouldn't be there didn't even make him turn his head.

"Please tell me vampires are totally fiction," Jimmy whispered.

There was a pause, then the same deep, ghostly voice said, "Cannot."

Jimmy sighed. "Well, that's just great."

They were at the Willard, a hotel so expensive that Chloe's eyes had almost bugged from her head when Luca took her there. For crying out loud, they were just a block from the White House! The Washington Monument was practically in front of the hotel. The luxury suite Luca had arranged for them was larger than her house, Chloe noted, and it was definitely better furnished and decorated. Who knew being a bloodsucker could be so lucrative? Then she laughed at her thought. They were in Washington, D.C., where bloodsuckers in thousand-dollar suits abounded. What better place for vampires?

The people here were very nice, but definitely odd, though she had to admit that people had a tendency to become odd when Luca was around. He'd checked them in using a fake ID and a very real credit card, gotten keycards, and then leaned forward to whisper something to the well-dressed desk clerk working the night shift. The clerk had quickly entered something into the computer and turned away, then when he'd turned back to the desk he'd seemed surprised to see Luca. "Ah, Miss Smith, I didn't realize that you had a guest with you. Do you need another key?"

"Miss Smith," Chloe muttered as they went to the elevator. "How . . . unimaginative."

Luca winked at her, and pinched her bottom.

On the way up to the suite, they weren't alone in the elevator. An elderly man got in at the next floor, greeted both Chloe and Luca in a friendly manner, then took a station at the front of the elevator as if he planned to spring forth as soon as the doors opened, though he definitely looked as if his springing days were over. But when the elevator had stopped at their floor and Luca and Chloe had stepped past the old man, he'd flinched, laughed, and said something to the effect that he hadn't seen Luca get on the elevator.

Senile, maybe, she'd thought at the time.

The suite, with its huge oval living room, took her breath away. All she could think was, it was a damn good thing she'd brought a dress, because this definitely wasn't a T-shirt kind of place. She wandered around, exploring, her eyes wide. "Why do we need a second bedroom?" she asked, then stopped in her tracks as a chill swept through her. Could Luca have gotten tired of her already? After all, this bonding thing didn't promise a happily-ever-after, just a tied-together-forever deal.

"It gives us another exit if we need one," Luca said. "That makes three: the foyer entrance, and a separate entrance in each bedroom. Always give yourself more than one way to get out, if you can."

Oh, good. She was thinking like a woman, everything was all about emotion, and he was thinking like a man, planning escape routes. Some things never changed even when the species were different.

She started to ask Luca if he was hungry, but caught herself in time. She herself was starving, so she ordered a meal for "Sue Smith" from room service and began to unpack as she waited for the food to be delivered.

While she unpacked, she stewed, nervously rearranging

the drawers. She put Luca's clothes away, too. Her thoughts were random and quick, flitting from one thing to another. Luca. Vampires. Warriors. Ordinary concerns, such as work. Shaving her legs. She should be living her life like a normal person with normal worries.

She was so hungry that when the doorbell rang in the foyer, she rushed to answer it. A dignified middle-aged man in a uniform pushed a rolling cart into the oval living room. The aroma of the burger was tantalizing; there was nothing like comfort food when one's world was falling apart. If she couldn't have her mother's meat loaf and mashed potatoes, a cheeseburger and fries were the next best thing.

Luca sat on the sofa, still and contemplative. No one did *still* like a vampire. The room service guy nodded to them both, then politely asked if he'd gotten the order correct. The meal was for one, with a single plate and one glass of water. Luca smiled. "Yes, that's right."

She signed the bill, added an extra tip even though the surcharge was outrageous, and handed over the leatherette folder. The delivery guy nodded, thanked her, and headed for the foyer, where he turned, thanked her again, and then said, "Sir, I didn't see you there. Is the order correct? It's for one, but I can bring another plate and a glass of water, if you'd like to share."

Chloe froze.

"The order's correct," Luca said, smiling politely. "Thank you."

The room service waiter exited and they listened to the foyer door close behind him. Chloe turned to the calm vampire sitting on the sofa as if there was nothing at all wrong in the world. She stared at him for a moment, her mind racing. Then she said, "He didn't remember you."

"No, he didn't."

"Neither did the man in the elevator, or the desk clerk. Or Valerie! I thought it was a glamouring thing you did to her, but it wasn't, was it?"

"No."

For a moment, she forgot that she was hungry. A chill swept over her as she thought of other things, the stunned look on his face when she'd called him by name, the careful, almost alarmed way he'd acted. "No one remembers you," she whispered.

"No. No one but you."

She swallowed. "Why do I remember you? Is it because I'm a conduit?"

He looked at her, an unreadable expression in his piercing gray eyes. "I don't know. No other conduit has remembered me, not that I've met many of them—that I know of, anyway."

She got the feeling Luca wasn't accustomed to encountering anything he didn't understand, not because she could read anything on his face, but because she felt what was inside him.

Chloe then turned her attention to something she could understand: hunger. She sat at the wheeled-in table and took a few bites, swabbing her fries in ketchup, aware that Luca watched her closely. Maybe the ketchup got to him, reminded him too much of blood, but abruptly he stood. "I have something to do in the bedroom. Don't disturb me."

"What are you going to do?" she asked. Sleep? Unlikely. Masturbate? Even more unlikely, not after the night—day . . . whatever—they'd shared. Not when she was right here, handy and frighteningly willing. "Some gross vampire thing I don't want to know anything about, I suppose," she guessed, trying to sound nonchalant even though she felt anything but, then she couldn't stop herself from smiling at him.

"I'm going to put myself in a meditative state so I can locate Sorin."

Chloe almost choked on her most recent bite of burger. Forget nonchalant. "*Locate* him? I thought we were hiding from the psycho!"

Luca smiled gently. "Either we find them, or they'll find us. I've never been the type to sit around waiting for anything to come to me. I want the advantage of surprise."

"Great," Chloe said as she took another bite of what very well might be her last cheeseburger; at least it was a good one. Come to think of it, she'd be perfectly happy to hide here for a while, if the alternative was hunting vampires. Forget her job; she was willing to be jobless and live in this beautiful suite with its oval living room. She'd never been in a physical fight in her life; in school she'd always been the peacemaker, the one who tried to mediate the inevitable squabbles that erupted between her friends. She wasn't a coward, she didn't think, but she was definitely out of her element. All that aside, she knew without a single doubt that if Luca was going to rush into battle, she'd be rushing right along with him . . . the jerk.

Instead of immediately returning to D.C. as he should've, Sorin found a room in New York and holed up for the rest of the day. He was tired, and he liked the city; in an odd way he fit in here. He'd been born a farmer's son, had lived most of his human life inside one or two square miles, as most of his contemporaries had. And still, he felt as if he'd been born to a place like this. Though reading energies wasn't one of his gifts, even he could feel the energy of this city; even he could get lost here.

He needed to get lost for a while. He needed time to think.

By not killing Phillip Stargel, he'd basically committed treason, though committing treason against a traitor was a convoluted idea. Jonas wasn't psychic, he wouldn't know exactly what had happened, but he'd realize Stargel was still alive, and active. If Jonas reported the truth to Regina, if Sorin told her the job was done and Jonas contradicted him, she'd gladly take his head—or try. No, she wouldn't do it herself, she'd simply set three or more vampires on him, and not even he could win against those kind of odds unless he were very, very lucky and they were very, very bad fighters.

Then again, Jonas had no reason to go out of his way to volunteer information. The way Regina had treated him, why should he? Instead of making Jonas a part of the higher order, she'd used and abused him, she'd treated him no better than the humans she kept prisoner.

At the end of a long day spent in a hotel room in Manhattan, sleeping some and thinking too damn much, Sorin decided he didn't regret his decision to allow the conduit to live. He'd never thought that the human race was without value—after all, he'd once been human himself, and vampires couldn't live without humans to feed off of. Nor had he ever really wanted to make slaves of them all, though when one of them pissed him off he'd think fondly of it, for a while. At the end of the day, he simply wanted to be a part of that life again, to be accepted for who and what he was. The constant hiding, changing his name and location on a regular basis, keeping the secret of his existence . . . that was what he wanted to leave behind.

As night fell, he became restless, and the thought surfaced that humans had their uses, beyond providing food.

He walked around until he found a busy nightclub,

where the line waiting to get in snaked down the block. Sorin walked to the front of the line, glamoured his way past the waiting throng and into the exclusive club filled with beautiful women, loud music, men trying to get laid, and copious amounts of alcohol. He couldn't lose himself in drink, but he did sometimes like the taste of a good whiskey and the memory it stirred.

He walked up to the crowded bar and patrons instinctively parted, moving smoothly out of his way. He ordered a Scotch whiskey, and as the bartender placed it before him a pretty brunette—a human who apparently did not have the protective instincts of the others around him—sidled up close to him. He looked into her dark brown eyes and she flinched a little as something inside her instinctively noticed the monster inside him. She didn't walk away; she should have, but she didn't.

She wasn't drunk; she'd come here for another reason entirely.

"I haven't seen you here before," she said.

"I haven't been here before."

Her smile was practiced, a little strained. "That would explain it."

Sorin took a sip of his whiskey. Normally he preferred vampire lovers to humans; the emotional component could be messy, and so many humans reminded him of children, they were so inexperienced and ignorant. But this one was looking for sex, nothing more, and tonight he could use the comfort of sex and nothing more.

"What's your name?" she asked.

"Ryan." He couldn't be honest with her, the way he'd been honest with Phillip Stargel. Besides, Ryan was the name on his fake driver's license and very real credit card.

"Ryan what?"

"Does it matter?"

"No," she said honestly. "I'm Janie," she said, offering her hand.

It didn't make much sense to him to shake a woman's hand. He took the offered hand, lifted it slowly, kissed the knuckles and allowed his lips to linger there. She shivered, and he heard her heartbeat pick up. She liked that. Modern human men were idiots, the way they treated women. They didn't know how to seduce, but then the women let them get away with expecting sex for the cost of a dinner, so there was blame to share. He could screw her in the men's room or in the alley behind this place, but where was the challenge in that? The satisfaction would be short-lived, and he needed more, especially tonight.

He bought her a drink, and finished his own. She wanted to dance, but he made it clear that he didn't dance. Not like this, anyway. He could waltz, he could tango, he could even jitterbug, and he was an expert at dances Janie and those like her had never heard of, but he did *not* gyrate in public as if he'd lost all motor control.

He turned to her, looked into her eyes again. Enough of the games. He didn't glamour women in order to get sex; that had never been necessary, and besides, where was the fun in seduction when free will was taken away? "I have a room in a hotel down the street."

Janie tried to look shy and uncertain, but it was too late for that. He could see through her too easily. "I hardly know you," she said, but he could hear the echo of pain behind her smile. She was lonely; maybe she'd had her heart broken and was looking for vengeance, or maybe she simply needed not to be alone tonight, the way he needed not to be alone.

She deserved some care, but he didn't have the time or the patience to play nice. "If you want to fuck me, follow. If not, I'll find someone else." With that Sorin turned away and headed for the door. Again, humans parted to make way for him, even though the room was packed and it wasn't easy to create that path. As he reached the exit he turned. Janie was right behind him, her little purse tucked under her arm.

Why hadn't he felt it before? Sitting on the floor in the bedroom, intensely aware that Chloe was in the next room, Luca reached beyond the walls, searching for Sorin's energy. Meditation, and the powers it gave, was something he'd picked up over the centuries. He didn't sense Sorin's closeness at the moment, but he quickly discovered his lingering essence, and more.

Excitement. Violence. Numbers. Blood. Anger. Magic. All of this was gathered in one place, a place of rebellion and savage hope.

The site of this power had a heartbeat, a life of its own. Once he left the hotel he'd have no problem finding it. He'd be drawn there, not only to Sorin but to the unusual power of so many of his kind in one place, in one state of mind. Extraordinary, he thought. He should've sensed it before now. The sheer force of it should've knocked him over as he'd stepped off the plane, or as he'd reached for Hector's essence.

But it hadn't. So why was he feeling it now? What had changed? The energy had been there, it was something about himself that had changed. As he brought himself out of the meditative state, Luca had a disturbing thought: Had his bonding with Chloe made him stronger? He'd been worried it would weaken him, divert his energy, splinter his attention, but why else would this particular meditation be so much more productive than previous meditations? What could a human like Chloe offer him, beyond sex and blood?

"Life's force," a woman's throaty voice responded.

Luca rose with powerful grace and turned to see a misty figure that was taking shape near the closed door to the parlor. It was a woman with a long blond braid, a leather shift, bare feet, and a long sword. He knew instinctively who she was: Chloe's Warrior.

"Why are you here?" Luca asked.

"I belong here. You do not. I have come to lay claim to my conduit."

"And you are?"

"Indikaiya." She gave him a small, mocking bow. "I must come through to your world. Your presence is interfering, vampire."

"Find another conduit," he said sharply.

"There is no time." The image of Indikaiya shimmered, but didn't disappear. "She is the strongest of my descendants, she has the power to hear me."

"You've endangered her."

"All of the conduits are in danger. Many of them have died. Do you think we'll let this go unavenged, vampire?"

He wondered if it would be a waste of time to try to reason with the primitive Warrior. Maybe, maybe not. Warriors and a few vampires had, on the rare occasion, fought side by side. "Not every vampire is a part of the revolution you're trying to stop. There are some among us who want to keep things as they are."

"Why? What vampire would not welcome more power?"

"One who believes that the human race should be preserved."

Even though she was shimmering and incomplete, Indikaiya's skepticism was clear. "Preserved as food supply?"

"And more. I shouldn't have to explain to you why humans are worth saving, even if they are fragile and short-lived and often their own worst enemies."

She regarded him thoughtfully. "If that's the case, you could help me," the warrior said. "Add your strength to Chloe's, tell her what to expect, what to do. Guide her. Tell her to call my name. She's fighting me; she doesn't listen, she tries to explain me away. You may not tell her my name, but you can help her in other ways."

"She doesn't understand, and she's scared."

"She doesn't have to understand," Indikaiya said softly. "She only has to open everything she is to me, surrender her power to open a portal, and call."

"Humans don't surrender to anything easily," Luca explained. "They protect themselves. These days they don't believe in anything they can't see and touch. It must be more difficult for the warriors to come into the world now, when no one believes in you anymore. When were you last here, by the way?"

"I was last called in 1777, though others have been here since that time."

"Ahhh. How many wars have you fought in?"

"More than I care to count."

And yet she continued to come back, again and again, to fight and perhaps to die over and over in the name of humanity. He'd never had the opportunity before to really talk with a warrior—the ones he'd met had always been in the height of battle, when conversation wasn't possible—so he was oddly reluctant to let her go. "Does it ever end or is this all you will ever know?"

Her expression was answer enough. She was determined . . . sad . . . but ceaselessly vigilant.

Indikaiya lived beyond this world, but she realized what was happening here. She likely knew more than he did. Of all the questions he might ask her, why hadn't he thought of the most important one first? "Do you know why Chloe remembers me?"

"I do."

Luca waited for the answer, but it didn't come.

"But I won't tell you." Was that a smile? "Not unless you help to bring me through. I promise to tell you before I take your head."

Luca tsked and shook his threatened head. "You seriously lack people skills, Indikaiya."

"You're not *people,* Luca Ambrus."

She had him there. "No, I'm not," he admitted. "But Chloe is bonded to me, so you know I'll do everything I can to keep her safe. We're on the same side, Indikaiya. Remember that."

Indikaiya gave him a haughty look, the perfect picture of a warrior princess, then she faded from the room. Luca stood there, feeling the remnants of energy brush along his skin. That was a wild woman; despite the fact that she knew he was protecting Chloe, he still wouldn't trust her not to take his head the first time she saw him, which brought up a dilemma, for certain.

He left the bedroom and went to the living room, where Chloe had fallen asleep on the sofa, her head on a pillow, her feet drawn up. As he entered she woke and sat up quickly, pushing her hair back and blinking several times.

"What a dream," she said as she stood. She looked tired. "I'd hoped they would go away, that the bonding did something because I didn't have any dreams last night, but I guess not." She gave him a wry smile. "Though I didn't sleep enough to have any dreams, so that might have had something to do with it. Anyway. I dreamed you and the Warrior were talking, and it was a woman! That explains the braid, anyway. Indi . . . Indi . . . Okay, just Indie, I guess. I didn't understand the rest of the name."

"How do you know it was just a dream?" Luca asked.

Chloe shrugged her shoulders. "Because I was asleep. Duh. But it felt different from the others, as if I were watching from a distance, not participating. And for once I wasn't scared half to death. It all seemed very . . . normal. Had to be a dream."

Luca stared at her, an idea so far-fetched that it jolted him to the bone beginning to form. The situation had changed, far more than he'd imagined. He'd bonded with Chloe, a conduit in the process of bringing a Warrior through from the other world. He didn't know if such a thing had ever happened before. The three of them were inextricably joined, a triad of power. An Immortal Warrior, a vampire-wizard, a chosen human. Shit. Indikaiya was no longer Chloe's Warrior, she was *theirs*.

Janie was impressed with his hotel suite. "Wow, this must cost a pretty penny," she said. "Are you rich or something?"

"Something," he responded. He'd been rich, he'd been poor, he'd been everywhere in between. Rich was better, but in-between had always sufficed. No one in their right mind liked being poor.

Janie wasn't shy. She knew what she wanted, and she'd been here before. As she worked the buttons of Sorin's shirt he leaned down and drew in her scent. She was not as sweet-smelling as Nevada, or as musky as his last human lover, but she smelled pretty damn good and he could tell from her scent that she was healthy— not that he could catch any human diseases, but he liked his women clean and healthy.

"Are you taking birth control?" he asked, because that was what a human man would do. Vampires could impregnate human women, but it was very unlikely, and even if she did get pregnant the overwhelming odds were she wouldn't be able to carry the pregnancy to full term. Breeds rarely made it into this world. So far as he knew, no breed had ever survived more than a few days.

Janie nodded, pushed his shirt back off his shoulders, and started working the button and zipper of his blue jeans. She was so small, so short, and standing together this way only emphasized the difference in their height and build. "Yeah. You're healthy, right?"

"Yes." Healthier than she could imagine. "You?"

"Oh, yeah. I'm very careful."

The fact that she was here belied that fact, but Sorin didn't think it would be wise to point it out to her at this moment. She was simply taking his word about his health, so she was either stupid, desperate, or so lonely she didn't care.

He picked her up and carried her into the bedroom. His clothes were more off than on and hers were loose and askew. By the side of the big bed he finished the job, and naked, they fell onto the mattress. She pulled the covers over their bodies as if she were suddenly shy.

Very slowly, Sorin pulled the covers back. "Don't hide. You're beautiful."

He could see her blush, smell the blood rising just under her skin. "Turn off the light, please."

"All right," he said, because abruptly she seemed so nervous. After all, it wasn't as if he couldn't see almost as well in the dark, so she wouldn't be hiding anything from him.

He turned out the lamp. Janie reached up and put her small hand on the back of his neck. She pulled his face down to hers for a kiss that was sweeter than he'd expected. Soon the kiss changed; Janie's body language changed. Her last bit of shyness fell away as he coaxed her to desire.

There was nothing wrong with getting lost in the physical. Men and women were created differently for a reason—a very good reason.

Sorin was aware of the precise moment when Janie let go of whatever had drawn her to him and gave herself over to the moment. Whatever man had driven her to another's bed, she forgot about him. She was fully Sorin's now, fully here with him.

When he pushed inside her his own worries faded, because she wasn't the only one in this bed who needed a refuge, a moment away from thought. She was warm and soft and willing, she took him in and cradled him there and they were, for a moment, alone in the world.

Sex remained the most powerful act Sorin had ever known. Beyond feeding, beyond violence, it spoke most strongly to his primal self. As a human, as a vampire, it was a pleasure that never faded, that never lost its power—not that he didn't possess more skill now than he had as a human. Seven hundred years of practice was bound to improve performance. Some vampires painted or learned to play the piano; some accumulated wealth or things or even humans. Sorin's interests had taken a different path.

Janie came quickly, and hard, but Sorin didn't follow. He hadn't brought her here for a quickie, which would be no more satisfying than a fast coupling in an alleyway. He slowed his movements, kissed her throat. That throat and the vein there were tempting, but he didn't bite. Not yet.

She closed her eyes and her hips moved in a gentle rhythm, matching his own. Just as she was on the verge of coming again—easy human—he withdrew entirely. She gasped and tried to pulled him back, but when he began to kiss his way down her body she quit fighting and just enjoyed the ride. He knew what he was doing, and left her breathless and flushed and shaking.

It wasn't long before he pushed inside her again, and she welcomed him with a sigh and a gasp. He teased her, brought her to the edge and back again, and then he pushed deep and they came together, a nearly perfect ending to a needed respite.

Their rendezvous became entirely perfect when he lowered his head and bit into her throat, nipping the vein, drinking deeply, tasting everything that she was: satisfied, sad, angry, happy, in love.

Not with him, of course, but still, she was filled with love that had done nothing but hurt her.

She hadn't felt the bite, but evidence of it would remain if he didn't tend to the site. He licked; she laughed, unaware of why he was raking his tongue across her very delicate neck.

"That was amazing," she said. "Really, I had no idea sex could be so . . . amazing." Then she laughed, because she couldn't find another word other than the one she'd just used.

Sorin turned on the light. Janie tried to pull the sheet up to cover herself, but he stopped her, took her chin in his hand, forced her to look into his eyes. "Whatever man hurt you, he isn't worth the pain he's caused."

"No man has . . ." she began, attempting to lie. The shine of tears gave her away. "He's an idiot. I don't know why I let him affect me this way. He cheated. I wasn't enough for him, even though I tried so hard."

"Do you want me to kill him for you?" He made the offer, wishing she'd take him up on it. He needed to kill someone right now, because nothing else had worked out right today.

She laughed and shook her head, thinking his offer was a joke. It wasn't.

"You love him."

"I wish I could love you instead," she said, reaching up to touch his face.

"That wouldn't be smart."

She nodded, rested her hand on his neck, and pulled him to her once more. "Maybe not, but we can pretend for a while, can't we?"

"Yes, we can pretend." As powerful as glamouring was, as truly amazing as a vampire's gifts might be, not even the strongest of the kindred could manufacture or take away love. Tonight, if he couldn't have the real thing, at least he could have the pretense . . . and damn if he wouldn't glamour her before she left, so the son of a bitch who'd hurt her would be in for a whopping surprise the next time she saw him.

That thought made him happy.

TWENTY-ONE

Sorin had left Janie sleeping and, decision made, headed for home. Well, for D.C.; it was home for now. His fellow rebels were the only family he'd known for a very long time. A common purpose had driven them together, and there was a strong bond in that commonality. Besides, if there was trouble, he seldom ran from it; truth be told, he usually ran toward it with relish. Why should this be any different?

Maybe he'd gotten away with what he'd done. Three of the four conduits he'd been sent to kill were dead. Other hunters had been assigned to the remaining New York targets, and they'd all been successful, from what he'd been told. He hadn't heard any talk about a missed target, no frantic phone call saying that Phillip Stargel was still alive, and what the hell had happened?

He stood in Chloe Fallon's driveway, long after full darkness had fallen, and stared at the empty house. The soldiers who'd been sent to watch Luca had arrived too late; their target had already departed. Lucky for them, he supposed. All the lights were off, not even the front porch light shone, but it was more than that which told him the house was empty.

The house was forbidden to him, but he could feel the life, or lack of life in this case, inside. There were no heartbeats, no gently hissing breaths inhaled, no whispers of life. Luca had taken the conduit away, probably trying to keep her hidden and safe, though why he would bother was a mystery to Sorin. It didn't matter where Luca took her, how hard he tried to conceal her; Jonas would find the conduit all over again. But then, Luca didn't know Jonas was working with the rebels.

He was tired of this. Killing the conduits was necessary, but what he wanted was for the war to truly begin, so he could fight in the open. The humans would resist, once they knew what was going on, and he looked forward to a good battle. Regina, however, had a plan and she insisted that it be followed. They were on the cusp of attack, on the verge of coming out in full force. First the warriors and the breaking of the spell, then the all-out battle that would change the world forever. Fine. He was ready for it to start.

"You rang?"

Sorin turned his head slightly and looked down at the hunter he'd called. Melody was his own child, turned more than fifty years earlier. He'd chosen her because she was strong-willed and beautiful and at the time he'd wanted to keep her for a while longer than her human years would allow. As he'd suspected, she'd become a strong and beautiful vampire, but, damn, she still hadn't learned caution. She was headstrong, spoiled, and had very quickly become annoying. He was fond of her . . . in a way. And in small doses.

She changed her clothing and hairstyle as often as a child changed a doll's clothes, pretending to be different people, playing at dress-up whether she was hunting or not. Tonight her long blond hair was caught in a high ponytail. Her faded blue jeans were tight, and like the black boots and leather jacket that were not quite right for the season, suited her. Her lipstick was blood red. She barely resembled the Pig Queen of Sunflower County, which she'd been when he'd turned her. He could still see her in her red bathing suit and white sash, her hair teased and sprayed in the style of the time, her smile brilliant. She'd been utterly irresistible, for a while.

"Plans have changed," he said. "I'd thought to have you watch the D.C. conduit for a few days, which is why I asked you to meet me here, but Jonas just told me that another Texas conduit is fast coming around. His name's Jim Elliott."

"Honey, Jonas is off his game," Melody said sweetly. "I took care of Jim Elliott days ago."

"This newest conduit is his son. The Warrior trying to come through made an adjustment very quickly, or else . . ."

"Or else what, sugar?"

"Or else the warriors are changing the game somehow." Contacting more than one potential conduit, perhaps. He thought of Phillip Stargel; the fact that they were using a child said a lot about how desperate and determined they were. They were trying to confuse the hunters or, at the very least, making sure that there was more than one site prepared for a warrior to come through. Maybe they hoped that the vampires trying to stop them couldn't get to every conduit in time. Unfortunately, they might be right.

Then again, it wasn't as if the task was an easy one. Times had changed for them all, for the warriors even more than the vampires. Tales were no longer passed from generation to generation; the Warriors had been forgotten. How much harder did they have to work, to get people to believe in them again so they would call them over?

"Just take care of the second Jim Elliott," he said. As he walked away from the house Melody fell into step beside him. She was quiet for a few minutes; almost thoughtful. "You're really tense," she said. "When was the last time you got laid?"

No need to share the details of his sex life with anyone, and certainly not with Melody. "Are you offering?"

"For you, sugar, any time."

"Time's the one thing we don't have. I have a job to do, and so do you."

Melody walked with a swing of her hips, the ultra-feminine sway naturally seductive. "Just as well, I suppose. You'd probably want to go back to the house, and if the bat-shit vampire queen was around she'd probably take my head out of spite because I'm prettier than she is. Jealous bitch," she added under her breath.

Sorin controlled a snort of laughter. Melody and Regina did not get along. The only thing that had saved Melody so far was that, as far as Regina was concerned, she was so unimportant. "Be careful what you say. She might hear you one day."

They walked a while longer, even though they could, and should, separate and run. Rest would come after victory. But the night was cool and quiet, and Sorin had done more than enough running lately. "Why did you join us?" he asked. "You didn't do it because of Regina. You actually like humans. So why are you here?" Many vampires hadn't joined, hadn't taken either side. The cowards were waiting to see how things shook out. If the rebels won, they would happily enjoy the benefits. If not, then they'd continue on as they always had, living in darkness.

"I figured you knew why," Melody said, her normally chipper voice almost solemn. "I'm here for you. I mean, I like the idea of not having to hide what I can do all the time, and hunting the conduits has been a lot of fun, but, the truth of the matter is, I'm here for you."

"You don't have to be; I'm not asking for that much

loyalty." Vampires usually felt obligated and tied to their makers for a very long time, especially if sex had been involved, and many makers used that obligation to its full advantage. He didn't.

"I know." Melody's usual brightness crept back into her voice. "It just seems right. I mean, I love this life you've given me. Vampire is who I am, who I was always meant to be. I tell you what: if we win—"

"When we win," Sorin corrected.

"Fine. *When* we win, you and I can take a week or a month or a year and celebrate until we just can't stand each other anymore. And if we lose, which I'm sure we won't but you know, anything is possible so I might as well plan for anything, then we'll commiserate in a nice, soft bed."

"Why not?" Sorin said. Even if he ended up as Regina's consort when all was said and done, which was a possibility as he was second in command and she'd need someone to watch her back, they wouldn't share a bed. He liked being on top in all ways; so did she.

"It's a date, then," Melody said cheerfully. "I'll take care of Elliott Junior asap, and then we'll talk about the D.C. conduit. It'll take a couple of days. I don't travel as quickly or as well as you do. Not yet, anyway. If I could get accustomed to sunlight just a little bit that would help, but I still can't stand it. And I used to have such a beautiful tan," she said wistfully.

"Give it time." A hundred years, maybe two or three hundred more; it all depended on the individual.

"I hope I can stay here for a while once that's done," Melody said, her southern accent returning in force. "I really am tired of working in the boonies."

"*When* we win, you will never have to go to the boonies again unless it suits you," Sorin said, and tugged on her ponytail.

"No, sir. I'll just fuck your brains out right here in the big city." She laughed, and inside the house they passed by at that moment, a human stirred. A moment later, a curtain fluttered as the human peered outside.

Sorin turned toward the watcher and growled, showing his fangs by the light of the overhead streetlamp.

The curtain dropped. Perhaps the human inside that protected house would convince himself that he'd been dreaming, or that what he'd seen had been a trick of the light. At the moment, Sorin didn't care. Soon enough, everyone would know the truth, and he would never again have to hide who—*what*—he was.

"Someone's coming."

Chloe lifted her head at the sound of Luca's voice. "Well, it isn't me," she said testily. Considering how often they'd made love, she was a little surprised that she wasn't, but right now she didn't want to even think about sex. She was so tired, exhausted from all the sex and the screwed-up hours, the dreams that had come back just when she thought they were gone. She really should be asleep, but honestly, would she ever sleep again?

"It's a vampire. A powerful one." He paused, his gaze gone vacant as he focused on something she could neither see nor hear.

"Sorin?" Her heartbeat increased, and what felt like a boulder settled in her chest. She didn't want to see the big blond ever again; the memory of him tearing at Valerie's throat made her shudder. If not for Luca, he *would* have killed Valerie right in front of her, and if she'd tried to help Valerie he'd have killed her, too. Knowing the vampires wanted her dead, in theory, was bad enough. To see Sorin in the flesh, hungry to do the deed, was the stuff of nightmares.

"No."

Any relief she felt was transient. He'd left his chair and stood, ramrod straight, facing the door to the suite. His broad-shouldered, powerful body looked perfectly poised to meet any threat that might come through that door.

"We're safe here, right?" Chloe asked.

"To a certain extent."

"That's not *at all* comforting! Just how certain is this extent?"

Luca turned his head to catch her eye. "They're searching for us. They don't know exactly where we are. When it's morning, we'll move to another hotel. It'll be safer then. Most vampires don't function very well in daylight."

But some of them did. *He* did. So much for settling in, unpacking, arranging her things in drawers as if she was going to be here for a while—and what an odd thing to worry about. She shook the thought away. "If they can find us here, won't they be able to find us wherever we go? And *how* did they find us?"

"Some vampires can . . . identify and locate energy. I can, and I know others who can. The search takes time, though," Luca said. "They found us a little faster than I'd thought, to be honest. We'll have to stay on the move, change locations every day."

"For how long?"

"Until this is over, one way or the other."

One way or the other. One way was for this Warrior of hers to stop dawdling and come through, already. The other way was for her to get killed. Great. She'd pick "one way" over the "other" any day of the week, if only she knew how to hurry the Warrior along. The thought of a powerful vampire out there, hunting for them, for her, made her feel painfully vulnerable. And what about Luca? He was endangering his own life, in protecting her. With a jolt, she suddenly realized she didn't want that. No matter what, she wanted him safe, she wanted him to live—

Luca turned his head to look at her, the expression in his eyes cold and hard. Before she knew it she was on her feet, alarm streaking through her, until she realized that expression wasn't aimed at her, that what she felt, he, too, was feeling. "Yes," he said. "I want you safe, I want you to live. I *will* protect you," he added grimly. "I won't let her hurt you."

Chloe blinked. "Her?"

The expression on his face subtly changed. "They, I should say. There are three of them, but the most powerful is a woman."

Three of them. Great. The more the merrier— The doorbell made her jump. Holy crap! He'd warned her that vampires were coming, but she hadn't thought he meant right *now.* And what kind of sneak attack started with ringing the doorbell?

Luca started toward the door. Chloe darted forward, grabbed his arm. "Uh, isn't this the time we should use one of those other exits?"

"No. I want to hear what they have to say."

"They're here to *talk?*"

"I imagine so."

He took her hand from his arm and maneuvered her farther from the door, all the way back to the entrance to the living room, as the doorbell sounded again. "Stay," he commanded.

"Woof!" she said, narrowing her eyes at him to let him know what she thought of the order.

He slanted a quick look at her, but the sharpness of the glance was offset by the tiny smile that quirked his lips. Still, she recognized the seriousness of the situation.

"Okay," she said in a lowered voice. "I'll stay."

Luca opened the door. Chloe could see the three vampires in the hallway; Luca only partially blocked her view. The three looked ordinary enough, she supposed; well, no they didn't. One was a beautiful, statuesque woman with red hair, wearing a simple black dress that probably cost a couple of thousand dollars, and killer high heels. The two men wore expensive suits; she knew Italian tailoring when she saw it. They looked human enough to her eyes, but then, so did Luca.

Luca would fight to protect her, but there were three of them and only one Luca, and she knew how strong vampires were. Chloe didn't fool herself into thinking for a moment that she would be of any use at all if a fight broke out here. No, she'd only be a liability, as Luca attempted to protect her. On the other hand, if these three were here to kill her, would they be dressed the way they were? They looked as if they'd be right at home at a White House function.

If she hadn't been so scared, she would have laughed at the idea of vampires having a dress code for killing, but female was female, and she'd bet there was no way the redhead would risk getting blood on that fabulous silk dress.

"Council members," Luca said very politely, but without any welcome in his tone. "Come in, please."

Chloe stiffened. Oh, shit; he'd invited them in. That meant—well, she didn't know what it meant, because this hotel suite, as lovely as it was, wasn't her *home*, so she supposed the vampires could have invaded at any time anyway, if they'd been so inclined. She needed to have a long talk with Luca, find out exactly how all these details worked.

The woman vampire fastened her gaze on Chloe, and abruptly she no longer looked entirely human. There was something feral in her eyes and in the way her muscles tensed, as if she were ready to spring forward, claws exposed.

"Alma," Luca said curtly, drawing her attention. "How unexpected that you've found me here."

Alma looked away from Chloe, focusing on Luca, and waved an indolent hand to indicate one of the men. "Benedict can locate specific energies, if he puts forth the effort. He hadn't tried in decades, but he came through for us."

"And you, Theodore?" Luca asked, turning to the other man. "Why did you tag along?"

Theodore was thick-bodied and looked ill-tempered, with his heavy dark brows and perpetual scowl. He gave Luca a long, cold look, one that struck Chloe as being . . . something else, something she didn't understand but was somehow different. Different from what, she had no idea. "I was curious to see what was keeping you from your duties to the Council."

Luca didn't hesitate in his answer. "Protecting Chloe is my only duty, at the moment."

Alma once more turned her attention to Chloe, her eyes hard as stone and mean as a snake's.

"Don't waste your time trying to glamour her," Luca said, menace lacing his tone. "We're bonded. She's immune to you. And she's *mine*." He didn't have to say, but implicit in the word "mine" was the dark promise that if anything happened to her he would have his vengeance on the offending vampire.

Alma turned her snaky stare to Luca. She actually looked shocked. "But . . . you're a blood born. Why on earth would you bond with *her*?"

Luca gave a cold smile. "My reasons aren't any of your business. All you need to know is that Hector's warning about an uprising was the truth, and there's a traitor on the Council. Chloe is a conduit. The rebels want her dead. I don't."

The one named Benedict took a step back, as if he could escape the news with physical distance. He looked distressed. "Rebels! What on earth are they thinking? Why do we have to go through this every couple of hundred years? Doesn't anyone remember that it's always a disaster? It's in everyone's best interest to maintain our world as it currently exists. Any intelligent vampire can see that."

"Apparently not," Luca said drily. "From what I'm able to sense, there are a large number of rebels involved and they're gathered very near. Didn't you pick up on the energy?"

Benedict looked stricken by the question. "N-no," he stammered. "I didn't. Are you sure?"

"Yes, I'm sure. They're not afraid of you, or they'd be gathering somewhere else, in California or Seattle or London. But they're *here,* and you all have a decision to make. You can fight with me, you can wait to be taken over by rebels, or you can hide and hope this war shakes out in your favor."

Theodore said, "Open war isn't the answer. Any war will result in our existence being made public, and from there on out the fighting will be constant. It'll never end. Any idiot can see this, if they know anything about humans."

"It appears that war is coming, like it or not," Alma said. "We can hardly sit back and wait to see if the warriors win it for us." She hesitated. "Or if, perhaps, the rebels are right and taking over will mean a better life for us."

"You don't look as if you have it rough now," Chloe said sarcastically, then wished she'd slapped her hand over her mouth before saying anything, because four sets of vampire eyes settled on her with expressions ranging from warning to outrage.

Luca kept his attention on the visitors, but Chloe could feel something of him with her, as if he were all around her. She knew, through her connection with him, that Theodore was somehow different from the other two. She couldn't put her finger on exactly *how,* but she knew that difference existed.

"We'll be lucky if many warriors arrive," he said. "The rebels' initial strategy has been to kill as many conduits as possible."

"I never thought to hear the words 'lucky' and 'warriors' used in the same sentence," Benedict grumbled, almost beneath his breath, "but I swear, it seems they are our best hope for ending the rebels."

Chloe could feel Luca's anger bloom, as if it had weight. She could almost see it, the color and form of it. "If that's your position, that the Council will just sit back and let the warriors fight our battles for us, then the Council has become useless. You're no better than any other group of politicians."

All three were offended by that remark, if she judged their expressions correctly. Well, who wouldn't be?

"You *will* protect us if the rebels come for the Council directly, won't you?" Theodore asked.

"No," Luca responded, his voice soft but pretty damn certain to Chloe's ears. If he'd told her *no* in that tone, she wouldn't bother to ask again.

"You serve the Council," Alma responded, her voice and expression going cold and haughty.

Luca snorted. "I worked with the Council, not for it. You were never discerning enough to tell the difference. But I hereby offer my official resignation. Council business is no longer my concern." His voice was so cold, Chloe shivered.

Benedict began to sputter and protest, but he didn't get far. Luca herded them all toward the door. The meeting was over, and it hadn't been violent at all. But boy, did she have a lot of questions for Luca.

When the vampires were gone, Luca turned and looked at Chloe. He was very angry, but there was something else in him that she couldn't quite grasp, something she never would've seen if they weren't bonded. Regret? Yes; regret, not for what he'd done but for what had been, or could've been. He'd just cut himself away from an organization that must have been a big part of his life for God only knew how long.

And he'd done it for her.

"What's the deal with Theodore?" she asked.

His eyebrows raised, very slightly. "You caught that?"

She rolled her eyes. "Bonded, remember? It's a two-way street."

"He's . . . perhaps an ally."

"You don't sound very enthusiastic. Or convinced."

"Theodore's decisions are always based on what's best for Theodore. He offered some assistance. A warning. I'm just not entirely sure why."

"I didn't hear him say any of that, but you know him and I don't. But I think I know why. He's looking out for himself. Even if I was a vampire, with all kinds of woowoo powers, I'd want you on my team," Chloe said honestly.

"I am on your team," Luca said, his gaze going warm as he reached for her. As if she had a single doubt . . .

Nevada crawled into bed and pulled the covers over her head. The new guards, female and *physically* appearing to be less dangerous than the old male guards, were likely to walk into the room at any time. They brought her tea, or threatened her family, or said they'd drink every drop of her blood if she didn't get the job she'd been given done. *Soon.* They enjoyed scaring her, like children jumping out and saying "Boo!" Except these weren't children, and they wouldn't stop at *boo,* if they were ever allowed at her.

It wasn't as if Sorin ever knocked, either. She had no privacy in this place.

In order to let her spirit travel to spy on the vampires—and check on her family—she had to conceal herself. The shower worked well for a short period of time, but she couldn't shower more than a couple of times a day without raising suspicions. And seriously, what if she fell while she was in the spell, and cracked her skull? So far that hadn't happened, but these trances were getting deeper and deeper, so she couldn't be certain what might happen. Maybe if the guards came in and caught her under the covers, they'd think she was taking a nap and leave her alone. At the very least, they shouldn't be suspicious of what she was doing.

Nevada wasn't sure she'd even be aware of an interruption, if her thoughts and spirit were elsewhere. Did any part of her remain with her body when she traveled? She didn't know, had no way of finding out.

It was stuffy beneath the covers, too warm and very dark. Nevada closed her eyes, took a deep breath, gathered the energy around her, focused, and let herself go.

Traveling this way was like flying in a dream. She felt herself, light and airy, leave the room, even though her body didn't move at all; it remained huddled under the covers. For a moment she was in both places, in her body and in the air, and then her connection with her physical self was completely severed. She passed the guards in the hallway, but they had no idea she was there. She floated down the stairs, through a few walls and down again, until she found herself in the large, windowless basement.

Abovestairs, the house appeared perfectly normal: bedrooms, bathrooms, a study, a formal living room, and a huge family room, complete with a large flat-screen television and video games, which the vampires really got into. There were other rooms she hadn't seen and had no interest in exploring. Servants' rooms above her, a library, a kitchen.

The basement was like a warehouse, the space divided by hallways that crisscrossed and with closed doorways. Just a quick look at this level told Nevada the basement served as prison and war room, barracks and armory. This was where the vampires planned and managed their war, where they kept Nevada's family, and goodness knows who else, prisoner. Here there were no pretty pictures, no vases of flowers and fine furnishings; it was as utilitarian as a shovel.

Tonight *she* was here. Nevada could feel the poisonous energy of the self-proclaimed queen, the female vampire who had put this plan into motion. Nevada hated her with a passion, hated her more than she hated Loman, or all the guards who'd tormented her over the past three years. She even hated the bitch more than she hated Sorin, who hurt her the most because she hated him one moment and thought of him as a friend the next. She kept thinking he was different from the rest, he was somehow better, which was reason to fear and hate him most of all.

But Regina was . . . God, she was awful. The energy Nevada felt around her was the coldest, most brutal and ruthless energy she could imagine. Regina was the reason Nevada hadn't yet told anyone that she'd found the last piece of the puzzle, that she now knew how to break the spell that protected humans in their homes. She'd told Sorin that she was close, but in truth she was beyond close. The job she'd been brought here to do was finally done, and she didn't dare let anyone know.

Nevada loved her family; she wanted to live, and she wanted them to live. But she couldn't bring herself to set these monsters loose on the world, no matter what the cost. If she could just figure out a way to set her family free before she told the queen to go take a flying leap, she could die satisfied. Her own death was a given; she'd accepted that a long time ago. The first time she'd looked into Regina's eyes, she'd known there was no hope for survival. She wasn't going back to school, wouldn't ever have another boyfriend, get married, have kids, sleep late and dance and eat birthday cake . . . there were so many things she would never do that thinking about them all had the power to paralyze her. She had to put all those thoughts aside and think about what she could do.

What was important was making certain that Emily and Justin would go back to school and eat birthday cake, that they would do all the things Nevada could not.

Would Sorin really work with her, would he let her family go if she promised to do as she'd been told? He'd said yes, but was his word enough? There was so much about Sorin that confused her, and the only way she could function right now was if she put him out of her mind.

Invisible to those she passed, Nevada walked down a long, plain hallway with concrete floors and gray walls. Behind a closed door, a man screamed. Nevada shivered to her bones. The screaming man was food, she supposed. That's all people meant to the monsters: food. Then there was sudden silence, and that was more frightening than the screams had been.

Sorin had promised her that as long as she cooperated, her family wouldn't be touched, wouldn't be food. Could she trust him? Not really. But she'd come to understand the importance of her part in this, and she believed that the vampires would do as they promised, for now. It wasn't as if there was a shortage of blood donors to serve their dining needs. They didn't need to feed on her family. Besides, now she had a way of checking up on them.

She reached the room where her family was being held. She could feel them inside, as sharply as she'd heard that poor man scream. They were *here*. The powers she hadn't even known about, before Sorin kidnapped her, literally grew stronger every day. She touched the wood door, but couldn't feel any resistance. The last time she'd visited, she'd just popped in, like dropping out of the air. This time she walked through the closed, locked door.

Emily's head jerked up. She looked directly at Nevada, her eyes wide. Nevada held a finger to her lips, to keep Emily from saying anything.

She took the time to look around. There were additions to the room: a cooler of drinks, a stack of books and board games, a handheld video game, and the remnants of a recent meal. For now, at least, it appeared that Sorin was keeping his word.

Her mother read; Justin was playing the video game. Her father stared into space, his mind elsewhere. They were all silent, much too quiet and reserved. Her family had always been a lively bunch, sharing jokes, laughing, taking all life had to offer. She'd think they were drugged, but she suspected that they had simply given up. They were resigned to being here.

She moved closer to Emily, so close that their arms brushed. "Do you see me?"

Emily nodded. She swallowed and looked down, then darted a quick look at their parents. "I don't understand," she whispered. "Is it really you? How are you doing this? How do I know you're not some vampire trick?"

Nevada smiled. "You got the *normal* name." It was a thing with them, and always had been.

"You got the *interesting* name," Emily responded, and a new light, the light of hope, brightened her eyes.

Then Nevada felt as if she was yanked backward through the door, into the hallway, and with a sharp thud, a gasp, and a pounding of her heart, she was fully and completely back in her bed.

But she was no longer under the covers, and Sorin's blue eyes were mere inches from her own.

TWENTY-TWO

Nevada looked as if she'd been caught with her hand in the cookie jar. Her face was flushed, her eyes wide and bright.

"Are you *napping*?" Sorin asked, incredulous. She knew how important her task was, how crucial her participation was to the safety of her family. How could she sleep in the middle of what had become her day?

"I . . . I . . ."

"Spit it out."

"I haven't been sleeping well," Nevada said. She wanted to sit up, but he remained bent over her so close she couldn't move without touching him. He didn't move back; he wanted her to be scared, but instead she just looked surprised.

"I barely slept a wink last night . . . during the day . . . whenever my last sleep cycle was," she explained. "I was exhausted. No wonder I can't sleep. I'm never sure if it's day or night, if I've been asleep eight hours or two. You know, a clock would be a nice addition to this room. Is that too much to ask for? A freakin' *clock*?"

She was trying to change the subject, but he didn't let her distract him. "You're running out of time," he whispered, his nose almost touching hers.

"I know; you've told me again and again," she said sharply. "But if I can't keep my eyes open, how am I supposed to work? I'm so tired I can barely think."

"Coffee? Red Bull? Any drug known to mankind and some not known? All you have to do is ask. You're a powerful witch, Nevada. Create your own remedy."

Sorin backed away from her and stood. With a grateful sigh, Nevada sat up and swung her legs over the side of the bed. "Maybe some coffee would be a good idea. I'm afraid to use any drugs; it might affect the spells. I'm just learning, you know; my magic is new, and more fragile than you can imagine."

"Your little sister is also fragile," Sorin responded, instinctively going for the threat that cut her the deepest. "Emily." He allowed the name to roll off his tongue as if it tasted sweet.

Nevada shot to her feet, her eyes wide with fear and anger. "Leave her alone."

"Do as you're told, and I will." Her reaction to his threat revealed her weakness; never let the enemy know what you fear, what you treasure. "If you don't, she'll be the first to die. You'll watch. You'll watch them all die, and I promise you they won't have easy deaths."

"You wouldn't do that to me," she whispered.

"Don't test me."

She paled, not an easy task for someone as fair as she was. Her delicate fingers twitched, then pushed back her fine red, sleep-mussed hair. He could see Nevada composing herself, reining in her fear for her family, perhaps because she herself recognized that her love was also her weakness.

"Do vampires have an afterlife?" she asked, a touch of sharpness in her tone "Do you have a soul or are you a monster who doesn't exist beyond the skin you wear and the blood you take?"

"I don't know," Sorin responded. Then he smiled, knowing his nonchalant attitude to that loaded question would speak volumes. "And I don't care."

Chloe and Luca checked out of the Willard early that morning, as soon as the sun was blazing in the summer sky. Luca didn't tell her where they were going; she got the very clear sense that he was winging it, that some sixth sense would tell him his next move.

She wished she could just go home. If she lived in a vacuum, that would be perfect. No one could come in without an invitation, and evidently the vampires couldn't set her house on fire or shoot her through a window because home was such a sanctuary it was damn near untouchable. But she didn't live in a vacuum. Luca worried about her friends, neighbors, and apparently even about stray puppies. The incident with Valerie had convinced him she was vulnerable through the people she cared about, and she couldn't deny it— like he would've done anything differently if it had been *his* friend being killed right in front of him.

"Any idea where we're going?" she asked, just to verify her hunch that he was making things up as he went. He didn't immediately respond. Maybe he really didn't know, though he didn't strike her as a man who *ever* didn't know.

She almost wished he didn't have anything in mind. Uncertainty would make him almost human, and he'd made it clear he wasn't human, never had been. Looked at objectively, that kind of called her sanity into question, that after just a few days she'd placed her life in his hands. Who was she kidding? She'd been willing to put her life in his hands almost immediately.

Maybe, maybe . . . there were too many maybes. She had too many questions and not enough answers. There was one question, though, that struck her as supremely important. "I hate to bring this up, but aren't you hungry?"

"Not yet. I'm old enough that I can go a few days without having to feed, unless I'm doing something that burns a lot of energy." He slanted a quick look at her as he skillfully navigated the tangled D.C. traffic. He was wearing dark sunglasses to protect his eyes, but she felt his look like a touch. "What I took from you the night before last was enough."

She went hot at the memory, the feel of his mouth pulling at her, the rush of sensation. Glancing over, she saw his hands tighten on the steering wheel. Okay, she needed to get her mind away from that, or, connected as they were, they might end up going at it the next time they were stopped at a traffic light. She cleared her throat. "You haven't been burning a lot of energy?" she asked, then could have kicked herself, because that wasn't exactly changing the subject.

"Not vampire energy."

"That's good. I think." Several safer items occurred to her. "About this blood born business . . . "

"I knew you wouldn't miss that."

"Then why don't you explain it? It isn't anything bad, I could tell that from Alma's tone. It was almost as if she were saying: 'How could you, a prince, sully yourself with this lowly peasant.'"

"Vampires don't have royalty," he said. "There are no continuous blood lines, for one thing. Power is individual, can't be transferred, can't be inherited."

"So you're not a prince? Then what does blood born mean?"

"It means I wasn't made vampire, I was *born* vampire. It doesn't happen very often; I know of only six other blood borns alive today, and one of them is on the Council."

"So . . . vampires can get pregnant?" The idea made her head spin.

"Very rarely. I haven't made a study of it, but the odds are . . . maybe once every two centuries."

"That fits my definition of rare," she muttered.

"Blood borns are the most powerful vampires, because we inherit from two vampires rather than having just our own inherent powers when we're turned."

"You double down."

"That's one way of putting it. But none of us are exactly alike, any more than humans are."

Different skill sets; he'd used that phrase before. One of his powers was that people didn't remember him. She tried to imagine what that must be like, and couldn't find anything good about it. That wasn't a power, it was a curse, almost like not existing at all. She didn't know why she was different, unless it was this conduit thing, but she would be grateful for the rest of her life that she had him in it, that she knew him and could touch him and hold his face in her memory.

Luca drummed his fingers on the steering wheel, his expression turning thoughtful. "I've spent my life fighting battles," he said. "That's what I enjoy, and what I'm good at. It's hard to find a good battle now, so to keep myself occupied I've been a . . . kind of enforcer for the Council. Keeping our existence a secret is best for everyone, but sometimes a vampire goes rogue and has to be dealt with. I have a talent for locating vampires through their energy, but I'm not the only one who can do that."

"Like Benedict."

"Yes, like Benedict, only better. I think some other tracker must have developed the power to detect conduits, otherwise how could they know who's a conduit and who isn't?"

Chloe didn't have to think about that very long. "So . . .

no matter where I am, they'll be able to find me." She might as well have swallowed a GPS.

"We'll have to keep moving. Knowing where you are isn't the same as knowing where you'll be five minutes from now, and we do have the advantage of being able to move during daylight, which limits the number of vampires who can come after us."

He frowned. "I wish I knew which tracker can do this. There's only a handful capable of it; they're all much better than Benedict."

"And he found us."

"Yes. Until you can bring your Warrior over, they won't let up."

So it was up to her. The only thing was, she didn't know what the hell she was supposed to do. While she was having the dream, tell the Warrior to come on down?

"Isn't there any way I can speed things up?" she asked helplessly.

"You have to call her by name, tell her to come. That's all."

"But I don't know her name! 'Hey, you' won't work?"

His mouth quirked. "No, it has to be her name."

"Indi-something. I couldn't make it out." She stared out the window, feeling helpless and frustrated. There had to be something she could do, some way she could work this out.

"Now that you know what's happening, she'll be able to make full contact with you much faster," he said. "Don't fight it. When you dream, try to hold on to the dream, so it'll play out longer."

"I have to be asleep to dream," she pointed out. "Sleep has been in short supply lately." But she was tired, so tired. If they could just find a safe place to rest, surely she'd dream. Wasn't it a kick in the pants that just a couple of days ago she'd have given anything to escape the dreams, and now she'd give almost anything to be able to dream?

She still didn't know what Luca had planned, but one thing was for certain: retreat wasn't on the agenda, which meant she had loose ends she had to tie up.

Chloe dug her cell phone out of her purse and punched in the number for her parents. She should've done this before, but she'd been a bit distracted. Knowing what was coming, knowing she couldn't, *wouldn't* run, this was a call that had to be made.

Her mother answered the phone.

"Hi," Chloe said, keeping her tone cheerful.

"Oh my God. What's wrong?"

As dire as things were, Chloe had to smile. She almost never called early in the morning, because of the hours she worked. "I *am* occasionally up before noon," she chided, and heard her mother's sigh of relief. "Anyway, I wanted to let y'all know that I'm taking a vacation, going camping with some friends from school."

"Camping?" The single word was filled with meaning. Chloe had never been a fan of the great outdoors.

"Yeah, I know. They tell me it'll be fun. If it isn't, I'll leave them to the bugs and dirt and come home early. Anyway, I didn't want you to worry if you called the house and couldn't get me. I hear there's spotty cell reception where we're headed, so I'll be out of touch for a few days."

"Are there any men in this group of friends?" The question was more hopeful than censuring, the word "men" slightly higher pitched than any of the others.

"A couple," Chloe said. If she could give her mother hope, in a time when there wasn't much to offer, then why not?

"Anyone in particular?" Did that question sing, or what?

"One, in particular," Chloe said, looking at Luca's profile. It was easy to put him in that category. Someone special. *One, in particular.*

Her mother knew better than to press for details.

"Be careful, honey." That was the standard warning. If her aneurysm burst while she was on a camping trip, she had no chance for survival. Then again, there was nothing either she or anyone else could do about it, and Chloe's decision had been to simply live, so her mother wasn't surprised.

Chloe wanted to tell her mother to stay in the house at night, to keep Dad inside, too, to bar the doors and not let anyone in, but she didn't. Besides, it had to be an emergency to get her dad to drive after dark. He said these days he didn't see well after the sun set. Who would've thought that could turn out to be a blessing? They'd be safe, for now. There was still hope, still a chance that the rebels could be stopped before nightmare swept the world. Chloe knew she'd never look at the night the same way again; she didn't want to do that to her parents, if it could be helped.

After she ended the call, Chloe looked around and realized that Luca was driving north, and had been since they'd set out, which put the morning sun on her right side, pouring through the passenger window. Had he chosen north deliberately, to keep the sun away from himself as much as possible? Maybe he was strong enough to bear daylight, but he didn't like it. It would be terrible to have to avoid the sunshine forever, she thought. For those who couldn't stand the daylight at all, half the day would be wasted, gone. Because he'd been born vampire, Luca had never been able to enjoy the warmth of the sun on his face, but did other vampires miss it?

She supposed living forever was a pretty decent trade-off, though honestly, who wanted to live forever all alone? Maybe Luca had friends he hadn't talked about. Maybe he'd even been married in the past. She didn't know how old he was, but he hadn't gone through life in complete solitude.

"What's it like?" she asked.

"What?"

"To live forever. To see the world change again and again."

"Interesting, maddening, dull, fascinating, sad, hilarious. All the things life is to you, I imagine, only . . . more." He glanced toward her. Traffic had thinned and he didn't have to pay such close attention to the vehicles around them. "And no one, not even a vampire, is invincible. I can die; both my parents died, though I suppose that, to be accurate, vampires don't die, they're killed. The world isn't safe, not even to an immortal."

"Do vampires go to, well, heaven?" She wanted to know, but once the words were out she wished she'd phrased the question differently. Having lived with the possibility of death for so long, she'd given more than a passing thought to heaven, or whatever life after death might be called. She believed. She *had* to believe that there was something more. "Do you believe there's something beyond *this* for you?"

"I know there are other worlds, other planes of existence." He shrugged. "Whether or not the kindred go there when they die, I can't say."

He didn't seem bothered by this notion, didn't seem to be annoyed that he didn't know. Maybe, after such a long time, the idea of going to another place wasn't a big deal.

"The world where the warriors live, what's it like? I think I saw it once, in a dream, but I can't be sure if what I saw was real or just a dream."

"From what I've heard, it's physically a lot like this one: green fields, blue skies, clear waters. The warriors live a normal life there, or as normal as life can get, between battles and wars."

"If this world is so ideal, then why would they ever leave?"

"To preserve the good that's left in *your* world." He glanced at her briefly, and again she wished she could see his eyes. "To preserve you." He abruptly changed the subject, as if talking about the warriors and life after death and worlds beyond this one was not what he wanted to do right now. "We're going to visit an old friend of mine. He'll give us a place to stay now, so we can get some rest."

Chloe wondered what would constitute an "old friend" to a vampire who'd been around for who knew how long.

And then she made a few more phone calls: work, to give them an update on her supposed illness; Valerie; a couple of other friends who might worry about her. She wanted to warn them all, as she'd wanted to warn her mother, but she couldn't, didn't. All she could do was stick by Luca's side and do what she could to stop the vampire revolution. She was amazed at how easily she lied. She was feeling pretty rotten, she told Valerie, and don't come over because she didn't want to give her whatever bug this was.

Phone calls done, she settled back and closed her eyes, though sleep was far from coming. Her thoughts kept spinning, darting here and there.

What good would she be in a fight against an army of monsters?

What choice did she have but to try?

Going to Ahron was a last resort. Luca never knew how he'd find the old man. Hibernating, having a crazy spell, maybe, if they were lucky, enjoying a lucid moment. They needed lucid today.

It wasn't coincidence that Ahron lived less than an hour from D.C. The Council housed and fed him, which was a good thing since he was, in his weaker moments, incapable of hunting for himself. Even on his best days, when hunting came as easily to him as it did to Luca, Ahron couldn't show his face in public. Hundreds of years had passed since Ahron could be mistaken for human.

If this was what true immortality did to a man, Luca could only hope someone would take his head before it happened to him. Ahron had been alive much longer than Luca had, though how much longer no one really knew, not even Ahron.

Ahron's face was perpetually young, but his hair was snow white and he had a frailness about him that gave away his age. His eyes were such a pale, vivid green they glowed. His skin was like porcelain, perfect and white and fragile-looking, as if it would crack if you tapped it with a fingernail. His fangs were perpetually extended, though he only needed to feed once a month, or even less often than that.

Even the Council members were afraid of him, which was why the elder wasn't housed in their headquarters. If Ahron ever displayed his full strength and abilities, which was entirely possible, the Council didn't want to be any-where nearby. The ancient vampire, a psychic since his turning and perhaps before, saw too much. In a lucid moment, he could see anything and everything. No secret was safe from him, no treasure or pitfall could remain uncovered. It was no wonder he was mad more often than not. Luca wanted to believe that it was Ahron's gift, not his age, that had transformed him, but who could know with certainty what had made him this way?

Ahron lived in the basement of a deserted warehouse. In the past, the Council had tried to keep guards in the building, but none stayed very long. It took a lot to spook a vampire, but Ahron was capable of sending the strongest among them running. Not that it mattered; the old vampire didn't really need bodyguards. While he was no longer capable of hunting aboveground, he could certainly handle any unwanted intruders. Trespassers who had the misfortune to wander onto the property at night didn't live to tell the tale of the creature who lived in the basement.

You couldn't always count on having a handy trespasser, though. The Council saw to it that meals—glamoured humans who'd happened to be in the wrong place at the wrong time—were delivered to Ahron's home every month.

Luca led the way down a narrow stairway and knocked on the steel door, though he knew that Ahron would've been aware of their presence as soon as he'd driven into the deserted parking lot. Knocking was the polite thing to do—and the safest.

Ahron opened the door, a smile on his face. Chloe gasped and grabbed ahold of Luca's shirt, perhaps searching for something solid with which to ground herself. Ahron's smile was that terrifying.

"Luca Ambrus!" Ahron said brightly, though he was too frail for that voice to have the hearty ring he tried to inject. "How nice of you to call. Did you bring me a snack?" His eyes flicked hungrily over Luca's shoulder at Chloe. "I just fed a week or so ago, or was it three weeks? Doesn't matter. She looks like a tasty snack. Perhaps even dessert!"

"This is Chloe," Luca said. "We're bonded, so she's mine. Chloe, this is Ahron."

"Too bad," the old man with the young face said breezily, as he opened the door wide. "Come in, all three of you."

For a moment Luca thought Ahron had suffered a mental slip, but suddenly he knew that wasn't the case.

The ancient seer saw not only Luca and Chloe, he also saw Chloe's Warrior. Indikaiya was with them enough for her presence to be sensed.

Chloe gave him a confused look, then hesitantly said, "I'm pleased to meet you," to Ahron.

"Are you?" Ahron stopped in his tracks, looking surprised. "How about that."

Luca hadn't been here in more than ten years, but nothing had changed. Ten years was nothing to him; the short amount of time was even less to Ahron. The computer was newer, and the television had been upgraded to a flat screen. The leather couch and matching recliner were the same, as were the paintings on the walls, paintings from the old masters such as Michelangelo. Did the human world even know these paintings existed? Their worth was unimaginable.

Ahron turned off his computer and sat in the recliner, moving slowly as if he were afraid he'd break if he sat too hard. "I suppose you're here about the revolution. Isn't it exciting?"

"I suppose that's one word for it," Luca said. He and Chloe sat side by side on the sofa. Her eyes were wide and, after greeting Ahron, she'd all but glued her lips shut. Considering she'd punched *him*—he still hadn't gotten over his shock—she must really be intimidated.

"Vampires should've taken over centuries ago," Ahron said with a wave of a delicate hand that was white as milk. "It's the most logical progression of events. We're stronger, we're smarter. Humans are our *food*, for pity's sake."

"I liked the hotel better," Chloe whispered under her breath, her words so low they were obviously intended only for him. She had no idea how sensitive Ahron's hearing was, how sensitive the old one was to all stimuli.

Ahron responded with a wide grin, as he fixed his gaze on Chloe. "My, my. That's twice you've spoken."

He looked back to Luca. "That's very generous of you, letting her talk. But allowing such liberties can be a mistake, as I'm sure you know by now. She serves two purposes, and I suspect she's adequate in both senses, but to allow her to speak to you as if she's an equal . . ." His green eyes glowed and he spoke directly to Chloe. "I've seen women like you come and go many thousands of times since I became vampire. You're very pretty, useful in your own way, but still, you *are* temporary. Don't be offended; it's your nature, like a flower is temporary." His smile faded. "Some are more temporary than others. I remember . . . bah. I don't know what I remember. I scare you, I see, and I should try not to scare you any more than someone would purposely frighten a child, but that is in *my* nature."

Like a switch, he turned his attention back to Luca. "I would offer to introduce you to someone I know who could lead you to the rebels, but you don't want to join them, you want to destroy the movement. It wouldn't be fair for me to interfere. I must remain impartial. Well, outwardly impartial, at least. The outcome of this clash is not set in stone. So little is, I have found. It's maddening to see so much and not know what is meant to be and what is mere possibility. My mind is filled with possibilities, potential outcomes, all riding on the swing of a sword or the path of an arrow."

Rambling was Ahron's stock-in-trade, but if you listened carefully enough, you could get his meaning. "Who is leading the rebels?" Luca asked. "How many are there?"

"I cannot tell you who leads, as you would surely use that information against the rebels. Besides, she would be very unhappy with me if I were to tell, and I would miss her company. Though she does not call as she once did," he mused. "Perhaps when the revolution is over and she is queen, she'll come to me again. Even better, perhaps she will offer me a new and better home, one where I can see the sun if it pleases me. I would make a superb minister of . . . something. I'm certain she sees that for herself."

So. The leader was a woman. He wasn't surprised; he'd always known the female Council members were far more dangerous than the males.

"How many?" Ahron continued. "Too many, not enough, more every day. Who among us does not wish to be accepted and embraced for who we truly are? Who does not wish to claim that which is his or her right?" His eyes glowed bright again; he changed the subject as if he'd been yanked from one time to another. "Your mother was incredibly beautiful, when I made her one of us. She stayed beautiful for many years. Even when she was carrying you beneath her heart and her health was not at its best, she was beautiful. I wish I had given her a child, I wish I had created a powerful blood born, but it was your father, the ungrateful bastard, who got her with child." A flash of hate altered his expression for a moment. "I was finished with her by that time, I did not care who she gave her body to, but you almost killed her coming into the world. She was never quite the same after that; beautiful women are often not the best of mothers, wouldn't you agree?"

"The rebels," Luca said, trying to turn the seer's mind back to the subject at hand.

"Yes, yes, your questions. Who? I can't say. I could, but I won't. How many, eh, who can know? When does the strike begin in earnest?" Again, his eyes flashed. Chloe flinched, and Luca didn't blame her. "Stop the Warriors, lift the spell, take the city. It's a good plan. Take the government as our own, rule their army, their government, and their people. From there it will spread, one city, one state at a time."

"What spell?"

"Soon I will need no invitation," Ahron said with barely disguised glee. "The world will be my own. Every home, *every one*, will be open to me. The spell that keeps me out isn't natural, it isn't right. When the spell is broken, nothing will stop me."

A chill touched Luca's bones. It had to be the sanctuary spell. The rebels must have a witch, either captured or paid, who was strong enough to break the spell. If the sanctuary spell was broken, Chloe would never again be safe, not even in her own home. There would be no place for any mortal to hide.

Sticking close to Luca was never exactly a chore, but Chloe stayed especially close while they were in Ahron's basement home.

Luca and Sorin, even the creepy trio who'd shown up at the hotel, could easily pass as human, if they wanted. Ahron couldn't. Nothing could disguise the kryptonite eyes, the skin that looked like milk glass, the fangs that were permanently extended. He'd actually been handsome once, she could see. He had the face of a man of around twenty, she'd guess, though what that translated to aeons ago, she couldn't guess. His careful movements and white hair marked his age, and against the young face that age was really strange.

Though he moved very carefully, like an old man, she had a suspicion that if he wanted to he could be very, very fast, which was all the more reason to stay close to Luca.

Were there others like Ahron, hiding around the world? If the rebels won the world might be overrun with monsters like this one. She'd known for years that she could die at any moment, though she'd always had hope that death wouldn't come too soon. In that respect, nothing had changed; it just might not be her heart that killed her.

Ahron liked to talk, even though most of what he said was nonsense. He talked about television shows and movies, his blog—proof that anyone could have a presence on the Net if they wanted it—and those he had once known. Talk about name-dropping! Alexander, Caesar, Mozart, King Henry . . . more than one of them . . . as well as many names Chloe didn't recognize. She got the sense they'd been no less important in their time; their names simply hadn't made it into the history books.

Useful information was scattered within the rambling, like rubies hidden in a pile of worthless stones. Names, numbers, places . . . She knew when those meaningful tidbits came, because she felt a surge of energy in Luca. One name in particular—Jonas—gave him a heavy jolt.

The day dragged. Ahron would occasionally look at her and smile, but it wasn't a friendly grin. It was more of a "Hello, dinner," expression of pleasure, as if he were sitting there wondering how she'd taste. Chloe knew hours had passed because she was so hungry her stomach had begun to growl. She placed her hand over her stomach and pressed down in an effort to still the protest. She didn't think Ahron needed to be reminded of hunger in any way.

The strange creature eventually seemed to forget that he had guests. He left his chair, sat before his computer, turned it on and, talking to himself as if he were alone, began to write his blog.

Luca took Chloe's arm and led her toward the door. "I'd hoped to be able to leave you here while I—"

"No," she snapped before he had a chance to finish. "You can't leave me here."

"No, I can't. Ahron seems to be aligned in some way with the rebels."

"That, and given half a chance he'd *eat* me."

Luca looked as if he wanted to smile, but this was not funny. His humor didn't last long. "I don't know of a safe place to leave you while I hunt the rebels. Ahron mentioned Jonas, and, unfortunately, Jonas is the most talented of all the trackers." He shoved his hand through his hair. "I've worked with Jonas. I can't believe he'd go over to the rebels, that isn't his style, but I have to accept what Ahron said."

She didn't like it. At all. So, what else was new? She didn't want to be involved in this vampire, warrior, human war, with the humans getting the raw end of the deal. But she was here, smack-dab in the middle of it all. There was only one solution, one logical choice.

"Take me with you."

TWENTY-THREE

It was fully dark when they drove away from Ahron's hideout. Chloe had never been so glad to escape from anyone, or anything, in her life. That's what leaving Ahron behind felt like: blessed escape. Luca didn't say much as he drove directly to the closest airport, parked in long-term parking, then rented a minivan, which was all the rental company had available for last-minute pickup. Though Luca was definitely not a minivan guy, he didn't complain. He handed over his fake ID and took possession of the vehicle, loaded their luggage into the back, then took the fastest route to the interstate.

"Can't you be tracked by your credit card?" she asked. She was so tired she felt punch drunk.

He glanced at her and smiled, but there was no real humor on his face. Talking to Ahron had not put Luca in a good mood. "You're assuming the Council or anyone else knows all my identities."

All? "How many do you have?"

"More than enough."

"If no one remembers you after you're out of sight, then why bother to have so many . . ."

"Just a precaution," he said absently. "These days you can't sneeze without a driver's license. Having several IDs simply makes things . . . easier. In case we're spotted, we'll switch cars as often as we change hotel rooms, from here on out."

They drove back into D.C., traffic picking up as they neared the center of the city. Luca seemed to know where he was going. If he had a specific destination in mind thanks to something Ahron had said, or his own abilities, he didn't say so. She didn't ask. They were both quiet.

The clock on the dashboard read three-twenty when Luca drove into an exclusive neighborhood, where the houses were huge and set very far apart. Chloe stared out of the passenger window, on alert and also entranced. Good thing they weren't driving her car; it would stick out like a sore thumb here. The minivan wasn't a lot better, but at least it didn't chug and shudder and make weird noises. These were estates, with gated drives and security cameras and enough lights to illuminate a small city. Her high school hadn't been as big as some of these houses.

"Somehow I expected Sorin and his buds would be in a warehouse like Ahron's, with no windows, no lights, maybe a few chains for their prisoners." Their food. Yuck. But then again, she'd been food for Luca several times now, and she not only hadn't minded, she'd enjoyed it. Maybe chains weren't always required.

As they drove past one estate with a perfectly manicured and massive lawn, a three-story redbrick mansion at the end of a long drive and a couple of very impressive cars near the front entrance, a sharp, raw sensation ran through her veins and she knew that was it. Her entire body shuddered, and she couldn't catch her breath. Luca had picked up on some energy, and she was feeling the backlash. The minivan slowed, then he steadily drove past.

"He's in there, isn't he?" she asked.

"Yes. How did you know?"

"I felt it. I felt your reaction to it. It's brighter than the others, too," she said, "and the sight of it makes me feel cold to the bone. Basically, I just know."

"You're right," he said, not sounding all that happy about the news.

"It's the bonding thing, I guess. You recognize the place, so I do, too," she said, her eyes on the tall, wrought-iron gates. They were standing open, maybe because vampires came and went with regularity, maybe because they weren't at all afraid of intruders. Any robber who tried to hit that house would be in for a big surprise.

Luca rubbed his face, looking perturbed. "The bonding links us, so, yes, you'd know if I'm upset or happy or horny. It shouldn't let you *see* energy."

"Well, it does." Her voice was a little sharp. If he didn't have an explanation, she sure as hell didn't.

Luca kept driving, because, hello, to stop directly in front of a vampire hideout and walk up to the front door wouldn't be smart. He parked a half mile or so away, on a side street where the homes were slightly smaller and less impressive, though still amazing. After a moment, he got out of the minivan.

"Are you nuts?" she asked as he closed his door. A little spying from the car she could agree to, but anything more at this point was crazy. Luca didn't say anything, just circled the van and opened her door like a gentleman—or a madman, because she wasn't going anywhere. She gave him a stubborn look and stayed where she was. "I thought we were just scouting things out, getting the lay of the land. We can't just walk in and start introducing ourselves!"

"I need to see more, and you know damn well I can't leave you here alone." He offered his steady hand to her.

After a moment's hesitation, she unlatched her seat belt and took the offered hand. "Crap," she muttered. "I'll have you know I'm not entirely happy about this."

"I realize that." Of course he did.

"Shouldn't I have a weapon or something?"

"You have me."

Well, that was the truth.

"I meant like a gun, maybe."

"Tonight is just for recon. When we attack, I'll see that you're properly armed."

Attack? They were going to attack? Chloe gulped. She was in this of her own free will, as far as she knew, and still the thought of attacking a house full of vampires gave her pause. She was determined, not stupid.

They walked down the sidewalk, which was deserted at this time of morning. There were hours to go until sunrise. The humans in the neighborhood should all be asleep, while the vampires were at their peak. Did the people around here realize, at a gut-instinct level, that there were some among them who were different? Not just different, but dangerous? Man, she'd love to be a fly on the wall at their homeowner association meetings.

Luca walked fast, but not so fast that she couldn't keep up. She could tell his mind was elsewhere, just as she could feel the energy emanating off of him, almost as if he were buzzing with power. She was a little surprised he didn't glow in the dark—like Ahron's eyes. Instinctively, she shuddered at the memory. Was she ever going to get that face out of her head?

"Why are you here?" she asked, her voice soft out of respect for the night.

"Because I refuse to sit back and wait for Sorin to attack again."

"That's not what I mean and you know it." Luca was many things; dense wasn't one of them. "My reasons are pretty simple. They want me dead, and they're threatening my world and everyone in it. But you . . . why?"

He sighed. "A victory for the vampires would be the beginning of a war that would never end. Humans don't break easily, not even when fighting means death. If vampires come out into the open more humans will be turned, but a lot more will die. It'll be a blood bath, literally. The result isn't good for anyone, vampire or human. And if too many humans die, well, it's stupid to kill off your food source."

She scowled; it really pissed her off to be referred to as a *food source.* "So choosing to help me was a purely logical decision."

He paused, then said, "Not purely logical. Don't talk anymore; we're getting too close to the house."

They were still over a block away. She started to argue that no one at the house could possibly hear them, but she caught herself in time. These were vampires they were trying to sneak up on; they had super sight, super hearing, super speed—hell, super everything. Nothing got past Luca, she knew that much. She nodded, saving her other questions for later.

Walking in complete silence at such an early hour of the morning gave Chloe a decidedly creepy sensation. Once, just a few days ago, she'd enjoyed her quiet walks home from the Metro, in the early hours. Since Enoch's attack, she definitely worried about things that went bump in the night. Something rustled in the bushes to their left, and she moved closer to Luca. He didn't seem concerned, so she assumed it was a cat or something; she didn't care, so long as it was a night creature that didn't want to kill her and suck out all her blood. Or was that backward? Maybe they sucked out all the blood first and *then* killed.

With every step they took, she felt an increased anxiety, an instinctive warning to turn and run. Instead she took Luca's hand. He wrapped his fingers around her hand, holding her close. The heat and strength of his grip offered comfort, and safety.

They were still well away from the mansion when he stopped, studying, listening. From here they couldn't see anything of the house except a piece of the roof. Tall, old trees surrounded the house on all sides, shielding it, protecting it from prying eyes. That might have been one of the reasons this particular house had been selected.

Tugging on her hand, Luca led her to a wrought-iron gate leading to the house next door to the mansion. The gate was locked, but he waved his hand and the gate popped open. Just like that.

She'd have to tell him later that he'd make a great thief, if he wanted to change careers. That thought made her wonder about what sorts of jobs he'd held in the past however long he'd been alive. For all she knew he'd been a thief at one time or another. The possibilities were truly endless. When they were safely away from here, she was going to find out how old he was; no more running from it. Yes, she might feel completely inadequate after she found out, but knowing was better than guessing.

It was dark in the neighbor's garden—or what had once been a garden. The land was untended, littered with dry, dead plants and tall grass. Did being so close to the vampires next door cause the vegetation to wither, or were the neighbors just too cheap to hire a gardener? This was a bad location for a garden, even Chloe knew that. The surrounding tall trees would block the sun. And why hadn't the neighborhood association done something about this neglected lawn?

The house was dark; either everyone there was asleep, or else they'd bolted long ago, listening to their instincts to get far, far away.

Luca released her hand. She missed the touch but kept quiet. He moved silently toward the well-lit house on the other side of the tall wrought-iron fence. How close did he intend to get? What could the two of them do against an unknown number of vampires?

He moved into the shadows, and she lost sight of him. She stood there, abruptly terrified, then she felt him reach for her with his mind and she knew what to do. Closing her eyes, she focused on him and could feel him plainly, see him as well as if he were standing beside her. He wasn't that far away, anyway. He was beside the fence; he'd stopped, too, and now that she was okay he closed his eyes, took a slow, even breath, and went entirely still.

Chloe hugged her arms, finding the warm night suddenly chilly. If she moved closer to Luca she'd make all kinds of noise; being around him made her feel clumsy, all because she was human. She also knew she needed to stop thinking, because her mental chatter might distract him.

She calmed herself, blanking her mind, leaving only a small thread of connection so he'd know she was all right. She couldn't have said how she knew to do that, she just did it. As she did, her senses seemed to open up more, the night becoming full of noises she had never heard before. She felt something inside her go still and quiet, and in that quiet screamed the voice from her dreams:

"Run!"

The warning was too late. She knew it, felt them coming, and instead of running, which would have separated her from Luca, she leapt toward him, closing the distance between them faster than she'd thought possible. With the suddenness that still surprised her, even though it shouldn't have, three vampires seemed to lunge out of the sky to surround her and Luca; the fence was behind them, the three vampires—two men and a very tall woman—in front of them. They had nowhere to go. At least, Chloe didn't. Luca could fly, she thought. He could get out of here. He was a blood born, he was probably faster and stronger than these three. *"Go,"* she whispered to him in her mind. She didn't know if the bond between them extended to actual words, so she wished him gone as hard as she could wish. He would fight for her, one against three, and he'd be killed—all for nothing, because then they'd kill her, too. Better that Luca lived, than that neither of them did.

He didn't budge, and she felt a distinct blast of anger at her because she'd tried to make him go.

He didn't seem surprised by the presence of the three vampires. He said calmly, "I'm here to see Sorin. He's expecting me."

The big female ignored Luca and nodded to a large, unattractive, massively fanged vampire who didn't appear to Chloe to be of the same species as Luca. He looked more animal than man. "Kill the conduit," the female said, and the ugly monster sprang, surprisingly agile for one who looked like nothing more than a lumbering beast.

Luca threw himself between the pouncing vampire and Chloe, hitting the attacker in midair, the impact sending them both flying away from Chloe. He had only a bare second of surprise before the other two acted, so he didn't waste that second. Grabbing the ugly vampire by his head and twisting hard, he ripped the vampire's head off and tossed it aside, all before they hit the ground. The two pieces of vampire quickly went to dust that was caught in the night breeze.

Luca rolled to his feet, turned, and saw the female change positions so Chloe was between them. The female had a Teutonic look, a strength in both features and body that few women had, vampire or not. The other male was young and apparently inexperienced, because he stood back with a slight expression of panic on his face. That expression said it all: this was more than he'd bargained for. But he moved to a position that triangulated Chloe between him and the female, then he looked at the other vampire for direction.

She ignored him, and took a different approach. She smiled, looked Chloe in the eye, and whispered, "Stand still for me, dear." She reached out a hand.

Chloe backed away and glanced toward Luca with terror in her eyes. The young one, threatening at the moment or not, stood between Chloe and the only reasonable escape route, not that Luca expected her to take it. She wouldn't leave him, any more than he'd have been able to leave her.

Then she looked back at the big female and said, "Fuck you."

The vampire actually jerked in surprise, then recovered and leapt, lips pulled back, fangs prominent, hand drawn up as if to swipe down with great force. Her nails were long, curved, more claws than fingernails. She was all teeth and claws, as if she fully intended to take a big chunk, and a long drink, out of her target.

That flash of surprise cost her precious time. Luca collided with her in midair, too, taking her down. She was stronger than the male, and a smarter fighter. She did her best to give him a good fight; her nails ripped his cheek as she tried to get his head in her grip. In the night, her eyes glowed blood red. She was old, old and experienced, but she wasn't as old as Luca, or as powerful. He broke her hold, flipped over her head so he landed behind her, and removed her head as he had the other's. For a moment it was a messy, bloody, unpleas-

ant sight, and then with a final scream from the de-
tached head, she went to dust.

He whirled on the remaining vampire, and froze.
While he'd been dealing with the female vampire, the
young one had seized Chloe. He had Chloe in a common choke hold, his wide, terrified gaze fastened on
Luca.

"You don't understand," the young rebel said, his
voice high and quick. "She's a conduit. They're going
to mess up everything if we don't take care of them.
You can get another human. There're a lot of them,
prettier than this one."

"How did you know we were here?"

The young vampire was surprised into answering.
"Jonas. He knew where you were."

Jonas. *Dammit!* He wasn't surprised that Jonas was
there—not only had Ahron mentioned it during their
rambling conversation, but when they'd arrived Luca
had searched for, and found, Jonas's essence in the
mansion. It did surprise him that Jonas would have
sicced the hounds on him; they'd worked together a lot
in the past, and if they weren't exactly friends, they'd at
least been friendly. Jonas was the most talented remote
tracker Luca knew. Changing hotels and cars wasn't
going to do them a damn bit of good if Jonas told Sorin
their every move.

"Do you know Jonas?" the fledgling asked. "He's
like . . . a pretty good guy, really. Works nonstop. He
said a conduit was very close, so, you know, we decided
we'd try to stop her. That's what we're here for, right?
I mean, if we could take out one that got so close to
headquarters maybe Sorin would make us real hunters
instead of grunts and guards." His voice wavered. "It
was a good idea."

Too bad the good idea hadn't worked out, Luca
thought. He asked, "Why didn't I sense you sooner?"

The vampires had been on them before he'd known they were coming.

The fledgling swallowed, hesitated. Luca stared into those wide, frightened eyes, reaching deep. His power of influence didn't work very well on vampires unless they were very new, or very weak. This one was both. It wasn't glamouring, not technically, but the influence was much the same. He asked the question again. "Why didn't I sense the three of you coming?"

"It was her." The young vampire gestured with a nod toward the pile of dust that had once been the female attacker, but he never took his eyes off Luca; if he had, he'd have forgotten that he wasn't alone with Chloe, that Luca was there at all. "She can shield almost anything. Well, she *could* shield almost anything, before you ripped off her head." He shuddered "We didn't know *you* were here, but Loman said we should be careful so she projected her shielding thing, and—"

"Who else knows we're here? Sorin? The other rebels?"

The kid shook his head. "No one. There wasn't any time. The three of us were close when Jonas called, and he said we had to hurry. And like I said, we were hoping to make an impression." He moved, and suddenly Luca could see both his hands; one held Chloe, the other held a long blade.

"A knife?" Luca asked with real incredulity. "You're a vampire. You don't need a weapon." He kept the kid's gaze locked with his, willing him to keep talking. He could feel Chloe's terrified gaze on him but he had to lock her terror away, keep it from affecting him, or he wouldn't be able to do what had to be done. He couldn't let himself think he might lose her.

"The hunters aren't supposed to leave too many clues when they kill the conduits, so, you know, humans won't figure out what's up before we're ready," the young vampire said nervously. "A knife just seemed like a good idea. Besides, I haven't been immortal long enough to be as strong as most of our kind. I don't have a gift yet," he said, almost whining.

"You should know by now that you are not immortal in the strictest sense of the word. If I take your head you'll be no more *immortal* than these other two."

He could kill the fledgling. He had the kid under enough control now that he could take him down without Chloe being so much as scratched. Luca started to do it, then had a better idea. He pushed deeper into the kid's mind. The vampire's arms dropped to his sides, and Chloe stumbled to the ground. In half a second she was up, lunging for Luca, moving a bit faster, crisper, than had been possible before they'd bonded. He caught her soft body against his, clamped her to his side, but didn't give her so much as a glance, not yet. He held the fledgling's watery gaze.

"Are you going to kill me?" the kid asked.

Luca smiled and said, "No. Not tonight."

Melody was worried. If Sorin found out she'd drained Jim Elliott—against orders—she was going to be in big trouble. The biggest, most final kind of trouble. She shivered a little as an unexpected rush of panic tickled her spine. She'd rarely experienced fear in her new life, but this moment was definitely fear-worthy. She might be Sorin's child, and maybe he still liked her a little bit, but if he found out she'd jeopardized the rebels' plans with her hunger she'd be dust before she had a chance to argue her case.

In her defense, she'd been hungry, and the human had been right there. How any vampire in his right mind could expect her to walk away from all that gorgeous blood, she didn't know. She hadn't been completely careless; when she'd realized what she'd done she'd tried to cover up the scene with a fire. After all, once a human was dead, healing the wounds left by her fangs was impossible. Dead was dead; *nothing* on a dead body was going to heal. Fire had worked before, when she'd gotten carried away, eating up all the evidence, so she hadn't seen any reason why it wouldn't work a second time. Maybe she should've stuck around to make sure everything had burned up: how was she supposed to know some nosy neighbors would call the fire department right away. That was a mistake she would not make again.

Using ordinary weapons to kill the conduits was a waste of her strength and hunger, but maybe from here on out she'd just do as she'd been told. She could use a knife on the younger Elliott, she imagined, or break his neck and toss him off a building. She needed to take care of him soon, so Sorin and the crazy bitch wouldn't check too closely into the botched mess she'd made of the first Jim Elliott. She didn't like being afraid.

She straightened her spine, thrust out her breasts, and reminded herself of who she was: a beauty queen who would never grow old and wrinkly, a woman who could hypnotize men without even bothering to call on her glamouring talents, a powerful vampire who could damn near rule the world. Her world, at least.

If she wanted to remain a part of that world, there could be no more mistakes.

Jimmy woke much earlier than he should've, considering how long it had taken him to fall asleep. Could he function on the day of his father's funeral on two hours of sleep? Looked as if he'd have to, like it or not.

Hell, he hadn't even made it to bed. He'd fallen asleep on the sectional sofa in the Lessers' basement/playroom, just a few feet from an air hockey table. Kate was asleep upstairs, but he'd been so restless he'd stayed down here for a while, then accidentally fell asleep. Now he felt jumpy, his skin actually crawling with goose bumps that had nothing to do with the temperature.

He plopped down in a recliner that faced the flat-screen TV. If he didn't think the noise would wake everyone upstairs, he'd play a video game or watch a DVD, maybe find a late-night—well, early-morning—movie on the TV. Instead he sat there in silence and pondered what Kate had suggested. Maybe it was true.

Vampires.

His common sense told him that wasn't possible, but lately common sense had gone out the window, not that he could give much weight to the blog he'd found. *Van Helsing, my ass.* But there were things he couldn't ignore, like all his dad's blood being gone, the wounds on his neck, the warnings in Kate's cards, and Jimmy's dreams that something was very wrong . . . what if it was all true? What if a vampire had killed Jim Elliott?

If he could accept that—which he couldn't quite do, even though he couldn't dismiss the idea either—then the next question was: Why? Why here and now? If people died that way every day you'd think it would be common knowledge. They themselves only knew about it because the fire had been put out so quickly. Maybe some towns had top-notch CSIs and coroners who didn't miss much, who could study a bit of residue and declare the cause of death with certainty, but in a small town those assets were as much fiction as vampires. Well, if vampires truly were fiction . . .

The television flickered on, then off again, startling Jimmy and making him jump. What the hell? He got up and searched the chair to see if he was sitting on the remote; if his butt could call people on his cell, it could probably turn on the television, too. But there wasn't a remote in the chair; they were all were lined up on the coffee table. He sat back down, leaned back and tried to relax. He closed his eyes; he hadn't had nearly enough sleep. Maybe he'd imagined it. Maybe he'd dozed off after all, and just dreamed the blink of light and sound.

Against his closed eyelids, light flickered. His eyes popped open. The television clicked on, then off. Then it came on again. The channel switched to an informercial where a man was hawking kitchen appliances. "Every home needs one of these . . ." The television went crazy again, flipping through channels, ending on an old movie. "Tonight, it all happens tonight whether you like it or not. Trust me . . ." Again, with the channel switching, this time ending very briefly on a war movie. ". . . surrender . . ."

Holy shit! What the fuck was happening? Jimmy's hair stood on end and he looked wildly around, but there was no one else there, just him and this television set, which was apparently possessed.

The television channel went back to the infomercial, and the same words repeated. "Every home needs one of these . . ." On to the old movie: "Tonight, it all happens tonight . . ." then to the war movie. Over and over, as if the television were repeating a code.

A code. He felt an electric wash of energy all over his body. Crap, was it possible? He leaned forward again, forgetting about the impossibility of what was happening, concentrating on the words. Was it a message? From his father? The spirit guide Kate said he had around him all the time? Someone—some*thing*—else?

"I need you . . ." ". . . acceptance . . ." "It's time . . ." "Now." " . . . now . . ." ". . . now."

He found himself on his feet. There was an unnatural glow off to the side, well away from the flickering television. And he knew, with a certainty he couldn't explain, that this was it. He could fight whoever or whatever was speaking to him through reruns,

infomercials, and old movies, or he could accept. If it
hadn't been for Kate, he had no idea what he'd have
done, but knowing her gave him the courage to face
that glow.

"Who are you?" he asked, afraid but determined.

The television went crazy again, finally ending back
on the war movie, where a man was shouting the word,
"Soldier!"

"Did you kill my father?"

From three different channels, the answers came.
"No." ". . . never . . ." "I wouldn't . . ."

This was either the most real, most bizarre dream
he'd ever had, or else his world had once more been
turned upside down.

He remembered some of what Kate had told him
about her beliefs, her experiences, the precautions she
took when she was trying to contact the other side.
"Are you good?" he asked. "Are you a godly spirit?"

The responses came fast and furious. ". . . I am."
"Yes, you moron!" followed by canned laughter.
"Yeah, that's the way . . ." ". . . forever."

"Fine, then," he muttered. "What am I supposed to
do?" He wanted someone to tell him what was going
on, he wanted not to be guessing anymore. He wanted
and needed a few concrete answers. He hadn't gotten
many of those lately.

This time the response wasn't as easy as the others
had been. The channels changed quickly, wildly,
before stopping long enough for one word to be
heard. ". . . you . . ." Again, channels flew past before
stopping for a second. "Must . . ." Jimmy stood very still,
he waited patiently as whatever was speaking to him
continued to search for the right word. " . . . believe."
" . . . accept . . . " and finally one word that was louder
than the rest. It seemed to resonate through him, to
touch his gut and his bones. *Ask!*

The television went silent and dark. Jimmy could still see the strange light that had tormented him lately, but now it felt more peaceful, stronger. And somehow, his. A word that had been just out of reach—a *name* he had never heard before—popped into his head, and he knew that name was a very important part of the puzzle.

He took a deep breath and said a quick prayer that he was making the right decision "Please," he said softly, "help me. Whoever you are, wherever you're coming from, I invite you into my world." Was he wrong? Were these the right words? He was feeling his way, as if he was putting a puzzle together in the dark. Was he inviting in something wrong, something that didn't belong here? No, what was coming was meant to be, was in some way a part of him. He squared his shoulders. "If you're a good spirit, someone sent to help, then please, come. Come, Rurik."

The light grew brighter, colors swirled through the bright light. Blue, red, green, even a coppery brown. Then the light kind of exploded; he threw up his arm to shield his eyes but he was a little late, and the flash momentarily blinded him.

When he could see again, he blinked hard, then blinked some more. Holy shit! He could barely breathe. Where the lights had been, there was now a man, kneeling on one knee, his head down: a big, flesh-and-blood man, wearing something plain and brown, but with a big sword strapped to his back. Long dark hair fell forward, hiding the man's face. Jimmy's heart was pounding so hard he could actually hear it, actually feel it, the blood throbbing through his body. He didn't know what he'd been expecting, but this wasn't it.

The man lifted his head, revealing his face. It was a face that reminded Jimmy a little of pictures of his grandfather as a younger man: the nose, the mouth, the dark eyes. These dark eyes were leveled at Jimmy. The man—the soldier, Rurik—effortlessly rose to his full height, which had to be a good six-foot-four.

And he spoke, with a touch of what sounded like a Russian accent. "We are running out of time. We need more."

Sorin glared at the young vamp, not believing what he'd just heard. They stood in the room where Jonas was being held, ignoring the tracker as he ran from map to map, from notes to laptop, and then back to the map. Poor Jonas was stretched to his limit.

"Tell me again," Sorin said, his command directed to the fledgling. God, was he surrounded by idiots? Was this what Regina gave him to work with? If this was the best the rebels had, they were doomed.

"Loman and Freda said they didn't want to do this anymore, they think we're going to lose, and they left. They"—he swallowed hard—"They both deserted. Freda said something about France. They wanted me to tell you, and I didn't want to tell you, but . . . but . . . but I'm not a deserter."

The last thing he needed was word about this getting out, Sorin thought furiously. Freda and Loman had both been with the revolution from the outset. They weren't among the best, but he'd thought they were at least *dedicated*. If the others heard that they had bailed, it wouldn't be good for morale.

"Where were the three of you when this happened?" Maybe there was something the fledgling wasn't telling . . . or didn't know.

"Jonas said there was a conduit nearby. Like, really close. He yelled out and we heard him. The three of us were just outside the door, so we . . ."

Sorin turned to Jonas, who was more frantic than usual tonight. "Is this true?"

"Maybe I was wrong," Jonas said, not looking toward Sorin but continuing his work. "There was *something* very near, an energy I couldn't quite read. I thought conduit, but then it was gone and it was too late for me to call them back, and since I'm locked in this room, a prisoner among my own kind doing the work of half a dozen trackers, there wasn't a whole hell of a lot I could do," he finished bitterly.

The man had a right to be bitter. And what choice did Sorin have but to believe him? They'd never spoken of it, but Jonas had actually covered up Phillip Stargel's survival. Sorin hadn't even asked, it had just been done. With a glance Jonas had made it clear that he understood . . . and that he wouldn't tell. If Jonas had told Regina that a New York conduit still lived Sorin would be, at the very least, ousted; at worst, dust. As it was, a black pin had been stuck in the map, marking the place of Phillip's "death." Because Jonas had kept that secret, there was an uneasy bond of trust between them, at least for now.

Sorin turned to the young soldier again. "So the three of you went looking for a nonexistent conduit." He wasn't sure he believed that, but for now it would do.

"Yeah. We looked for a while, and then Loman said he was bored, and Freda said this revolution wasn't going the way she'd thought it would, and they started talking about France and . . . that was it."

"And you didn't go with them," Sorin said.

The soldier fiddled with his earlobe. "They, uh, didn't ask me." He quickly caught himself. "And like I said, I'm no deserter."

Distracted as he was by the bad news, Sorin couldn't help but notice Jonas's sudden stillness. He'd been running back and forth all night, talking to himself, making notes. Now he stood still and silent in the middle of the small room.

"What's wrong?" Sorin snapped. "Do you need to feed?" Maybe he'd simply run out of steam and needed nourishment.

Jonas shook his head, then walked to his box of pins. He dug through, chose one, then walked slowly to the map of the United States. Without hesitation he stuck a white pin, the first on the map, into Texas.

"It's begun," Jonas said. "A warrior has arrived."

CHAPTER TWENTY-FOUR

Chloe couldn't stop shaking. She'd tried. She'd attempted to force herself to quit trembling from head to toe, to take total control of her body, but it didn't work.

Knowing what she did, she shouldn't be surprised that they'd been jumped by three vampires, but accepting that a battle was coming and watching as vampires intent on killing her leapt out of the night with scary-ass teeth bared were worlds apart. Yes, Luca had protected her. And yes, the attacking vampires had eventually gone to dust, which sounded so neat and clean but really wasn't. Unfortunately, the transformation from headless to dust wasn't immediate.

There had been a too-long moment of grossness, as well as severed heads that continued to see and tried to talk for a split second, which was about a split second plus a million years too long. And whatever magic or biology that had made the vampires' blood conveniently disappear along with the bodies did *not* extend to the blood that had soaked Luca when he'd pulled their heads off. He'd been covered in it, his shirt and face and hair, even his jeans. So much blood . . . Just what she needed to make the day complete; the sight of the man she was sleeping with, the man she'd trusted her life to, soaked in the blood of vampires who'd tried to kill her.

At least they had clothes in the van, so as soon as they'd found a secluded spot after leaving the posh neighborhood that would forever have a place in Chloe's nightmares, Luca had pulled to the side of the road, changed his clothes, and done his best with what he had to clean his face and hands.

It was near sunrise when they checked into a hotel, chosen because it had an underground garage and sat at the intersection of two major roads, making for an easier escape if they had to make one. In the light of the lobby Chloe could see specks of blood Luca had missed in his hasty clean-up, but the desk clerk didn't seem to notice. It was a glamouring thing, she knew. Luca made sure the hotel employee didn't see anything that would alarm him.

She remained alarmed, however, whenever she looked at Luca and saw a streak of red in his dark hair, or that smudge of blood under his jaw.

They didn't have a suite this time, just a room with a big bed, a television, and one uncomfortable-looking chair. The heavy curtains, which they could pull over the window, was the best thing about the room. Not that it mattered; they wouldn't be here long. Tomorrow they'd have to move again, and then the next day . . . again. She wasn't going to bother to unpack this time.

Temporary or not, she was grateful for the four walls around her, glad for the comfort of this home away from home.

Which brought another thought to the forefront of her mind. "Can they come in here?" she asked. "Without invitation, I mean?"

"I'll protect you."

She took that as a firm "yes."

"You couldn't just lie and tell me we'd be safe here for a while," she grumbled.

"Of course not." He sounded remote, as if something was on his mind. Well, that wasn't surprising, but Chloe felt shut out, and unreasonably hurt.

They both headed for the small bathroom, driven by the same urge. Luca needed to get the remaining blood off his skin, out of his hair. Chloe wanted to wash the stink of Ahron's airless home from her skin and the memory of the attack from her mind.

As she quickly peeled off her clothes, Chloe worked up her courage and asked, "Are you going to make me forget what happened?" *Please?* Yesterday, or even just hours ago, she wouldn't have asked, she would have simply gone into his arms. This new distance she felt in him was intimidating, as if she trespassed on some private ground.

Luca, stripping off his clothes much faster than she could, didn't look directly at her. "No," he said tersely as he reached into the shower and turned on the water.

"Why not?"

"Because you don't need to be relaxed. You need to remember that you aren't safe."

"I'm safe with you." Wasn't she? After all, he'd taken care of three vampires in order to save her. He'd killed two and sent the other one running home with his mind muddled and his tail between his legs, figuratively speaking.

"Not really."

She swallowed an impulse to cry and, using sheer willpower, pulled herself under control. Had she done something wrong? If he'd already gotten tired of her, it had come on fast, because before the attack he'd been holding her hand. Now he acted as if he couldn't bear to look at her. What had happened?

She stepped into the shower; Luca was right behind her. She turned her back on him and lifted her face to the water, willing herself to not think about anything.

For a moment, it worked; for a long, wonderful moment they stood there, sharing the strong, hot spray of water that could wash away some of what had happened. Blood, sweat, dust . . . but not memories. She glanced down, watching the swirl of pink water as the remaining blood was washed away, staring as all that was left of the vampires who had tried to kill her disappeared down the drain.

If only she could go back in time and forget all that she knew! In just a few short days, her world had been turned completely upside down. Vampires, conduits, warriors . . . in many ways she wanted to be blissfully ignorant again, with no worries beyond making rent and preparing for her parents' upcoming visit. She hadn't asked for this, hadn't asked to be bonded to some super vampire. Then again, Luca hadn't asked for it either, and he kept risking his life for her, kept putting himself between her and everything that threatened her. If it weren't for vampire rebels and Immortal Warriors, they never would've met. But going back would mean she'd never met him, and knowing Luca, being a part of his life, was worth any risk she could think of.

Besides, she thought, shaking herself back to reality, time travel wasn't an option . . . as far as she knew. Wouldn't that be a trip? What else existed in the world that she didn't know about? If there were vampires, and warriors who lived in another world just waiting to step into this one, what else existed just beyond her knowing? She didn't want to find out, not right now. Whatever was wrong between her and Luca, she wanted to put it right.

She turned around, reached up, and touched Luca's face. The female vampire had scratched him, leaving long, deep, ragged furrows in his cheek, but all the evidence was gone now. She'd watched it heal before her eyes, closing up, his perfect skin reknitting. After a short while even the scar had faded away and his face was as smooth now as it had been before.

"When this is over, if we both survive, will you make me forget you the way others forget?" she asked sadly.

"If I can."

She wasn't surprised by his answer. In all honesty, she'd like to forget the terror, but she didn't want to forget him. Which would she choose, to feel safe again, or to have Luca? It went against her common sense, but given the choice, she wanted Luca. She had never supposed he'd stay with her her entire life, but at least she wanted to remember him, to keep the memory of him in her mind as well as her heart.

"You don't belong in my life and I don't belong in yours," he said.

"So when this is all over, if we survive and the vampires don't change everything, I'll forget all about you, and you'll forget me . . ."

"I won't forget you." His words were sharper than was necessary. "Ever."

"Because of the bonding." She'd known he was reluctant to bond with her, but had she truly realized how much it would cost him? She knew she couldn't bear the thought of losing him.

"It doesn't make any sense at all to care for a human," he growled. Water ran down his face, across his finely sculpted lips. It looked as if the last of the blood had finally washed away. No pink rivulets ran down his body; it had all washed down the drain, gone but not forgotten. Never forgotten. "You don't live long enough to warrant the investment."

That was pretty damn cold. If she hadn't been able to hear the anger and confusion in his voice, she'd have been crushed. After all, bonding with her had been *his* suggestion. It wasn't as if she'd even known such a thing was possible.

"Damn you," she said, and went up on her toes and kissed him. After the night she'd had, it didn't seem too much to ask: a kiss, a physical connection that could make her forget everything that had happened and what still might come. Luca was the one pleasure in a very unpleasant day . . . week . . . *life*. He was the one good thing to come out of her world being turned upside down.

For the first time, she fully accepted that she might not live to see the end of this war. Was that really any different from the life she'd lived to this point? Since she'd found out about the aneurysm, she'd known her life was uncertain. But for right now, she had this, and she had Luca.

No matter what it cost her, she didn't want to give him up.

Maybe it was the bonding thing that made her so easily able to let go of all reservations. Once she and Luca touched they were one mind, one body. She felt his heartbeat, their breath was in sync, her desire and his were the same. She touched him, and all his reserve fell away. There was no awkwardness when she wrapped her arms around his waist and pressed her body against his, no fumbling, no second thoughts as the kiss deepened and he wrapped his arms around her. There was just him, the two of them together, their mouths clinging hungrily together, a meeting of skin beneath the spray of hot water.

Before she got entirely lost in sensation, Chloe had one last thought: it was worth every moment of terror she'd experienced to find Luca. He was worth the pain, the anxiety, even worth her life.

He lifted her up, pinned her to the shower wall with the hard press of his body. He nipped at her throat, at her breasts, drawing drops of blood that he then licked away. There was no pain when he bit her, just a rush of pleasure, a deep tingling that shot through her body, a feeling of rightness in a place and time when it seemed that *nothing* was right.

Chloe Fallon, who was always so level-headed, who lived in the real world, who never leapt without looking fully and carefully, had no second thoughts about giving everything she had and everything she was to Luca.

He was tired, but before he slept Luca propped himself on his elbow and watched Chloe for a while. The heavy curtains blocked out most of the light, making the room so dark he'd have no trouble sleeping. The Do Not Disturb sign was hanging on the door handle, so the maids wouldn't bother them. There was no way to be certain they were completely safe, but he had to sleep, and there was no way he'd go off and leave Chloe alone.

He was completely pissed off. It wasn't just the bonding. That was bad enough, but the fact that he'd even *thought* of offering bonding to her should have alerted him. There was nothing he could do about it now, though.

She was human. She was frail, mortal, delicate, and wouldn't live nearly long enough. He'd been in love before. Love always ran its course, in time. It changed, morphed, died. A relationship with a human had always been impossible, but now it wasn't, and he was caught.

It was too late. Love was rarely logical. Sometimes love was a choice, and other times it wasn't. Sometimes it fell on a man like a ton of bricks, whether he wanted it to or not. She was human, he would inevitably lose her . . . and he loved her.

Fuck.

* * *

Nevada crawled into bed. She couldn't keep her eyes open any longer. With the windows in her room boarded up, she hadn't had a true sense of time since being brought here. She hadn't been kidding when she'd told Sorin that she wanted a clock, though he hadn't brought one. Still, the days and nights usually unfolded naturally enough. She slept when she was tired, she worked when the vampires were most active, which she assumed was after dark and before dawn. The house that sometimes bustled had grown quieter in the past little while, so she could assume it was morning. Not that it mattered; the magic and the excitement of seeing her family, too briefly, had drained her.

She was scared, as well. Sorin knew she'd been up to something, he just didn't know what. If he found out she could travel beyond these walls, if he knew she could see her family and actually speak to Emily—if he found out she was capable of spying on them all, she'd be dead before her body hit the floor.

She *was* going to die. She'd accepted that long ago. But not until she saw her family free, dammit! And somehow she had to find a way *not* to let Sorin and Loman and others of their kind loose on the world. Whatever she did, she knew it wouldn't go over well with her captors. No, she didn't have much of a chance at all. She might as well not even hope for a happy ending.

Tired as she was, eyes heavy and scratchy, Nevada lay in the bed unable to sleep. Her heart was beating hard, her mind raced. She'd love to peek in on her family again, or allow her spirit to roam the building, searching, listening for clues as to how she might see her family freed, but she was too tired for magic, too exhausted to do anything except lie in bed, wishing for sleep and blinking tears from her eyes.

There had been a time when she'd slept in complete

darkness, secure in her own room, certain that nothing could touch her. That had been before she'd been taken, before she'd known who she was and what she could do . . . before she'd known that monsters were real. Now she slept with the bathroom light on and the door wide open, and a table lamp on—two lights shining, in case a lightbulb burned out in the night. She didn't want to be in the dark ever again, didn't want the freakily silent vampires to sneak up on her, not even Sorin. Maybe *especially* not Sorin.

Not that seeing the vampires coming would change where this was going. The end was coming. She felt it; she even embraced it. But was that end for her alone, or was it also coming for everything and everyone she loved?

If he hadn't seen it with his own eyes, he never would've believed it. Jimmy followed the sword-toting man up the basement stairs, through the house, out the front door, where the sky was just turning gray with dawn.

Once outside, the man stopped, lifted his head, took a deep breath and slowly exhaled, as if the air smelled wonderful to him. Then he turned to Jimmy, his expression hard and serious. "We will need an army."

"Uh, I don't exactly have one of those handy. Who the hell are you?" He'd asked that question before, but hadn't gotten an answer.

"I am Rurik."

"Yeah, I kinda figured that out for myself, but that doesn't really answer the question." A name didn't *begin* to answer all his questions. "I'm Jimmy, by the way. Jimmy Elliott."

"I know," Rurik responded impatiently. "You are my—" He paused, his brow furrowed. "You are mine," he finished.

Oookay. Let's don't go there. "Why are you here?"

"To stop the vampires. To turn the tide. Without us, they will win."

Jimmy scratched his jaw. He shouldn't be surprised that Kate had been right. Vampires. He'd really wanted to believe that she was wrong on this one. "Without *who*?"

The sky was coming alive, the day beginning. The lightening sky washed across the strong lines of the man's face as he answered. "The warriors who serve mankind for all eternity."

"But . . ."

"No more questions." Rurik turned toward the rising sun. "You must take me to Washington, D.C."

"My father's funeral is—"

"You will honor your father after the battle is done." Rurik turned his head and glared at Jimmy. "You will honor his death by defeating those who took his life. Do you have a weapon?"

"Hell no!" Jimmy responded, glancing at the hilt of the warrior's sword.

"You will need one."

"I'm not . . . that's not . . . I think there's been a mistake. I'm not a warrior."

Rurik smiled. It was white and wide and terrifying. "You will be before I am finished with you."

Melody was lying back on the hard hotel bed, waiting out the daylight hours, waiting for sleep to come, plotting how she might kill Jimmy Elliott the younger, when her cell phone rang. She couldn't drain him, she reminded herself. There would be no more draining the conduits. She repeated that a couple of times, making it a mantra. From here on out she'd follow the rules. She'd have to, if she wanted to keep her head. She simply wouldn't drink from the conduits at all, that way she couldn't get carried away.

The cell rang again, and she grabbed it from the bed-side table, smiled when she saw Sorin's number. She missed him. Maybe he was a hard man—a hard vam-pire in the midst of hard vampires—but he was also hot. And great in bed. And powerful. With the coming of a new order, it couldn't hurt to align herself with someone who was up there from the get-go.

"Miss me?" she asked as she answered the phone.

"You're too late," Sorin snapped.

"Too late for what?"

"The conduit you were sent to kill has brought his warrior through."

Melody sat up, no longer at all tired. Daytime or not, she was fully awake. "Well, crapola. What do I do now?"

"He'll be coming here," Sorin said. "He'll *try*. It's your job to make sure he doesn't make it."

The one window in the room was covered with lined curtains, but Melody could see the tiny crack of light that edged the fabric. Daylight had arrived in full force.

"I'm not strong enough to go out in the daytime."

"You'd better get strong enough," Sorin said, his voice so soft she almost couldn't hear him. "You can't let the warrior have a twelve-hour head start."

"He can't fly, either without a plane or on one, not without ID and such. He won't have time for rounding up a fake ID if he's already headed your way," Melody said as she swung her legs over the side of the bed and stood. "He'll be traveling by car, maybe with his con-duit, maybe on his own, if he knows how to drive. Can Jonas still pinpoint him?"

"Yes."

"Good." Melody threw her small suitcase onto the bed and opened it. The clothing she'd packed for this trip wasn't sufficient for her to go out in the daytime, since most of her outfits were designed to show a lot of skin, but she'd manage. She'd call the front desk. With a decent enough tip or a touch of glamouring, she could get someone to make a trip to WalMart for long pants, a floppy hat, a scarf, and gloves. The sparkly flip-flops she'd packed wouldn't do, either. She couldn't let the sun touch her toes. Talk about ruining a pedicure! "I won't be at my best today, but I can make some headway." She didn't have any choice. "I'll finish the job tonight."

"You'd better, or don't bother coming back."

Melody wasn't smiling, but she tried to put a hint of good humor into her voice. "Come on, sugar, you wouldn't hurt me. I'm your own child."

"You're right. I couldn't kill you."

Now Melody managed a smile.

"But neither would I stop Regina from doing it."

Sorin ended the call without even a simple "good-bye." Great. Both as a human and a vampire, Melody had always been on much better terms with males than she had with females. Women never liked her; men always did. Regina wouldn't hesitate to take Melody out if the warrior she'd been assigned to stop reached D.C.

Which meant if she didn't complete her task tonight, she might as well get her ass as far away from Washington as possible. Not that she wasn't going to try to do as she'd been ordered; the idea of being with Sorin was too attractive to give up without at least trying.

Melody put her cell on the bedside table, picked up the hotel phone, and dialed the front desk. She wished she had the power of Voice, the way some older vampires did, but she had to be looking into her subject's eyes when she glamoured them. Luckily, she didn't need any special powers to get men to do as she asked. All she had to do was get one of them to her door, and then she could do her thing and get what she needed.

"Hey, honey," she said in a friendly tone, wondering if the man who answered the phone was the same one who'd checked her in, not too long ago. She hoped so; he'd been checking out her boobs and wouldn't hesitate to rush to her room to get another look. "I need a really big favor . . ."

TWENTY-FIVE

Luca woke early. Chloe slept against his side, her soft breath brushing over his chest, his arm around her. The sweet scent of her filled his senses. Lying there with her, he felt dangerously content. Contentment had no place in a battle; it dulled the edge that kept him alive. But with her, at this moment, he was content.

He allowed himself only a few moments to savor the feeling, then he turned his thoughts to Jonas. It bothered him that Jonas was involved with the rebels. Maybe he shouldn't be surprised, but he was. Not only surprised, but worried, and with good reason. Jonas was capable of locating anyone, anytime. Which made him wonder: If Jonas had detected Chloe's energy outside the rebel compound, why hadn't he also realized that she wasn't alone? That Luca, whose energy signature Jonas knew well and would surely recognize, was also nearby?

He had to at least consider the possibility that Jonas had known very well that he was sending those three vampires toward Luca, and that he hadn't warned them they'd have something more than just a human to deal with. Was he working with the rebels or against them? That was two strong vampires dead and a weak one neutralized, and Luca didn't imagine the rebels had a lot of members to spare.

Unexpected violence aside, the night had been successful. He'd gotten what he'd been looking for. He knew where the rebels were gathered, he had a good idea of their numbers, and he'd confirmed for himself that Jonas was involved. While he didn't have a precise number, he'd detected enough energy within the mansion to realize that even with his enhanced abilities, he couldn't take on that many vampires by himself.

Calling in the Council was out of the question. He didn't trust them; hell, he'd turned them away when they'd tracked him down. Even Theodore, who'd sent him the warning to stay away from headquarters, wasn't entirely trustworthy. The majority of Council members were likely steadfast and intent on stopping the revolution, dedicated to maintaining order as they knew it. The problem was, he didn't know who those particular Council members were, and when dealing with vampires as individually powerful as they were, even he used caution. One on one he could handle them; if two of them came after him, that was a different story.

He had slept for several hours, enough to feel refreshed. The bedroom wasn't quite as dark as he'd have liked, but the morning had been overcast and the curtains were thickly lined, so he'd rested well enough. He could have slept in the bathroom, but then he wouldn't have Chloe curled against him. That was enough to make enduring the light worthwhile.

She was sleeping deep, hard, worn out by the long hours and brutal violence. Between the excitement, the sex, and the fear for her life, she'd been emotionally drained and physically tested. He looked down at her sleeping face, feeling the hot ties of the bonding, both emotional and physical. If not for her he might be back in Scotland by now, letting this drama play out without him.

Wouldn't he?

No. For one thing, he'd never been able to keep his distance from a good battle. For another, a traitor had murdered Hector, and that alone called for vengeance. With or without Chloe, Luca had chosen his side.

By late afternoon, Chloe still slept on. It was still hours until summer sunset, but periodically he closed his eyes, stilled himself, and searched for vampire energy anywhere close to their hotel. A couple of times he felt a brush of energy, but it wasn't close by and was soon gone, so their location was still safe. He'd let her rest as long as he could.

He sat in the single chair in the room with his cell phone in hand, thinking. He was a part of the vampire community; he wasn't the most social of the kindred, but he did have a few friends he could call on in an emergency, and this was definitely an emergency. He couldn't afford to waste time. With every hour that passed, the odds increased that Jonas would send hunters directly to Chloe's location, no matter where Luca tried to hide her. He needed to strike at the rebels soon, before they had a chance to prepare for him.

At the same time, rushing into battle was stupid; it was bad planning, and Luca had fought too many battles to get sucked into that trap. As angry as it made him that Chloe was targeted, he had to keep a cool head. Guarding Chloe was his first priority. He'd keep on the move, take the time to pull in reliable reinforcements. Every time he had that firmly fixed in his mind, though, his gut would insist that he take the fight to them *now*. It was urgent that he attack *now*. Tonight. There was no other way.

Some of the vampires he'd normally call wouldn't see anything wrong with the rebels' plans. Some of them might have already joined with them. A lot of the kindred were fed up with the status quo, and wanted to exist openly, free to use all the strength and power they possessed. He had to be very sure about who he called, who he trusted, because Chloe's life depended on it.

Finally he began to dial. Like it or not, he had to take the chance even though nothing was certain and no one could be implicitly trusted—no one except Chloe.

"I've never been to Memphis," Jimmy said, still nervous even though he and Rurik had been on the road since just after dawn. Maybe it was the sword the warrior riding in the passenger seat held so confidently, the sharp tip resting on the floor mat, the intricately designed grip caught in big, rough hands. Maybe it was the shotgun in the backseat. According to Rurik, that was Jimmy's weapon. They'd bought it at a flea market just off the interstate, three hours after heading out of town. Jimmy had never owned a gun before, though he'd gone hunting with his dad a few times, years ago. Hunting hadn't been his thing, he'd been bored stiff, and after a while his dad had stopped trying to get him interested.

"I hear they have great barbecue around here," he continued. "It's probably not as good as Texas barbecue, but maybe we should give it a try. You know, just to compare the two." They'd stopped twice for food already. Rurik had a huge appetite.

"We can stop if you are hungry, but we cannot linger." Rurik's fingers beat a steady rhythm on the hilt of his sword, as if he were anxious to use it. He definitely wasn't much of a talker. He issued orders, ignored questions, and fiddled with his sword. Now and then the sunlight caught the blade, and a glint that reminded Jimmy of the weird flashes of light he'd been seeing lately would fill the car. He had to wonder: Was that what he'd been seeing all along?

Light bouncing off the shiny blade of a long sword? If he'd understood that sooner, he might never have invited Rurik in.

He needed to make a pit stop, too, so he pulled off the interstate at the next exit. He spied a weathered sign for a barbecue place, which turned out to be attached to a gas station and convenience store. That would do. One-stop shopping: he could fill up the tank, take a piss, and get something to eat. With Rurik as his passenger, the fewer stops they had to make, the better.

Rurik would want to eat in the car again, rather than taking the time to sit at a table in the restaurant, and that was fine with Jimmy. A six-foot-four dude wearing what looked like homespun and carrying a very sharp sword was tough to explain, and he refused to leave the sword behind in the car. Best to get Rurik in and out quickly, wherever they had to stop.

The Warrior remained in his seat while Jimmy filled the tank. When that was done he pulled to the front of the building, put the car in park, and turned to Rurik. He tried once more. "Look, nothing has happened the other times we stopped. You should leave that thing in the car."

Rurik knew Jimmy was talking about the sword. They'd had this conversation before. "And be defenseless? No. You should carry your weapon as well."

Yeah, that would work. Two men, a sword and a shotgun, and a convenience store; it sounded like the makings of the lead story on the evening news. "No, thanks. I'll take my chances."

Jimmy wanted to call Kate and explain what was going on, but what the hell could he say that he hadn't said in the note he'd left sitting by the coffeepot? *Emergency. I have to go. Call later. Love you.* He'd even turned his cell phone off, once Kate and his mother had started to call. There was simply nothing he could say to ease their worry.

It tugged at Jimmy's heart that his dad was probably in the ground by now, and he hadn't been there. He couldn't get that out of his head, as he and his passenger hit the restroom and then headed to the attached restaurant to order barbecue sandwiches. He wondered if the funeral service was over, if the rest of the family had made it in . . . if Kate and his mother would ever forgive him. Thinking about things like this could make him crazy, if he let it.

Jimmy had asked for a sweet iced tea when they'd ordered their sandwiches. Rurik wanted a six-pack from the convenience store. The man loved his beer, and he apparently had a great tolerance for it, because he didn't seem to be at all affected by the six-pack he'd consumed earlier.

Naturally, people stared: not at Jimmy, but at Rurik. The clerk behind the front counter, where he paid for the gas and beer, was especially concerned, darting constant looks at Rurik. The guy looked as if he were about to dial 911. Jimmy leaned slightly forward and offered an explanation.

"My cousin is posing for some video game artwork and animation this evening, and he likes to get into character beforehand. I hope he's not freaking people out."

"Well, you can hardly expect to walk into a store with a sword and not freak people out a little bit," the cashier said with a less-than-brilliant smile. He paused. "What video game?"

"We can't say," Jimmy answered in a lowered voice. "It's all hush-hush right now. But you'll recognize it when the ads come out, since you've seen my cousin in costume."

The cashier bought the story, and relaxed a bit more.

"Hey, you," he called, looking past Jimmy's shoulder. "What's your name? You know, in case you get famous or something."

"I am Rurik." As always the Warrior spoke with an accent.

The cashier's smile faded. "Yeah, yeah, stay in character, asshole."

Jimmy showed his ID, paid, handed Rurik the six-pack, stepped outside, and took a deep breath. Next time they had to stop he was going to leave Rurik in the car. The Warrior would just have to piss on the side of the road or into an empty beer can until they got to D.C. Jimmy thought he'd handled himself okay so far, but he wasn't an actor or an accomplished liar and he really couldn't take much more of this. His heart was beating a mile a minute.

He skidded to a stop. A woman dressed in long pants, a long-sleeved T-shirt, gloves, a floppy-brimmed hat, and a scarf leaned casually against the passenger side of the car. She was definitely not dressed for a southern summer afternoon. Despite all the garb she had on, she was a looker. She was so good-looking, and built like a brick shit house, that it took him a minute to register that she was leaning against *his* car, as if she were waiting for them. He didn't know her, so that gave him a start, like he needed any more surprises today.

The woman lifted her head sightly, revealing a lush mouth that curved in a smile as she glanced past him. Her attention settled on Rurik, and stayed there. "Hey there, sugar," she purred.

Rurik dropped his six-pack. Two of the cans burst open, spewing beer in an arc as the Warrior drew his sword. For a split second Jimmy wondered what the hell he was doing, and then the woman sprang toward the Warrior, godawmighty, almost *flying*. Her movement was too *big* to be normal, and dammit all, those were *fangs*.

Jimmy dropped the sack of sandwiches and his Styrofoam cup of iced tea, and ran. He punched the button on his keychain remote to unlock the doors, then yanked the rear driver's side door open and dove into the backseat. He grabbed the shotgun, backed out of the car with it cradled in his hands. He could barely think. *Oh shit, oh shit.* That was pretty much all his brain was capable of. His hands shook, and his heart pounded so hard he could feel it hammering against his chest.

For one blessed moment he thought that maybe he wouldn't need the shotgun. Without hesitating, Rurik ran the vampire through with his sword. Jimmy blew out a breath of relief, one that turned to a strangled cry when the sword didn't even slow her down. She backed away, leaving the bloodstained blade behind, and danced to the side, away from the sword, to swing out with a balled hand. An unbelievably powerful blow connected with Rurik's jaw and sent him to the ground. He landed on his back, hit his head on the concrete. His sword fell out of his hand and went clattering across the parking lot.

The vampire snarled like a wild animal, and in the shade of her hat brim Jimmy saw them again. Fangs.

She pressed one small foot, clad in a white tennis shoe, on Rurik's chest. "I've never tasted warrior blood before. Bet I get a charge out of it, sugar."

Rurik's eyes were still dazed, but he turned his head toward Jimmy. "She killed your father. Go for the heart or head."

The vampire smiled. "If it was dark I'd take you both on at the same time, but I'm not at my best during the daytime. Guess this'll have to do." For a moment she looked into Jimmy's eyes, and everything kind of went away. He felt a strange tingle at the center of his forehead and a chill down his spine, and for a second or two he felt completely disconnected and numb. The vampire dismissed him and dropped down like an animal to grasp Rurik's hair in one hand, jerking his head back as she opened her mouth and exposed her fangs, poised to tear out his throat.

Jimmy pumped the shotgun and fired. He couldn't get her heart from this angle, not without hitting Rurik, too, so he aimed for the head. And missed. It had been a long time since he'd handled any kind of weapon. The shot grazed the vampire's hat, knocking it off.

She howled as the sunlight hit her face, automatically lifting her free arm to shield herself from the sun. "I told you to stay right where you were," she snarled at him. "Damn sunlight. I can't even glamour properly."

Jimmy pumped the shotgun again and moved closer. Rurik had insisted that he load the shotgun after they'd purchased it, thank God, but Jimmy hadn't believed he'd need to defend himself so soon, so he hadn't put one in the chamber, for safety's sake; that meant he just had this one last shot, rather than the maximum three he could have had. This one had to count; he didn't think the vampire would give him time to grab a couple of shells from the car and reload. She jumped up to face him, her movements unnaturally smooth and quick.

Rurik had shaken off the knock on his head; as soon as she released her hold on him, he moved fast, grabbed the vampire's legs, and literally lifted her high in the air. Damn if she didn't look like an old-fashioned car-hood ornament, or a wooden woman on the front of a pirate ship, with her back arched and her breasts thrust forward. She hung there, high in the air, and Jimmy knew he'd never again have this chance. He didn't hesitate; he aimed for the heart and fired.

This time, he didn't miss. The blast hit her in the middle of her chest, getting the heart and a lot of other flesh. Rurik released his hold and the vampire dropped like a rock, splatting hard on the pavement just a few feet in front of Jimmy. She took a deep breath, screamed with raw fury, and lifted her head. Her cheek had taken a beating when she'd slammed into the ground, and her clothes were soaked in her own blood, but she was still alive, and *fuck, she was getting up!*

"You must destroy the heart or the head, not simply damage it," Rurik said as he rose to his feet and reached for his sword in one smooth motion. "Remember that," he added calmly as the damaged vampire rose from the ground, moving much more slowly and clumsily than she had before. Rurik lifted his sword and swung it with an incredible strength, neatly severing the vampire's head. Her head spun away, screaming one last time. Her once-lovely face blistered in the sunlight, then her entire body—both parts—turned to dust.

Rurik leaned down and picked up the vampire's scarf, wiped his sword with it, and returned the blade to its scabbard. "Thank you for coming to my defense," he said without emotion.

Holy shit, now what did they do? Jimmy looked toward the convenience store, where several faces were all but pressed to the glass. The clerk was jabbering full-speed into his cell phone. "Well, fuck," he said, as he started walking back to the convenience store. When he was almost there, he decided it really wasn't a good idea to walk into a crowded store with a shotgun, whether he had any ammo left or not. He turned around, watched as Rurik wiped some blood from his face, then picked up the sack of sandwiches and the unexploded cans of his six-pack.

He couldn't believe the guy still wanted to eat. As far

as he was concerned, he never wanted to see a barbecue sandwich again for the rest of his life. The chopped
meat reminded him too much of how the vampire had
looked when he'd shot out part of her chest.

"Get in the car," he said to Rurik as he put the shotgun in the backseat and walked back to the convenience store. He opened the door, plastered a smile on
his face as he stuck his head inside. "Please tell me you
didn't see the cameras. We wanted your expressions to
be genuine. Hope we didn't scare anyone too bad.
Wasn't that great? The producer is going to be here in
just a few minutes. He'll want signed permissions from
all of you, if you want your likenesses to appear in the
video game." He wondered if any of them could see
past the act, if maybe those closest could hear his heart
hammering.

"Where's the woman's body?" one lady shouted hys-
terically. "Oh my God, she just *exploded*!"

"It's all special effects these days," Jimmy said, keeping that idiotic grin in place.

"I saw . . ." a man began, but stopped and didn't say
anything else. What could he say? There was no body,
just a limp pile of clothes and some ash. And who in
their right mind would believe for a moment that what
they'd witnessed was real? He had a hard time believing it himself.

The clerk spoke into the phone, "Never mind," and
disconnected his call to turn his attention to Jimmy.
"I'm not giving any permission without some cash
upfront."

"Sure," Jimmy said, trying to sound reasonable when
what he wanted to do was turn and run like hell. If he
made it to D.C. without having a heart attack, it would
be a miracle. "I don't have the power to make any deals
on my own, but the producer will be here in ten minutes, tops. My cousin and I have to get out of here so

we can make the next shot before we lose the light. It's, like, way down the road, so we've gotta run." He gave a wave, turned, and stepped over what was left of the vampire, which wasn't much: some bloody clothes, a partially shredded hat, and dust. The dust was scattering in the summer breeze.

Sunlight flashed on something metallic, catching his eye. The edge of a cell phone stuck about an inch out of a bloody pocket. Without thinking he leaned down and carefully plucked the dust-covered, bloodstained phone from the pocket. With it caught between two fingers, Jimmy gratefully plopped into the driver's seat and dropped the phone in the console between the front seats.

Rurik indicated the cell. "Why did you take that?"

"This is war, right? One of the aspects of war is the collection of information. Want to know who that freak's been talking to? This is how we find out." If he could ever bring himself to touch the damn thing, that is.

Jimmy glanced at his passenger. Rurik hadn't escaped the skirmish unscathed. His jaw was red, and would probably be bruised before too much longer. The vampire had scratched his throat when she'd grabbed it, though a scratch was far from the fatal wound she'd obviously planned to inflict. The plain brown shirt was splattered with blood. His clothes weren't soaked, not like the vampire's had been, and it was difficult to tell that those streaks were actually red against that dark brown, but still . . . gross. There was a lot of blood loss involved in shotgun blasts and severing a head. Who knew?

As he cranked the engine, Rurik nodded curtly. "You are very clever, but you are not skilled enough with a shotgun to be of much use in a battle with vampires."

Jimmy's first thought was *Thank God, maybe I'll get out of this alive after all.*

And then Rurik continued. "We must get you a proper sword."

It was after dark when they checked out of the hotel. They'd checked in too early and left too early, and had ended up paying for two days when they hadn't even been there twenty-four hours. It didn't seem fair to Chloe, but in the scheme of things an inflated hotel bill wasn't worth obsessing over. She had more important things to obsess about.

Luca drove directly to a rental car lot, dropped off the minivan, and leased a gray sedan that looked pretty much like every other car they'd passed on the road. It was completely forgettable, which was probably why he'd chosen it. For a moment, Chloe wondered if he'd glamoured the girl behind the desk, or made some kind of excuse for trading in a perfectly good van that had been rented just last night. But that thought was quickly followed by a "duh." No explanations or vampire tricks were necessary when he wasn't going to be remembered.

"Where to now?" she asked as he pulled onto the road, breathing a sigh of relief when she realized that he was driving away from the rebel vampire headquarters.

Luca had been quiet since she'd awakened to find him all but ready to go. He'd given her time to take a shower, but had made it clear that he was in a hurry. He was driven, and thanks to their bonding she knew how strong that drive was. Now he glanced at her and said, "We have a stop to make, before we attack."

So much for her relief. "Attack? Just the two of us?"

"I hope not. While you were sleeping I made a few calls, pulled in some friends. They're trustworthy."

Chloe gulped. Great. Her life—heck, the fate of the world—was in the hands of *trustworthy* vampires. "We can't . . . wait a few days to see who shows up? Maybe give it some thinking time and come up with a battle plan?"

"No, we have to do it now," Luca said, his voice emotionless, but she could feel his agitation. That wasn't like him. Luca was normally icy calm.

"Why?"

He hesitated a moment, then his jaw hardened. "I don't know. I've learned to trust my gut instincts over the years, and my gut is telling me that we can't wait."

Okay. Battle time, then. That changed things. She didn't want to be separated from him, but she was practical enough to know that in a fight she'd be more of a hindrance than an ally. She'd distract Luca, take his mind away from the enemy. He'd be so focused on protecting her, he might make a mistake—and end up paying for that mistake with his life. She couldn't bear it if that happened, if she lost him because he was focused on her instead of on what he was doing.

"Take me home," she said, her voice smaller than she'd intended.

"No."

"Think about it," she pleaded. "I'm safe there. No vampire can come into my home uninvited. I know you're worried that I'll do something foolish, but I swear, even if they bring my mother to the door I won't go outside or invite them in."

"Yeah, I'll buy that," Luca responded, rolling his eyes.

Chloe crossed her arms. "There's no need for sarcasm."

He drove fast, when he could. If anyone else had been behind the wheel she'd have been panicking, but if ever anyone was in control, it was him. She trusted him implicitly.

"I have to tell you something," he said.

That didn't sound good. A chill ran down her spine because he sounded so serious. If Luca was worried, she should definitely be worried, too.

"There's another reason I can't take you home and leave you there. Ahron mentioned the rebels breaking a spell. I don't know if you realized what he was talking about or not, but the spell in question is the sanctuary spell that keeps a human's home safe from the kindred."

She hadn't thought the situation could get any worse . . . yet there it was. Worse. "Can they do that?"

"Ahron seemed to think so, and that's enough to concern me. They must have a witch on their side."

Witch? What next? Werewolves and goblins? That settled it, though; she didn't want to go home.

They crossed the Virginia state line.

The storage facility was an ordinary collection of metal units, like thousands of them all over the country. Luca had rented this space for the past twelve years. Before that, he'd leased a smaller unit in a different town, but over the years his collection had grown and he'd had to get this larger space.

He unlocked the metal door, guided Chloe inside, and flipped the light switch.

At first glance, the unit was as ordinary on the inside as it was on the outside, but the wooden crates and metal lockers that lined the walls were filled with weapons, any weapon he might possibly need in his line of work—or for a war.

He opened one wooden crate and drew out a broadsword that was wrapped in oilcloth, to keep the blade from rusting. When he carefully unwrapped it, Chloe gasped.

"Holy cow," she muttered. "Is that thing as sharp as it looks?"

"Yes, it is." He could take on three unarmed vampires with his hands alone, but considering how many rebels he'd have to face tonight he'd need every advantage he could get.

He reached past another, lighter sword and grabbed the short-bladed weapon he had thought of for Chloe. He'd be with her all the way; he'd do his best to keep the rebels away from her, but it would be foolish not to arm her. He placed her sword beside his own and moved to a metal locker. For several minutes, he went from locker to locker, from shelf to shelf. For himself, he chose a modified shotgun and two high-caliber handguns, along with enough ammunition to take on an army.

Arming Chloe was a bit more complicated.

"Have you ever handled a gun?" he asked, turning to face her.

"No. I'm sorry," she said helplessly, knowing she was a liability to him.

Too bad. A couple of shots to the heart or the brain with a powerful enough weapon would drop most vampires in their tracks, but the target was small, and even a half-inch off target meant an angry, wounded vampire was coming after you. There wasn't time for shooting lessons; he had other weapons with which she could defend herself.

He hoped she wouldn't need them. The only way any vampire would get to her was if he was dead.

It was a long way from Texas to D.C. by car, with an armed and still slightly bloody warrior sitting in the passenger seat, getting more impatient with every passing hour.

He drove fast but steady, eating up the miles, but Jimmy wasn't exactly sure what they were closer to. He wasn't sure he wanted to know any more than he already did.

The vampire's cell phone began singing Elvis's

"Hound Dog." He jumped, and the car swerved into the left lane, earning him an angry blast from the horn of a pickup truck.

Rurik simply stared at the cell, lying in the console. As they'd been driving through Tennessee the Warrior had studied the cell. He'd even cleaned it up a bit, using the leftover napkins from their sack of sandwiches to wipe away most of the blood and dust. But he didn't touch the phone now, he simply glared at it. Jimmy grabbed the cell, glancing at the name and number that came up on the screen.

Sorin. That was one of the names the vampire had entered into her address book. The call was from a D.C. number, judging by the area code. Jimmy didn't want to listen to the phone ring anymore, and he sure as hell didn't want to talk to anyone the vampire who'd murdered his father might have in her address book. He hit the "fuck you" button to reject the call, and dropped it back into the console. Maybe he should turn it off, but it might be a good idea to know who was trying to call the dead bitch.

"I like this world, very much," Rurik said thoughtfully.

"Yeah, so do I," Jimmy responded.

"It is worth saving."

A chill ran down Jimmy's spine. It was so easy to get caught up in his own little world, his insignificant life, that the larger picture became fuzzy at times. He'd never given much thought to the world as a whole. Kate did, though, and he wished she were here now, but at the same time he was very glad that she was far away from whatever they were driving into.

"Where you're from . . . it's not the same?" Might as well try a little small talk.

"Not entirely. My home is more simple than yours. You have things here that we do not have."

"Like beer?" Jimmy asked, looking at the discarded cans on the floorboard.

Rurik grinned. "We have ale, plenty of it, but we do not have Budweiser."

Jimmy laughed, for the first time in what seemed like a very long while. A preference for a specific brand of beer made Rurik seem almost ordinary . . . almost. "What else do you like?"

"Your women. They're . . . soft. Not like the females in my world."

"Your women aren't soft?" Damn. Did that mean they were hard, like, literally?

"They are all warriors, like I am. Strong, determined fighters. They are good women, all, and some of them are very beautiful. But your women are different. They are . . ."

"Softer," Jimmy supplied, when Rurik faltered.

"Yes. I also like your french fries and . . ." he paused for a moment, as if searching for the right word, "classic rock, and cherry pie."

"Women, music, beer, and pie. Rurik, you're just an all-American guy." It occurred to Jimmy that Rurik had to have been here before, in order to appreciate all these things. "When was the last time you . . . popped in?"

"Nineteen sixty-eight."

Jimmy got that chill again. *Vietnam.* His great-uncle had died there.

"Dude, you don't look all that old."

"I've been around for a very long time," Rurik said. "And of course, I watch when I am not here. From the other side, we see everything."

Great," Jimmy grumbled. "Even my most private moments aren't sacred."

Rurik smiled again. "You are assuming that your private moments are of interest to anyone other than you."

True enough, but from here on out he'd always wonder . . . if there was anything for him from here on out.

"Okay, tell me the truth," Jimmy said. "I can take it." At least, he hoped he could. "You're a warrior, you're from another world, you've been around for, like, forever, you fight in wars . . ."

"When I am called, and when it is necessary. There are times when many of us come, and other times when only a handful are called."

"And this time?"

Rurik's jaw seemed to tighten before he sighed and answered. "Many of my kind have been called, which is a testament to the severity of the situation. I am sad to say, not many have made it through. Not many at all, unless since I have come here, others have also been able to make the journey. Many of the conduits, like your father, have been murdered before they could call their warriors over."

Oh, shit, if this wasn't a recipe for disaster, he didn't know what was. Not only were they going to be fighting vampires, they'd be badly outnumbered. He wanted to bail. He wanted to drop Rurik off, then turn tail and run—back to Texas, back to Kate. If there was a war with vampires, well, that didn't mean he had to be a part of it in any way other than as a deliveryman. He'd done enough, hadn't he?

He didn't need to ask but he had to know: "Why are you here now? It's the vampires, right?" Maybe he'd read the situation wrong and there were just a few of them, something Rurik could handle on his own.

"Yes, the vampires. The monster who killed your father, she was not alone. There are many more like her. They wish to enslave humanity, to end the world you have always known. If they win, if they ascend to power, then the beauty of your world will fade, and soon die. There will be no more music, because the human spirit will no longer sing. Your women will no longer be soft and innocent. Humans will become cattle, slaves . . . less than human."

He was already speeding, but Jimmy's foot pressed harder against the gas pedal. After a while, Rurik smiled once more, though the joy he'd expressed earlier was gone.

"I also like speed."

Sorin contained his fury as he watched the white pins being stuck into Jonas's maps. Most were in the U.S., including one in New York, but others were placed on the world maps throughout Europe, Asia, and Africa. Maybe the warriors were spread out so far because they realized what was happening to their conduits, and maybe they came in from thousand of miles away because that's where their only capable descendants lived. Whatever the reason, the revolution had suffered its first failure. They hadn't been able to stop them all.

But they'd been able to delay the warriors' entrance, and some had surely been halted entirely. Fewer warriors to face was a victory, of sorts. There were more black pins than white. But that didn't lighten Sorin's mood.

A warrior had come through in Texas, and Melody wasn't answering her phone. The warrior was still alive, according to Jonas. Had the warrior killed her, or had she deserted when she'd failed? Either scenario was possible. Given what he'd said to her, if she hadn't been able to take out the warrior she'd have gone to ground somewhere, hiding rather than taking the chance that Regina would kill her.

Regina was livid. She was angry with Jonas, ready to take Nevada's head. She'd expected her plans to be executed without flaw, and they hadn't been.

"Do I have to do *everything* myself?" Regina faced

Jonas, her anger coloring everything about her. Her posture, her normally beautiful face, the way she balled her small hands as if she were hungry for something to strike. Her fangs had extended, as if she were hungry for something else entirely. "You were supposed to locate all the conduits before any of the warriors could come through. Tell me why I shouldn't end your pitiful existence here and now."

"I can still be of service," Jonas said, frazzled and tired, and not as afraid as he should've been. Maybe he was ready to die. Maybe he was tired of being Regina's whipping boy, the puppy she kicked when she was having a bad day . . . and sometimes when she wasn't. "I'm still able to track the warriors. I'll know when they get here."

And the warriors, who'd been watching everything from their own world, would know exactly where the rebels had gathered, who their leader was . . . and how to kill them all. They would also be enraged at what had happened to their conduits. To know exactly where the warriors were as they came closer would be a great advantage, and Regina wasn't ignorant of that fact. Her rage faded, and she stepped back from Jonas. He was safe enough, for now.

Nevada was not. Regina had to have some outlet for her rage, and the despised little witch was her next target. She flew out of Jonas's room and climbed the stairs like a woman on a mission. She pushed past the two surprised guards, opened the door to Nevada's room, and stalked inside. Sorin was right behind her.

"I've waited as long as I intend to wait," Regina said in her ice-cold voice "If you can't break the spell now, then you won't live to take another breath."

Nevada stood, and calmly faced them. A bubble of light, one he recognized, surrounded her. Perhaps she'd known what was coming, or maybe she'd simply been practicing, but she'd protected herself with a sanctuary spell. He waited for the shield to fall, because they'd interrupted her as she'd been working and she'd told him often enough in the past that any distraction pulled her out of her work. Her focus should break, and disrupt the spell . . . but nothing happened. The shield didn't fall, but seemed to grow brighter. What was she doing? Didn't she know her family would pay the price for her rebellion?

"I'll break the spell when my family is free," she said, her own voice cool and even. "All I have to do is smash this vial." She held up a small glass tube, and the gleam from her magic bounced off the vial and what was inside it, something both bright and dark, light and heavy, pulsing with power.

Regina turned toward the door and the guards who watched. "Bring me the sister," she ordered. "Emily."

Sorin watched Nevada's face. She should be terrified. In the past the mere mention of her sister's name had brought fear into her eyes. But not tonight; tonight she looked confident and assured. He didn't like it. Hell, what else could go wrong?

For several long minutes the two women faced each other, each one steady and silent. If anyone had asked Sorin which of them was the stronger, he wouldn't have hesitated in his answer: Regina. But at this moment Nevada seemed to be as strong, as much in control, as the vampire queen. She'd grown in many ways since she'd been imprisoned here; she'd become much stronger than anyone had imagined she might.

Nevada closed her eyes and whispered a handful of words in one of the languages she'd learned here, in this room. If they'd known how powerful she would become, would they have ever risked bringing her here? Was breaking the spell worth creating this new and forceful creature?

Yes. Breaking the spell was worth any price, but if they'd realized it would come to this, they might've assigned someone to learn alongside her. Maybe then they could at least understand what she was saying when she spoke in the language of spells.

Then again, perhaps one had to be a witch in order to learn.

One of the guards, the dark-haired Danica, came back to the doorway. She was flushed and frowning, not a good look for any vampire. "Your majesty, we can't enter the prisoners' room."

Regina turned to glare at the young vampire. "What do you mean?"

"It's as if they're in their own home."

Regina whirled back to Nevada. "Your doing, I suppose."

"Yes," Nevada said, and smiled.

Anger and frustration flared in Regina's expression, then she composed herself. "How long will you let them stay in that room and starve? Perhaps my people can't enter, but that doesn't mean I'll allow them to leave. I won't release your family, witch. Not ever."

"Then you'll never get what you want from me," Nevada said without a hint of concern. She didn't seem at all agitated, as Regina did. That alone made her appear stronger, more in command. "The spell must be broken soon or all the work I've done is wasted, and I'll have to start again. It takes a long time, to start from scratch. Let my family go, and when I'm sure they're safe I'll do as you wish." She added, "The protective spell I've put on them will go with them, of course. Not that I don't trust you, but . . . just to be sure. You understand, don't you?"

"I don't think you're that powerful," Regina said, sneering.

"You doubt me?" Nevada shot back. "Try me, bitch. Come and get me."

Sorin took a single step forward. Was Nevada trying to get herself killed? Didn't she have a clue how strong Regina was?

Regina was surprised by Nevada's defiance, but she didn't take the bait. She turned to the guard in the doorway. "It appears we have no choice. Release Nevada's family. Let them all go." She mouthed something else at Danica, but Sorin couldn't read her lips from his position. Whatever she'd said couldn't be good for the humans; Regina didn't easily give up anything she considered to be her own.

Danica left to do as she'd been told, and a confident Regina looked at Sorin, turning her back so Nevada couldn't hear her. She whispered, "It isn't as though we can't find them whenever we wish. The protective spell the witch cast won't last forever." She leaned closer. "Did you know she could do such a thing?"

He shook his head. They'd taken Nevada, trained her, tried to force from her what they wanted and needed. Somewhere along the way, his little witch had grown very strong, too strong for Regina to allow her to live. She'd signed her own death warrant.

"Now what?" Regina asked as she faced Nevada.

The shield around Nevada intensified once more, grew more colorful. Sparks shot through it. Nevada said, "Now we wait."

TWENTY-SIX

Of all the places in the world Chloe didn't want to ever visit again, this was number one on her list. She should be running in the other direction. She didn't want to be here—not that she really had much of a choice in the matter.

Last night vampires had tried to kill her just a few feet away from where she and Luca now crouched. The memory of the attack was so fresh she'd probably be hearing whispers and creaks and bumps in the night that weren't really there—that is, if she could hear anything other than her pounding heartbeat. She knew why she was a target: conduit, warrior, war. She knew this had to be done. That didn't change her mind about the joy of being here again.

She didn't want this excitement, she sure as hell hadn't asked for it, but it was hers nonetheless. Hiding wasn't an option. If the vampires managed to lift the spell that kept a human's home a vampire-free haven, no one would be safe. And she had to admit that, even though at the moment her flight-or-fight instincts were leaning toward flight, she wasn't going to send Luca out alone, not when she could be beside him. He didn't need her protection, she'd likely be more of a distraction than a help, but this had become her war from the first moment she'd dreamed of her Warrior, and she couldn't hide from it.

Accepting that this was meant to be, that she *had* to be here, calmed her quite a bit. She'd faced worse and survived, after all. A failed relationship or two. D.C. traffic. Running out of shrimp on a Friday night. Sorin threatening Valerie. Ahron, strange and scary as hell. Three vampires out for her head. She'd get through this, too.

She and Luca were both dressed all in black. Black pants, shirts, and shoes. They looked like a couple of secret agents in a slick movie, only in the movies the secret agents never got so scared that they worried they might wet their pants.

At least tonight she was armed. Not only had Luca presented her with a short, very sharp sword, he'd also armed her with an oversized, heavy flashlight with a powerful full-spectrum bulb. A blast from that flashlight wouldn't kill a vampire the way sunlight would, but it would hurt. Aim for the eyes, he'd said. Most vampires would be blinded by the light, at least momentarily and maybe for a good long while—unless they were wearing sunglasses, the way Sorin had been the first time she'd seen him.

If for some reason the light didn't work, the sword was her next best bet. Luca had told her to stab the heart three or four times to make sure it was destroyed. Removing the head was best, he said, but it also took strength she didn't have. She couldn't expect to tap a vamp on the side of the neck and be done with it.

Her stomach turned a bit when she remembered the brief sight of last night's severed heads, and all that blood. Multiple stab wounds directly in the heart would be just as messy. Could she do that?

Hell yes, she could.

In addition to the flashlight and the sword, she had

her trusty pepper spray tucked in one pocket, just in case. Though, seriously, if she tried both the light and the sword and a vampire was still coming, the pepper spray wouldn't do her a whole helluva lot of good.

If she was well-armed, Luca was a walking armory. One short shotgun and two handguns were strapped to his body, and he wore a bandolier of shotgun shells. A sword in a leather sheath hung from his waist. He had knives strapped to his ankles, knives strapped to his wrists. Since she knew he was capable of killing a vampire with his bare hands, the weapons were, maybe, overkill. Then again, if he thought he needed so much in the way of weapons, she should be doubly worried.

Chloe passed the time distracting herself, pumping herself up—mentally, at least—and trying to convince herself that this night was like any other. To tell the truth, though, at the moment she'd give almost anything to be dealing with unsatisfied customers and shrimp shortages, to be balancing accounts and smoothing the way between employees who had personal issues. She'd love to worry about her bank account, school, and her parents' scheduled visit. Had she once thought those problems were difficult? Lately her problems had been getting progressively worse. That trend had to change soon. Right?

She peeked at the mansion; it looked as if every light inside was on—every one outside, too. The place was lit up like a casino, so brightly illuminated it had to be tough to tell from inside if it was day or night.

After watching for a while, they moved closer to the house, sticking to shadows while they still could. Chloe followed in Luca's footsteps. Literally. Sneaking around wasn't her strong suit, not that she would ever be as silent as Luca. She heard her own footsteps, but he didn't make a sound. Her breathing was too heavy; his was completely silent. Everything seemed to crunch and snap beneath her feet; he moved like a ghost. As they reached the property line Luca dropped down behind a hedge. Chloe followed suit, hunkering down close to him. She kept one hand on the sword that hung at her side, to keep it from making too much noise, and with the other hand she tightly gripped the heavy flashlight.

Luca watched the brightly lit house and waited, tension on his face and in the way he held his body, his full attention focused on what was about to happen. He'd made his calls, but he didn't know who might actually come—or if anyone would. The two of them might be on their own, one vampire and one human against who knows how many vampires set on ruling the world. Luca wasn't an ordinary vampire—she couldn't believe she'd used "ordinary" and "vampire" in the same sentence—but he was just one man. He couldn't survive against such overpowering odds.

But he was of the mind that if they cut off the head of the snake, it would die. Whoever was in charge, whoever led this revolution, she had to go. If the rebel leader was here tonight Luca was going to take her head.

Sorin would likely lose his head, too, and that suited Chloe just fine.

Watching, waiting, her fear began to fade. Intense fear wasn't going to do her any good at all, and gradually she began to feel the rightness about attacking tonight. They couldn't wait, couldn't run and hide. The monsters had to be stopped, and if she was a walking basket case she'd do Luca more harm than good. She knew what to do: light in the eyes, blind the vampire, then stab it in the heart. If they were still kicking after that, she'd hit them with the pepper spray, then stab them some more. It was a decent enough plan. If she was lucky, she could wallow in fear after the fact.

They hadn't been watching long when what looked like a family left by way of the front door. A man, a woman, a teenage boy, and a girl ran in a tight knot, as if they were afraid to be separated even by inches. Their clothes were rumpled, the men's faces unshaved, every head of hair unstyled and unkempt. They sprinted, as if they couldn't get away from the house fast enough. The woman tripped and the man, her husband perhaps, caught and righted her without even slowing down, dragging her along for a moment.

"They look human," Chloe whispered. It was hard to be sure, since judging by the few vampires she'd seen, most of them could easily pass as human.

"They are," Luca responded.

"What are they doing here?"

"Unwilling blood donors, I suspect," Luca said.

"And they're escaping through the front door? Why are the vampires just letting them go?"

"They're not." Luca nodded toward a corner of the house, and Chloe saw a tall, thin man—vampire, she was certain—watching the family. When the foursome was a short distance away, the watcher began to follow.

"Are the vampires just playing with them?" Chloe whispered. "Is this some kind of sick game?" Let the prisoners think they can escape, then hunt them down and . . . she didn't want to know what would happen next.

"Maybe." Luca narrowed his eyes. "Maybe not. There's some kind of magic around the humans, a kind of protective field. Maybe that's what let them get free. The magic won't last long, though; it's already wavering a bit."

She couldn't see anything like that, but she took Luca at his word.

"I suspect when the magic fades the rebel who's following will move in and kill them all. Quickly, if they're lucky." He was very matter of fact about it, but then again, he'd seen a lot of death in his years, all kinds of death: natural and unnatural, expected and unexpected, quick and not so quick.

Chloe's heartbeat raced again, her mouth went dry. She knew there was a lot to be done here tonight; she realized the importance of what was to come in that big house. But to just leave the foursome to the vampires was wrong. She couldn't accept their deaths the way Luca did. "Shouldn't we do something?" Everyone in the little family had looked so scared, especially the young girl, and Chloe knew those poor people didn't have a chance against even that lone vampire.

Luca turned his head to look at her. It was new and exciting and scary, the way he caught her eyes and held them, the expression in his. Between the bonding, the intensity of their time together, the love she was beginning to feel . . . just looking at him was an experience like no other.

"Stay," he said, and before she could argue with him, he was gone. He moved so fast he was a blur in the night, beside her one moment, gone the next. It was hard to tell, but she got the distinct impression of flight. Because she couldn't focus on Luca, she looked instead at the vampire who'd begun to trail the escaping family. He was unaware that he wasn't alone until it was too late.

Luca didn't tear off the vampire's head, not this time. The sword was a silent weapon. With a movement so fast she couldn't follow each and every stroke, Luca swung that gleaming blade and separated the vampire's head from the body.

Chloe closed her eyes, and a voice that had been absent whispered in her ear. That voice was clearer, more distinct than it had ever been. She went still, recognizing the Warrior from her dreams. *"Your vampire saved the humans."*

"He's on our side," Chloe mentally responded. In her mind's eye, the Warrior began to take shape in the lightning-pierced mist, a woman with strong, clean features and a long, thick braid.

"Perhaps I will not kill him, then. Perhaps." After a pause the Warrior—Indi-something, Chloe remembered—said, *"It's time, Chloe. Bring me in. Open your heart and ask for my help and I will be there. Call me to you."*

"Not if you're going to kill Luca. No. Promise me—"

Luca returned as suddenly as he'd left, and the image of the Warrior faded away. "They're safe for now," he said as he knelt beside her. "Anyone else I can kill for you?"

Nevada was at peace for the first time in a very long while. She held her fate entirely in her own hands. The shield she'd built around herself remained strong as she closed her eyes and projected her spirit to Emily. The vampires hadn't lied. Her family was away from the house that had been their prison for so long, they were running toward safety. They didn't realize that they were running away from her, too, or that their escape would end in her death.

Her spirit floated alongside her family, falling into step with Emily, who immediately became aware of her presence. With a little work, Nevada thought, Emily could become a very powerful witch, but she hoped with everything she had that her little sister never knew what she knew, that she never learned about secret languages, musty volumes filled with spells, and hidden abilities that had the power to change her life.

"When will you meet us? I mean, *really* meet us?" Emily asked without slowing down. "Where?"

"Who are you talking to?" their father asked.

"Nevada," Emily said breathlessly. "She's here, and not here, and I can see her but . . . I don't know how to explain."

"I love you all," Nevada said. "Keep running, don't stop until daylight. No place is safe tonight, not even home."

"Where are we supposed to go?" Emily asked. This time, she wasn't interrupted by another family member.

"Away from here. Anywhere that's away from here."

"What's going to happen?"

"Something bad is about to start." Nevada wanted to believe that the vampires would forget all about her family, but she knew all she could give them was a head start. After that, it was up to them.

"They're everywhere, Emily. The vampires are everywhere. Tell the others, and stay safe, and . . . I love you."

"Where are you? Where can we meet—"

Nevada dropped back into her body, back in the room where the vampires kept her body even when her spirit roamed free. She didn't want to lie to Emily, but she couldn't very well tell her the truth either. Sorin and the vampire queen were watching closely. Did they realize what she could do, that she'd been spying on them for weeks now?

It didn't matter, not tonight.

"I suspect somehow you have discovered that I've held up my end of the bargain," Regina said, ice and displeasure in her voice. "Now it's time for you to deliver on your promise. Break the spell that keeps humans protected in their homes."

Nevada wanted her family to be much farther away before she gave the queen what she demanded. "Not just yet," she said calmly. Knowing she was going to die had removed her fear. She was in control, as much as was possible.

In the past few days, she'd called on every ounce of magic she could muster. She'd even cast a net, of sorts, asking for help—*demanding* help—calling, in every way she could think of, on any and all who would fight the vampires with her . . . or else after she was gone. She didn't know if the spell had worked, she couldn't know if anyone at all would show up to try to stop the end of their world, but she had tried. She'd insisted that the time was now, the vampires had to be stopped *now*. Other than that, all she could do was wait.

Considering her luck, she'd probably just doomed a few good guys who might've been susceptible to her magic. A cop or two, a few firemen drawn here not knowing why . . . a soldier, maybe. Those who'd been born to serve and protect might've been affected by her spell. Unless there were a whole helluva lot of them, she wouldn't be the only one to die tonight.

She looked at Sorin, who'd been tormentor, captor, and on occasion the only friend she'd known since being kidnapped. Why did she see so much more in him? Was it a syndrome of some sort? Did she see more in him because she'd needed to have hope in order to survive this long? Whatever the reason, she did almost like him, sometimes.

"You've done a lot of bad things, but you're not like her," she said, speaking to him as if Regina was no longer in the room, or else was of no consequence. She was actually doing her best to piss off the queen, so maybe in a fit of anger the death she delivered would be a quick one. Nevada didn't dare hope for much better than that, not anymore. "You're more than a soulless fiend. Somewhere deep inside you, you're so much more than what you've let yourself become. You don't see it, but I do."

He didn't answer, but the expression on his face made it clear he wasn't moved by her observations.

It was Regina who responded. "Sorin, since you're such good friends with the little witch, perhaps I'll let you have her before the night is done. A gift, for all your tireless service. Once Nevada does as she's told, she's all yours."

"Indie tried to come through," Chloe whispered as she and Luca crept closer to the big, well-lit house.

He stopped, looked at her, and realized with startling sharpness that though he had no choice in the matter, she didn't belong here. It was far too dangerous for her to be here, but then the world itself was dangerous tonight. He knew that, but he couldn't stop himself. The attack had to come *now*.

"Indie?" he asked, though he knew damn well who she meant.

"Indi-something, the Warrior. I didn't let her."

For the second time in just a few days, Chloe Fallon had succeeded in rendering him speechless with shock. The first time was when she'd remembered him, the second time was now. He opened his mouth, closed it, then tried again. "You didn't let her?"

"First she has to promise me she won't kill you. If she won't promise, she can stay where she is," Chloe said stubbornly.

He fumbled for words. He, who for two thousand years had dominated his world, couldn't think what to say to this human woman. "Sweetheart . . . other warriors will come through. She isn't the only one. Are you going to protect me from all of them?" The idea of anyone protecting him from anything was . . . flabbergasting.

"Maybe."

"We need her help. We need all the warriors who can come through."

"I won't let her kill you." She was as yielding as stone on that point.

"Do you really think you can stop her?"

"She's mine, right?"

If only it were that simple. "She's yours until she's flesh in this world, and then she's here to kill vampires."

"Vampire *rebels*," Chloe corrected. "You're one of the good guys."

"And she's supposed to make this distinction, how?"

"Maybe the vampires trying to stop the rebels could wear uniforms, or an identifying armband." She gave him a shoulder bump to show him she was joking.

"Great idea," he said drily. "So far, we'll need exactly *one*."

In theory, the Council was interested in keeping the order as it had been for thousands of years, but none of the Council members were soldiers. Maybe in the past they had been, but now they were politicians. Some of them might go into hiding until this all shook out, a few might pound their fists in indignation, but they wouldn't fight. Luca had called half a dozen potential soldiers asking for assistance, and none of them had arrived. Some were physically far away, that was true, but others could've been here by now. They weren't. He couldn't stop a revolution on his own, but for Chloe's sake he had to try. Her world was worth saving, and if the rebels succeeded that world would be destroyed.

He sighed. "Did you forget that, if she comes through, you're in the clear? They'll stop hunting you?"

She gave him a sad, sweet little smile. "No," she said quietly. "I didn't forget." She seemed to catch herself, as if she knew she'd given too much away. "Besides, in the clear? Who are we kidding? I'm a tasty human smack dab in the middle of a vampire nest. Indie or no Indie, I don't think the rebels are going to offer me a get-out-of-hell-free card any time soon."

She tried to make light, to joke when there was nothing to joke about, but there was a world of meaning in her eyes. They were too connected for him to miss even the most subtle nuances—not that Chloe had ever been particularly subtle.

For a moment he wondered how he'd gotten himself into this untenable position, but then he looked at Chloe. He'd denied emotion for so many years he almost hadn't recognized it when it had slammed into him with the force of a hurricane. There was no logical reason for him to care for her, no reason for him to risk his very existence for a human who'd be dead in a few years no matter what he did tonight. But love wasn't logical. Love was messy and inexplicable and even unavoidable. He was here for her; he was here for love.

That thought had barely formed when he felt the burst of energy behind them that signaled a vampire's arrival. He whirled, thrusting Chloe behind him as he lifted the shotgun barrel. Chloe stepped from behind him, moving up to stand by his side, sword in one hand and flashlight in the other. The expression on her face was as fierce as any warrior's.

Then he recognized the new arrivals and said "Hold," thrusting out a stilling hand so Chloe wouldn't strike, or turn on the light that would instantly alert the rebels; that was, if Jonas hadn't already alerted them.

Isaac and Duncan stepped forward; both were wearing wide smiles, both were armed, much as he was, and ready to fight. Luca breathed a sigh of relief. His army was pitifully small, but he and Chloe wouldn't be fighting alone tonight after all.

Sorin understood Regina's offer. After Nevada broke the spell, when she was no longer necessary to them, he'd be expected to screw and then drain her.

The thought made him sick to his stomach.

How could he do either of those things when she reminded him so much of the daughter he'd left behind when he'd been turned? The red hair, the pale skin, the delicacy of her bones and her face—and her scent. Most of all, her scent.

One human female, against a necessary revolution. One woman, against future aeons of existence lived at the top of the order. He shouldn't even be questioning the order. He could kill her quickly; it would be a kindness. But he couldn't do what Regina wanted.

Nevada turned her head to look at him; her gaze caught and held his. She was inferior and breakable, but her recently discovered magic was very powerful. In many ways Nevada's appearance of inferiority was deceptive. If he allowed her to live, what might she do? Her life wouldn't go on as it had been before he'd taken her. No one's life would go on as it had before.

He could kill her, he could keep her, or he could defy Regina and let her go. There was only one acceptable choice, for a soldier in this war that had just begun. And only one for a man who'd once been a father.

"Now," Regina commanded, her gaze pinned to Nevada's. "I've kept my part of the bargain, now you keep yours."

Nevada took a deep breath, lifted her chin, and broke the vial she held. A sliver of glass cut her finger, and the smell of blood filled the air. The magic bubble that had surrounded her fell, dissipated as if it had gone to dust. Like blowing snow, it drifted around the witch who'd created it. For a moment it was as if she wore the remnants of her spell, sparkling and pretty. Then it was gone.

When her work was done he could almost see Nevada's power fade away, as if all she'd done tonight had drained her.

Regina took a cell phone from a pocket in her long gown and placed a call. She said one word. "Now." And a moment later, she smiled. One of her soldiers, somewhere in the world, had just entered a human's home uninvited.

Satisfied, Regina looked at Sorin. "Kill her." She flicked an unconcerned glance to Nevada. "By the way, your family is being followed. As soon as I give the word, they'll all be dinner to a very hungry soldier who understands that those who displease me should suffer the worst sort of punishment." With that parting shot she left the room, leaving Sorin alone with Nevada and his orders.

Nevada didn't try to run, didn't cower or cry. If anything, she looked even more determined. "I don't suppose I could convince you to save my family, after you kill me."

"Why should I?"

Finally, tears filled Nevada's eyes. Not for herself, but for those she loved. "Because you're not like them, you're not like *her*."

"I am exactly like her."

"No, you're not!" Desperation and anger colored her voice, and her cheeks. She blushed bright pink, her eyes sparkled hot with helpless rage. "You could've hurt me a thousand times, but you didn't. I suspect even when you kill me, you won't do it the way she wants. You're not cruel."

Angered, uncomfortable, Sorin loomed over her. "You don't know what you're talking about. I've killed thousands in my years as a vampire, I've been cruel and violent and hungry to the point of pain. I've left a trail of blood wherever I've gone. Humans mean nothing to me; *you* mean nothing."

All she did was stare up at him, resolute.

He was close enough to grab her, close enough to do what had to be done, but . . . he didn't. What the hell was wrong with him? She reached out and touched him. Her hand settled gently on his cheek and rested there, where

Phillip Stargel had patted him. Her fingers moved, gently. "Remember," she whispered. "Remember what it was like to be human, to love, to do anything to protect your family the way I've tried to protect mine."

And he did, in a rush of almost forgotten emotion that nearly dropped him to his knees.

"I'm ready to die, Sorin," Nevada said. "I've accepted that. But my family . . . save them. It's my dying wish. You owe me that much."

"I owe you nothing," he said, his voice low and rasping.

She ignored his words, showing neither fear nor sorrow. Serene, trembling very slightly, she closed her eyes and tipped her head back and to the side, offering him her throat. The scent of her, of her skin and her breath and the blood on her finger, drifted up to taunt him, to rouse his hunger—and his memories, memories that were best left buried.

Laughing children, a loving wife, the comfort of a warm fire at the end of a long day. Contentment . . . yes, dammit, he had once been content.

And now he was damned.

Fuck it. He'd never liked the bitch queen anyway. "Let's go," he said, grabbing Nevada's arm and dragging her toward the door. She tripped along, unsteady, surprised. And judging by the expression on her face, very annoyed.

In the past three years Nevada had seen glimpses of the hallway outside her door, and she'd visited some rooms and passageways via remote viewing, but the rest of the big house had always been a mystery to her. It wasn't as if she'd seen every detail when she'd walked about in spirit only. She didn't see much now, as Sorin hustled her down the stairs, past other vamps who didn't dare to question his right to have her.

The house was very nice, for a vampire lair.

The kitchen he led her into was almost untouched; she recognized the remnants of her own meal—the meal she'd assumed would be her last and had been unable to eat.

"Where are you taking me?" she asked. She had hoped he'd kill her quickly and with a minimum of pain. Nevada realized that she had to die, but that didn't mean she wanted to *hurt*.

"I'm letting you go," Sorin said curtly. "When you're out the back door, head west. Run. Run as fast as you can and don't look back."

She stopped in her tracks. She was nowhere near a match for Sorin, strength-wise, but she caught him by surprise and his hold on her slipped. "You can't let me go!"

He stared at her as if she'd lost her mind. "I don't understand. I'm risking everything to let you go, and you're arguing with me?"

She could hardly explain to him that, fully expecting to die, she'd tied the breaking of the spell to her heartbeat. She hadn't been sure that the bitch would release her family before the spell was broken, so she'd had to make it work. Still, she'd known she was going to die, so attaching the whole shebang to her heartbeat had made sense. The world wouldn't be vulnerable for more than a few minutes. As soon as she was dead, the spell would be back in force and human homes would once again be safe from vampires.

She hadn't counted on Sorin actually releasing her. He couldn't do that! Her best hope had been that he'd help her family. This . . . this was cruel, because it gave her back the hope she'd lost a long time ago. She really wanted to live, but her survival meant every human in the world was vulnerable. Could she recast the original spell to make home a sanctuary from the vampires? Of course she could, but, God, how long would it take? How many people would die in the meantime?

The world would be a safer place if she died tonight, but she was weaker than she'd thought; she liked the idea of living, of finding her family and keeping them safe. She wanted to see the sun again, fall in love, laugh, lose herself in a silly movie or a sad book.

"Never mind," she said. "I'll go. Thanks. Which way is west? Just point."

Sorin's eyes narrowed, and he moved so he effectively blocked her path. "What are you up to?"

"Do you really want to know?" She'd been right about him, after all. He could've killed her, he was *supposed* to have killed her, but he hadn't been able to do it. She'd been right in seeing more in him, in sensing the *more* that lay beneath his skin, behind his eyes.

He surprised her then, at a time and in a place she thought held no more surprises. The vampire who'd kidnapped her, held her prisoner, threatened her and her family, and in the end saved her, took her face in his hands, leaned down, and placed his lips on her forehead. She was sure he also inhaled deeply.

Nevada held her own breath for a moment, and a moment was all she had. An explosion of glass and an unearthly scream from the front of the house interrupted the gentle kiss. Moving so fast she felt as if she were flying, Sorin carried her a few feet to the left and all but threw her into a small storage space beneath the back stairs. She grunted and her arm slammed against the wooden wall as she landed. The door slammed, and Nevada found herself trapped in a small place, in complete darkness, while outside her new prison what sounded very much like war raged.

She took a deep breath and closed her eyes. Anything might be happening out there, anything at all. But was it possible that the net she'd cast had caught a hero or two, after all?

CHAPTER
TWENTY-SEVEN

Three vampires and one human attacking a stronghold filled with an unknown number of rebels was ridiculous, but Luca didn't see that he had any choice. Surprise was the best advantage they had. It wasn't the first time in his long life that he'd gone into battle against long odds.

He would've given anything to have a safe place to leave Chloe, but like it or not the safest place for her was with him, no matter where he had to be, even if that place was here.

Duncan had always had a flair for the dramatic. He leapt through a large bay window, glass shattering as he gave one of his demonic yells. Isaac was a little less flamboyant, and was satisfied to burst through the front door.

Luca was right behind them, his senses on full alert as he homed in on the center of the energy that filled the house. The sharp pang of a hunger for power pulsed from beneath his feet, and it was so close, familiar. For a moment he was washed in that energy, and the pieces of the puzzle fell into place. He should've known. She'd always wanted more, for herself and for the kindred.

The vampires in the house weren't prepared for attack. This wasn't the time they'd planned to begin the fight in earnest, and they certainly hadn't expected resistance from their own kind. Many of them were new, new to rebellion and to the life of a vampire. They were all unarmed—thinking themselves safe here, thinking they had time before they launched their attack. They were confused by the sight of three vampires and a human woman who wielded a flashlight and a sword, both rather clumsily.

Before the rebels gathered their wits and were able to fight back, Luca was swinging his sword. With attackers coming from all directions, a properly wielded blade was the most efficient weapon; he could use his unnatural strength to its fullest. Eventually he might need the shotgun and the handguns, but those weapons operated at human speed, and sometimes they weren't fast enough. The sword was a part of him, an extension of his body. He'd been fighting with a sword since before he'd turned ten.

In the wide foyer, the formally decorated parlor, and the hallway splintering off the center of the house, bodies tangled in battle. Luca counted himself lucky that so far those they faced were young and inexperienced, as well as ill-prepared. Chloe's flashlight was effective on fledglings who were still so sensitive to light; it was enough to keep them away from her, which was all that was necessary.

Even when the rebels realized what was happening and attempted to defend themselves, they failed. None were as battle-trained as the three vampires who fought like whirling dervishes, at the same time doing their best to keep Chloe in the middle of them.

Between them, Isaac and Duncan had fought in almost as many battles as Luca had, and like him they'd served the Council in past years, as hunters or bodyguards. Like Luca, they saw the value in maintaining the secrecy of their existence. They also enjoyed a good fight now and then, and good fights were hard to come by in a modern world.

Swords flashed, slicing through vampire flesh, sending rebels to blood and then to dust. They didn't attempt to wound their opponents but inflicted only killing blows.

Beyond the bloodshed and the dust, Luca caught sight of a familiar head of blond hair, as Sorin ran from the rear part of the house and disappeared through a doorway, shutting the solid wooden door behind him. Given the energy Luca felt, the surging power beneath his feet, that door probably opened on a stairwell that would lead down to a basement. Running wasn't like Sorin; if anything, he loved a fight as much as Luca did. There had to be an important reason for Sorin to head *away* from a battle.

He moved in that direction. A young vampire, young in all ways, flew down the stairs from the right and leapt toward Luca, fangs extended, hands clawlike as he attempted to strike. It wasn't even a challenge to take the fledgling's head. As Luca fought, he worked his way toward the door where Sorin had gone. Chloe remained close, but not so close that he had to worry about catching her with the tip of his sword. The blade he swung was never beyond his control.

Among the three of them, they dispatched most of the rebel soldiers who'd been on this level of the house when they'd attacked, but more continued to pour in. Reinforcements had been called, through shouts and mental powers and even cell phones; some of them had been close by. Though they weren't the strongest of their kind they were soldiers, ready to fight to the end. Luca decided two competent fighters could handle the incoming, if those two were battle-trained.

He turned to Duncan. "Block the doorway. No one comes or goes." He jerked open the door. As he'd suspected, it opened onto a plain, steep stairwell. Chloe pressed close to his back, so close she was a part of him. He knew precisely where she was standing, and whether or not anyone was targeting her. He was struck by the certainty that it was meant to be just that way. Just before he closed the door behind them, he caught a glimpse of Duncan and Isaac taking up their stances near the doorway. Luca didn't know what he'd find below, other than the woman he'd come here looking for, and he didn't know how many other entrances to the basement there might be, but no reinforcements would take *these* stairs up or down, not as long as Duncan and Isaac survived.

They'd fought tougher battles than this one.

"Oh my God, oh my God," Chloe muttered as they hurried down the stairs, but she didn't hesitate, didn't drop down and hide her face in her hands and wail. He wanted to laugh, he wanted to stop and kiss her until she was breathless. She had no idea how brave she was. He'd tell her so, when this fight was over.

They reached the bottom of the stairs. This was no cluttered, utilitarian basement. It was cut into hallways and rooms and was larger than most homes. Though he didn't see Sorin or any others waiting for him, he knew they were close by. He sensed their presence, and probably at least a few of them sensed his. He wouldn't remain undetected for very long, so he might as well not even try to hide.

He lifted his sword into position, drawn back and ready to swing. It was perfect for taking heads, which was what he intended to do. He wasn't even going to give the traitor a chance at a fair fight, he was going to take her out as if she were a rabid wolf. The uprising depended on her. With her dead, it would roll to a stop. With the revolution halted there would be no reason for the warriors to come in at all, and therefore no reason for Chloe to be hunted. That alone was reason enough to fight.

Sorin was furious; furious with Regina, with Nevada, with himself. He'd believed in the cause, fought for it, killed for it many times over. But lately he'd been having nagging doubts, inexplicable moments of weakness: first Phillip Stargel, now Nevada. Dammit all to hell, all humans were *not* created equal. Some deserved protection. Some were good for nothing but serving as a source of food. Did they have to protect all in order to save some?

When Nevada had touched his face and said "remember," he had. He didn't know if she'd cast a spell on him or if it was simply the scent so similar to his daughter's that had brought the memories flooding back. It was more than the face of a child he'd adored, more than memories of his human life, good and bad. He remembered love. He recalled intensely how it felt, how it flooded his being and made everything else seem unimportant.

He didn't know what he was going to do, but he couldn't go on this way. Maybe he could get Nevada to a safe place, then simply disappear. He was through with Regina, with this war, but he wasn't a soldier who would desert in the middle of battle.

He found Regina in Jonas's prison cell, as he'd thought he would. With warriors coming in and more and more conduits being awakened, Jonas's job had become even more important than before.

"Warriors?" she snapped as soon as she saw Sorin.

"Luca," he said. "And others, including the conduit he's taken up with."

Regina whirled and glared at Jonas. "You didn't tell me there was a conduit in my own house!"

"My senses are overwhelmed," Jonas said, shrugging

his thin shoulders. Sorin could hear the deep weariness that was so pronounced tonight. Jonas didn't have a lot more to give; he was all but spent.

Regina looked at the maps around her, and Sorin did the same. But for one, all the pins in the maps were white and black, representing conduits killed and warriors who'd arrived. The one green pin was stuck in D.C., and though the map wasn't detailed enough to indicate it, he knew the conduit represented by that green pin was in this very house.

Her face twisted with rage. Her movements so quick they were a blur, Regina whipped a long, narrow-bladed knife from the sheath that hung against her hip, and buried it deep in Jonas's heart. She pulled it out, stabbed it deep again, then again.

"You're no good to me if you can't keep up when things get tough," she said viciously. "You're useless if you can't tell me when traitors are at my door!"

Jonas hung there for a moment, his gaze dulling even as he looked at Sorin—not for help, it was too late for that—but with a deeply sad expression of pleading in his eyes. *Stop her.* Then he went to dust.

Sorin looked down at the pitiful heap of empty clothes. This was the end of the line for him, and he knew it. If Regina would so easily kill someone who was still useful, someone who had, as far as she knew, served her well and faithfully, then no one was safe, not him, not anyone. Her eyes glittered red as she kicked at what was left of Jonas, that small pile of clothes and dust. No one was safe from her.

And he'd helped her get to this point. He'd commanded her army, killed conduits, and been instrumental in planning the attacks that were still to come. He'd taken Nevada and her family, cajoled and bullied his little witch into doing what was necessary. He'd set aside the fact that she smelled and looked like the daughter he'd left behind when he'd been turned, the daughter he'd watched from afar for as long as he'd dared.

Some humans—like Phillip Stargel, like Nevada . . . like Diera—deserved to be preserved and protected. Regina, self-named queen, would preserve no one if she had her way, he could see that now. To her, everyone was expendable.

"I have to join the fight," he said, and as the words left his mouth they took on new meaning. Could he take her here and now? She still held the knife, and she was stronger than she appeared to be. She was older than he, and she was blood born. It might be worth the risk, but if he died here, in an unarmed and unplanned attempt to kill her, who would get Nevada out of the house? Diera had grown up without the protection of her father; he wouldn't leave Nevada that vulnerable.

He didn't have to fight against the revolution; he just had to walk away. Luca or a warrior would take care of the queen, sooner or later.

Sorin gave Regina a crisp bow and left the room. He walked down a short hallway and stopped, listening; there was a fight taking place ahead of him. He couldn't reach the stairway without taking this hall, and the way was blocked by an ongoing battle. He hesitated, then shrugged. What the hell.

He rounded the corner, paused to take in the situation. Luca Ambrus fought three rebel vampires; he was armed to the teeth, but he didn't need weapons to be lethal. Luca was all but washed in blood and dust. He'd killed a lot of vampires in a very short period of time and he wore the evidence all over him.

The conduit Chloe Fallon also held a weapon, though she was obviously unskilled with it. The blood of the kindred had splattered across her clothing, here and there, but it was obvious Luca had been placing himself between her and danger.

Why had he brought her here? Was he trying to get her killed? At the moment Luca was keeping himself solidly between the rebels and the conduit, but more soldiers were headed this way, so he couldn't keep it up indefinitely. She had her back to a wall, but there were pockets of opportunity that a rebel was sure to take advantage of sooner or later.

One soldier managed to slip around Luca, and the Fallon woman pointed a flashlight at his face and turned it on. The vampire screamed, dropped his knife, and lifted his hands to cover his eyes as he spun away, useless in the fight for the moment. Not a normal flashlight then, and a fairly effective defensive tool.

Nevada could use one of those . . .

The blinded soldier drifted too far to one side and was wounded by the wildly swinging blade of another rebel. When he floundered and stumbled into a dangerous path, Luca took his head.

But in the space of a heartbeat, reinforcements had arrived. Luca now fought four, and others would soon be here. An expertly wielded blade slashed close and Luca dodged to the side; another soldier took advantage and shifted, moving closer to Chloe, his blade aimed at a vulnerable spot. She didn't even see him; her attention was focused on Luca.

Almost without thinking, Sorin surged forward. The rebel soldier wasn't even alarmed to see Sorin coming, thinking that his commander was joining the fight. That was true enough, just not the way the vampire assumed. In one smooth move Sorin made his hand into a claw and rammed it into the soldier's chest, ripping the heart from his body and plucking the sword from a hand that was in the process of going from flesh to dust.

Luca's head whipped around. The conduit had turned at the last second, and saw what had happened. Their eyes met; he saw both fear and relief in hers. He could not even begin to imagine what she saw in his.

Sorin used the sword he'd taken from the rebel to sever another head, and then another. He shifted so his back was to the conduit, his body placed so that, between him and Luca, she was guarded. The tide quickly turned; it took only a few moments for the rebels to grasp the fact that their leader was against them. Almost as one, those who were still alive turned and fled.

And Luca turned to Sorin, sword raised.

"No!" the conduit shouted, shoving against him. "He— I don't know why, but he's fighting *with* us."

"I know," Luca said. "I just don't understand why."

Sorin lowered his sword, taking the chance that he wouldn't soon be a pile of dust, like the others. "Hell, Luca, neither do I."

For the moment Isaac and Duncan were holding their own upstairs—she knew because no one else had come down the stairs—and the vampires in the basement had backed off. They weren't gone, though. Even Chloe, totally untrained in battle, knew that much.

The basement was like a maze, with crisscrossing hallways and closed doors and echoing noises she couldn't quite place. With Luca on one side and Sorin on the other, she was as safe as could be, all things considered. She never would've thought to trust Sorin, but he'd saved her life tonight, more than once.

"Why did you bring her along?" Sorin demanded angrily as they worked their way down a hallway. The two men worked in concert, making sure each room was clear before they let her walk past the door. They were moving deeper into the basement, searching for Regina.

"Where could I leave her? Jonas knows where she is every minute. She isn't safe anywhere, unless I can stop this madness."

"Jonas is dead. She killed him."

Luca's eyes went as cold and gray as frost.

"The sanctuary spell is broken," Sorin continued.

"Already? It's done?" Luca asked.

"Yes."

Chloe felt as if her insides were being ripped apart. No one was safe now. Not her parents, not her friends . . . no one. They were too late.

Luca cleared another room, moved past the door. "What changed your mind?" he asked.

Sorin slanted an inscrutable look at Chloe as he mirrored Luca's movements. "Some humans are worth saving," he finally said. He gave her a wicked grin. "They're too yummy to let anything happen to them."

Chloe edged closer to Luca. *Yummy?* She tightened her grip on the flashlight, which so far had proved to be much handier than the short sword.

"They deserve to live," Luca said, without arguing about the yummy part.

"*Some of them* deserve to live," Sorin clarified, and then he sighed. "The problem is, how do you decide which ones?"

They reached an intersecting hallway. Luca halted, his head tilted a little, then he shot out a muscular arm and shoved Chloe behind him. The next instant a half dozen vampires exploded from the shadows toward them. Someone fired a gun, the sound deafening in the close confines of the basement. Sorin jolted, then grinned and launched himself forward, not even slowed down by the bullet he'd taken. If the shooter wasn't accurate, a gun wasn't much good against a vampire.

Another shot blasted her ears, and Chloe instinctively fell back. Maybe those bullets wouldn't do much damage to the vampires, but they'd kill her.

Luca and Sorin took up a back-to-back position in the hallway, and between them they blocked any of the attacking vampires from getting past. She backed up a little more, out of reach of those long, slashing blades. Blood arced, and choking dust filled the air. These vampires were better fighters than the first wave had been; reinforcements had arrived. Luca and Sorin were holding their own, but were harder pressed. Sorin shifted in her direction and she backed up a few feet, out of his way. She felt stupidly helpless. All she could do was watch and pray and try not to trip them up—

Maybe not. Maybe there was something she could do to help.

Chloe leaned her sword against the wall, close at hand if she needed it, but even though it was short it was heavy, and she knew she didn't have a chance against a vampire in any kind of a sword fight. The flashlight was heavy, too; she almost needed both hands to lift it. She steadied it, aimed it, and turned it on. The powerful beam hit one of the rebel vampires, touched his neck and cheek, and instantly blistered his skin. Before she could adjust her aim to shine it into his eyes, the rebel whirled and kicked the flashlight out of her hands. It went flying across the concrete floor, rolling away, and the light went out.

Chloe grabbed for her sword, but even as she did she knew she wasn't fast enough. The vampire she'd burned with the light was coming for her.

Luca spun, already swinging his sword, and took the vampire's head.

Chloe dove for the flashlight. Maybe it wasn't broken. Maybe the battery had just been jarred loose, and she could get it working again.

"Call me!" The Warrior's voice came more crisp and clear than ever. There had been a time when that voice had terrified Chloe, but now it was a strange comfort. *"You need me."*

"Promise me!" Chloe silently demanded. She grabbed the flashlight, leaned against the wall as she shook it, turned off the switch, then turned it on again. Nothing.

Swearing under her breath, she unscrewed the cap, then retightened it. Her knees were shaking, she trembled down to every bone. The flashlight flickered, then went out again. The din of battle was deafening in the hallway, blood was everywhere, dust clogged the air. Oh God, she was breathing secondhand vampire.

"Call me!"

"You have to promise. Luca is mine! *He saved me, he's fighting for us!"* She loved him, too, but that wasn't an argument likely to sway a warrior. *"You'll need him."*

For a moment there was silence from the Warrior in the other world. Then, reluctantly, she said. *"I promise. Call me, now!"*

Chloe looked for Luca; he and Sorin were being drawn farther down the hallway by the rebel vampires who continued to arrive on the scene. The fight was a blur of silver, flesh, blood, and that bitter gray dust. She anxiously watched him, trying to focus on him.

"Ask! Call my name!" Indie's request burned with urgency.

"Indie! Come on in," Chloe said.

"Name!" Indie demanded, the sound fierce.

Chloe closed her eyes and tried to remember the dreams she'd had, the name she'd heard. Why was it so hard? It was like trying to remember the title of a movie, or the name of someone you hadn't seen in a long time, the right answer was there, on the tip of the tongue. Indi-something. Indie . . .

"Relax, and listen."

Chloe took a deep breath, she opened her eyes, and there it was. She knew it as well as she knew her own name. "Please help us, Indikaiya."

There was a burst of light, a glow that hurt her eyes. She leaned against the wall, gripping the broken flashlight. Luca and Sorin had moved even farther away; she could hear Luca calling her name. No, the call was in her head, like Indie's voice, but it was just as clear as if he'd been standing beside her.

Move closer. You're too far away.

But she couldn't move, not yet. Indie was taking shape before her. There was that braid she'd seen first, now hanging over well-shaped muscular shoulders, the hint of Indie that had so haunted Chloe because it hadn't made sense. Indie was a tall woman, strong and determined—and armed with a sword.

In seconds, Indikaiya was solid. She turned to face Chloe, and she smiled, with pride and love and a fierce joy. The Warrior had a strong and striking face, not pretty, exactly, but somehow beautiful. She looked like a long-legged European model . . . if models had muscles and wore short leather shifts.

"Thank you," she said, and then she turned and ran, following the fight that had called her here.

Chloe called after her, "Luca and the big blond are on your side!" just in case. She'd come here wishing Sorin dead, but she wouldn't want to rob Luca of a much-needed ally in this fight, even if that ally had once tried to kill her and had bitten Valerie.

Indie disappeared around the corner Luca and Sorin had turned moments earlier, and when she was out of sight, Chloe took a deep breath. She attempted to regain her strength, to steady the shaking of her knees before moving forward. Bringing the Warrior in had exhausted her—and she'd already been pretty damn spent—though she hadn't really done anything except somehow create a portal between worlds. Who knew that would take so much energy?

She kept her gaze pinned straight ahead, bracing herself to do as Luca had instructed and move toward him, though goodness knows she didn't want to get too close. So far the rebel vampires had been drawn to the fighting, but that might not last. At any moment one of them might realize that the human in the invading "army" was all but helpless . . . and momentarily alone.

Chloe caught a hint of movement out of the corner of her eye, and forced herself to turn, trying to brace herself for an attack. Instead of a brutal vampire like she'd expected, a tiny, dark-haired woman was striding down the hall, an expression of concern on her face. "Are you all right?" she asked. "Dear, I don't think you should be here. It isn't safe."

"That's the understatement of the century," Chloe said warily, trying to will some strength into her legs. The woman smiled as she came closer. Chloe instinctively gripped the flashlight tighter. The sword was several feet away, and she wished it was closer, like in her hand. Vampires all looked different, some creepy, some beautiful, some downright ugly, some ordinary. If this woman wasn't a vampire, then what was she doing down here—

The dark-haired woman moved so fast, her hand slashing, that Chloe caught only the blur of motion. She reacted instinctively, her own hand moving with incredible speed, smashing the heavy flashlight across the woman's nose. The woman howled with pain, even as Chloe felt a hot sting, but when she looked down she saw the bloody blade in the woman's hand, and her own clothing beginning to run red with the river of her blood. The hot sting became fire, spreading, overtaking her, engulfing her.

Confused, she stared at the blood. Where was the dust? No, no dust; she wasn't a vampire. Her brain couldn't seem to work. Something was very, very wrong, and her legs wouldn't hold her up. She dropped bonelessly to the floor.

TWENTY-EIGHT

If this was the way vampires lived, then being a bloodsucker paid a whole helluva lot better than engineering.

Jimmy followed Rurik's increasingly abrupt and loud directions to find himself in an exclusive part of D.C. where the homes were movie star worthy. The guy who'd admitted he couldn't drive, a warrior who was primitive in so many ways, made a decent navigator. Once they were on the right street, finding their destination became easy. Most of the houses were quiet, some were actually dark. But one . . . one was swarming with men and women who fought on the lawn and inside, visible on the other side of a broken picture window.

Great.

Jimmy stopped in the middle of the street and Rurik threw the passenger door open. He was obviously anxious to join the battle, but he stopped and leaned into the car.

"Your job is done. You are free to leave. But if you wish to fight, if you wish to be a warrior . . ." His smile was bright. "It would be my pleasure to fight with you again."

With that Rurik turned and ran, not waiting for a response.

For a moment Jimmy sat there and watched, a part of him screaming that this couldn't be real, another part having no choice but to accept all that he'd seen and heard. He wasn't a fighter, never had been. He hadn't even liked hunting deer with his dad. Then again, he'd never been in this situation before. What if one more warrior made a difference? What if he represented the tipping point between good and evil, between safety and danger for the entire fucking world? Knowing what he knew, could he run away and live with himself?

He pulled sharply to the curb, shut down the engine, and got out of the car. As he retrieved the shotgun and a box of shells from the backseat, another car pulled up to the house. A man dressed in deerskin jumped from the passenger seat, then reached inside to grab a quiver of arrows and a wicked-looking bow.

The car that had dropped off the new arrival hit the gas before the warrior had a chance to close the door. Jimmy watched the car and the man behind the wheel make an escape.

As Jimmy stuffed shells into all his pockets, he watched the taillights of the escaping car. *Coward.*

Regina staggered back, blood streaming from her broken nose. Despite herself she covered her nose with a protective hand, even though she knew it would heal within minutes. The damn little *bitch*! How dare she? Regina stared with satisfaction down at the dying human. The stab had been a killing one; the conduit hung on, but she didn't have long. Even a few minutes of life, however, was longer than Regina was prepared to grant her, if only for the insult of breaking her nose. She bent over the conduit and lifted her knife again, intent on cutting the girl's throat and watching her last breath bubble out.

Chloe Fallon lifted the damn flashlight that was still in her weak trembling hand, shook it, swore, and then an unnatural light burst to life and shone directly into Regina's eyes, blinding her.

She staggered back, screaming with pain from the burst of light so close to her sensitive eyes. Damn her, damn her! She couldn't see, but it didn't matter. She didn't have to deliver the coup de grace. The Fallon woman would soon be dead anyway, so she should forget about her and concentrate on escaping. She smelled the fresh blood and had to fight the urge to drop to the floor and drink. Without her sight, though, she had to be cautious. Immediate escape was the best strategy.

Her eyes burned, the skin on the left side of her face hurt, but it was a familiar burn, one she knew would quickly heal. Any vampire who'd attempted to take on the sun too soon knew this feeling. Her eyes, though, her eyes hurt.

Regina was very familiar with the basement; with one hand against the wall to guide her and her other senses fully engaged, she made her way along the corridor, away from the battle and toward the hidden exit.

Of all her followers, she'd depended on Sorin the most. In him she'd seen someone who could almost be her equal in ruthlessness—almost, because only Luca was her true equal. But Luca had taken up with that measly human, while Sorin had inexplicably turned traitor. What had happened? Seeing him fight alongside Luca had been a shock, but why should she expect anything different from him, or anyone else? Why should she expect loyalty without fear? She'd make him pay for turning against her.

But that was for later. This wasn't over. Right now she was outnumbered, the warriors had arrived, and Luca, that blood-born son of a bitch, had made matters worse. Even if she could see, the battle wouldn't be an easy one. She should've had Luca killed when she'd had the chance. When he'd shown up at Council headquarters, she should've done the job herself. He never would have seen her coming.

She wouldn't have that chance again.

At least she'd made him pay for his interference by killing his precious little conduit, the human who'd turned him against his own kind. She would've loved to have spent more time with Chloe Fallon, to make her suffer, but there had been no opportunity to savor the moment, or the blood. What a shame.

The fighting continued, noisy and messy. Now and then she even heard the blast of a firearm from the ground level of the house, above her head. Sorin had often advised her to provide the army with more modern weapons, but she hadn't seen the necessity, not when her soldiers could kill with their hands and their teeth; only the newest and weakest needed anything else in battle. A few swords, whatever ordinary weapons they needed to take out the conduits, a handful of guns in case a few warriors made it into this world . . . nothing more had been necessary.

She'd never expected it would come to this, that her followers would be fighting their own kind. If she'd had a bomb she'd blow them all to hell and start over, building a new army. What was another fifty years or so when she had an eternity? But she had no explosives, and she'd be damned if she'd wait a moment longer than she had to.

Already her vision was beginning to return; no one healed more quickly than a blood born. She climbed the narrow stairs beyond the hidden doorway, opened a hatch concealed by a patch of perfect grass, and slipped into the night, far from the house where the fighting still raged. It was her battle, her war, but it didn't make sense to sacrifice herself in a skirmish where the odds weren't with her.

There would be other battles. This fight was lost but the war itself was far from over.

Nevada drew her knees in, buried her head in the folds of her skirt, and closed her eyes tight.

Unfortunately she couldn't close her ears.

Outside her dark hiding place, it sounded like the end of the world. Who would be foolish enough, courageous enough, to attack a nest of vampires? Maybe the conduits they'd been trying to kill, though she didn't think those humans were any better fighters than she was. Maybe her spell requesting help had been more effective than she'd imagined it could be. If only they'd arrived sooner, before she'd completed the task Sorin had brought her here to do.

She couldn't help but wonder how many humans were in danger tonight because she'd lifted the spell that had once kept them safe in their homes. She hadn't expected to live long after her work was done, she'd expected to die—and to take the breaking of the spell with her. She'd always realized that Sorin was more than the others, that he was better, but she'd never imagined that he'd actually *save* her.

If she'd known that was even possible, what would she have done differently?

For a while she couldn't concentrate enough to practice her remote viewing spell, but as the sounds of battle waned a bit, she lost herself in that mental place that allowed her to travel, and stepped out of the storage space and into battle.

No one could see or touch her, but she saw them. Some of the vampires she recognized; she'd seen many of them in her time here. They'd delivered food, towels, sheets, soap, clothing—the endless supply of things a woman needed during three years of life. They'd threatened and taunted her; they'd imprisoned her family. Those who fought against them were different. Two who blocked the doorway to the basement stairs were vampires, too, but she hadn't seen them before. They were obviously fighting against others of their kind, keeping them out of the basement, for some reason.

If Sorin could risk everything to save her, maybe there were other vampires who weren't all that impressed with the queen and her plans. She could hope, anyway.

Away from the doorway, into the hallways and entryway and parlors, rebel vampires also fought against others. Male and female—though most were muscular and fearless men—they were armed with swords, arrows, long wooden staffs filed to a point at one end, and guns of all types. They were dressed in varied styles, as if each had stepped out of a history book. They were very effective against the vamps; they knew where and how to strike. What were they?

A former guard she recognized jumped a soldier who held a gun in each hand. Using what looked like a butcher knife, the vampire cut the soldier's throat. The gunman bled, fell to the floor . . . and faded away. Solid one moment, then misty, and then gone. Okay, so they weren't exactly human, though they appeared to be ordinary flesh and blood.

What on earth had her spell conjured up?

A very tall, dark-haired man with a sword he handled well cut the head off a vampire. The vamp looked disgustingly bloody and gross for a moment, then went to dust.

The dark-haired swordsman swung about, looked directly at Nevada.

And winked.

Nevada was shocked back to her body. Whoever—whatever—the fighters were, they could see her. At least, that one could. The others had been busy fighting for their lives, so she couldn't be sure if they all had the ability or if it was just . . . him.

Luca felt a sharp pain slice through his heart. He wavered. "Chloe!" Her name came automatically. He dizzily looked around, trying to find her. He, Sorin, and Indikaiya had already reduced the number of rebels significantly; the battle was waning. Many had already decided retreat was their best option, and he couldn't blame them. Even in the narrow confines of the hallways, the threesome fought together as if they were veterans accustomed to watching one another's backs. A warrior, a turncoat, and a blood born made for an odd, but very effective, team. Sorin and Indikaiya wouldn't miss him in the fight, not now when there were only a handful of rebels remaining. He dispatched one, sent another one running, and turned back toward Chloe.

She wasn't in sight. Why hadn't she stayed with him? Why hadn't she kept close, as he'd told her to? He ran, his heart pounding with pain and panic. The flow of battle had separated them, and now . . . she was dying. They were bonded; she was inside him, a part of him, in more ways than he'd known was possible, and because of that, he knew.

He found her lying on the floor in a puddle of blood, alone, barely breathing. The amount of blood made the bottom drop out of his stomach. From the position of the wound, he knew the knife had cut into her heart. She'd been left here to die, left for him to find. She'd be dead in minutes.

Luca dropped to his knees, released his hold on the sword. It clattered against the floor loudly, echoing hollowly.

She was still conscious—barely breathing, her brown eyes dull with encroaching death, but still conscious.

Somehow she focused on him, weakly trying to lift one hand to him. "Did we win?" she whispered.

He lifted the hand that she couldn't, cradled it in his, fighting back his pain and panic. "Not yet."

She took a shallow breath. "Haven't you . . . ever seen a war movie? You're supposed to tell me . . . the battle is over and the good guys have won . . . and without me . . ." She stopped, gasped. "*Not yet* isn't at all inspiring."

"I'll try to do better." He gently gathered Chloe in his arms, tears burning his eyes. She stifled a weak cry as he moved her. In the distance, beyond and above him, the battle continued, but he didn't care. Let it go on without him. All that mattered to him in this world was right here, in his arms. He hadn't had her long enough, he thought savagely. Just a few days. But she'd made him laugh, she'd made him angry, she'd brought color and joy and *life* to him.

Her chest lifted with another of those shallow breaths. "Can you . . . lick this . . . and make it better?"

"No," he said, his voice thick. He could barely see her through the thick film of tears. Angrily he blinked them away. He didn't want to miss a minute, a precious second, of her life. He would have tried to make her vampire, he'd have done anything to keep her with him, but she'd told him she didn't want to be a vampire. He didn't know if he could do it, anyway; she was too close to dying, there wouldn't be enough time.

"Vampire," she whispered, groping weakly toward him.

"Yes." She'd never called him an endearment, he realized, but she'd called him something far more important: his name.

"Luca," she said, and with a start he realized the bond between them was still there, that she was still feeling what he felt. "Luca . . . make me . . . vam-pire."

He was so shaken he wasn't sure he'd heard correctly. "Chloe?"

"I love . . . you. Stay," she managed. "I want . . . to stay." This time her effort to draw in air was nothing more than a shudder. "With . . . you," she finished.

He froze, suddenly, terribly afraid there wasn't time. If she died, if her heart took its last beat, it would be too late. Savagely he tore at his wrist with his fangs.

Maybe she had a chance. Maybe. She had already taken a significant amount of his blood when they'd bonded. This wouldn't be like starting fresh. He didn't have time for a fresh start.

Shaking, he placed his bloody wrist at her mouth. "Drink, Chloe, drink."

Her lips moved, but the blood dribbled out of her mouth, down her cheek. The dull haze over her brown eyes was growing. Fiercely he pressed his wrist down on her mouth, forced the blood against her tongue. It began dribbling out of her mouth again. He growled, rubbed her throat, forced her to swallow. "Dammit, Chloe! Drink!"

Fuck! He didn't know how much she'd need. Turning a human wasn't a precise process, there wasn't a recipe for it, or a formula. There was no set number of feed-ings, no specific amount of blood needed. All that was required was for the vampire blood to overpower the human blood, to become dominant, to thrive.

She wasn't swallowing. He made a wordless sound of grief, of fury, and ground his wrist even harder against her mouth. Over and over he rubbed her throat. "Please," he sobbed, not caring that he was crying like a baby. "Chloe, please. Please don't leave me. Drink, sweetheart, please drink."

Her hand moved.

Slowly, as if the effort was almost beyond her, she lifted her hand, gripped his arm, and held his wrist to her mouth.

On his knees, bent over her, he shook with sobs. Slowly her mouth began to suck at his torn wrist. She made a soft, hungry little sound, then suddenly she was clinging to his arm and sucking hard, as if she were starving.

He sat down hard on the floor and held her on his lap, cradling her as she fed. New vampires were unpredictable, hungry, often feral. "I'll take care of you," he whispered against her hair, gently rocking her back and forth. A war had started, but he'd have to constantly keep an eye on her, watch over her, train and teach and protect her—but he'd also have to protect others from her. She came first. If she was too wild he'd leave the war to others and take her to Scotland. Or to Ahron, if the trip to Scotland was impossible in her new state.

But she was alive. That was all he cared about, all that mattered. She was his, and he intended to keep her. War be damned, and Marie be damned.

Chloe finally released her death grip on his arm, licked his wrist, then leaned her head against him and sighed as she closed her eyes. "My head is spinning," she murmured. "Am I drunk?"

"No."

"Are you sure?" She opened her eyes, grinned up at him, and sat up as easily as if she hadn't nearly died just a few minutes earlier. As curious as a child, she lifted her blood-drenched shirt and watched as the wound knitted shut. "Wow. I feel . . . giddy." She laughed. "Oh, man, I feel so *good*. I can fight now, you don't have to protect me like you did when we got here. I bet I can kick your ass."

"I wouldn't go that far," he said, wiping his cheeks dry. She'd need protection for some time to come. She looked so happy, as mischievous as a child, that suddenly he laughed.

"Everything looks different. Luca, there are so many things I want to do. There's so much to see . . ." And then she blinked twice and her face fell. "No more sunshine," she said, her giddiness gone.

"Not for a while," he said. "As you get older, you'll be able to go out again."

"No more chocolate," she said in a mournful tone.

"You won't want it," he assured her. "Not for a few hundred years, at least."

"But I have you." She placed her arms around his neck. He waited for her to bite him again, to feed a new hunger she couldn't control. Instead she rested her head against his shoulder. "When I was dying, nothing else mattered."

He gathered her more tightly against him, wordlessly giving thanks that she was still with him. Her reaction was . . . curious. She wasn't behaving like other new vampires. Maybe it was because they were bonded, because she'd fed on his blood instead of regular vampire blood, that she was stronger than he'd imagined she would be.

And she was a conduit. She was different from the beginning. It would be interesting to see how this developed.

She began twitching as strength coursed through her body. The world would look different to her now. All her senses would be sharper, more sensitive.

She'd seen her last sunrise for a while.

"I feel so odd," she said, standing in a flash, looking around her as if everything was new. In a way, it was. "Where's the bitch who stabbed me? I want a piece of her. I'll teach her. I'll pull all her hair out, I'll tie her guts into bows—"

"Small woman with dark hair?" Luca asked, breaking into that litany of physical mayhem.

Chloe stopped, rolled her shoulders, took a deep breath. "Yeah. How did you know?"

His own anger bit hard and deep. Marie had killed Chloe in order to distract him, or else she'd done it out of spite. Whatever the reason, he couldn't allow the act to go unpunished.

And Marie *had* killed Chloe. Chloe's life as she'd known it was over. She wouldn't go back to work, watch movies with Valerie, attend school . . . go home to her parents, who'd lost their child tonight. As a new vampire she wouldn't be able to hide what she'd become. It took time to learn how to behave, move, and restrain natural instincts around humans. Chloe likely wouldn't have those skills until all those who knew her well were dead and buried.

But she had him. For better or worse, she had him.

After what seemed like hours, the sounds of battle faded away until there was only an occasional sound of swords clashing, or something breaking. Nevada still didn't move. What would she find if she stepped out of her hiding place? Had Sorin survived? Who was out there? Who was winning—or had won?

She knew that it would be best for everyone if she died here and now. The protection spell would be reinstated the moment her heart stopped beating. Given time she could use her magic to recast the spell, but how long would that take? How much time did humans all over the world have left?

But she couldn't take her own life, couldn't pretend that she didn't want to live.

The sounds of war diminished, and then finally faded entirely. It was probably safe to peek outside, to see what was going on. But she had no idea what might be on the other side of the small door that separated her from . . . chaos.

When the door opened, she flinched and then blinked against the light that flooded her small space. Sorin was there, holding a sword in his hand. He wasn't alone. Behind him stood a tall woman dressed in a leather shift. She also carried a sword. There was the fighter who'd seen her even though she'd not been present in body, and a man about her age cradling a shotgun; his pockets bulged with a few cartridges for that weapon.

They all looked as if they'd been fighting for their lives. Sweaty, breathing hard, bloody, a couple of them bleeding from minor wounds . . . not the vampire, of course . . . they looked at her expectantly.

Maybe they were here to kill her because they knew. Maybe they would take the decision from her.

Sorin offered his hand, and Nevada took it. He helped her from the small closet, held her hand until she was standing steadily. Nevada lifted her chin bravely, looking up because they were all so blasted tall! "I suppose you already know what's happening here. Kill me and the protection spell will go back into effect. I tied the breaking of it to my heartbeat, because I was sure the queen bitch would kill me as soon as I broke the spell." She took a deep breath. "I don't want to die, but I understand." She closed her eyes and waited for the slice of a sword or the blast of a shotgun.

Nothing happened.

Nevada slowly opened one eye, to find that Sorin and the dark-haired soldier had placed themselves in front of her and held their swords up and ready. They were both positioned and willing to defend her from the others, even though they'd all fought on the same side tonight.

It was the female with a braid who spoke. "Down, boys. I for one have no intention of killing an innocent human."

The man with the shotgun nodded. "Seriously, it would be like shooting a kitten."

Sorin and the other man both relaxed, slightly.

"Can you fix it without dying?" Sorin asked.

"Yes, with time," Nevada responded.

"How much time?" the dark-haired man asked. He had a touch of a Russian accent that was kind of sexy.

"I don't know," Nevada confessed. "Days, weeks, months . . ."

"We don't have months," Sorin said sharply.

"I know," she whispered guiltily.

Since no one made a move to kill her, her two body-guards relaxed. The new arrival turned and looked down at her. Again, he winked. "I knew a witch once. She was not nearly as pretty as you."

"You saw me."

"Of course I did. Those of us who travel between worlds see others who travel in a similar way."

Between worlds. She shouldn't be surprised. He caught her gaze and held it, and Nevada felt something she hadn't experienced in a very long time. It was unexpectedly nice. "My name is Nevada."

"I am Rurik, beautiful one." He bowed gallantly. Sorin snorted, and so did the female. "Never fear. While I am in this world no one will dare to kill you."

It didn't seem fair, even to her, that her survival meant others could—would—die.

And still, she didn't want to go. Not now, when things had just gotten interesting.

When the others moved away, Sorin took her arm and leaned down to whisper in her ear. "Did you put a spell on me?"

"No!" she said. "Is something wrong?"

"Yes," he responded. Then, "No. But when you said *remember . . .*"

"That wasn't a spell. I just . . . I saw that the memories were within you but you'd buried them deep. I saw that you needed them to come to the surface."

"Perhaps I'd buried them for good reason," he grumbled.

Nevada looked around. "Is she dead?" she asked. It wasn't necessary that she use a name; Sorin would know who she was asking about: the queen.

"It appears that she escaped," he said, and she heard real regret in his voice.

They followed the others into the dining room connected to the kitchen, which had been badly damaged but wasn't destroyed like the rooms she'd seen when she'd traveled out of her body. Many of the fighters who'd come from another world to help had survived and had gathered here. They had their heads together, making plans for what was to come. Some tended minor wounds.

They were fighters, soldiers. Her part in this was no less important.

Nevada gathered her own internal strength. She could do this. "I'll need a place where no one will find me, for a while. I'll need my books, the vials, the herbs I've collected over the years. And my crystals. They're important to the process."

"We can't stay here," Sorin said.

"My family must be protected," she insisted. "You know damn well if that bitch queen can get her hands on them and use them, she'll do it."

"For the weakest among us, you make many demands," Sorin grumbled.

It pissed her off to be called the weak link, even if it was, in some ways, true. "Maybe I'm physically weak, but you need me. I'm the only one who can do what must be done to fix this."

Sorin gave a gentlemanly nod of his head. That was enough of an answer for her.

Rurik turned and looked at them, his gaze moving sharply from one to the other. Nevada hoped he didn't think they were a couple! But then again, that hardly mattered at the moment.

Did it?

Chloe wanted to run, to fly. She was certain she *could* fly, if she tried. Everything around her looked different. She saw colors she had never noticed before, heard everything, as if the world breathed.

Luca held on to her, gently but also firmly, as they climbed the stairs to the ground floor of the house. It looked different from when they'd last seen it. There was dust and blood everywhere, rumpled clothing strewn about, walls and furnishings crushed. A discarded sword or two were lying in the dust.

Isaac and Duncan were still guarding the door, though the fight was over. There was a deep gash in Duncan's face, but it was healing before her eyes. Amazing.

She could do that now. Did she still have an aneurysm, or was that healed? Who the hell cared? Even if it burst now her body would immediately heal itself. She was free, free of the specter of death that had hovered over her for so long.

They heard voices from the back of the house and headed in that direction, Isaac and Duncan trailing behind.

The first thing Chloe noticed, as they came upon a group in the dining room, was that two of them, a redhaired girl and a young man with a shotgun, smelled wonderful. She was drawn to them, she wanted to get closer, but Luca stopped her with a firm grip and a word.

No.

And as if they knew what she was thinking, Sorin

and one of the warriors placed themselves between her and the yummy smell.

Hunger. That's what she experienced as she smelled the humans. *Hunger.* But she had more control than they seemed to think she had. She'd been able to resist chocolate ganache cake when she'd been dieting. She could resist the humans now.

The vampires seemed surprised that she didn't leap on the humans in the room. Luca's grip eased. A little.

"She has unusual control for a fledgling," Sorin said, but he didn't move away from the redhead.

Luca gave her a deeply speculative look. "She does," he agreed.

Indie stepped around the protective males. Her expression was grim. "What has he done to you?"

"He saved me," Chloe said calmly. "I was dying, and with my permission, he changed me."

The redhead peeked around Sorin. "Chloe!" she called.

Not trusting herself much more than Sorin and Luca did, Chloe didn't move closer. "Do I know you?"

"I'm Nevada. Apparently, I'm a, uh, witch. I tried to send you a warning when I found out that the vampires were coming after you."

"Remember," Chloe whispered, as the contact she'd dismissed came back to her. "You warned me they were coming and then told me to remember."

"That's why you didn't forget me," Luca said, relief in his voice, relief that he finally had an explanation.

Nevada blushed. "I guess the spell didn't work exactly as it was supposed to."

Chloe smiled. Nevada drew back a bit, obviously afraid, and Chloe realized that her fangs, a new development, were extended "Thank you," she said. "Don't mind the fangs. It's nothing personal."

The redheaded witch looked confused.

"If I hadn't remembered Luca, nothing would've happened as it should."

Luca stepped around her, maintaining his grip on her arm. She looked at that hand and raised an eyebrow, and he released his hold. Reluctantly. "I'll be good," she whispered.

He stood slightly in front of her, and she knew he was alert to the possibility that she might, at any moment, pounce on the delicious humans. He didn't yet know that part of what she'd brought with her to this new life was her discipline and control. She'd show him, though it might take some time.

"How many warriors are there?"

"A handful here, others on the way," Indie answered.

Luca faced her. "Can we work together?"

"I don't see that we have any choice," she responded, obviously unhappy about the prospect of fighting beside those she'd come here to kill.

"Marie escaped," Luca said. "This won't be over until she's dead. We can kill every soldier she's recruited and in a few years this will start all over again, in another place, when we don't expect it and aren't prepared. If she's determined to do this, nothing but death will stop her. And as a blood born, she won't be easy to kill."

"She's not indestructible," Sorin said.

Chloe stared at the blond vampire. She knew where everyone else here stood, and why, but he was a mystery. "For all we know you're a spy. You changed sides pretty quickly. Why should we believe anything you say?"

He looked her in the eye. "In the beginning I saw the pretty version of Regina's plan. It was an ideal, a perfect world for us. But over time I saw the wrongness of her thinking. When she killed Jonas, an act I'm sure she already regrets, I knew it was over, for me. She's going to kill anyone who gets in her way, human or vampire.

If she has her way, there will be nothing left of the world we know."

"He saved my life tonight," Nevada said softly. "Sorin can be trusted, I swear."

The human with the shotgun raised his weapon slightly in the air, as if he were a schoolboy asking for permission to speak.

"I'm low man on the totem pole here tonight, so maybe I should just keep my mouth shut, but seriously, warriors, vampires who are apparently on the right side of things, me, the spell being broken . . . it can't be coincidence that all this happened on the same night. How is that even possible?"

Nevada blushed, blood flooding her cheeks. A new and tantalizing scent filled the air, but Chloe recognized it for what it was. It was also forbidden. She had the strength to set aside any impulses that would make her no better than the monsters who'd made terrible plans for the world.

"That was me, again," Nevada admitted. "I . . . I cast a net, asking for help. Any and all help. I didn't know what else to do." She gave in to a little smile. "And it worked. How cool is that?"

Chloe felt the surge of Luca's annoyance.

"You got me here with a *spell*?" he asked tightly.

"Well, not *just* you," she said.

"You don't appear to be even a quarter of a century old, and yet your magic affected me not once, but twice. That's impressive."

Chloe suppressed a smile. Luca might admit aloud that Nevada's magical abilities were impressive, but inside he was seething. He definitely didn't like the idea that he could be affected by spells cast by a small, and very young, human.

They began to talk battle plans, recruitment, strategy . . . which almost bored Chloe to tears. After a while she found herself studying the throat of the shotgun-toting human. He *did* smell good, and surely he had blood to spare. He had a deep scratch on his arm. While she couldn't see the wound from this angle, she knew it was there. It smelled heavenly.

Though she hungered for a taste, she was not beyond her own control. She could just lick off the excess without biting, without taking something she shouldn't . . . Luca took her arm again, and held on tight.

He knew her every thought, her every desire.

Chloe looked down at the hand on her arm, but her thoughts were immediately yanked from hunger to the startling realization that her life had changed. Her black shirt was soaked in blood. Luca's hand, his clothes . . . they were both drenched in that which nourished vampires and made them strong.

She looked up, caught Luca's eye. Instinctively she leaned into him. This certainly wasn't where she'd thought this night would end.

"There has to be a shower in this house," she said.

"Upstairs," Nevada said. The little witch was probably as anxious for Chloe to get cleaned up as Chloe herself was. It wasn't a pretty sight—not that she and Luca were the only ones wearing evidence of battle. "My bathroom has plenty of towels. I'm not sure about the other rooms." She gave simple directions, and they were on their way before she'd finished. Talk of what might come next continued in their little group of vampires, warriors, and humans.

Away from the scent of the humans, Chloe's desire for a taste of blood faded. She closed her eyes and took a deep breath as they moved quickly, incredibly quickly, up the stairs. Reaching beyond the house, beyond the stench of death and the tantalizing scent of blood, she took in the summer scent of flowers, grass, air, and water. She could swear she actually smelled the moon.

Luca didn't go to the room Nevada said had been hers, but chose another. This bedroom was stark, minimally furnished and without any personal touches. In the attached bath, a towel hung from a decorative rack. It would do.

Moving quickly, Luca removed her clothing and his and turned on the water. Together they stepped into the large brown-tiled shower, standing close within the spray that was pleasantly cold, then pleasantly warm. Chloe looked down once, and watched the pink swirl of blood and water circling the drain. It wasn't at all appetizing. She closed her eyes and leaned into Luca.

The stark truth was that everything that had once been hers was now gone. Though she was very much alive, the life she'd always known was over, so in a way Chloe Fallon truly was dead. She knew that was the way of things, had known it when she'd told Luca she wanted to live.

As sharply sad as it was to leave everything she knew behind, she didn't regret the decision she'd made. This was the end of one life, that was true, but it was also the beginning of another.

"Even my love for you is sharper and deeper than before," she whispered. "I didn't think that was possible, but it's more solid, more certain. It's like until now I've been seeing everything in black and white, and now there's color all around. You're a part of me, Luca."

"I am."

"There's so much to learn, so much I don't know. But I don't suppose there will be any rest until the psycho who stabbed me is taken care of."

"Not much, no." He sounded . . . displeased.

Water rained down on them; that water now remained clear as it washed away. She looked up at

Luca, saw him so clearly, so sharply, as if he were also new. "Do you regret giving me your blood, making me like you?"

"Never." His answer was so quick and certain, she couldn't doubt his sincerity. "If I sound annoyed it's because I want to take you away from this war and spend years teaching and training you. And I can't do that, not yet."

Chloe knew she should mourn her old life, and she was certain there would be moments when she did. Friends and family would be hard to leave behind. But right now, with an uncertain war coming and Luca at her side, she wasn't at all sorry to be who she'd become. Everything she'd ever done, every choice, every accident, every seemingly meaningless step had been leading her here.

"I believe I've been waiting for you all my life," she said, the certainty of it grabbing her in the gut.

For a moment Luca was silent, and then he whispered in her ear. "Trust me, love, I've been waiting longer for you. Much longer."

Indikaiya's grip on the hilt of her sword tightened, as she instinctively prepared to strike. The sight of Chloe—her conduit, her *descendant*—as a vampire turned her stomach and broke her heart.

The surviving warriors, the witch, the boy with the shotgun, and a handful of vampires congregated in the basement of the mansion where the battle had taken place, since dawn was upon them, and even the vamps who could tolerate the light didn't like the idea of facing the morning sun. She'd come here with the intention of killing every vampire in her path, but she'd not expected that any one of them, much less a small handful, would actually be willing to fight on the side of right.

Luca and Sorin had both dispatched more than their fair share of rebels, and Chloe had made it clear that she'd not been turned against her will. Indikaiya had no excuse to dispatch Luca Ambrus. Annoyance was not an acceptable reason for removing his head.

In the past few hours, everyone who'd fought in the battle had gotten cleaned up and changed clothes. Chloe had found a suitable outfit in the witch's closet, and the males had rummaged through rebel soldiers' things. Nothing the petite witch owned would fit Indikaiya, so she'd settled for a silk shirt that smelled like Sorin and a pair of trousers a much smaller vampire had once worn.

The boy with the shotgun, Jimmy, was talking on his cell phone, trying to make impossible explanations to a girl he called Kate without actually telling her anything she should not know. He was a potential warrior himself, if a reluctant one. He had not run, not before the battle, not during . . . and not after, as plans for continuing war were made.

Rurik was flirting outrageously with the little witch, and Nevada, who had an important task before her, was shyly flirtatious herself.

The two humans, Jimmy and Nevada, were constantly surprised by the appearance of a "new" vampire in their midst: Luca. At first it had been amusing; now it was simply annoying. Nevada had mentioned that given time she could come up with a fix for the problem . . . and then a few minutes later she'd mention it again. The warriors did not have this problem. Many of them were as old as Luca, some were as powerful, in their own way. They all came from a different world and were not affected by his magic.

Chloe, Luca, and Sorin had gathered at the end of the hallway, and spoke with animation. They were an odd group, with mixed feelings that were, at the moment, ignored in the name of a common cause. At first Chloe had kept a wary distance from the vamp with the long blond hair, but her attitude had gradually shifted. She was no longer quite so on guard with Sorin; she was actually beginning to trust him. No vampire could truly be trusted, not in Indikaiya's experience.

Warriors continued to arrive. They'd missed the initial battle, but there would be others. And it looked as if the war they'd come here to fight wouldn't be so simple as vampires against warriors. There were four vampires who'd killed their own kind tonight, who'd protected the humans, as Indikaiya had come here to do. She was not foolish enough to dispatch an ally in a war where she needed every ally she could get.

Chloe said a word to Luca and stepped away from him, heading toward Indikaiya with a smile. The rising sun had dimmed her new vampire's energy, even though she hadn't seen even a hint of light. Luca watched her closely, especially as she walked past Jimmy. But she passed the human without anything more than a quick glance; she was very much in control of herself, which was rare for a new vampire.

"You nearly drove me crazy," Chloe said gently as she came near.

"My apologies," Indikaiya said, the words accompanied by a curt bow that would've been more appropriate in another time. "Of all my descendants, you were the strongest, psychically. Your mother could not hear me at all, and the others . . . they were simply not capable."

"It's okay. You were doing what needed to be done. I know that now. But man, when all I could see was a braid and I was hearing your voice out of nowhere . . . definitely nutsville."

"It was necessary."

Chloe lowered her voice. "I just want to make sure

that you're going to keep your word. About Luca. You said you wouldn't kill him."

"He still has his head, and his heart."

"I'd like to keep it that way."

Luca Ambrus needed protection less than any being on this earth, as far as Indikaiya could tell, and yet here was Chloe, shielding the blood-born vampire as best she could. "You love him."

"I do."

Indikaiya was attuned to the power in the room, to every vampire, the two humans, to the warriors—some she knew well, some who were new allies—and suddenly she was aware of a new and different energy, something rare and powerful: another descendant.

A half breed in the belly of a new vampire; a vampire who was also a conduit, both impregnated and turned by a blood born. Such a thing had never happened before.

Chloe had no idea that she was carrying a child conceived before she'd been turned. Indikaiya didn't think Luca knew, either . . . though with his gift he would likely figure it out very soon. She was only able to sense the child because she was so attuned to those in her bloodline.

Like it or not, the war Indikaiya had come to this world to join would not be a simple one. Vampires like Luca and Sorin would be fighting beside the warriors, not against them. Chloe and her child needed to be protected, just as the humans would be. There would be those, human and vampire, who would do their best to make sure the half breed didn't come into this world. Indikaiya herself would argue that such a being should not come to be, and yet this was Chloe's child, Indikaiya's own blood.

This would be a war fought in shades of gray, and she much preferred black and white. Good and evil.

As if to prove her point Sorin caught her eye, smiled and, heaven above, winked at her.

The sooner they killed the vampire queen and ended this foolish revolution, the better off the human race, and Indikaiya herself, would be.

WARRIOR RISING
BY LINDA HOWARD AND LINDA JONES

The Immortal Warrior Indikaiya, and others of her kind, are fighting a war with the vampires in order to preserve the human race. For Indie, what should have been a simple, black-and-white war has become tinged with many shades of gray. Her blood descendant, Chloe Fallon, has not only bonded with the blood born vampire Luca Ambrus, but to save her life she had to be turned vampire. Not all vampires are aligned against the Warriors; Luca himself, and some of his friends, are fighting on the side of the humans. Indikaiya came into this world to fight against vampires, and she finds herself fighting beside some of them, in a war where she can't afford to turn her back on any ally.

Then there's Sorin. The powerful vampire is everything she dislikes in a vampire, and more. He too has chosen to fight for the humans. As Indie and Sorin fight side by side in this war she discovers feelings for him that have no place in her world. There can be no happy ending; Sorin is vampire, she is a Warrior. If she chooses to turn her back on her calling and remain in this world, she will age and die, while Sorin does not. When the war is done, she must return to the other world where the Warriors wait and watch over their human charges.

Sorin was once a leader among the vampire rebels, but now he's driven to protect the humans, to stop the ambitious queen. In all his very long life he's never known anyone like Indikaiya. She's a surprise in a world he thought held no more surprises. A reward for a man who hasn't earned rewards. For Sorin, Indikaiya is his one pleasure on the path to redemption.

Published by Ballantine Books